OCT 2008

DEADLINE!

BOOK ONE

D0106664

a serial novel by

Paula L. Tutman

Warning! Rough and explicit language, sexual
situations and an extemely addictive storyline

Deadline!
Copyright 2008
Paula Tutman
All rights reserved
First Printing May 2008

ISBN   0-9815845-4-3
       978-0-9815845-5-3

Written by Paula L. Tutman

Cover by Windward Design

Published by
Dailey Swan Publishing, Inc.

Dailey Swan Publishing, Inc
2644 Appian Way #101
Pinole Ca 94564
www.Dailey Swan Publishing.com
www.deadlinethebook.com

Acknowledgements

For several years I've kept a list on my refrigerator of people who've helped me with this project. I walked by it several times a day and looked at it, thinking it would be the next most important thing in the world to me if my book ever got published—the first thing, of course, being the manuscript

I got help from so many people, and so much encouragement, that every couple of weeks I found myself adding a name or two of someone who did something big or small that was pivotal to me finishing the project, meeting a deadline, or reworking a section of the book to make it that much better.

A month before my agent called me and said, "Are you sitting down? Dailey Swan wants to publish your book", I became concerned about that slip of paper that had been hanging out on my fridge. I decided to put it in a safe place. And in such a safe place it remains, untouched, unfound and unused. Damn it! Why do I keep putting things in safe places? I always forget where that is. Which means in spite of all the names I'm listing, I've absolutely forgotten some. It is a huge regret.

Help comes in many forms, and this book is the incarnation of several different manuscripts I've been tinkering with for some time. I ignored it completely for two whole years to write two other books. I returned to it when I became lonely for its characters. It was called *Silver Spur Chop Suey* then. I had trouble writing the last chapter, it was just too frightening to finish, but painfully I did.

A friend of mine said the book was just too big — a lot of people told me that, but when she suggested that I split the book in to two sections, it changed the entire manuscript. I started over, got rid of stuff, added other stuff, started again. *Silver Spur Chop Suey* became *Deadline! Book One*, the serial novel.

I have a system of writing that I call, from God's lips to my fingertips. It means that I hear a 'voice'. I hear the writing and text as it looks on the page. When I'm not writing 'in the voice', I generally hear the crap meter alarm running. I also do exhaustive research. I send the manuscript out to people who will tell me the truth. They'll tell me if something is working or missing or exciting or just plain bad. My favorite critique was from a producer at WDIV TV 4 in Detroit, who told me he called in sick two days because he couldn't put the manuscript down. Two other acquaintances said the book was just plain bad. That wasn't my favorite critique but I took it to heart and set out to make the book better. Their suggestions were on the money. One of those readers was my boyfriend at the time. Ex-boyfriend, good suggestions, great trade off.

So please forgive this outrageously long list. It is my first published novel, after all, and I am so very grateful to the people who actively helped me, encouraged me and gave me the blueprint for some pretty fascinating characters by living their own lives out loud.

Thank You!

I can't write a word before running it past my mother, Elaine B. Tutman, my father William L. Tutman and my twin sister, Lisa Tutman-Oglesby. They were patient, thorough readers with swift corrective pens at the ready. I love you.

Three wonderful and faithful friends who changed the shape of the project with their ideas and dedication are Val Clark, Joyce Suber, and Johnny Menifee.

My deepest gratitude to the following: My literary agent, Diane Nine. My talent agent and dear friend, Mendes Napoli. My publisher Casey Swanson and Dailey Swan Publishing.

Fred (Hoppy) Tutman and Mike Herman, thank you for explaining all that legal stuff.

Big thanks to Jesse Cory, Jason Schultz, and the team at Ohm Creative Group for the beautiful website, Deadlinethebook.com. Take a peak for insights into the writing of *Deadline!*

Rachel Holland is the photographer who took those amazing photographs.

I've had incredible support from my management at WDIV TV4 in Detroit, including Alan Frank, Steve Wasserman, Neil Goldstein, Bob Ellis, Brooke Blackwell and Deborah Collura.

Parts of the book were borrowed from my life at WLKY TV 32 in Louisville, Kentucky, WATE TV 6 in Knoxville, Tennessee and WJZ TV 13 in Baltimore, Maryland.

Nelsina Jackson Murphy, Jim Gockowski, Ralph Merkel, Jim Hall, Joe Smith, Joel Boykin, Steve Davitt, Leona Gould-McElhone, Ro Coppola, Benita Alexander Noel, Ted Pregitzer, Vic Skelley, and Steve Jones, Alan

Cork — do you happen to see a little of yourselves in the book? Thank you for being rich characters in my life.

Dr. Margaret Bennett, Sue Nine, Bryan Dulsky, Lynda Ruffind, Cheryl Johnson, Asha Blake, Cesar Gonzalez, Anne Eames, Suzie Franks, Bernie Smilovitz, Mike and Sandy Bauer, James Jackson, Dr. Audrey Lucas, Mary Levock Tutman, Susan Sherer, Vladae Roytapel, Bonnie Wainz, Cynthia Kidder, Mark Armitage, Devin Scillian, Pat Berwanger, Christy C. at LOC, Jean Harding, Carey Ocasio, John and F.K. Marsh, Shandel Small, Mary Callaghan Lynch, and Martha Reeves (yes of the Vandellas) — thank-you for your help and friendship and encouragement along the way.

Thank-you so much to the follwoing people who liked the manuscript, hated the manuscript, but read the manuscript and helped make it better: Vanessa Rumber Sams, Irene Marton, Dean Clark, Keith Anderson, Todd and Angela Robinson, Brad Marshall, Neil Rubin, Susan Kaplan, Cathy Champion, Ross Eberman, Bruce Clifton, Bernie Zettner, Betty Holmes, Michael Marton, Jill (Jablonski) Miller, and Barb Roethler.

And finally I'd like to acknowledge that most of this book was written overlooking the shores of Lake Huron in Bluewater, Ontario at Brentwood on the Beach with Joan and Peter Karsens — an easy smile, a hardy laugh and a martini at ready.

PROLOGUE

"I hate my life today!

The clock is ticking, I have less than three hours before news time, and I have to have something to feed the monster.

Feeding the monster. That's what we call it.

The monster is bigger and more powerful than any of us. It's hungry four times a day and it needs a snack just about every hour on the hour.

The monster is the newscast, and it must be placated no matter what, at 5:30 in the morning, at noon, at 5:00 in the evening, and 11:00 o'clock at night.

It doesn't matter if your story is half-baked or well done. At your designated slot, you must feed the monster. The monster is always hungry and if it doesn't eat, you die. That's how it works. And that's why I hate my life today."

Every television news reporter, any given day.

CHAPTER ONE

Murder has its own smell. Its own feel. Its own air.

And on that brisk night on the outskirts of Detroit, in the little town of Pixley, the atmosphere was rank with all of it.

Those who've never felt the presence of the kind of evil that attaches itself to a murder scene are all the better for it. But for journalists, who make their daily bread cloaking themselves in the misery of others—their eyes hold a barely perceptible sadness, their skin, thickened by the constant grind of stress and deadlines has a different pallor, and their souls seem non-existent from the comfortable distance of an easy chair plopped in front of the television set at news time.

PS Garrett was the last reporter to get to the little gas station and carryout in the tiny farming town on the outer edges of Detroit's northwestern suburbs. She knew she'd be playing catch-up. But, luckily, her camera crew had been in place and working on her behalf for an hour or more.

As she pulled into the gravel parking lot and surveyed the area, she could see Channel Three had at least two reporters on the story. She scanned the horizon for Sherman Hall and breathed a sigh of relief that he wasn't there.

Channel Nine seemed to have at least two reporters on the scene as well. She was less afraid of them, since they had the most incompetent reporters in the market and no one watched them anyway.

She drove her shiny red sports car to the far end of the large parking lot to find parking as discreet as possible. She'd never been a fan of driving her own vehicle to news stories, but sometimes it couldn't be avoided. So when she did have to use her own car, she always tried to park out of the way, backing it up against some sort of barrier so that her license plate couldn't easily be read.

So many years on the front had made her battle weary and paranoid. She never knew if someone out there might be interested in jotting down her license plate number, perhaps to track her down at home later to make trouble because of a story she'd done.

PS rummaged around in her reporter's bag for a newspad and pen, jumped out of her car and ran over to the Channel Six live van parked on the periphery of the crime scene. She hopped into the passenger side of the vehicle and settled in for a long evening.

Jerry, the microwave truck technician was already feeding videotape back to the TV station.

"Hey Jerry, what gives?" PS asked as she scanned the horizon with a suspicious eye. Sherman was still nowhere in sight. It made her almost as nervous as it did relieved. If he wasn't there, where was he?

Jerry looked up from his frantic toiling in the back of the large van. "Oh, so you're the screw they turned for this one."

Jerry was one of the greatest at Channel Six. He had the smile and the temperament of a kindly old grandfather, though he couldn't have been more than ten years older than the young thirty-something reporter. He was also a consummate professional, and PS always knew she was in good hands when she worked with him.

"So Jer, what's the deal here?" She asked, needing some shred of direction before hitting the pavement to get the story.

Jerry returned to his frenzied button pushing. He was busy fiddling with gauges and knobs. He had been feeding videotape to the station, but just in the few seconds since PS had gotten into the van things started going wrong. The tape feed was halted, and suddenly Jerry became frantic, flipping switches and making adjustments on the gazillion knobs and buttons on the instrument panel bolted to the back wall of the van.

"Can you flip the switch just beneath the scanner, please?" He asked with a gasp.

"Sure."

The reporter flipped a small white switch to the up position, and Jerry started talking on the two-way radio to the engineer who had been monitoring the tape feed back at the studio.

Jerry returned to his frenzied button pushing.

PS glanced at the clock on the dash. Eight fifty-five and the live truck technician seemed close to cardiac arrest as the news gathering equipment continued to fail him.

The microwave unit was a masterpiece of gadgetry. There were dozens of blinking lights, little monitors with moving, flashing lines that looked like the graphic equalizers on a home stereo. Other monitors had little green lines that looked like a Richter scale, they arched and contorted like laser snakes on a Black background.

Very often, when something went wrong—and something went wrong very often—these technicians knew how to re-route energy sources and bypass circuits to get the tape back to the studio and get the shot on.

That night, Jerry's knowledge was going to be put to the test.

Things were always different at murder scenes.

In the front seat of the van, the stress level was mounting.

PS was at a disadvantage. That seemed to happen a lot at Channel Six. Her television station didn't even know about this story until a producer caught a glimpse of it on a news-brief on Channel Three.

Now, as she sat in the news vehicle, starving for information about what tape had been shot, and what interviews had already been collected, her other hunger spoke up.

PS had already been seated at her favorite restaurant, Silver Spur Chop Suey. She had just taken a swig of her cocktail and had a broasted chicken wing perched at her lips when her pager sounded.

She reached into her reporter's bag and rummaged for mints, gum, or a stray piece of chocolate that might have survived her last attack of deadline-induced anxiety or *deadlinitis*.

The reporter's bag was a large tapestry camera bag that she had gotten into the habit of carrying several years before. In it, she kept everything she could possibly need for up to a three-day period—extra make-up, soap, deodorant and a few candy bars that seemed to need replacing around the 15th of every month.

She started carrying the bag after being stuck at a prison lock-down for several days without so much as a toothbrush, or change of panties.

All totaled, PS stood up in front of a live camera twenty-one times during that ordeal. The last sixteen were done without benefit of foundation, powder or lipstick.

And it showed.

Bob Tucker, the station's news director was furious. "This is Detroit," he howled. "Not Amarillo, Texas. When I see my reporters on the air, I want them to be fresh, and polished, and professional looking. I don't care what they're doing at channels Three, Nine or Fox. Here at Channel Six my reporters will be slick in their presentation. Presentation is everything!"

Tucker never once complimented the reporter on the exclusive interview she wang-dangled with the mother of the inmate who was holding three guards hostage. He never once said, "good job", when the photographer nabbed the only video of the warring inmates hanging their demands out of a second story window on a sheet while the crews from the other stations slept in the back of their vans with their jackets pulled up over their heads.

Tucker only focused on his reporter's lack of lipstick and the rat's nest in her hair.

When news managers are drunk with victory, they always find something the foot soldiers could have done differently in the trenches. There's always more street reporters could have gotten—more video photographers could have shot.

That was the last story PS ever covered unprepared. Now she carried a reporter's bag and it has served her well ever since.

She looked up into the rear view mirror and could see that Jerry had started re-feeding some video. It was video of yellow crime scene ribbon stretched around the small dingy building. The camera blurred and then focused on a short, balding man who was crying as he walked several police officers around the perimeter of the building.

That must be a relative, PS thought as she cracked a piece of hard candy between her teeth.

"There. How's that? Did it steady up?" Jerry yelled into the mic in the back of the van. His voice was strained and over-modulated as he spoke into the two-way radio that had been sitting by his side.

He didn't wait for an answer, instead reached above the tape deck that was bolted onto a shelf. He grabbed a knob that came off in his hand. "Dammit to Hell!" He yelled.

A voice crackled over the two-way radio. "Stop. Stop the feed. We've got a lot of noise in your video, I'm going to have to re-tune your shot."

"Crap!" Jerry yelped. "We're too far away. There must be something blocking the path of the microwave."

"A hill or something?" PS asked curiously.

"God only knows. I mean, we're way the Hell in East Jesus. It could be anything. I hate these stories!

Dammit to Hell!"

Jerry stopped the video player, rewound the tape that had been rolling, and frantically started pushing more buttons.

"How's that?" He asked the technician back at the station.

PS knew she was in trouble because Jerry was one of the cool-headed live truck techs. When he was panicked, it pushed the up button on everyone's panic level.

As she watched him fiddle and listened to him talk to the engineers back at the station in that elevated voice, she knew this was going to be another one of those stories they got on the air by the skin of their chinny chin chins, if at all.

PS wasn't sure where to start, but she knew it had to be somewhere. And without Jerry available to fill in the many gaps, she made ready to jump out into the February air to fend for herself—blind. She wasn't excessively concerned, after all, it was just another murder scene. She'd been to dozens of them. Besides, Channel Nine had sent two of its rookie reporters. No real competition there. Not even with a couple of green producers to help out. She'd competed with the two Channel Three reporters on several other occasions and was reasonably sure that combined they'd have trouble finding the story-line at a flower show, let alone the scene of a double murder.

Late though she was, the story was do-able. So she was at least able to breathe.

She opened the van door and once again, surveyed the crime scene. The van tech from Channel

Three was pulling cable from his microwave truck to a tripod that had been set up on the periphery of the yellow crime tape that surrounded the little gas station. The two Channel Three reporters were standing near a news car, obviously comparing notes. One of them looked up and pointed in PS's direction. When their eyes met, she shifted her gaze uncomfortably toward a clump of police officers, standing around doing nothing in particular.

But then a chill ran down the front of her chest. Her skin began to prickle, and she felt an uncomfortable tinge in her left shoulder. As she reached up to rub the discomfort away, PS Garrett glanced up to see the imposing figure of a man walking across the parking lot. It was Sherman Hall strolling leisurely toward the other two Channel Three reporters.

A lump formed in the middle of her throat. It was worse than she had originally thought. Now, it was personal. She could no longer afford the luxury of being briefed by Jerry. He had his own problems. Now, she had hers. She had to get out and start digging.

Now!

There were lots of people milling about the crime scene: spectators, the curious—the kind of people who see a lot of flashing lights and stop their cars to see what's going on—the same kind of people with rubber necks at highway car accidents. And there was certainly no shortage of police officers.

These kinds of crime scenes always seemed to have a surplus of police officers, whose jobs seemed to be to just stand around.

Channel Nine's live truck was parked next to

16

Channel Six's and PS could see one of the reporters in the front seat talking on a cell phone. Another Channel Nine reporter ran up, looked into the Channel Six van as PS peered frantically from the open door of her van. He rolled his eyes, then jumped in on the driver's side of his vehicle. He exchanged a few words with the female reporter who had been on the phone. She turned around and looked at PS—as if to say, *What are you looking at?* So PS diverted her gaze out of courtesy and embarrassment.

Color bars popped up on the monitor in the back of the Channel Six van and a calm returned. Jerry looked up and smiled just as PS began to exit the vehicle. "You weren't worried were you?" He asked with a wink.

PS glanced at the dashboard. It was already 9:15. She'd be on deadline in less than an hour. "Me?" She answered with false bravado, well aware there was a hungry newscast waiting to be fed. "Nevah! Is everything okay, are we going to make our slot?" She asked.

"Yeah, just a few gremlins in the system. Nothing to worry your pretty little head over." Jerry looked up and flashed another of his million dollar smiles. It eased some of the tension in the front seat, but not much.

"Thanks, Jer. I appreciate it. So can you tell me what the deal is here, or do I need to go out and scavenge for scraps?"

Jerry chuckled and began to fill her in as he tended the tape transmission. "Looks like two kids, teenagers really, got canceled by some lunatic."

"Teenagers? Funny, the assignment desk didn't mention that little detail," PS said, not really surprised at all.

"They probably didn't know. Apparently it's a botched robbery—gunman didn't even take any cash. Anyway, some hayseed who stopped off for cigarettes apparently stumbled over the bodies and called the cops, and that's what brings you to our fine city today. Tom's out there shooting some more tape, but it's been tough. The cops are pretty squirrelly on this one for some reason. Don't even think about slipping beneath the crime scene tape to get a closer look. They're itchy tonight, and you know what that rhymes with."

Jerry glanced out of the van window. "Hey, there goes the police Chief."

Jerry nodded his chin toward the little gas station, and then turned back to PS "Guess you better jump out of the nest, Little Bird, see if you spot your other cameraman out there somewhere, it looks like I'm going to be tied up in here for a while."

"Chirp, chirp," she responded with a forced laugh, glancing out the window just in time to see Sherman Hall getting into the back of his own live van.

She half walked and half ran as she headed toward Chief Grainger.

He was a big, gruff guy who'd been doing this police stuff for a long time. He knew all of the local reporters, and he knew the drill.

That night his usual quick pace was slowed to a deliberate amble as if each step hurt him. As the reporter approached him, he looked at her and gave a half-hearted, but approving smile.

"This one really sucks," he said out loud just as she reached him.

It was getting chillier and frost danced off each word. "This one is really bad. Crazy bad. We've got ourselves a mean, kid-killing bastard out there somewhere."

And then he muttered under his breath, "Everybody should be afraid tonight."

PS shivered and pulled the lapels of her blazer around her neck. It had been an unseasonably warm February, but now it was downright cold, and she hadn't thought to throw a heavier jacket into her car. Her fingers were starting to ache from the chill, so she blew on them and rubbed them together, as much to stay warm as to mask her mounting unease.

She looked around. This was no different from any other crime scene, really, yet this one felt different. The air was thicker, more difficult to breathe, and even in the chill, her face felt a little hot and sticky.

There was a different breed of evil in the air. One she hadn't experienced before but recognized immediately.

She glanced toward the little gas station. The building was wrapped in yellow police-line tape and the sky awash in flashing red and blue lights. Steam rose from the hoods of the dozen or so police cruisers scattered about the property.

A nagging discomfort in her left shoulder turned to an ache and PS resisted the urge to massage it and instead turned her attention back to the

Chief, whose already slow pace had become laborious. His feet crunched as they slowly hit the gravel in their spit-shined patent leather shoes. "Chief, can I quote you on that?" PS said as she mustered a cheese-eating grin trying to keep things light. "You know, kid-killing bastard, everyone should be afraid tonight. All that stuff. Can I quote you on that?"

She looked up at the Chief with what she hoped would be a sympathetic smile.

He didn't return it. Instead, he sighed and a crease formed above his brow. "You bet," he answered. "You bet you can quote me on that. I mean it."

The Chief of Police stopped walking and turned to face PS who'd been trotting behind him, the *click, click, click* from her high heeled shoes a soothing sound to him. He liked this reporter. A lot. She played the game differently than the others. She always seemed to be more empathetic than the long line of hard-assed, tough-minded white men who dominated the police beat, who ruled the world with their deep baritone voices, London Fog trench coats and smug assumptions.

There were very few women who had the stomach to cover the crime blotter effectively or successfully for very long. PS Garrett was the only woman and the only black person. She also had a softer approach. It made her stand out.

The Chief knew for a fact that she could be just as tough-minded and dogmatic as the others. But he liked her style. And more than once he had to remind himself to stop staring at her pretty brown legs. No matter how cold, or how rainy or how anything it was outside, PS Garrett always wore skirts that perched respectfully at the top of her knees to show off those pretty brown legs.

Her eyes were big, and bright and curious. And her below-the-shoulder-length hair always seemed to be attractively disobedient in the breeze. Her bangs swept slightly to one side with the exception of one wisp of rebellious hair that always seemed to dangle in front of her left eye.

She was constantly trying to discipline it, absent mindedly trying to sweep it behind her ear. But it always managed to swing back to the front of her face. It made her nice to look at. And on nights like these in particular, Chief Grainger needed something or someone nice to look at.

The Chief had hoped she'd be the one from her station sent to this scene. They didn't have a lot of bad news in this part of town, mostly vandalism sprees. But every time PS Garrett came, she was a welcomed reprieve from the arrogance of her male counterparts.

"Chief, I just got here," PS said urgently as she tapped her bare wrist where a watch might be. It was for emphasis. PS had tossed all of her watches years ago. It was her one way of proving to herself that she wasn't a slave to time. Though deep in her heart she knew she was baling cotton on a schedule with the rest of them. "I know you have a lot to do, but can you fill me in enough to get me on the air?"

"It's good to see you, PS," the Chief said. "What took you so long to get here?"

"The usual, Sir. You know. If it's news, it's news to us."

The two chuckled.

"I know I'm late, and I apologize, but I see the others have already been on the job for a bit. Can you catch me up?"

Grainger knew what she needed. He had been served up many times in the past to feed the monster and he really liked this particular chef.

The Chief sighed again, swallowed and paused. He then began to speak in the methodical way that all police spokespersons regurgitate the facts. But that night the Chief didn't seem to be as detached as usual.

"Customer walked in to purchase some petrol and found the white male, 16 years old, slumped behind the register. A teen-aged minor—white, female, 15 years old was a few feet away in a pool of blood on the floor. As you can see, it's the Gas 'N Go."

The Chief pointed to the front of the store that had large gold letters confirming the shop's name. He sighed and continued, "I been here a dozen times myself to get coffee."

The Chief pulled out a red bandanna from his rear pocket, wiped his brow, looked inside the hanky—as if to inspect what he'd collected—put the handkerchief back into his hind pocket and labored on. "It seems this sixteen year old kid, Danny Weinstein, had been tending his daddy's gas station and quick stop. It was customary for this Weinstein kid's fifteen-year-old girlfriend to keep him company."

PS listened intently to what the Chief was saying, all the while her eyes darting about the crime scene to keep tabs on the whereabouts of the other reporters and to keep a look out for her own cameraman who

22

had been wandering around. The very fact that none of the other reporters was standing around trying to steal tidbits of her conversation with the Chief made her all the more concerned. This was a hot scene. Everybody there should have been paws up, begging for details. She wondered what they might already know that she was still trying to find out?

She could see that Channel Three police reporter, Sherman Hall, moving around his live unit several dozen yards away. He was tall, strikingly handsome and always well dressed.

She pursed her lips as she saw him conferring with someone who looked to be a producer-type.

"Chief, have you released the girl's name, yet?"

"No. I can't give you her name yet, 'cause we haven't contacted her next of kin. If you find out what it is, and I have no doubt you will—if you haven't already, I'm gonna have to ask you not to use it 'til you get my say so. That's all I need is to have her mamma or daddy driving down the road or playing cards at a friend's house and hearing their daughter's been murdered. Let 'em hear it from me first."

Chief Grainger paused to give PS a stern look. She nodded in acquiescence, and the Chief finally continued. "Nothing this bad ever happened on this stretch of highway."

Indeed, Pixley was a sleepy little agricultural community surrounded by small lakes and tributaries, perched fifty-five miles northwest of Detroit. Even though the road that went through town was a main thoroughfare for motorists who wanted to avoid the interstate traffic—the hamlet where the Gas 'N Go was located was more likely to get the patronage of locals rather than tourists.

"Those two were nice kids," the Chief continued as he began to slowly walk toward the command cruiser that was now surrounded by several patrolmen and a State Trooper, his feet crunching the cold gravel with each step, PS gently tipping behind him in his tracks. "Danny had been helping his dad, who still suffered flashbacks from the Vietnam war. The dad's been in bad shape for a long time.

"The old man's divorced. I'm told his wife left him and the infant boy to fend for themselves, so Danny was more than a son to his father. He was his world. Best buddies, I'm told. Sometimes we wondered just who was the dad and who was the son, the two seemed to take turns."

The Chief shook his head. It was obvious that he was hurting. "I used to know the family way back when. I didn't know the kid real well anymore, I'd seen him when I stopped in on occasion, but I know he was a decent kid."

Chief Grainger paused again, looked up and searched the sky. PS followed his gaze. His voice trailed off into a whisper.

She listened carefully to the Chief and wrote down as much as she could.

"Whew!" The Chief continued. "A decent kid. Never any trouble like those young punks who smash mailboxes and shoot birds. Never got any trouble from this one."

The Chief stopped walking and began to stare

at the front window of the little gas station. "This one is bad," he said, shaking his head. "This one is real bad. "

And with that, the Chief was finished. He had work to do. He simply picked up his pace and walked toward his cruiser without saying another word, leaving PS Garrett alone on the asphalt parking lot of the Pixley Gas 'N Go.

She looked around and spotted a small group of locals on the other side of the parking lot. She decided to head in their direction, meandering over so as not to be threatening. She didn't want them to see her coming and turn to walk away.

As she approached, one of the women of the group looked up and angrily addressed her. "What do you want? No comment. We have nothing to say here."

"I'm sorry to bother you," the reporter gently persisted. "I saw you all standing here and I didn't know whether or not you knew the victims. I don't mean to be intrusive."

"Well you are. Get the Hell out of here, would you?" The woman screeched at the top of her lungs.

"Jackie. That's not right. She didn't do nothing to us." A short man with a scraggily blonde beard, mustache and a ponytail put his hand on the angry woman's shoulder and gently moved her aside. "I'm Larry, we live in the same complex with Danny and his dad. That's his dad over there with the police."

PS followed Larry's gesture and saw the balding man she'd seen earlier on the tape in the van as it was being fed back to the station. He was in a sweatshirt and cut-off blue jeans, talking to police officers and lead-ing them around the property. PS turned back to Larry. "I'm sorry. Did you know the family well?"

"He was a good kid. A real good kid."

"The best," spat the weeping woman who was so angry at the reporter a few moments before. The two other people—who PS could now see were both men, turned their backs and huddled their heads to-gether. It was clear they were not comfortable with her being there, but they weren't so interested in get-ting her to leave either.

"What can you tell me about the two kids in there?"

PS could tell these people were in grief, and could also tell they wanted to talk. They just needed some reassurance. She didn't dare try and drag a cam-era over though, even if she had spotted her MIA pho-tographer. That would have blown the deal. These people were going to be more valuable to her story off camera.

She tried to inconspicuously get a glance at the watch on the hand of the woman who had screeched at her. She desperately needed to know the time.

No luck. So she swallowed her mounting anxiety and stepped in toward the group, knowing that she'd have to commit much of what they said to memory. If she even pulled out a newspad and started jotting down notes they'd clam up in a hurry. Right now she needed to be their confidante. Just an ear, listening to whatever it was they wanted to talk about.

By then, Jackie, the woman who greeted PS so angrily at first, had decided that if her companion was willing to talk, so was she.

She took long drags from her cigarette and blew the smoke toward her feet with a hissing noise. She and her male companion exchanged the butt between them as they took turns talking and staring in the direction of the Gas 'N Go.

The woman looked like a character out of 'Easy Rider', with her grungy ill-fitting blue jeans that *belled* at the bottom, and tattered, black satin baseball jacket that was pulled tightly around her body with her crossed arms. Her mousy brown hair was oily and separated and hung lifelessly to her belt.

PS became self-conscious of the three gold bracelets that dangled proudly about her own wrist. They had been gifts from her favorite boyfriend, who was also named Danny, and she hadn't taken them off since his sudden departure. She tugged at her wool blazer from Nordstrom to cover the egotistical display of jewelry and made herself more comfortable with the people she'd approached.

"He was a real fine person," Jackie said and looked at her partner who nodded his head in agreement and took a long drag off the cigarette. "I liked his girlfriend, too. What was her name?"

Jackie searched the sky and snapped her fingers trying to coax the girl's name out of hiding. When it didn't come she turned to Larry, who thought for about a minute. "Tammy, her name was Tammy."

He took another quick drag off the cigarette butt as his reward and handed it back to Jackie, who hit it hard and handed it back to Larry.

PS stifled the urge to wave the smoke away that was now filtering into her nostrils.

"Yeah, that's it. Tammy Moore. I liked her, too. She was kind of heavy, you know, chubby." Jackie chuckled a little, coughed up what was some sort of nicotine phlegm, swallowed and then looked at PS with what appeared to be a little embarrassment.

The young reporter gave her a reassuring smile, as if to say, Yeah that happens to me too, and obliged her with a chuckle. Jackie cleared her throat and continued. Her voice sounding an octave lower and more gravelly than before. "His girlfriend, Tammy, you know—had a bubbly personality. She was different than the other girls around here. She had style. Class. Yeah."

Everyone in the group chuckled and nodded their heads in agreement. Jackie struggled on. "She wore these big Black framed glasses, you know the one's you'd see in those old sixties movies? Glasses like them. She laughed a lot too, and loved animals." Jackie drew out the word loved so it sounded like a musical note. "She was a nice girl. She liked children too. Yeah. And junk. She loved junk, mostly other people's junk. She collected old jewelry and sunglasses. She used to always come around asking me if I had any good junk. I gave her an old pair of cat-eye glasses I found at my grandma's house. She loved them ole glasses. Said she was going to glue some rhinestones and glitter on 'em. That crazy kid." Jackie smiled.

She sighed, and huffed a little as if to blow off steam and grief. Frost trickled out from behind her pursed lips. The sadness welled up in her voice and tears began to roll down her pale cheeks. "The Chief told me she had a pair of antique cat-eye glasses in her pocket that fell out when her body was being examined by one of them cops in there." Jackie stopped talking and began to choke up. "They were good kids. They wouldn't hurt anybody. Hell, if someone asked 'em for money they would have given it. I know they would have. They didn't need to be killed."

"Hell, Grainger told me the son-offa-bitch didn't even take no money." The scraggily man with his back turned, spat.

In no time flat, Jackie had worked herself up into a frenzy and her voice had become high pitched and squealing by the time she began to cry. "They were good kids. Good kids."

"That's enough," Larry said to the reporter as he shifted his body to cradle Jackie's face into his shoulder. "That's enough. We've said enough."

Then one of the other men in the group, the big guy, who had turned his back when she first walked up, decided it was time to say something. He was a really tall, gruff looking guy with a long red beard, and a handlebar mustache. He was wearing a Black leather jacket that looked to be a little snug. It hung open at the front and PS could see the words on his T-shirt, which read—0 to horny in 6.3 beers. "I think it's time for her to go."

He was speaking to the others, but looking directly at PS.

The young reporter thought he might be right.

"Thank you folks," she said and bowed slightly in respect as she began to back away. "Thanks for your time, I appreciate it. I'll be sure to mention on TV how well thought of these kids were."

"We'd appreciate that," Larry said. He buried his head into the shoulder of his companion.

The big guy, who'd been menacing a moment before, turned his back and continued to talk quietly with the skinny man who never once looked up in her presence.

Larry kissed Jackie gently on the forehead. "I always liked her," he said, gesturing toward the retreating reporter. "She always seems so friendly on TV."

"Hey, wait a minute," Jackie demanded as she lifted her tear streaked face from her companion's shoulder. "There's something I always wanted to ask you."

"Yes, Ma'am. What's that?"

"What does the PS stand for?"

PS Garrett got that question a lot and always had the same answer ready. "My parents were kind of, you know, avant-garde. They thought I'd appreciate picking out my own name when I was old enough. They were wrong. PS doesn't stand for anything."

But to herself the young reporter thought, Pretty Sad. That's what PS stands for. Pretty Goddamned Sad.

She walked away with the name of the second victim, and a lump in her throat, trying to convince herself that it was just thirst and knowing in her heart that it wasn't.

CHAPTER TWO

Her deadline was creeping up and PS wanted to go back to the Chief but knew he'd said all he could, or would. Reporters always wanted to know more than they were supposed to. It's the nature of their business. And police always needed reporters to know less than they did. It's the nature of their business.

She didn't want to push Grainger, so instead of walking directly toward him, she just kind of walked toward his general direction to observe anything else that might be going on while keeping an eye out for her photographer. She knew she already had video and soundbites. They were being fed back to the station when she arrived. All she had to do at that point was scavenge for icing—anything new and interesting that the other stations might not have.

She meandered closer, and closer still to the Chief, trying not to be intrusive. Finally the few cops who'd been standing around walked away, and she decided to approach.

"Chief," she asked gently. "Does it look like robbery?"

"I couldn't say right now," he sighed and looked toward the small shop that was bathed in yellow crime tape and flashing lights.

"Chief?" She firmly pressed. "Can't say or won't say?"

PS Garrett knew that she was treading on shaky

ground, but she was also counting on her ability to read Chief Grainger well enough to know when to stop.

"I will tell you this. We've got ourselves a killer out there. A cold-blooded killer. And I want you to warn people. Tell 'em to be careful. Tell 'em to stay in. Tell 'em to keep an eye out on their neighbor. That I can say."

"Chief," PS pressed. "Those are pretty strong words. Don't you think we'd send this community into a panic if I told them to lock their children up and hide from the boogie man?"

Granted, it would have made a great soundbite, but she couldn't, in good conscience, create panic in a community that hadn't had a murder in seven years. "I mean, I'll say it if you want Chief..."

"No," he broke in. "I've already said it. Your cameraman did an interview with me earlier."

PS turned to Tom, her missing photographer who'd just wandered up.

"You did an interview with the Chief?" She whispered.

Tom nodded his head.

"You can't do that!" She said with deep concern.

"I can if you pipe down and don't mention it to the shop steward. Fuck the union, on a night like tonight," he said with a wink.

PS turned back to the Chief. "Okay, then can we do another quick interview—on camera?"

She turned and winked back at Tom. The two knew it was always better to have a reporter's voice on tape conducting interviews. Not everyone in the shop was a team player. And this would protect a photographer's right to help his reporter fight the battles in the trenches.

On camera, the Chief gave the bare facts of the crime. He said the female victim had not been officially ID'd yet, though he knew who she was. They were still looking for her next of kin for notification and positive identification. He extended a plea to the public to call the police station if anyone had any information that might help solve the crime, even if it seemed insignificant. Grainger also repeated that very unusual statement he'd blurted out earlier—"That everyone ought to be afraid tonight."

He then brushed an imaginary piece of lint off his uniform and slowly strolled off leaving the TV crew standing in the chilly Michigan air.

"Was that a trip or what?" PS said to Tom as he was putting away the microphone and turning off his portable battery light, or bat light.

"Pheww! I'll say," Tom said as he lifted the camera off his right shoulder and slung in down to his side with ease. "This one is eerie."

"It feels different, doesn't it?" PS answered.

"Creepy, like someone's watching."

Out of instinct, the TV crew glanced hurriedly around them.

"Who would kill two defenseless kids? I talked to those people standing over there," PS said, gesturing to the victims neighbors she'd spoken to earlier. "And they said the Chief told them, who ever did this, didn't even take any money. Who the Hell would kill kids for no reason?"

33

"I don't know, but I hope I don't run into him."

"Hey, what time is it?"

"How on earth does a reporter get away without owning a watch? Isn't having one a pre-requisite?"

"Hey, screw the speech. What time is it?"

Tom raised his arm to look at his watch. "9:40."

"Good. Time is still on our side. Let's see what else we can find."

Tom and the reporter continued to wander the crime scene in the opposite direction of the Chief and headed toward a bank of police cruisers that were running idle with no one at the wheel. As they walked past the police cars that hissed and puffed beneath their hoods, a voice whispered from the shadows of one of the empty cruisers. "Are you Channel Six?"

The TV crew spun around startled. They couldn't see who was talking but PS replied, "We're from Channel Six."

"Yeah," whispered the invisible man. "I watch you all the time. You're my favorite channel."

"Thanks." PS said as she strained to see who was speaking so secretively.

"Hey, I know you." The voice continued. "You're that reporter with the initials."

"That's right, Sir. I'm PS Garrett. And who are you?"

A long lean face emerged from behind the police car. It was grotesque and monstrous—with deep gashes and scars. Before she could help herself, she gasped and stepped back as the wild figure of a man moved toward her. She instinctively reached back to

34

grab Tom's arm for security.

As the stranger moved closer, the red and blue flashing lights from the police cruiser brushed his face, revealing deep wrinkles and sunken eyes. He was ghastly, a tortured looking soul who appeared equally consumed with a need for alcohol and a bath.

Without even realizing it, PS and Tom took another step away from the stranger.

"I found them," he said as he continued to emerge from the shadows.

"I beg your pardon?" PS asked as curiosity coaxed her forward.

"I'm the one who found those kids. I was going in to get some cigarettes and I saw the girl laying there in a pool of blood. It was horrible, and that ain't all I seen neither."

PS didn't even look back at Tom. She didn't have to. This act was a well-choreographed dance. He instinctively raised the camera and before PS could protest, switched on the battery light perched at the top of his light stem. He reached over and handed her the microphone. She hastily grabbed it, knowing that the light had already cost them valuable seconds to get the interview.

The white light was blinding, a stark contrast to the cool red and blue flashing lights of the police cruisers, and the stranger stepped back a bit and shielded his eyes as if he were a mole or a vampire unexpectedly greeted by sunlight.

The light also caught the attention of a sheriff's deputy who had apparently moved away from the cruiser to catch a smoke.

"Hey, you there!" He yelled. "Stop!"

He raced over, dropping his glowing orange ember to the gravel.

Before any information at all could be persuaded from the stranger on tape, the young pimply faced deputy whisked him away from the TV crew, and into the police car. The deputy shot back a nasty look, walked around his vehicle and plopped into the front seat on the driver's side, still glaring.

"Dammit!" PS said to Tom. "That would have been good."

She struggled for a moment to contain her anger, and then as calmly as she could muster asked, "Why in the Hell did you turn on that light? You couldn't shoot that interview in available light?" *You moron!* She screamed to herself.

"I wasn't thinking, PS. I'm sorry. My hand automatically reached up and switched the damn thing on before I could stop myself. I'm so sorry."

The two were talking amongst themselves, nose to nose quietly and when they looked up saw that Sherman Hall and his cameraman, Dirk, were standing in front of them.

Dirk was an odd, fidgety fellow who had peculiar twitches. He seemed to involuntarily lurch and hiccup. His head always seemed to spasm from the neck. It always looked as though he were slightly shaking his head, 'no'. And apparently, he never got rid of that case of the crabs from college, as he was always squatting his knee to the right and snatching at his fly after scraping his hand up from his testicles having given them a good tug.

The more agitated Dirk was, the more urgent the need to scratch, scrape and tug. He also chirped and whistled as he spoke.

The behavior always caught PS off guard, though Sherman Hall didn't seem to even notice it.

Tom wondered how the poor fellow could even hold his camera steady with all of that jerking and squeaking. PS didn't care. She couldn't stand to be around him, he smelled like stale raisins and it infuriated her that he wore a wedding ring and was rumored to have children.

"How can a man like that be married?" She'd always complain after an encounter. "If he were a woman, he wouldn't even get a date. It's just not fair. Men can look like anything and still get married!"

As much as she hated to be around him, she could hardly take her eyes off of him. He was something to behold, indeed.

Sherman Hall on the other hand was something else entirely. She could hardly take her eyes off of him. He was about 6'3", broad shoulders, jet Black hair with a little graying perfectly placed at the temples, chiseled chin, and deep green eyes.

She hated the way his monogrammed French cuffs always peeked so neatly out from beneath his overcoat, even though she loved it.

But as attractive as Sherman Hall was to her and ninety-nine percent of the female viewership, PS believed that he was a skunk. She hated that every single story that pitted them against each other was a hard fought battle. No matter what the circumstances he was always one step behind her, if not one step ahead.

Sherman Hall seemed equally as disgusted by his counterpart. She used her beautifully shaped legs as a weapon. She had perfect lips that were always neatly lined. The top lip was like a twin peak, perfectly proportioned with her beautiful face. The bottom lip was bee stung and pouty. And he always had to resist the urge to reach out, and sweep away that one little spray of hair that constantly dangled in front of her face.

He hated the way she managed to blend in with the locals at any story scene.

PS Garret was a master chameleon. She was able to get people to reveal information that Chinese water torture couldn't pry out. There was something about her that made her likable, and seemingly trustworthy. People were dying to tell her their stories—their secrets. Whereas he had to work twice as hard to get anyone to even come to his microphone. He had to beg, and ingratiate himself, where it seemed effortless for PS Garrett. And he hated it.

He hated her, even though he loved her.

After years of the two reporters competing against each other on the streets of the Detroit police beat, no clear winner could be declared. They were each other's nemesis. And the rivalry was bitter.

Dirk spoke first. "And what was that all about?" He said, squatting and scratching so vigorously it made PS's scalp itch.

"Are you kidding?" Tom protested. "Why would we tell you anything?"

"There's nothing you can tell us that we don't already know. Maybe you should be asking what I can

38

tell you," Sherman Hall said as he puffed his chest and moved into the breathing space of PS.

Polo. She thought to herself. He's wearing Polo cologne today. No it's not. It's that stuff in the sapphire blue bottle at the department store. That's my favorite.

In spite of himself, Sherman was intoxicated by the scent of the small framed reporter in front of him. And he hated himself for it.

There was an underlying current of respect and admiration the two felt for each other. The kind that true warriors, evenly matched in combat might experience. But disdain and insecurity always won out when the two confronted each other face to face.

"Sherman Hall, back off," PS said, stepping away from him, a bit intimidated by the fact that he knew he had elements to the story that she didn't have. "Why would I ask you anything?"

"Because maybe if you did so nicely, I'd throw you a bone."

"Only a dog like you carries bones in his pocket, Sherman Hall, and I don't need your leftovers, you arrogant suck! Come on Tom, let's go re-edit our story with that soundbite we just got. I can tell you for sure, you don't have anything like that on tape," PS said as she marched away with Tom in tow, her hips swaying just enough to distract Sherman Hall.

"You know as soon as we go on the air, he's going to know you don't have shit," Tom whispered.

"Oh, I know. But he makes me so mad. At least I can make him sweat for another hour or so. Let's go. We gotta turn this chicken shit into chicken salad."

Sherman Hall was so arrogant. He always acted like he had the upper hand of a crime scene even when he didn't. He always played the 'good ole boy' card with other cops, used his looks and suave to take the upper-hand.

And that cameraman of his, she was so disgusted when that weirdo, Dirk Danbury, would pass out cigars to cops, county execs, and other people of power, position and information. Though, she wondered who in the Hell would accept a cigar from the right hand of that creep.

The two of them just didn't play fair, and it usually worked in their favor. Sherman Hall was a particularly painful thorn in her thigh.

PS looked back at the police cruiser and could see the face of that odd-ball guy watching them as they walked away. The intermittent red and blue light, hitting the glass window of the back seat made him even spookier. She broke eye contact and turned away. That really would have been a good interview.

"I know why the cop had to squire him off. The last thing this department needed was for us to get information from a witness that would screw up the investigation. I'm glad you at least got some quick video of him before the cop was able to marshal him off," she said aloud. But she was more than a little pissed Tom had flashed on the light. Had he shot the interview in available light, she'd be able to back up her threat to Sherman. And given he had an hour or more jump on her to begin with, she wanted him to eat some sort of bird, even if it wasn't crow.

Oh, how she hated to be beaten by that reporter, Sherman Hall. She just hated it!

As the Channel Six crew members made their way back to their live van, Tom fired off a few extra shots of Danny Weinstein's dad who was still standing at the edge of the yellow crime scene tape with several police officers and filled PS in on what he'd been able to find out.

Tom said the boy's father had apparently heard there'd been a shooting at his Gas 'N Go from some report or something on a scanner or radio. Tom saw him as he raced to the scene when none of the other stations was around. The photographer said it was pretty clear they didn't even know who the dad was, since, as near as he could tell, no one had tried to get video of him as he showed the cops around the property that was now entirely protected by well-placed sentries in police cruisers.

As much as she loved her work, PS hated this kind of story.

Most times when kids like these got corked, they were kids who everybody liked.

Of course, no kid deserved to die like this—on a lonely stretch of highway mowed down by some heartless reprobate with bad upbringing. If they were bad eggs who deserved to die, it would be less of a story. Dope dealers, for instance, got mere mentions on the news, if any time at all. Unsympathetic characters.

Of course if that drug dealer or addict dragged some innocent soul along with him in the process of dying badly, then that would be a story worth covering.

41

The more tragic the story, the more air time it was granted. And as tragic and unfair as this double murder was, it was one Hell of a good story.

The Channel Six crew stopped one more time to survey the crime scene before getting into the van.

As they stood on the periphery, scanning the area for more elements to the story, PS's eyes kept drifting to the front plate glass window of the Gas 'N Go.

Tom watched the crowd to see if anybody in particular stood out. He was keeping his eyes peeled for more family members. Perhaps one would come and drift far enough away from the crime scene so they could pick them off for a quick interview. Or maybe they'd catch the boy's father as he headed toward his vehicle.

They both dreaded such interviews, but they're a necessity. Soundbites from grieving family members raised your stock in the newsroom. And while people swore they hated to see them on television, neither Tom nor PS had ever once noticed anyone turning the channel at the sight of a sobbing relative.

PS's eyes kept drifting back to that front plate glass window for some reason. Her reporter's sense was telling her there was something there worth paying attention to.

Finally, she couldn't stand it another minute. There was something there trying to speak up.

Her skin started to crawl. When she pushed her blazer sleeve up over her wrist, she could see goose bumps. Her left shoulder started throbbing even in the unseasonably warmer air.

"Tom," she said as she squinted and strained to figure out what was bugging her mind's eye. "There's a smudge or something just beneath the words Gas 'N Go on that front window. At first I thought it was dirt, but I don't think so anymore."

"Well, let's take a look," Tom said as he erected his tripod and hoisted his camera on top of it.

What PS really wanted to do was to walk up to the yellow tape and take a peek for herself, but that was the line of demarcation. On a night like tonight, getting too close would be asking for real trouble. It would have meant being taken off the police beat because word would spread like wildfire that she was a cheat—no cop within a two-hundred mile radius would even talk to her, unless it was to give her a speeding ticket for going one mile over the speed limit.

She had to fight her reporter's sense to move closer. "Can you get a tight shot of that smudge? Right there, just under the 'N'. What is that?"

Tom trained his camera lens on the plate glass window, and zoomed in.

At first he said nothing, he just made adjustments to his telephoto lens. But then he stopped. He was standing there, still, completely silent.

"Well?" PS insisted. "What is it? Can you see?"

Tom said nothing. He turned his head from side to side, to make certain no one else was paying attention to them, and then he pressed his right eye back to the viewfinder.

"Well?" She commanded impatiently.

"Shhhhhh! Quiet would ya'!" Tom answered in a whisper, in a voice that sounded like a distant echo.

His words were barely audible which was unusual because Tom was generally boisterous, even during the worst of stories.

He had a quick smile and an easy laugh, and he knew how to brush off the stink of a sad story. The more grisly the scene, the more it seemed to roll off his back like duck water.

"What is it?" PS exclaimed in the same hushed voice. "Is it something or nothing?"

Tom said nothing, instead fiddled with his lens, apparently trying to fine-tune the image.

"Hey man, we're on deadline! What's the deal?"

"Here," he finally said, satisfied that he had gotten the best picture possible. "Take a look for yourself. And pipe down will ya?"

Tom was a good bit taller than the reporter, everybody was, so she had to tiptoe to peek into the eye of the view finder. And as she craned her neck and peered into the rubber tube, even she was struck dumb.

"What the Hell is that? Are those some sort of letters?" She asked.

"You're reading them backwards," he answered quietly, looking around to make sure no one was paying them any mind. "Flip 'em around."

"Huh?"

"Flip them around, you're reading them backwards."

She made the mental adjustment, reading from right to left. And right there beneath the N in the gold lettering on the Gas 'N Go window, almost too small to see from a distance with the naked eye, but crystal clear with a camera and a telephoto lens, were words written in what looked like blood, '*Watch, Watch.*'

The blood drained from PS's face and an icy cold draped her shoulders as she looked around to see if anyone else had noticed.

Tom nudged her. "I don't think anyone else is paying attention."

"Surely the police have seen this," she whispered. "The crime lab technician must have already gotten photos of it."

"But that doesn't mean anyone from any of the other stations has seen it," Tom quickly assured.

PS's heart rate began speeding up, and her forehead started feeling warm. She was trying to keep her cool because she didn't want to alert any of the other reporters, but she was having a bit of trouble containing her nervousness—her excitement—her nervousness. "What the Hell does that mean?" She asked Tom.

"I don't know," he answered, shaking his head and nonchalantly taking his camera off the tripod and setting it on the ground facing away from the building. "But it would appear our murderer is showing off and can't wait for us to see more."

The uneasiness that had crept into the reporter's shoulder earlier was now a sledge hammer banging out the William Tell Overture.

"This was no ordinary would-be robber," she said in a muted tone. "This was slaughter. Obviously this guy fancies himself a modern day Charles Manson or something. What kind of monster would scribble with the blood of a human being? Hell, with the blood of anything?"

Now she knew why Chief Grainger wanted to warn his people to watch their step and their neighbor's step. There was a bad guy out there somewhere—not your garden variety convenience store heister. This guy was something else entirely.

"I mean, it's one thing to shoot someone." PS said in hushed tones, glancing about nervously. "That's brutal, but it's not a contact sport. You just point the gun and pull the trigger. Pow! That's it. Your dirty work is done. But when you reach down, scoop up a finger full of blood and write a cryptic message on the glass wall in front of you, that's a different kind of crime altogether."

PS turned to look at her partner. Tom was a little excited at this point, too. "There is definitely some sort of rabid animal out there," he whispered, a wild half smile on his face. As horrible as what they'd seen was, Tom knew that they had struck gold. PS knew they had struck gold. THEY HAD STRUCK GOLD!

PS continued, "Now I know what Chief Grainger was so spooked about."

With confidence anew, she meandered over to Chief Grainger. She didn't want to seem too anxious, because all reporters watch each other on stories like these, some more closely than others. She didn't want to alert anyone that she'd found something—but measuring her steps proved difficult. It was close to 10:00, she was officially on deadline and she wanted to make sure the filet mignon was done just right before being served to the monster at 11:00.

Chief Grainger was holding court with one of the reporters from Channel Nine. PS didn't know his name. She didn't know many of the names of the reporters at Channel Nine. It just wasn't worth her while.

As she got within earshot of his conversation with the other reporter, she stopped to keep a respectable distance.

Kind of an etiquette thing.

On stories this competitive, only the very rude, inexperienced and insecure walk up while you're talking to a potential source of information.

Instead, she stood close enough so the reporter could be annoyed by her presence, and hurry things along—but far enough away as to not overtly eavesdrop, though she made certain she could still hear what was being said to the competition.

She wanted to make sure that the Channel Nine reporter wasn't inquiring about the smudges on that window.

Once the Chief looked up and acknowledged her, she used it as an opening to move in.

She greeted the other reporter, apologized for the intrusion and gently dragged Grainger away, loudly going over very obvious details of the crime scene she had gotten earlier.

"Chief, I just want to make sure I have this right. We have two teenagers, one sixteen and the other fifteen, right? Now which one was fifteen, the boy or the girl..."

It was all an act—just pretending to confirm a few things so as not to rouse the suspicion of the Channel Nine reporter who was now watching her walk away with the official source of information on the crime scene. And the last thing she wanted to do was to attract attention, especially from Sherman Hall.

"What's going on here, Missy?" The Chief scolded. "I know you better than this. What's on your mind?"

When she was comfortably out of earshot of any other reporter, she fessed up.

"Um, Chief. We just saw something in our camera lens on that plate glass window, and I don't remember you mentioning it."

"I beg your pardon?"

Chief Grainger sounded irked for the first time that night. "What are you talking about?" He demanded.

"Chief Grainger, no offense," she assured. "But I'm talking about the blood st..."

Chief Grainger shushed her mid-word. He was angry, and his voice was raised. PS became concerned that his tenor would alert the other reporters. She glanced nervously about.

"I said I don't know what you're talking about," he insisted. "You're mistaken."

"Am I, Chief?" The reporter replied, lowering her voice several dozen decibels in hopes that he would do the same. "Mistaken about what? I don't remember you allowing me to finish my sentence. I'm sorry I bothered you."

Now she was angry. She'd known Chief Grainger for a long time. They'd worked on several big stories together. They had a good working relationship, and he'd never been dishonest with her before, as best as she could tell.

One thing was certain, however. She knew something about this crime no one else in the media seemed to know. She knew what she had seen on that plate glass window. It would have been nice to get a confirmation, but it wasn't necessary so she decided to bluff. It was a dangerous move, but one well worth the risk.

PS Garrett slowly turned away from the Chief and began to walk away, her hips gently and seductively swaying more out of agitation than flirtation.

She decided to play a little poker. She moved further away from the Chief, but not without first saying over her shoulder, "I was able to have a lengthy interview with that witness who was over there in the cruiser before one of your boys pried him away."

A bold-face lie. But if the Chief wanted to play it like this, that was fine with her. "After our little talk, Tom put the telephoto lens on the camera. We got a clean shot of it."

By now she was a good three feet from the Chief. She was walking away, but taking her time about it. But he wasn't following. So she upped the ante a bit.

"And besides," she continued. "That guy you tucked away in that cruiser seemed pretty shaken up, and so do you, Chief. Sounds to me like the headline at the top of the hour should be, maybe something like, 'Rabid killer inks cryptic message in victim's blood.' Like I said, sorry to have bothered you."

She stopped walking and spun around to face the Chief. She didn't like doing this. She liked this guy. But she couldn't let that stop her from getting to

49

the truth. She had a job to do, and part of that job was informing the public that a mad man was on the loose. The other part of that job was beating the competition. PS Garrett aimed to do both.

The Chief was no dummy. He knew what she was doing—leading him into the dance. He knew this was play-acting—that she was baiting him. But, she was baiting him only because she had the bait. She had the goods, he knew it, and he knew only he could determine how it was presented on the air. He knew he didn't have editorial control, but his words would carry weight with this particular reporter. He knew she wasn't inclined to exploit the crime like that Sherman Hall guy from Channel Three. He didn't like that guy. He was a little too smooth, too cocky.

PS was staring the Chief in the eye. If he was going to tell her a lie, continue the charade, she wanted him to do it while looking her dead in the eye. She didn't think he could. And either way, she'd have her answer. She'd have exclusive video for the top of the 11 o'clock news. She'd be a hero. She'd win the night.

Sure the others would catch wind of it, and turn their cameras to the smudge, but she would have had it on the air first and that's all that counted.

She stood there for a moment more. The clock was ticking.

Chief Grainger looked at her for a nanosecond, tugged at his shirt collar, cleared his throat and narrowed his eyes.

She waited for his response for several seconds that seemed more like hours. When it came, it came like a sneeze—abruptly and with some sense of great release. "Dammit! You're the only one who's noticed that."

"Oh yeah?" She muttered, almost inaudibly and grinning on the inside.

She had stared down the Pixley police Chief and he had blinked. But now the Chief had to be handled sensitively. She didn't want him to gather the others to tell them about the smudges in a sense of fair play. She had to be cool, play down the discovery.

"But," the Chief continued. "I need to ask you not to mention it in your story tonight. We're conducting an investigation here. If that information gets out, it could hurt us."

PS Garrett's jaw dropped. This was heresy.

"Chief, for crying out loud. How?" She whined.

She didn't like how this was going. The balance of power was shifting.

"You're a good reporter," The Chief answered. "I've watched your work. I've known you for a lot of years. You're as good as they come."

"Chief?" She broke in, considering his words to be more flatulence than flattery. "What the..."

Grainger barreled on. "You do a lot of these police stories. You know there are some things about a crime scene we can't divulge.

"Say we find a potential suspect and we question him about what happened. He might say something about the blood, or who knows, maybe we can trip him up somehow."

"But, but..." PS stammered.

Again, the Chief would hear no part of it. He was gathering momentum. "If you go on television

51

tonight and talk about those words on that window, every kook in town will be sitting in our office claiming they did it. We'll never be able to sort through the mess."

The reporter's stomach sank and her hands began to tremble. The Chief was right and she knew it. Deep down, she'd known it all along.

She bit her bottom lip in solemn resolve. She knew the right course of action. But that didn't mean she had to take it. Sherman Hall had beaten her on a story earlier that week. The cards had been stacked against her all along on this one, until the Ace popped out of the hold. She hadn't asked for it, it was a gift. And PS Garrett didn't like squandering gifts.

She didn't want to hear what the Chief was saying. She didn't want to hear it! She didn't want to hear it!

Grainger was getting agitated, shifting his weight from one side to the other as he continued to try to sway her. He looked like Squealer, in George Orwell's Animal Farm—prancing from side to side.

The more PS chewed on the matter, the more he pranced. He knew it was entirely up to her. Anything found in the viewfinder of a camera was public domain. Any reporter would have a right to it. But the Chief needed the scales tipped in his favor.

"I know it's good television," he continued. "I know it's gruesome stuff, and you like to lead the newscasts with that sort of thing."

PS's nostrils flared. What the Chief was saying was true, but she didn't want to hear it. She stuttered to defend herself, but the words came out garbled in a gasp.

Grainger took advantage of the communication stall and quickly said, "I'm not condemning you, it's your job. I understand that. But I'm asking you. No, I'm appealing to you as a person. Please don't divulge that information. It could mean the difference between catching a killer—a rabid animal—or letting him go free.

"If you don't use the information, I'll consider it a personal favor, and I'll owe you one."

SHIT! Now that's just playing dirty.

"Yeah, well what if the other stations go with it?" PS snapped. "It'll be my tail. You know that."

"They don't know about it."

"How do you know for sure?"

"I know."

"How do you know?"

Now it was her turn to be agitated.

"I'm asking you to do the right thing. I'm telling you, to the best of my knowledge, no one else has noticed. It's not that noticeable from the outside, I don't know how you saw it. I'm asking you to not hurt my chances of catching a killer. A monster. I'm asking you to do the right thing."

PS was beyond her deadline. She could feel it with her internal clock. An hour before any given newscast, an automatic alarm seemed to sound inside the walls of her chest.

She shut her eyes and turned her face to the heavens. She was being toyed with and it was pissing her the Hell off.

Nope! She decided. She just couldn't justify it.

If her news director found out that she had censored the news, she would be selling tacos to pay her mortgage. Nope, it just couldn't happen.

She glanced over and saw Sherman Hall busy at work in the front seat of his live van. She dug her three inch heels in deeper. Nope, she just couldn't do it.

Of course even without that bloody little tidbit she still had a good story for the news. All the elements were there, all of the emotion.

What am I thinking? This is loony talk. PS thought to herself. *How could I not show those pictures? The public has a right to know.*

PS furrowed her brow and tugged frantically at the bang that had just slipped back down in front of her eye. *The Chief himself said everyone should be afraid tonight, and I need to show everyone why. Not telling this story is not responsible journalism. This is censorship.*

"It is not my job to tailor the news or to manipulate it," PS finally said aloud. "It's a matter of the public trust. It is my job to tell all that I see and hear. I am an observer. The eyes and ears of the people at home. To not tell a pertinent fact of a story because you ask me not to is high treason. A hanging offense. How could I live with myself?"

"But then again, if you did show the video," the Chief said. "It might hamper the search for a killer. How could you live with yourself then?"

Crap!

"That's not fair, Chief," she argued.

"Truth is not fair, PS. It just is."

PS didn't like it, it wasn't her job to edit the facts, but at least the Chief would owe her a favor, and she had been known to need a few favors from the local constabulary from time to time.

And besides, she wanted this beast caught as much as anyone else. She thought about it again. Added up the story elements she'd already gathered in her head. Did she have enough to win? Probably not. Did she have enough to compete? Yes.

She looked back over at the Channel Three live truck and thought, *I hate my life today.*

"Okay, Chief. Deal. I won't show the video until you catch a suspect."

"Until the trial. Please."

"The trial? Come on!"

"Please."

"And you owe me, right?"

"I owe you."

"You owe me big."

"I owe you big."

Chief Grainger extended his hand to shake on it.

PS relaxed the grip and tried to walk away, but the Chief held on.

"You know I'm a woman of my word," she assured him. "I said I won't use it, and I won't use it no matter what. I won't even tell anyone I have it. I wouldn't dare. If the boss knew I was sitting on this and didn't use it I'd be asking you for a job."

"What about your cameraman?" The Chief asked hesitantly.

"We're a team. He'll understand. I promise."

The Chief cupped her right hand with his left, and gave it one last strong shake. The two exchanged deep eye contact as that adorable wisp of hair floated back and forth across her eyelid. She unclenched her hand from the Chief's to sweep her stubborn bang behind her ear, turned and ran back to the live truck to have a little heart-to-heart with Tom.

She was nervous about the arrangement, but knew it was the right thing to do.

She talked to Tom and he agreed with the Chief. He gave her the tape for safekeeping, and she tucked it into her reporter's bag until she could lock it safely away in her desk drawer the next day.

PS felt buoyed. Even though she had been called in late, she still managed to cover all the bases. Even though the other guys had at least two news crews each, and field producers to boot, she had held her own.

She called the producer to go over the elements of her story.

The phone rang about fifteen times before someone finally picked it up. PS's spirits sank. It was the producer most likely to have a contract on her life by the age of forty. "Hey Salina, who's doing the eleven tonight?"

"You're talking to her," Salina spat in her own inimitable low, husky, mean-spirited voice.

Salina Kingsley. She had a hard smoking, hard drinking, hard living, no loving approach to everything in news gathering. And she had a mean mouth as her basic way of dealing with reporters, especially PS Garrett.

PS ignored her tenor and feigned as much cheerfulness as possible. "How's it going?"

Nothing. Dead air.

"Hello, is there anybody there?"

"Yeah, I'm waiting to hear what the Hell you want. I'm on deadline here."

"Me too, Salina, I just wanted to go over the details of my story with you. It's a good one. I think we did a pretty good job of playing catch-up out here," PS said in hopes she would get a little kudos and encouragement.

Nothing.

Giving kudos wasn't a part of Salina Kingsley's repartee.

A little of the air escaped PS's balloon, but she forged on. "Yeah. Well, we got some video of one kid's father. And some pretty good interviews with the Chief. He's really spooked by this thing. I think you should play that up in the lead."

"Oh, so now you're a producer. Did you want to time my show out for me too?"

"Salina, what is your problem?"

"My problem is it's 10:15 and I'm just hearing from my lead story. Where the Hell have you been?"

"I've been working this story," PS screamed into the phone. "A story I got to very late because you didn't know it was going on until you saw it on somebody else's station."

And then PS screamed in her head, *YOU BITCH!* But said, "The reason you haven't heard from us is because we've been humping out here to play catch- up."

"What do you want here, a standing ovation? You did your job. That's what you're supposed to do. That's why you get paid the little bucks!" Salina sneered.

"You know, Salina, actually I just thought that after working a double shift and busting my ass after you missed the story in the first place, you could be a little kinder, but I guess I forgot for a minute that you were raised by wolves. Perhaps you should take a minute, Salina, and slurp up your Prozac or did you miss this morning's rabies shot?"

PS slammed the cell phone down and heard the sound of plastic splintering. She didn't care. This story had to be good. If it wasn't, Salina would be all over her.

Her blood pressure jumped a few points. It was 10:16 and she still needed to write a script and feed voice tracks back to the studio in time for the editor to cut the package or story. It took less than five minutes to put her thoughts down, the story pretty much wrote itself. In the end she had a complete, and tidy little bundle of events that would be edited back at the studio into a package that contained taped tracks of her voice, that would have video edited on top of it, interviews with spectators and officials, or snippets and chunks of interviews called bites, or soundbites, and bits of natural sound or nat sound to give the story atmosphere and texture.

She also jotted down her Chyrons or titles, those words superimposed at the bottom of the screen. Without them, the audience might not know who the interviewee was — who was doing the talking inside the package.

PS gave Jerry her notes, and suggested a little extra tape to feed. She told Tom where she wanted to stand for her live shot—she wanted to be a little further south of the building, away from that smudge on the window.

She rummaged around in her reporter's bag for her make-up case, and her hand grazed the tape. She drifted off for a moment, remembering those horrible bloody letters on the plate glass window. She wondered what the murderer meant by, *"Watch, Watch."*

She moved the tape aside and grabbed her essentials—eye liner, translucent powder, lipstick. She slipped her small listening device, or IFB, into her ear, straightened her blazer, rubbed her shoulder and put the day's struggle behind her.

It was done.

"Houston, we've got a problem," Jerry's voice whispered from the back of the live van.

"What now?" PS groaned.

"They just lost my signal again. Apparently we're having trouble with the transmitter."

"What?" She screamed. "I can't believe this."

She looked at the clock on the dashboard. It was 10:20 and the editor back at the station only had the raw footage they'd fed back earlier—no voice tracks or instruction with which to edit the story. "This is crap!" She hollered. "This is the third time this week we've had transmitter problems. How in the Hell do they expect us to do our jobs?"

10:21, and Jerry's frantic button pushing was to no avail. With each mounting minute, PS's rants became more enraged. "What size market is this anyway? Number seven or one hundred and seven. For Christ's sake! Podunk, Mississippi could probably get this tape fed back faster."

10:21 and 35 seconds. Still, no luck. Now PS was the one who was rabid.

Jerry looked up as if to say, *Get out of here would you, you're making me nervous.*

PS pursed her lips and obliged. It wasn't his fault. They were all victims of the same sloppy management that failed to keep the gear maintained, was too indecisive to send a crew to the scene before the story was spotted on a Channel Three news-brief, and so busy counting beans that they were forced to accept the number two slot in the ratings, even though Channel Six was capable of being number one.

But she couldn't resist just one more rant as she climbed out of the van. "Little things, Jerry! Little things! It only takes the little things to get the Goddamned news on the air."

Then she looked up at the heavens in despair, "God, can we have a little help here. Just a little dub will do ya'."

She walked across the parking lot to her live shot location and made herself ready to go on at the top of the hour with no pre-edited story. She'd just have to wing it. Tap dance. "I'm not a reporter," she spat. "I'm a cotton picken' entertainer."

Her head ached as she tried to figure out how

she was going to pull off this story with no script and no story on tape.

"How's it going?" Tom asked politely.

He knew the answer, but she obliged him with a temperamental scowl. "We'd be better off with a couple of cans and a ball of string."

Tom shook his head empathetically, connected the cables to her earpiece, moved the television monitor closer so that she could see the newscast and walked back behind his camera. He came back to straighten her twisted collar, and gently reached up to sweep that dangling wisp from her face.

She looked up and smiled.

She surveyed the crime scene and played with a script in her head. She'd be live in two minutes. Even without edited footage, She had to make ready to compete. The studio could just run video, and she could watch it on the portable monitor at her feet and kind of give a play by play. It wouldn't be pretty, but it would get the job done.

10:58. PS Garrett could feel the butterflies flutter from her stomach to her chest. She was as ready as she was going to be.

She glanced over a few dozen yards to Channel Three's position. They had two reporters standing by. Sherman was nowhere in sight. He must have been live at another location. That was a huge concern but one she couldn't give any attention to at the moment. PS surmised they were going to do tag team reporting. Now that was a station that had its act together.

She swallowed a big piece of cotton and looked further down the line to size up what Channel Nine was doing. They also had two reporters, and a couple of field producers working the beat—and nobody ever watched them! They were dead last in the ratings. And here she was trying to compete with Stone Age equipment and a fading picture on the monitor.

It was a bad night when you were worried about what Channel Nine might have that you don't.

"Stand by," Tom instructed, and raised his left arm above his head.

PS turned her head toward the little gas station and could see police photographers stepping gingerly around the pools of blood, snapping pictures of the bodies, the blood, the registers, those words, everything. Crime lab technicians were still taking measurements and dusting for prints.

The man who had lost his only child stood still, numbly nodding and shaking his head to the questions being asked and re-asked by detectives in the shadows near the building.

PS turned back to face the camera. Just past the bank of live trucks, radio mobile units, and print media vehicles, she could see the road and the cars as they slowed down, obviously aware that something bad was going on in the glow of television camera lights bouncing off the yellow crime scene tape and the frenetically flashing lights atop police cruisers.

By now the community-at-large had probably heard it on the radio, or by word of mouth, or one of Channel Three's newsbriefs.

PS felt overwhelmingly sad for the parents of the young girl inside. She tried to glance at Tom's watch. Golly, she thought. Tammy's mother and father might just now be getting the news. If not, they'd surely know after seeing the first block of the 11 o'clock news, no matter what station they were watching.

The first block of the news is synonymous with above-the-fold in a newspaper. It's the section of the news before the first bank of commercials.

Goose bumps popped up on PS's forearm.

She was slipping. Normally crime stories didn't bother her. She'd covered dozens and dozens of them. She had become immune to the pain that surrounded them—grown accustomed to recognizing the slightest hint of feeling and emotion and shooting it down before it became a drain on her soul.

But that chilly night, she actually felt grief for not one murder victim but two.

She looked over her shoulder to see the shadowy figures moving about the Gas 'N Go, seemingly in slow motion.

A large white van had just pulled up and parked outside the shop.

The meat wagon.

She stood there in the chill, taking it all in, digesting the drama as it unfolded like a Monday night Movie-of-the-Week. It didn't feel real, but it was. She had the video to prove it.

Once again, she turned and trained her eyes on that smudge just under the N of the Gas 'N Go lettering on the window, and that ominous warning to *"Watch, Watch"*. A rubber, gloved hand came up out of nowhere and began to rub at the smudge, wiping it clean away.

Just for a moment, PS tried on the grief of that poor man quivering several yards away from her in the shadows. He was probably blaming himself for letting his son watch his shop so late at night.

She ached for him.

What kind of person would commit such a horrendous crime? Where was he now? Was he watching the activity from a window at the motel across the street? Maybe he was eating dinner at a nearby restaurant. It was conceivable that he could be one of the nosey on-lookers, straining for a closer peek of what was in front of the yellow crime scene tape. Maybe he was still among them, cold-blooded, remorseless, amused.

The front door of the Gas 'N Go had been slung open and an empty gurney was being wheeled in to collect one of the bodies.

PS focused and looked at Tom. He smiled at her and winked reassuringly. They were both thinking the same sickening thought. If Salina timed it right, they'd be in the live shot while the bodies were being removed from the building. That would be compelling video for sure.

PS parted her legs a bit to get a good footing on the cold parking lot gravel. She didn't want to wobble or topple in her heels during the live shot.

She was relieved when a voice crackled over the IFB into her ear. "We've got some video edited, so you can just talk over it if you want."

It was the voice of the assistant director in the control room. The air traffic controller at the master board, if you will. He was responsible for lining up the live shots and making sure the director took the right camera for the right story.

He was thoughtful and supportive, unlike that bitch, Salina Kingsley who was probably sitting next to him by now, barking orders.

Great. PS thought to herself. I won't look like a complete ass, after all.

She gave a barely perceptible nod to acknowledge that she'd heard the assistant director back at the studio. Tom lowered his arm, slicing the cold spring air with his finger outstretched to cue the reporter to begin talking to the anchors who were back at the studio watching in the monitor behind the anchor desk.

And before telling this sad story to thousands of people at the top of the 11 o'clock news, PS Garrett felt afraid. Very afraid.

PS wrapped up her live shot, pulled the IFB out of her ear and wound the cord around her fingers before tucking the unit into her blazer pocket.

Tom suggested that they all swing by Silver Spur Chop Suey on their way home. It was PS's favorite restaurant, and Tom thought she deserved a stiff drink and some commiseration.

Jerry, who was now rolling cable around a big metal spindle agreed. Already, word had made its way around the crime scene that a group from the other stations would be there—maybe even a couple of cops when they got off duty.

PS didn't need any more convincing than that. "Great idea fellas. Maybe we can buy those cops a few rounds and they'll fill in all the blanks of the investigation. Maybe I'll even get a head start on the drinks."

"You need it, honey," Jerry said in a kindly, fatherly sort of way. "Good job tonight."

"No. Great job," Tom chimed in.

Tom and PS bumped shoulders in a toast and exchanged the knowing glance that sealed their little secret of the tape that was safely tucked away in the reporter's belongings.

PS trotted across the asphalt, unaware that two people from opposite sides of the parking lot were watching her intently as she left.

Sherman Hall, who'd just pulled back up to the scene in an unmarked news vehicle and was gloating about his clear victory over Channel Six in the news coverage that evening. And a silent stranger, with blood on his hands, as he sat in a stolen car watching—first, the crime scene he had created, and then, the television reporter he had always wanted to meet.

CHAPTER THREE

PS Garrett jumped in her car and sped out of the parking lot.

One mile down the road, and the stink of the night was already starting to fade. Five miles further, the images were mere ghosts. Her mind turned to other things—bills to be paid, Fido needed cat food and her teeth cleaned. PS hadn't talked to her parents in weeks and made a mental note to call them the next day. And she couldn't wait to see Willina, her best friend, so she could vent about Sherman Hall and that bitch, Salina Kingsley.

She dialed Wil up on her cell phone and the two agreed to meet at Silver Spur. Even though it was a *school night*, it took very little to convince Willina Johns to join a party.

PS opened her sunroof. She wanted the cold air to filter into her car. Several miles east of Pixley and the air was soothing and cleansing, not chilling.

She drove through another small town as a shortcut to get to the freeway. She made note of the cute little shops she passed, knowing she would never have time to come back.

She noticed a throb, an annoyance. Chalked it up to the awful night, but then realized something was poking her in her back-side. She felt around and realized she was sitting on her pager that had been tucked away in her blazer pocket along with her IFB cord. She scrunched up in her seat, pulled the jacket from beneath her bottom, grabbed both the pager and the listening device and tossed them onto the seat beside her.

At a stoplight, she gazed over at the concaved picture window of a storefront. In its reflection her eyes glazed over and she could see images of that small balding man, weeping as he walked police around the perimeter of his store. She could still see the disarming splash of flashing police car lights as they peppered the horizon. And she could imagine what the bodies of those two innocent teenagers must look like. Crumpled on the floor, the look of terror frozen on their faces, their bodies—bloodied and returned to the fetal position. And in her mind's eye, she enlarged the crimson words, *Watch, Watch*.

She shuddered, and then started at the sound of a horn blowing behind her. She looked up and the light was green. She put her hand up through the sunroof and waved an apology then she shifted into first, stepped on the accelerator and sped ahead of the car behind her.

"She waved to me," the man sitting in the car behind her said aloud. "She waved to me. I knew she liked me."

He then lifted the fingers of his left hand to his nose and sniffed. He liked the smell of human blood. He then made a mental note of the license plate number on the small red car that had been sitting at the light in front of him.

PS Garrett got to the Spur ahead of the other news crews. As she got out, the proprietor, Mack was

68

waiting at the door. "Willina called and said you were coming here."

Mack handed the reporter a tall Kool Aid glass filled with a dark and potent mixture of Kaluha, Godiva Chocolate Liqueur and Half N Half. "Brown Cow?" He offered.

"Hey, thanks," PS said gleefully as she grabbed the concoction and greedily tilted the glass to her lips.

To PS Garrett, Brown Cows were the elixir of life. The cocktail cured colds, stopped allergies in their tracks, removed paint and wiped away a day of grief and frustration. She'd come to depend on them, just to smooth out the edges until the weekend. And on the weekend, she used them to forget that Monday was on its way.

"Sad story about those kids, huh?" Mack said shaking his head as PS walked through the door.

"Did you see it, Mack?" PS was excited that Mack had tuned into Channel Six for a change. He was an avid fan of Channel Three and no matter what PS said to him, she could never get him to tune into her station. "You saw it?"

"You bet," he answered. "It's terrible what happened, and that poor man. What's his name? Stan? He was crying like a baby on that interview."

"Interview? Mack, what interview?"

Mack had obviously been very touched by what he'd seen and had his head bowed.

PS asked him again. "Mack, what interview?"

"You know. The one you got with the father before he made it to the gas station. He was saying

69

how he had to go to an AA meeting, so the boy volunteered to watch the shop for him.

"I nearly cried myself when he said it should've been him instead of his kid. He's right you know, no parent should have to bury his kid. Sad, very sad."

The glass PS had been holding nearly slipped out of her hand as she stood just beyond the door of Silver Spur Chop Suey with her mouth open. Her heart sank as what Mack was telling her began to sink in. "Mack, I didn't interview Mr. Weinstein. I only had video of him coming out of the gas station."

The young reporter's confusion turned to anger, that anger to fury and that fury into a full scale, throbbing headache. Not because Mack had clearly been watching that other station again, that much she expected, but because another station had obviously scored such an important interview.

She had been nailed! The victim's father! Those are the interviews you hate to get and love to get at the same time. They add life and color to a story. As much as the public rails at the media for going after that kind of interview, they always tune in to see the sobbing relatives. A story is not complete without the sobbing relatives.

"My news director must be going berserk!" She yelped.

She felt around in her blazer pocket for the pager and then realized she had left it in her car.

Good thing. It was probably exploding with nasty messages from the boss, or worse, Salina Kingsley. And it would not have mattered that she had been sent in to the scene late, or that the other stations each sent two reporters instead of just one. Most irksome of all was, it didn't matter that she was the only one who knew about those bloody words scribbled on the window and she didn't squeal for the good of the investigation.

No one was going to give her credit for skipping dinner to work a double, or for coming in that morning even though she had the sniffles.

NONE OF IT MATTERED!

The only thing that mattered at that moment was that Channel Three had interviewed the victim's father.

PS wondered who else got an interview with the dad. If it had been one of those losers at Channel Nine, she felt as though she would have to look for a rusty razor blade and end her life for sure.

All of a sudden, drinks with the competition didn't seem like much fun. PS began to storm out the door, until Willina came sauntering up from the parking lot. "Hi, what ghost did you just see?" She said with a broad grin on her face.

She usually had a broad grin on her face. In fact, she had very little to frown about, living a seemingly charmed life with the only real stresser being the remote chance her boyfriend's wife might find out she existed. And even that possibility didn't seem to bother her much. She was pretty sure if Henry had to choose between the mistress and the Mrs., the mistress would win.

By almost any standards, Willina was a standout. She was a statuesque 5'9 in her stocking feet, though PS couldn't remember the last time she saw her best friend bare foot.

Willina's idea of sensible shoes were three inch spiked heels instead of five inch spiked heels. She claimed that she was straight off the plantation—Black. But, PS was suspicious of her family tree. All of her brothers and sisters had deep toned, dark skin and broad features. Willina was honey brown. She had sharp features, from her delicately slender nose, to her high cheek bones. Her eyes were narrow, almost Asian in appearance, though not quite as almond-shaped. The eyes behind the lids were striking—deeply intelligent and intense, and an unusual shade of gray rarely seen in people of color.

Her body, however, was true sister. She had 25mph curves that were enviable—large, firm D cup breasts, a slender waist and an ample backside that most men seemed to find irresistible.

When she spoke, it was with command and thunder. Her only initial flaw, her diction and grammar.

She had the appearance of coming from breeding and money, but her dialect always gave her away. She was raised in the hood.

She was more street smart than book smart. But even with the lack of speech training, you could tell that this woman knew exactly what was going on, and understood the world better than most.

Wil opened the door to Silver Spur Chop Suey as PS started tumbling out.

Breathlessly, PS gasped, "Oh my God, Willina, you're not going to believe this."

"Oh, I probably will. Hey Mack, what's up?

"Same ole' Wil. Whatta ya drinkin' tonight?"

"I feel like something new, something fresh and fruity. What do you have?"

"Miller or Pabst Blue Ribbon?"

"Mack, this place is a dump. You know that don't you?"

"Miller or Blue Ribbon?" Mack persisted with a laugh.

"Split the difference, mix the two. I'm feeling adventuresome. What's up with drama queen here?"

"Drama queen? I'm the drama queen? Here my livelihood is on the line and the two of you are arguing over what kind of beer there is in this slop hole!"

"Ouch!" Mack protested, genuinely hurt by the comment.

PS realized what she had said, and touched Mack on the arm. "You know that's not what I meant. I love this place, and I love you. But I'm just in shock right now."

"Okay," Willina said as she moved passed PS and Mack in the doorway. "Let's talk about it."

PS followed her inside the restaurant. "I totally got my ass beaten on a story tonight."

"Okay."

"I got sent in late, I didn't have much help..."

"You're talking about the double murder in Pixley, right?"

"Uh huh."

"Yeah, I saw that. Oh, the father of that boy was so sad to watch, I had to turn off the TV."

"Willina, you saw it too? What station were you watching?"

"I don't know, I had been flipping around. Why?"

"I didn't do that interview. I didn't have any interviews. I didn't have anything? Do you know what's going to happen to me at work tomorrow?"

"My guess, is that bitch, Salina Kingsley is going to blow you some shit. She's going to make you feel incompetent and you're going to let her. Can she fire you?"

"No," PS admitted as she sat down and took another deep swig from the Kool Aid glass that had survived the slip from her hand. "Only the news director can do that."

"Is he likely to fire you?"

"Well, I doubt it. I mean, I do have a contract."

"Well then, it seems to me the best thing that could happen to you is that you get fired, they have to pay off your contract and you get an extended paid vacation and we go to Paris for a couple of months. Now what's so tragic about that?"

"Wil, you don't get it."

"I get it. You don't get it. This is a job. I'll give you a good, well paying job, but it's just a job. Some days you have good days, and some days you have bad days."

"Willina, what do you know about good days and bad days. You're a kept woman."

"This isn't about me, this is about you. And I have worked before."

"Yes, but when you get sick of a job, you leave

74

it and ask for an increase in your allowance from your married boyfriend."

"Hey, there is something to be said for being a courtesan."

"Oh, is that what we're calling it now?"

"Did you want me to stay and talk this out with you or not?"

"I'm sorry, Wil. It's just that my work is important to me. People count on me to get the news. And I don't take that lightly."

"I know you don't, honey. But why do you let these bumps in the road bring you to a halt. This is not a slit-your-wrist incident. Okay, so this one got past you. You gotta learn to shake that crap off. Let it roll like water off a duck's back."

The front door of Silver Spur Chop Suey swung open, and in walked a horde of hungry, thirsty news people.

PS took another deep swig from her glass, and pretended none of this bothered her.

"Quack, Quack," Willina chided. "Quack, Quack. It's all part of the game. Work is just a game."

As un-luck would have it, everyone showed up—except those cops from Pixley. Apparently the Chief had appealed to their better senses and asked them to spend their off time somewhere other than in a bar with a bunch of hungry, probing reporters.

This was PS's hang out, and every once in a while a stray reporter from another news outlet might wander in, but PS had never seen anyone from Channel Three cross the stoop until that night.

Khrista Horn, the reporter and weekend anchor

for Channel Three was there, as was that arrogant snot, Sherman Hall.

PS felt he always held his nose so far in the air, it looked like there was a constant stink just beneath his nostrils. She believed he probably couldn't get out from beneath the smell of his weirdo photographer, Dirk who walked in smoking what was left of a large cigar.

A second Channel Three photographer also strolled in. He was a gorgeous Hispanic who often worked as Sherman Hall's back up photographer. He was tall and broad, and always wore muscle shirts that seemed to define his well-formed chest. He spoke with a thick Latin accent that always melted PS.

Her position toward Sherman often thawed a bit when he worked with Manuel, instead of that creep Dirk. But for some reason, Dirk seemed to be the star reporter's first choice as a partner on the streets.

Edith R. Hillard from Channel Nine was even in attendance. That was a rare sighting, indeed, since the Channel Nine people more resembled vampires. They only had one newscast, and that was at 10 o'clock at night. They would come out during the evening to suck the blood out of a story that almost no one was going to see and then they'd disappear into the day.

Mack was in his glory, begging Krista and Sherman for autographs.

PS wanted to hurl as he hovered over them— never allowing their glasses to go empty and making it clear that whatever they consumed—was on the house.

"Steady, steady, girl," Wil encouraged. "Suck this one up, it'll be good for you."

It didn't take long before the various reporters and photographers abandoned their small individual conversations and got down to the nasty business of comparing notes for the night. And as it turned out, all the other stations did have an interview with the victim's father. They found out where he lived and caught him coming out of his apartment as he made his way to the crime scene. He had heard about the double shooting on the radio only moments earlier. He was in shock, and didn't know he had every right to tell those nuisance reporters and their probing cameras to go to Hell.

"He was a reporter's dream!" Laughed Sherman Hall. "Timid, and in shock. Does it get any better than that?" Sherman howled and slapped the table with glee. It shook, and PS grabbed her drink and steadied it as she listened, having nothing to contribute.

"Apparently, he still had hope it wasn't so," Sherman continued. "He wrung his hands and cried and gave the reporters background on his son."

"And that's when that newspaper reporter asked if he had a recent picture of his son," Khrista contributed.

"Yeah, that's right. That's right," Sherman screamed in a voice that surely made dogs howl for miles around. "Stan Weinstein even pulled out a snapshot from his wallet."

"I know," Edith R. Hillard chimed in. "I couldn't believe it. I thought I would wet myself right there. It was like taking a calf to slaughter."

"Snatching candy from a baby," offered one of the radio reporters. "My only regret was, I don't need pictures to get my story across."

The table erupted in spontaneous laughter.

It was a disgusting display of insensitivity. Anyone else listening to this conversation would have had one more justification for hating the damned media.

PS sat listening to all of that noise, thinking to herself, *Oh my God, the other stations even had a picture of one of the victims. This is worse than I thought.*

"You know, while we were all standing there talking to that Weinstein character, I did have one question I didn't dare ask out loud," Sherman said, having piped down a bit.

Everyone leaned in so as to catch every word.

"Yeah, and what question was that?" PS asked feigning interest.

"Where the Hell was Channel Six?"

Everyone at the table shouted with laughter. Khrista Horn laughed so hard, her drink squirted out of her nose.

"I mean, those guys are everywhere!"

Sherman was on a roll. He'd already stuck the knife in, and now he wanted to turn it. "That is, if you believe their commercials," he shrieked with laughter. "I mean, what the Hell was that all about? Couldn't those guys see this was a huge story?" He yelled. "Who's running your assignment desk anyway? Stevie Wonder?"

More laughter.

"Obviously it was somebody who wonders what a real news story is." Dirk squeaked and burped as he took a long drag off his cigar butt, before spewing stiflingly stale smoke into the air.

Channel Six was indefensible.

All newsrooms are inherently the same, only the call letters change. Every reporter sitting at that table had been in the same position at one time or another. They all lived and died by equipment, planning, and timing.

Beep, Beep, Beep. The sound of a pager pierced the air, and everyone automatically reached for their belts. Even PS grabbed at her blazer pocket instinctively. But then remembered she had left her pager on the passenger seat of her car.

Reporters and photographers alike pressed pagers to their ears, or pushed display buttons in order to determine who was being summoned by the *All Mighty* via electronic tether.

"It's me, it's me. It's mine," announced Edith R. Hillard from Channel Nine. Everyone settled down as she read her display. "Ooooooh look!" She squealed as she turned her pager around for all of us to see. "It's my news director congratulating me on beating the pants off Channel Six."

The entire table went nuts—laughing, talking, conveying congratulations.

What a prize! A message from the news director. That was like hearing the horns of heaven. It makes everything—the murders, the deadlines, the stress—the everything—worthwhile.

Rarely do kudos come from the news director. When they do it's so valuable that reporters lock the messages into their terminals so they can re-read several times a day for several days to come.

"Let's ask the Channel Six reporter what the message from her news director says on her pager!" Sherman Hall said in a loud raucous, had-far-too much-to-drink, sort of voice.

TV news is a mean business. In order to survive, reporters must learn to forget the people who make the stories and to remember only the events. They learn to keep score on who got what from whom at the scene.

In the end, it's not about the man who lost his only son, or the woman who will mourn the violent death of her daughter. In the end, it's not about the bad guy who got away. In the end, it's not about the public good or public bad. In the end, it's who got the best or first interview, who told the best story, who gets the applause when they walk into the studio the next day. In the end it's who did the best job keeping those commercials from bumping into each other.

"I'll tell you what my pager says, Sherman Hall," PS said as she got up to leave.

She held up her hand and pressed her fingers down to flick him the bird. "That's what it says."

She walked toward the door of the Spur with almost everyone laughing.

"Don't go," Sherman said under his breath. "Don't go angry."

"Wha'd you say man?" Dirk squeaked.

Sherman watched as PS opened the front door and walked into the night. "Nothing. I didn't say anything."

"What did he say?" Willina asked Dirk. She wasn't nearly as offended by him as she was amused.

"Who knows. All I know is that every time that buddy of yours comes around, it turns my partner here into a grade A asshole."

PS unlocked her car, but stood in the chilly air for a few minutes to cool the steam pouring from her ears.

She liked looking at the stars, and that night, the sky was vibrant and clear.

There it was! Pleiades, her favorite constellation.

Pleiades, also called the Seven Sisters because of the seven stars that make up the cluster. She called it the little cat, because that's what it reminded her of.

Gazing up at the stars reminded her that there was beauty and wonder in this world. It helped her to remember the things that she loved that brought her peace—things like vibrant flowers, and the stripes on saltwater fish, slicing an eggplant long-ways, to see the image of the sun.

Looking up into the night kept her hopeful.

It made her think of Danny. Her Danny—who'd left without warning so many years ago. She shivered and gasped, and then quickly chased that thought away.

She became uneasy with the sense that she was being observed—scrutinized. Her reporter's sense was setting off alarms. She glanced around and didn't see anything or anyone and looked back through the glass door of the Spur. It was filled with smoke and laughter and drinking. And through the pack of jackals she saw Sherman Hall staring out after her. Probably gloating.

Once again she questioned the decision to tuck away that video. Did she really have a right to protect the public?

She took a few extra seconds more to consider those horrible smudges on the plate glass window—and those ominous words painted in blood. She wondered what the killer or killers meant by that cryptic message, *Watch, Watch.*

Was it some sort of cult or satanic worship ritual?

Once again she chased away a shiver that was working its way down her back. It didn't feel like early February. Frost was actually dancing off her breath instead of snow, and her car windows had ice crystals on them instead of sleet.

"I did the right thing," she whispered to the wind. "Those cops have a killer to find, and if I'd broadcasted that bloody message, not only would it have created a bigger panic in the area, but it would have made it that much more difficult to catch the killer.

"Maybe it wasn't the best decision for me as a reporter, but I had a responsibility as a person to not derail the investigation."

She jumped in her car, feigning satisfaction she'd done the right thing, put it in gear and headed up the highway toward home. She settled in to the soothing *thump, thump, thump* of the bass that was filling her car, courtesy of her favorite jazz station. She reached to turn the radio up, and that's when she heard it—the faint *beep, beep beep* of her pager.

With one hand, she reached behind her reporter's bag on the front seat and fumbled around until she'd located it. She slowed down, lifted her knees to the steering wheel to help keep the car steady on the road, and pushed the display button to read the message on the face of the pager.

And yes, it was her news director.

CHAPTER FOUR

PS Garrett tried to roll out of bed, but couldn't make her body move. It was as though someone was sitting on her back, and using a shoe to pound on her head. "Get off! Get off! Get off!" She screamed aloud to her hangover in hopes that it had been listening.

It hadn't.

With great effort, she coaxed one leg to swing over the side of the bed, and then the next. Moving her right arm proved more difficult. She'd fallen asleep on in, cutting off the circulation. It had no feeling at all, and as she slowly raised her body marveled at how heavy the numb stump felt. It was as if it was dead.

PS often fell asleep in an odd position that turned various body parts into deadweight.

And as usual, when the feeling slowly began returning she yelped in pain. "The needles, the needles, I hate the needles."

With all of her limbs in some working order, PS hopped over stacks of clothes on the floor and maneuvered around books and shoes that had piled up, ignored for weeks to get to the bathroom.

That's it. She thought to herself. I'm staying home today to clean up this mess. She walked into her master bath to brush her teeth and wash her face. She grabbed for a bath towel, but it was soiled and rancid. I guess it's time to do laundry again. She thought.

She remembered that she had done a load of linen several weeks ago, and ambled to the back of the condo to investigate the dryer in her laundry room.

Fido greeted her at the bedroom door. The large orange tabby had been a constant companion since her boyfriend Danny had left three years ago. The cat was their first child together. And while most of PS Garrett's world was mired in chaos and confusion, the twenty-two pound feline was a single source of stability. All of the love she felt for Danny had now been transferred to the cat.

"Are you hungry, sweetie?"

The cat mewed and purred, and bowed as it kneaded the floor in front of her owner.

"Well, thank you. And good morning to you, too." PS hoisted the hefty cat up into her arms and slung her over her shoulder as she navigated around the piles of clutter that had magically found their way to her living room floor.

As she walked through the living room, she absent mindedly turned on the television. The morning anchor was reading the story about the Pixley murders. "That's it. I'm definitely not going in today," she said to Fido.

She walked into the kitchen, put the cat down on the counter and opened the *kitty cabinet* to find some breakfast kibble for her companion.

From another cabinet, she pulled down a delicate bone china saucer, used it to scoop out some kibble and placed it on the counter. She then pulled out a matching teacup and went to the refrigerator to get Fido some milk. But stepped back when she opened the door. The smell was over powering.

She held her breath, gingerly grabbed the culprit and walked over to the sink. "Sorry, kitty. No milk today. Mama's been a bad girl."

She grabbed her TV remote, clicked over to Channel Three just as they were re-running Sherman Hall's package from the night before. Stan Weinstein was being interviewed. He was sobbing and shaking and showing reporters the picture of his only son who'd been murdered at his Gas 'N Go. He said he hadn't even gotten over to the scene yet, he was on his way there when he was stopped by the horde of media at his stoop.

That's when a voice in the pack asked him, "How do you feel?"

PS Garrett cringed. "How would anyone who found out their child had been murdered feel, you idiot?" She screamed at the television. "Light weight!"

PS Garrett despised that question and any reporter who asked it outright. Bar none, it was the most idiotic question in the reporter phrase book. And anytime she heard someone ask it, she believed in her heart that they were bush league, small market, budget, Sam Donaldson wannabees.

Any experienced reporter knows there are ways around the obvious.

One could ask, for instance, What's going on in your heart today? Or, What can you tell me about Joe Schmoe? Sometimes a well placed, What do you want to say to the person responsible?—works well. And there's always, Can you tell me what police are saying?

Of course it all really amounts to, 'How do you feel,' but it sounds better cleverly disguised.

Indeed, the entire exercise of grilling someone who's been traumatized so much that it begs the question, How do you feel?—is callous, it's insensitive, it smacks of everything vile and disgusting that makes journalists the vultures they are.

As much as PS hated that aspect of the job, she understood it well. She was not an herbivore. Her profession craved meat.

"I'm devastated," Stan sobbed. "I don't know what I'm going to do. I'm devastated. Who would do such a thing. Do you mind if I go now?"

PS watched the end of the package and pursed her lips. She couldn't let Sherman Hall win the final round. She just couldn't. And besides, she glanced into the fridge and everything was green, unless it was originally green like the head of lettuce in the corner, and then it was yellow. The only things ingestible in the house were cat food and Kahlua.

She may as well go in.

She hurriedly got dressed, picking garments off the clothes pile and sniffing them to ascertain their degree of wear-ability and scooted out the door. As she got to her vehicle, she could see that there was something on the windshield.

It was a modest bunch of wildflowers, obviously picked from the vacant lot across the street. They were scraggily, and sopping wet from the night's frost. It had been an unusually warm February and a few sparse blooms had taken hold over there. But it would have taken more than an hour to scavenge enough mature plants for a makeshift bouquet that size.

It also looked like some sort of message had been scribbled on the glass, but the melting frost had pretty much soaked it away. She did a 360, scanning the area to see if someone was watching her, or if there was anything out of the ordinary.

Nothing.

Her skin started to prickle, and that dull ache she always seemed to get in her left shoulder began to speak up. She tossed the flowers to the ground, quickly got into her car and sped off toward work, her windshield wipers making short work of the remaining flecks of pollen and whatever it was that seemed to have been scribbled on her windshield.

The condo was filled with children who thought it was cool that a local celebrity lived in the complex. PS chalked the wildflower incident up to fan mail and dismissed it.

With her head still pounding from the night before, she decided to make a slight detour on her way to work. Willina had told her about a small coffee shop that she frequented that served a light breakfast.

She pulled into the tiny strip mall and walked into Perk Up.

To say that a coffee shop was out of PS Garrett's element would have been an understatement.

She walked up to the counter where an extremely youthful, extremely happy twenty-something year old greeted her. "Good morning Ma'am!" She chirped as though she had met an old friend.

The greeting was so friendly PS Garrett looked around to see if there was someone standing behind her. There wasn't. So she spoke in as cheery a voice she could muster. "Good morning."

"What can I get for you, Ma'am?" The clerk sang.

"I'd like one of those banana muffins, some strawberry cream cheese and," PS paused. Should she go for the orange juice or the coffee? Her head was still pounding from the night before. "And a coffee, please."

"Greeeeeeeeeeat!" Squealed the young clerk so shrilly it made the reporter jump. "What kind of coffee would you like?"

"I beg your pardon?" PS asked genuinely confused.

"What kind of coffee would you like? There are our daily specials."

The coffee clerk pointed to a chalk written sign in front of the register. There was Peruvian Far Trend, Kenyan Gold—which sounded to PS more like a kind of marijuana than a coffee—something called the Baker's Blend, and Deep Dark Bean—which sounded too dark and evil for a neophyte coffee drinker like herself.

PS didn't know what to say. She didn't know that choosing coffee was such a process. All she wanted to do was wake up, and make her head stop hurting. "I just want coffee," she blurted.

The perky clerk furrowed her brow in confusion. "Okay, um, what kind of coffee?"

PS looked at the clock on the wall. Shortly, she'd be late for work, and she didn't want to be so much as a minute late after what had happened the

night before. "Just plain old coffee, thanks," she insisted. "There is such a thing as plain old coffee isn't
there? I mean, I see those commercials with Juan
Valdez. Just give me what he's drinking."

"Alrighty. Would you like large or small?"

"Large is fine, thank you."

PS sighed a bit in relief. Now that the coffee
thing was settled maybe she could get her meager breakfast and get the Hell out of there.

"Ma'am?" The sales girl asked from behind large
silver canisters to the side of the register.

"Yes?"

"Would you like regular or decaf?"

PS was starting to get annoyed. "Just coffee."

It took eight minutes and thirteen inches of cash
register tape for a coffee, a muffin and a pat of cream
cheese. It wasn't even a real breakfast with meat and
eggs, and the tab came to nearly $8.00. Now PS was
really irritated.

She took a sip of the coffee and wrinkled her
nose. *How do people drink this crap black?* She thought
to herself.

She walked over to the condiments counter and
searched for sugar. *Jesus!* She thought to herself. *There
are four different kinds of sugar. Is anything easy anymore?*

She chose the large brown packets. Eight of
them. She tore the tops off with her teeth, opened the
lid of her huge cup and poured the sugar in. She then
grabbed one of the little wooden stirrers and whipped
it around the cup. But she couldn't figure out where to
throw the trash. Absolutely nothing in the area re-

sembled a garbage receptacle.

There was a large wooden cabinet with a flap, she opened the flap, but inside lay large pieces of china. She turned around and surveyed the shop, but again, couldn't find anything that looked appropriate to toss her refuse.

She balled it up in her hand and decided the large plastic basin on top of the cabinet would have to do.

She took another sip of her coffee and it was still unpalatable. Fourteen big brown sugars later, and PS finally figured out that the small metal shoot in front of her was the trash bin. It so closely resembled a spoon holder, had she not stood there so long trying to sweeten her coffee, she would have never figured it out.

She stood on her tiptoes to see what it was she had been throwing her earlier trash in. It was a basin of soapy water holding cups. Make that, holding cups and sopping wet brown sugar packets.

As PS walked to her car, she noticed a crumpled piece of paper on her windshield. "Cripes!" She griped. "How do you get a ticket getting a cup of coffee this early in the morning?"

She looked down on the pavement. *No blue lines, so it's not a handicapped spot.* She thought to herself. She looked at the sign on the building and it said 'parking for Perk Up customers only'. And her $3.71 cent coffee, $2.50 muffin and .50 cent pat of cream cheese definitely qualified her as a Perk Up customer.

She walked up to the car, tossed her muffin sack

through the open sunroof and onto the passenger side of her car, and then grabbed the piece of paper off the windshield.

It wasn't a ticket, it was a small slip of scrap paper of some sort. On it was a short scribbled note that simply read, 'I enjoy watching you!'

PS looked around the small strip mall parking lot. There didn't seem to be anyone else standing around. *That's odd*, she thought to herself. People stopped her all the time to tell her how much they enjoyed her on television, or to discuss a story they'd seen. But she had never been left a note on her windshield. *Why didn't the person just walk into Perk Up and say hello in person?* She wondered. It would have taken a lot less time than finding a scrap of paper, jotting down a note and then disappearing.

Her reporter's sense was telling her this was not mere fan mail.

She thought about the makeshift bouquet of flowers on her windshield that morning. "Can this be connected?" She said aloud. *It can't be.* She continued to think. *I'm too far away from home.*

She looked at the note again. There was something oddly familiar about the handwriting. She couldn't quite figure out what it was, but she felt like she had seen that handwriting somewhere before. She slowly mouthed the words written on the piece of paper, *I enjoy watching you, watching you, I enjoy watch, watch, watching you.*

She tumbled the words in her head. Where had she seen that writing before? She couldn't figure it out.

For a moment, she became frightened. *Am I being stalked?* She wondered to herself. No, that's ridiculous. *Willina says I'm paranoid. And she's right. I've been completely on edge ever since Danny left. This is just an over zealous fan, that's all.*

An awful feeling of dread washed over her. She didn't know why but she suddenly felt like she had to get into her car right away or run. She hastily opened her door, hopped in, put the key in the ignition and closed her sunroof while simultaneously locking her door—not realizing that she had dropped the note on the asphalt in her haste.

She scanned the parking lot again and saw nothing or no one. "I'm just being paranoid," she said aloud. "If Wil were here, we'd be laughing by now."

She stepped on the clutch, put the car into first gear and decided that the price of being on television is being watched.

She drove out into the street and headed for the Channel Six studio downtown.

Thirty seconds after her car had pulled into traffic, a pair of hands scooped the note from the asphalt. The silent stranger stood and watched the little red car as it zoomed down the street. *She didn't even keep my note.* The stranger thought to himself. *That pisses me off. She doesn't even know I exist. I'll show her I exist. I'll show her and Rose. When I'm through, the whole world will know I exist. Nobody will ever call me nobody again.*

In a television newsroom, the day after a major crime event is almost as important as the day of. The next big stratagem is to advance the story. Going over the yesterday events becomes old news, and in the television business, old news is not news.

There's always some new little detail the day after. The cops will have a suspect, or the cops will have a composite sketch, or someone will have come forward with the description of a vehicle. Sometimes family members will speak out about the crime. Danny Weinstein's dad had already done that the night before, and then disappeared into the comfort of not-known-to-the-media relatives.

But by noon the following day, there was till no suspect in the Gas 'N Go murders in Pixley, and no significant way to advance the story.

The station, after its royal class ass-whipping the night before, assigned a total of three reporters to the story.

The name of the girl still hadn't been released. Her parents were apparently out of town, but Larry Pink, the station's assignment editor sent reporter, Susan Michaels to Pixley to find classmates and family members. Everybody knew her name, which meant reporters could get reaction to her untimely end. They just couldn't say her name on television without the say so of police—as if no one in a twenty-five mile radius couldn't guess after seeing the report.

It was all part of advancing the story.

One of the newer hires was sent to Pixley to find out more about Danny Weinstein. He somehow found out that the boy's mother lived forty-five miles west of Pixley, and even though she hadn't seen her child since he was an infant, she was fair game for a television story.

As expected, PS had been placed on covering the investigation, though silently she was dubbed, The Loser.

None of the producers would look her squarely in the face. She got the worst possible pick of cameramen, and was given Sylvester the least experienced and most inept photographer in the stable.

Even one of the interns asked if she would go upstairs and pick up a candy bar from the vending machine for him.

PS said, "No."

Salina had let it fly that after the broadcast the night before, Bob Tucker, the news director had marched to the file cabinet in his office and pulled out PS's contract. When he realized she was signed for another two years, he reportedly kicked a trashcan.

PS wasn't sure if it was true, or just some of Salina's berating. It didn't matter. It was never a good day after being beaten on a big story. That's just how it was.

Every station in the market had reporters tail police as they tracked possible leads. The way everyone played cat and mouse with that story, one would have thought they were covering the search for JFK's assassin.

Cameras were everywhere police were.

Reporters were taking notes, and photographers rolling tape as cops bird-dogged every viable tip the public offered—and the police had gotten dozens of tips. Many of them incredibly useless, off-the-wall tips. But tips, none-the-less.

One woman just outside of town called police to say she saw a man at a grocery store who looked like he was capable of murder. That was it. He looked like he was capable of murder. Nothing else—no torn prison shirt, no shackles and broken chains on leg irons, no trace metals on the hands or swastikas engraved on his forehead. He just had a suspicious look.

She told the Pixley authorities that she was standing in line, buying milk and bananas at a Livonia quick stop, which was a good forty-five miles from the murder scene, when she noticed this man in front of her who just had an evil look. She said he was wearing tattered jeans and a dirty T-shirt. On the back of his left hand was a faded, fuzzy blue tattoo that said, 'OUTLAW.'

When he turned around and glanced at her, he never even pretended to smile. He just glared.

Naturally, she headed to the nearest pay phone and dialed 911. When 911 couldn't help her, she called Channel Six to tell her story.

She was livid when Larry Pink told her that the way someone looked wasn't enough reason for suspicion.

That one was not considered a solid lead, even though that day Channel Six was aching for a way to advance the story.

Lots of people didn't even bother calling police first, they called the television stations. It was like they thought TV news could do something about a murder suspect just because that's how it looks on television.

Some of the tips the newsroom got were so ridiculous, one of the writers kept verbatims of them on a big white magnetic board in the newsroom. She wrote them down in bright red magic marker, in big bold letters, so they could be seen from across the newsroom.

"I think my neighbor down the street did it. He hates kids."

"Pixley police are in a union contract dispute. They took out a hit so the community would be too afraid not to pass the proposed millage tax increase."

"Check out the store's insurance policy. I think the father might be involved."

"Here's my tip. Tell Barbara Bennett not to wear her hair up any more. It makes her look old."

Zoe, the news writer with far more personality and intelligence to remain just a writer for very long, started a pool. Everybody in the newsroom pitched in five dollars a piece, and they decided that they would vote at the end of the month. Whoever received the most inane, stupid, idiotic, useless tip would collect the pot.

It was a good idea. With some two hundred dollars in the kitty, everyone was encouraged to help answer the phones, which had been ringing off the hooks in the newsroom since the murders.

By three o'clock when the only way to advance the story was to say that the Pixley police didn't have a single solitary lead on the murders. The station consolidated its reporters. And PS was placed on the next biggest story of the day, the death of a man snuffed out by a semi while trying to protect his child.

PS wouldn't be the lead story.

It would be the ultimate in humiliation—to have absolutely no hand in the-day-after coverage of a major crime event.

PS spoke in her clear, strong, ringing, TV alto voice while sitting erect in the studio chair, facing the camera with the flashing red tally light with the big ugly Styrofoam '6' behind her. "Barbara, police tell me much of the difficulty in moving the child who, luckily, was only grazed by the fender of that semi—was unlocking the little boy's hand from the grasp of his father who was killed instantly when he apparently jumped into the path of the fast moving tractor trailer to save his son.

"Reporting live in the newsroom, PS Garrett, Channel Six news at five. Now back to you in the studio."

In the TV monitor, posted next to the unmanned robotic newsroom camera—PS could see that Barbara Bennett, the first string anchor, responded with a sympathetic nod. She then turned to another camera in the main studio and continued reading the TelePrompTer. "We'll keep you posted on the child's condition. John?"

She turned her head to face her co-anchor, and right on cue, her small round, perfectly made up face framed by the impeccably coifed hair, melted into the fine chiseled, well-tanned face of John Eisenburg who had equally impeccable hair, perfect make up and a booming baritone voice that earned him his seven figure salary.

"Thank you, Barbara."

John shifted in his chair to face the other camera. "In other news today, the mayor of Warren missed his appointment before a circuit court judge in a bizarre case of ethnic intimidation..."

PS stole a glance at the clock on the far wall. 6:25.

If she hurried, she could beat traffic on her way to the Spur. She wanted to apologize to Mack for leaving the restaurant so abruptly the night before. But most importantly, she wanted a triple Brown Cow and a double order of broasted chicken wings and spicy lo mein noodles. It was just the bootleg psychotherapy she needed to smooth out the last two days.

Silver Spur Chop Suey, or the Spur as the regulars called it was an oasis. Cheap, friendly, no rules, lots and lots of alcohol.

It sat along a burnt out strip of Woodward Avenue just outside the city limits. The exterior was kind of Motown blue, that odd shade of blue on the top of the Motown records label—not royal, and certainly not peacock, the only way to describe it is Motown blue.

Everything about the Spur said old, cheap and dirty. It had a fuchsia and light blue neon sign that flashed between colors.

If you were coming from the south, you couldn't miss the glare of neon—flickering between the low-keyed painted signs of the Triple X adult bookstore, and the Brazilian Lights Coffee Shop, both of which sat on either side of the Spur. If you were coming from the north, the restaurant—that word used as a technical term only—could be identified by the neon flashing Silver Spur hop uey. The C and the S burned out years ago and Mack, the big, torn T-shirt wearing, chain-smoking, beer-belly-toting, Channel Three watching, redneck who owned the place never bothered to get it fixed.

PS Garrett and Mack couldn't appear to be more ill-matched on the surface. But they were soul mates for reasons only they fully understood. They consoled each other, anesthetized each other's emotional wounds, and intermittingly fought like cats and dogs.

The argument always settled with a drink and a kiss.

Mack bought the place more than twenty years ago. He said it used to be a Bible bookstore. That's why he settled there.

He had been married to a first generation Chinese immigrant who'd died in a fire along with their two children two decades ago.

He said he felt like a lot of souls had lived in that building. And he liked the company. Mack believed this was the place his soul could be saved. PS felt the same thing. So whenever there was healing to be done, PS Garrett strapped on her appetite and her thirst and headed to Silver Spur Chop Suey, or Silver Spur hop uey, whatever the case may be.

PS needed the healing to begin. She could

hardly wait for the day to end, and now that it had, she rushed to make her escape from the studio before Salina Kingsley walked back in from the control room.

Peter, the maintenance engineer, had been watching the story of the semi accident on one of the newsroom wall monitors, and was waiting to discuss it with PS.

He knew that if he walked up to her before the all clear, he could have ended up on camera.

Eight seconds into the next story, PS whispered into her mic, "Am I clear here or what?"

"Oh, yeah. Sorry about that. Good work today," the voice of the assistant director answered in her IFB.

She was grateful for the kind words. The first she'd heard in two days.

She started *undressing* from the camera, first taking out her ear piece and tucking it into her pocket and then removing the small microphone from her blazer lapel. That's when Peter struck, walking up to her with compliments on her report.

In the Channel Six newsroom, it was common knowledge that Peter was the man most likely to talk you to death. When he got started, there was no stopping him. His mouth was like a run-away locomotive. No breaks. The smartest thing anyone could do was walk the other way when they saw him coming, or else get sucked into the deep, dark abyss of a 'Peter' conversation.

So even though Peter was telling PS what a good job she'd done on the story, and how thought-provoking it was—all really important stuff—PS struggled to not to encourage any further chit chat as she hurriedly tried to extricate herself from her live shot position in the middle of the newsroom. But Peter had already managed to get his hook in by grabbing her gently by the arm.

He started talking about the tandem semi trucks and how dangerous they are. He then went into a thoughtful dissertation about, "Whether those trucking companies are even paying enough taxes to justify those mechanical beasts that eat up our roads and kill our innocent."

It's not that Peter didn't know what the Hell he was talking about, but at the moment PS just didn't give a flying fig.

A photographer walked by and put his hands behind his ears and wagged them at her, sticking out his tongue and mouthing the words, "Na na nanna nah."

Salina Kingsley strolled by quickly and mouthed the words, "Better you than me, suckah! Serves you right."

A writer sauntered by behind Peter and mouthed the words, "Have a nice life."

The news director, Bob Tucker, walked by and just shook his head.

PS's stomach started to growl, she badly needed a drink.

A triple.

It had been a rough day. She hated talking to grieving friends and relatives, even though it was necessary. And she didn't feel like reliving the day from Hell with Peter, an all around great guy, who just happened to talk too damned much about nothing in particular.

"Pete," she tried to break in.

Foolish of her to even try to get a word in edgewise.

Peter began talking about traffic signals, and how they should be timed so there would be a delay for right turns. "That way when the walk sign flashes, a driver has more time to consider pedestrians who may be in the crosswalk."

PS's head was starting to hurt. Things started going gray. She went into auto pilot, saying "yeah," and, "uh huh," in all the right places.

She wondered how Peter ever got married. She could hear him talking, somewhere off in the distance, his stale coffee and pipe tobbaco breath wafting in her general direction. She took small measured breaths to minimize how many of his words found their way into her nasal passages—his blah, blah, blah, just melting into a cacophony of faint noise.

If he were a woman who talked this much, she thought to herself, He'd never get a second date. How is it that he shut up long enough to father a child? This man goes on and on. He grabs on to your trousers like a little dog and shakes his head from side to side, grating and grating on you until you want to kick him.

PS was always acutely aware of who had on wedding rings and who didn't. She was also acutely aware that she was one of the ones who didn't.

His voice faded in and out again as she slipped back and forth into semi-consciousness.

Salina Kingsley walked by again, with her brief-case tucked under her arm, swinging her umbrella with her free hand. PS pretended not to notice her go by.

Somewhere in the distance Peter was talking about how that truck never stopped, even though at forty yards away the signal turned yellow.

"He should have stopped," Pete droned on. "Instead of barreling through with that right turn on red. I sure hope that little boy makes it. You know, my son is about that age."

"Yeah, Pete. I know that." PS whispered, faint with anger.

Pete continued on and on, oblivious to her pain. Not seeing the discomfort on her face, or that her knuckles had blanched from being clenched.

When she regained consciousness, the clock said 7:30.

7:30! I should have been pulling up to the restaurant right about now, and I haven't even left the station. She screamed in her head.

She looked around. The team on the assignment desk had already gone through shift change. In the faint distance, she could hear the night-side photographers receiving their orders. She could hear that one of the night-side reporters had called in sick, and the other one was traveling with the satellite truck to the other side of the state to cover a miraculous live partial liver transplant from a parent to her child.

Good, she thought to herself. We'll have a good news lead story tonight. Now what am I going to do to save myself?

She knew she had to get out of there, lest she be tagged to replace the absent reporter.

She continued to scan the newsroom for escape. It was different at night—calmer, less frenetic. Writers she barely knew had already parked themselves at the various computer terminals and had begun to write for the 11 o'clock news. Most of the brass had gone home, though she could see that the lights were still on in Bob Tucker's office. He must've been burning the late night oil over some little detail. Perhaps he had more beans to count.

Barbara Bennett was in her office, sitting in a recliner reading a magazine, a throw blanket over her ankles, a pink steam hair roller dangling smartly to her brow from a spray of streaked blonde hair. John Eisenburg meandered about the newsroom, making polite conversation with those who crossed his path.

PS drowned Peter's droning with a mental calculation. Barbara and John probably made more than eight-thousand dollars per minute for actual work performed during the day. They came in around four. Read the news for an hour and a half. Went out for dinner, or sat around to relax until ten, and then read the news at eleven for another half hour.

How do I get a gig like that? She thought to herself. *Probably some pictures of Tucker nude with animals wouldn't hurt.* She chuckled to herself at the visual.

She glanced at the clock again.

7:32.

Enough was enough. She knew she was in the dog house, and everyone in the newsroom had to go

105

through the motions of hating her. But she had been a pal to Peter long enough. Long enough!

"Pete, I'm sorry, man, but I've got to go, I'm late. But it's good to talk to you," she jumped in.

She then ran out of the newsroom and, out of morbid curiosity or maybe it was just being a reporter, she couldn't help but look back. Once again, Pete was operating on a delayed clock. He barely registered that the reporter was no longer standing in front of him, listening. He was still standing there, droning on and on to an empty chair.

No one else dared go near him.

CHAPTER FIVE

PS jumped in her car and raced up Woodward Avenue toward Silver Spur Chop Suey, unaware that a beat-up old white Toyota that had been sitting down the street from the station garage had stealthily fallen in behind her.

When she got to the Spur, Willina was already on her third beer and waiting.

"What kept you?" She asked with amazing clarity for a woman who had already consumed nearly half a six pack.

"I ran into that engineer, Peter."

"You mean chatty Cathy?"

"Yup."

Willina shook her head in disgust. "You poor thing."

She then gestured to Mack who was glued to the television watching a Channel Three prime time special on the lack of adequate security at the airport. "Don't stop at one glass, bring two. This woman has been to Hell and back."

"You can say that again."

"Okay. Mack, don't stop at one glass, bring two. This woman has been to Hell and back."

PS chuckled and rummaged around Willina's plate for a chicken wing that might have escaped her notice. There were none.

"Hey, Wil?"

"Um hmm."

"Hear me out on this one."

"Okay. What's up?"

"Well, something weird has been kind of going on."

Willina put down her beer and paid close attention to what her friend was saying. Willina had known PS for more than a decade. She knew her friend was fragile in many ways. And something in the tone of PS's voice caught Wil's attention. "Okay, what's weird that's going on."

"Well, I've been getting messages."

"Messages in your head?" Wil asked with such seriousness it broke some of the tension PS had been feeling.

"No you bumblehead! Somebody has been leaving me messages on my car windshield. And this morning when I went to my car, somebody had left me a bunch of flowers under the wiper blades."

"Like roses?"

"No, like weeds and wildflowers pulled from the side of the road. It's kind of creepy."

"P. You live around like, a thousand children. You have your own little ready-made fan club right there in your condo. You said you're always getting little notes and gifts."

"Yeah, I know. But this one feels different. It feels creepy."

"P. I don't want to minimize what you're feeling. But you have been under a lot of stress lately. You don't think things are going so great at work, when really things couldn't be better. You're making more money. You lead the newscast almost everyday. The only sore spot is that bitch, Salina Kingsley and she's been there since you've been there and nothing has changed."

"Keep going," PS said, feeling as though her concerns were unfounded after all.

"P. you haven't been the same since..." Willina stopped mid-sentence. She had been meaning to broach this subject with PS, but hadn't found the right moment. She knew she would meet resistance and she knew she would have to choose exactly the right moment, when dealing with her friend on the old boyfriend thing.

"Well, since..."

Mack ambled over with a piping hot plastic plate of lo mein noodles and two tall glasses filled with the magical elixir, Brown Cow.

"Mack!" PS interrupted. "What's up with you and Channel Three, anyway? Now, not one of those people had graced your stoop before last night."

"It was great, wasn't it?" Mack said excitedly.

"No Mack, it wasn't."

"P," Willina broke in. "Let it go, girl. It's not that big a deal."

"Yes, it is."

"Don't take it personally. You guys suck! I mean not you, but your news coverage. You know it yourself. Tell the truth. If you didn't work for Channel Six, would you watch them?"

PS took a long swig from one glass and then the other.

Willina looked at her with concern.

"What are you looking at? I just didn't want the other glass to get lonely."

"I'm just checking you out that's all," Willina said as she finished off her own drink.

"And what's that supposed to mean?"

"I just don't think you're doing so well, that's all."

"Excuse me?"

Willina had been concerned about PS since her beloved Danny left three years ago. She had watched the downward spiral of her friend. Already high-strung, PS Garrett added edgy and paranoid to the list of negative character traits one might collect after being traumatized and heartbroken. And the way he left. Willina couldn't blame her for teetering close to the edge.

She just didn't want anything to push her completely over.

"Don't get pissed off about it. I'm just telling you like it is," Wil said gently.

"Okay, so I have two horrendous days at work. And look at this. Do you see this?" PS turned her head to the side and gestured to her ear. "It's gone! One of my ears has been talked off by Peter, Peter, the hour eater. You're sitting here sucking down three beers, and I bet you're about to order a fourth..."

Just then Willina raised her hand to gesture to Mack for another.

PS continued, "And you're blowing me crap about having a couple of drinks. Look at me! I have no ear!"

"That's not what I'm talking about. You need to let him go P."

"What? Let who go?"

"P. You need to let Danny go. He's gone, he's not coming back, you need to move on. It's affecting your life."

"Wil, don't. We don't need to talk about this."

"It's the one thing we don't talk about anymore."

"Not this close to an unlucky streak. I can't handle this conversation." She said as she pressed one of the glasses to her lips.

"Do you think you should see somebody?"

"I'd love to. You got somebody? Is he tall, handsome? Somebody like who, Wil?"

"You know, somebody like a thera..."

PS interrupted. "Are you saying you think I need to seek professional help? Are you crazy? Do you think I'm crazy? If you think I'm crazy, girl you're crazy."

Willina sensed it was time to pull back. The conversation needed to be lightened up. She didn't want PS to be angry with her while she was nursing an unlucky streak at work. "Okay then. Let's talk about something else," Willina said casually. "You need to get laid."

"What?" PS said as she spit her drink out over the table.

"I don't know how you do it, but I couldn't live without a man."

"That's evident, in that, you sleep with someone else's man."

"Let's not get off the subject." Wil countered. "I'm not saying fall in love, get married, have children kind of sex, I'm talking about rubbing an ache, scratching an itch. You know relieving some tension."

"Where do you get this crap from?" PS said gulping down another mega swig from her Flintstone's Kool Aid glass.

"Why do you avoid it? Men approach you all the time and you give them short shrift. I think it's time for you to look around and choose a prospect."

"Oh, and I guess eligible men are just growing on trees in Detroit."

"Last time I looked they were."

"Willina, you're full of it. I'd love to meet a guy. And he doesn't have to be the one. He could be the one-right-now. But the opportunity hasn't presented itself."

"Bullcrap."

"Bullcrap? What's wrong with the word, shit. You can't say the word shit or something? What? Did you give up the word shit for Lent?"

"No, shit's a bad word and I'm trying to trim it from my vocabulary repertory. It's a very un-ladylike word."

"Shit." PS scoffed.

"That's right. And you look awful saying it. No wonder you can't get laid."

"Bullshit," PS countered.

"And there you go again. Every time you say that word you lose an opportunity with a prospect."

"This is crap," PS huffed.

"That's better. Now let's get back to business. Sherman Hall."

"SHIT!"

"Stop that, now listen."

"What about him?"

"He's a prospect."

"That prick?"

"I think there's something there. And you know I have an antenna when something's there. I can smell sperm cooking a mile away. My little sensor goes, beep, beep, beep. And it's been going beep with Sherman."

"You're looney. That guy's a creep."

"I'm telling you, the other night when he was here at the Spur, he couldn't take his eyes off of you."

"Well, you see Willina Johns, that's where you're wrong. That guy can't take his eyes off himself. I'm willing to bet he couldn't screw straight because he'd be too concerned about if he looked good during the deed. Unless he did it doggy style facing a mirror so he could check his expressions."

"Oooooh girl. See how long it's been. Doggy style is not a bad idea. And what's wrong with watching? Besides, Sherman Hall's got it going on."

"And how do you know?"

Mack brought Willina two more beers and a double order of wings. And Willina settled in for one of her renowned dissertations, PS affectionately called, The World According To Wil.

Willina's face turned deadly serious. "What I'm about to tell you is privileged information. Got that?"

"Uh, huh," PS scoffed.

"I have never shared this secret with any other member of the female domesticus species. Got that?"

"Uh, huh."

"Whoever understands the intricacies of what I am about to tell you can dominate the male species.

And we all know, whoever dominates the male species, dominates the world."

"I see. And you mean to tell me that you are a world dominator? Is that dominator, or dominatrix?"

"Stop that and listen," Wil said seriously.

"Okay, go on. But this had better be good."

"As I was saying before I was so rudely interrupted by a nincompoop," Wil plocked PS on the head with a napkin. "I am large and in charge. Look, I don't have a regular job, I live in a luxury condo in West Bloomfield and the diamond bracelet I have on has five carats. That ain't rabbit food. Can I get a witness?"

"Amen," PS laughed and raised her hand to slap Willina five. "I can honestly say, you rule!"

"Okay then. Shut up, listen and learn. I can tell everything about a man, including how good he is in bed, by the way he walks. "

"Shut up!" PS protested.

"It's true. And if you can tell how a man is in bed, you can tell other vital things about his character."

"Get out!"

"How he shall fuck, so shall he live."

"Wait a minute. You can say the word fuck, but you can't say the word shit?"

"P. Shut up and listen."

PS lifted her drink to her lips with a chuckle and piped down.

"It's all common sense, really. But then that's something you don't seem to know much about."

PS looked up from her lo mein noodles and shot Wil a nasty look.

114

"For instance," Wil continued. She got up from the table to demonstrate, "If they walk with their backs straight—with measured, even strides like this…it's a sign that they are strong, confident and giving lovers.

"Now, if they swing their legs straight out in front of them from the hip, like this…"

Willina straightened her legs like a peg and took long, strong strides, with each foot planting flat on the floor with each step, "See how their legs barely bend at the knees? Now watch, this is important, their feet fall in line, north-south with the rest of their body, that means they're strong and creative in bed."

PS began to giggle hysterically. "You're out of control. You know that, don't you?"

"Shhhhhh! This is important stuff. Now, if they walk with their knees slightly bent and they have long legs, but a short torso, they're sloppy lovers. It's bad when that happens.

"If they take short baby steps, and they walk with their knees slightly bent, and they balance themselves on their toes with each step without letting their heel hit the ground, they have latent homosexual tendencies or they're Autistic. Either way, probably not a good idea."

"C'mon. Give me a break!" PS protested.

"No, it's true. Listen to me. If they're slightly bow legged, and only gently pigeon toed, they're athletic in the sack. If they walk from the hip, that is, it takes the whole bottom half of their body to propel their legs forward, they're selfish lovers of the worse kind, because they don't think they're selfish, they think they're God's gift to sex. If they shuffle along…"

Willina scraped her feet along the tile floor, waddling like a penguin to demonstrate, "They're sloppy and careless in bed, and likely uncircumcised."

"Oh, come on," PS scoffed.

"No, it's true."

"Wil, now you stop it."

"Listen to me. I'm telling you, that little flap of skin affects the way a man carries himself."

"I don't believe it."

"Believe it."

"Yeah, okay. Whatever you say. I guess you have had basis for comparison."

"Don't get mean."

"Now, who's not being honest?"

"I didn't say it wasn't true, I just said don't be mean about it."

"Fair enough. Keep going."

Willina reached over, took another swig of her beer and continued her performance. "If they're fly footed—you know, they walk with their feet pointed out like a penguin. Like this...they're trainable, but only with a lot of work and patience."

A very nice looking man strolled by on his way back to the bar from the rest room. He was very well dressed in a sports coat, contrasting slacks and a crisp white shirt with no tie. He had a strong, long, gait. He shifted his weight slightly from side to side as he walked un-rushed back to his stool.

When he passed the two women at the back of the pub, he looked over and politely acknowledged by nodding his head, but kept going.

"Hmmmm," Willina said, smacking her lips.

"That one is feeling confident. He probably got a promotion at work, and he has a few gifts for his wife in those packages under the bar. But I would say, he's capable of infidelity and probably won't take the lead in bed. He prefers to be serviced instead."

"Come on! Give me a break. How did you get all of that from his walk?" PS snarled. "As for those packages, they're probably dirty movies he just purchased at the triple X next door."

Willina countered as she sat down and took another swig of her beer with one hand, and one of PS's broasted chicken wings with the other. "Well, he had a long stride. His legs were straight, which means he's definitive. He's a man who knows how to get what he wants. But did you see how he shifted his weight from one leg to the other as he walked?"

"Yeah." PS answered in rapt attention at the notion that Willina might actually have something here.

"That means he waffles. He can be dominated. He probably had a strong willed mother who bossed him when he was a boy. My guess is, he likes to play good boy, bad boy in bed. And he's not really satisfied unless the woman is doing all of the work."

"Okay, what about this guy?" PS pointed to a man who had just entered the Spur. He was tall, neatly shaven, wearing pressed blue jeans, and a designer shirt that clung to the breasts of his well defined chest. He had on brand new gym shoes that squeaked a little when he walked in and took a seat.

Willina cocked her head to one side and watched the man closely, the wheels visibly turning in her head as she sized him up. "Well, that guy is a brute. Look at him. His body is completely straight, but did you see how his head leaned back a little when he walked? Also if you look carefully, you see he led his steps with his pelvis. And look how he puffs his chest out a bit. This is a man who walks with his dick. He thinks he's all that, and more. And based on how pretty his face is, I would guess the women are probably throwing their panties at him. He's pretty muscular, so he probably works out. If I had to guess, he has something to prove in bed. He wants to show women how strong he is, so he forces himself on them, just a bit," she smiled to herself. "I bet he's rough, and pushy in bed. He probably even wants the woman to wash his dick when he's through. I'll take his number. I like it rough."

PS roared with laughter. "You know Wil, this is all very fascinating stuff. Have you ever thought of writing a book?"

"I'm working on it. I'm working on it. Maybe you'll help me one day with the book proposal."

Another man worked his way through the maze of tables and chairs as he joined a rather rotund woman at a table across the room. His whole body wriggled as he walked. His feet pointed due east and west as he walked south and his behind bobbed up and down slightly with each step.

The two women watched the man attentively as he moved past them and then turned to each other at the exact same time and exclaimed, "VIRGIN !"

They howled.

"Hey, ladies, ladies," Mack said, moving quickly

toward them. "Keep it down will you? I run a class establishment here."

"Oh, in that case, Mr. Laudy Dah," PS laughed. "Please clear these Kool Aid glasses from our table and bring us our check. We're ready to go."

"All done here?" Mack asked.

"Yup."

"It's on the house." Mack said.

"Why?" PS asked suspiciously.

"I owe you one from last night. Okay?"

"Well, if that's the case," Willina said emptying her beer can down her throat. "I'll take one more to go."

"No you won't," PS said "You still have to drive a few miles. Do you still need me to follow you to the dealership?"

"Yup! It's time for my five-thousand mile check up. We just need to drop it off at the Beemer place up the road."

"I thought those luxury car places gave you loaners. Why do you need a ride from me?"

"I knew I'd be hanging out with you until late, and I didn't have time to stop off earlier today. They said there'd be one waiting for me at my place when I got home this evening," Willina said with a broad grin.

"I wasn't kidding earlier, Ms. Johns. You rule."

"I know, I know, I got the stuff to show," Willina sang as she got up from the table and headed toward the door, making sure she made eye-contact with each man at the bar on her way out into the street.

Willina offered no apologies. She was a survivor and a free spirit. She claimed to be the best mistress this side of Pacos. PS didn't doubt it. She just wished she was a little more like her friend.

PS was a survivor too. The two women just chose different methods to survive the odds.

On their way home from the car dealership, a beat up old car sped up from behind them, passed recklessly on the left and nearly ran the two women off the road.

PS was driving, and swerved onto the shoulder and then back onto the street in front of the vehicle to keep her car from rolling into a ditch. It took PS a few seconds to recover as she pulled back into the roadway. Next, the driver started speeding up, and hitting his brakes as he got inches away from her back bumper, basically menacing and tailgating.

"That asshole!" PS screamed as she opened her sunroof, stuck her hand up and flicked him the finger.

The driver went berserk. He started honking his horn and screaming. He then crossed the solid yellow line, barely missing a car on the left to get in front of the two women. He kept slowing down and then hitting his brakes, trying to get them to run into him. The whole time he was yelling and shaking his fist in his rearview mirror.

"What is this idiot doing?" PS asked, becoming concerned. "He almost ran us off the road."

She reached back to grab her purse that was sitting on the floor behind her, but couldn't get a hold of it. "Wil, grab your cell phone will you? Call 911."

Willina rummaged around in her purse for a second. "Shit! I left it in my hands free unit in the car."

"Well, grab my purse and get mine."

But Willina was whip lashed into the dashboard as PS slammed on the brakes. The idiot in front of them had come to a complete stop in the middle of the road. Then the nut got out of his car and stormed toward them, gesturing wildly holding what looked like a tire iron. He took huge strides and his entire body leaned forward as he charged the little red sports car.

PS was terrified. She couldn't back up, because there was a car behind her. She couldn't pull off on the right because of the sidewalk. And there was oncoming traffic to her left.

"What on earth is this asshole doing?" PS said, her voice quaking as the angry motorist got closer to her vehicle.

Willina said nothing. She just watched the approaching maniac with amused curiosity. When he got about fifteen feet from the vehicle, Wil reached over and pushed the button that slid the sunroof completely back. She then calmly pulled a pistol from her purse, stood up in her seat so that her upper body was up through the open sun roof, pointed the gun at the approaching motorist and calmly said, "Back off, Motherfucker."

As Wil leveled the gun at the approaching motorist, the vehicle directly behind them, and then another screeched tires as they pulled out into oncoming traffic to pass them in order to distance themselves from the fray.

The approaching mad-man stopped dead in his

tracks. His face turned red with anger. And he yelled. "You stupid bitch!"

"Did you call me a bitch?" Wil said, finally getting angry. "You know I could shoot you for that right now and be justified. I won't even spend any time in jail. They'll say it was temporary insanity or justifiable homicide. And what do you know about bitches anyway. You are threatening me, you bastard. I can blow you away right now in self-defense. In fact, I think I will."

Willina steadied her arms, lowered her head and gently placed her left eye at the head of the site lines of the pistol. She took a deep breath, exhaled with a sigh and pulled the hammer back on the gun.

PS shuddered at the click. Her face contorted in utter shock. She was speechless. "*I'm a reporter.* She thought. *I report on this kind of crap, it doesn't happen to me.*"

As horrifying as this scene was, what Wil was saying made sense. The man was threatening them. If Wil did pull the trigger it would be in self defense.

PS dreaded the thought. A dead motorist in the middle of Squirrel Road. Willina blowing away the smoke from the barrel of her pistol with calm bravado. The police would be questioning the two women on the side of the road as the medical examiner pulled a sheet over the cold body that was beginning to attract flies.

And the television cameras. PS shivered. *Oh my God, the television cameras would be rolling. The competition would have a field day. I would be the lead story on every news show on every channel for the next week.*

"Wil, don't!" PS pleaded under her breath.

"Why not, he's threatening us?"

"Willina, please," she said once more, now almost begging.

"P. Why are you pleading for this butt hole's life? He's the one who should be pleading," Wil demanded.

She then steadied her aim at the jerk who finally realized he had picked on the wrong women to harass.

Willina continued her lecture to the creep who, by then had slowly raised his hands up in the air and was standing in front of the car with his knees wobbling.

Willina was in full rant. "What did you think we were going to do? Lean out the window and say 'please, Mr. Big Strong Man, please don't hurt us little ole' defenseless womens. Is that what you thought we'd do? Do you think you have the right to physically accost someone because they did something you don't like? Is that how you feel powerful, you prick? I'm tired of talking. Wiping you out will be a public service."

Willina tuned up her aim once more, and was obviously readying herself to shoot.

"Okay, okay. I'm sorry. Don't shoot. I'm sorry, I said."

The man put his hands higher in the air in surrender, and slowly backed up. "I said I'm sorry okay? Please, don't shoot me."

Willina watched him carefully as he got back

in his vehicle never lowering the pistol until the door to his vehicle slammed shut.

"Prick!" Willina scowled as she plopped down in her seat, and then she yelled, "Pull off, now!"

PS floored the accelerator and passed the nut-case on the left before he had time to turn his car back on. She then made a fast illegal left hand turn and tore up a one-way street, and down another before slowing down.

When the two had back tracked several miles and ended up behind the point where they had first encountered the lunatic driver, PS pulled into a strip mall parking lot to catch her breath.

Willina was still sitting there with her pistol on her lap, smiling.

PS took about ten deep breaths and swallowed a gallon of saliva and looked at Wil in both relief and anger.

Silence.

"I wouldn't have shot him, you know," Wil finally blurted.

"Oh?" The reporter said. "That's not what it looked like back there."

"I couldn't have, even if I'd wanted to."

"And why not?" PS asked. "You looked like you knew what you were doing."

Willina turned the gun over in her hands and began to laugh. "Because, I don't have any darts for it."

She handed her friend the gun. It was a plastic toy. On close inspection it barely resembled a real gun at all. PS looked at Willina, the gun, and back to Willina again. "You mean to tell me you just backed down some raving lunatic with an empty dart gun?"

"Yup," she said proudly putting the toy back into her purse.

PS didn't know whether to laugh or scream. She wasn't sure if Wil had endangered their lives or saved them. Adrenaline was coursing through her veins. She could hear her heart pounding in her head and her hands were shaking. They went *ratta tat tat* on the steering wheel.

PS Garrett then slowly pulled herself together and backed out of the parking lot, and headed toward Willina's condo. She was afraid to look in the rear view mirror for fear she would see that her hair had turned gray and that she had aged fifteen years in the last ten minutes.

Wil didn't say a word for the first mile or so, and then she quietly said, as if she were really thinking out loud to herself, "He wouldn't have done anything anyway. He didn't have the confidence. Did you see how he walked? He can't even fuck."

Grateful that, true to her word, PS was keeping a lid on the video of the bloody message, Chief Grainger kept her apprised of everything going on in the Pixley murder investigation. If the police station received a valid tip, he called her first.

For her, he sorted the information that was being considered as significant and the calls that were being tucked away as remote possibilities.

He told her he wouldn't forget their deal, and would spread the word to law enforcement throughout the area that he would consider it a close personal favor if they cooperate with this particular reporter as much as possible, no matter the story.

It was an even trade. Being in favor with police throughout southeast Michigan could easily slip PS a few notches higher on the news-pole as she became the favored journalist at crime scenes around the tri-county area.

It was because of that understanding that Chief Grainger let PS in on the one big tip police thought might actually lead somewhere. A man who'd gotten gas at the Gas 'N Go early the evening of the murders called police to say he'd seen two black men in dark clothing getting out of a green sports utility vehicle. He said he remembered them vividly because they looked suspicious, and, "They were playing that rap music stuff loudly." That's what initially caught the possible witness's attention. And, because he thought the two guys looked like thugs who were up to no good, he went around the side of the Gas 'N Go to pretend he was putting air in his tires. That's when he saw the license plate. It was easy to remember because it was a vanity plate that read 2BAD4U.

The tipster said he was sure the guys were casing the shop, but he couldn't wait around to see what happened so he made note of their license plate and went along his way.

Three days later when, in passing, he heard about the shooting at the Gas 'N Go, he contacted the Pixley police. The chief let fly that the man on the phone would be in the flesh at the police station that

126

afternoon, and it might be a good idea for her to be waiting outside after his official interview with investigators.

PS grabbed a cameraman, told the 5 o'clock producer that she'd be back with the lead story and headed north to Pixley to wait outside the cop shop.

Grainger had given her a description of the man, so PS had a pretty good idea of who she was looking for.

The unmarked news cruiser sat outside the police station with Sylvester, the photographer and PS intent on the front door. The two kept themselves amused telling knock knock jokes and making up riddles from gruesome crimes they'd either covered or that had made national news.

"What was Jeffrey Dahmer's favorite cut of meat?" Asked Sylvester.

Sylvester was no Ansel Adams with a camera. His major charm was the ability to turn a deathly boring detail into something survivable with stupid jokes, ridiculous stories and outrageous challenges—like trying to see who could hold their breath the longest.

He was one of the regulars at Silver Spur Chop Suey, and made no secret that he was a beer lover—and he had the belly to prove it. And he loved morbid jokes.

"I don't know," PS answered. "What was Jeffrey Dahmer's favorite cut of meat?"

"Ground Chuck!" Sylvester hooted.

He threw his head back to giggle. PS snickered a bit, but without conviction. Her stress level was on the rise.

Undaunted by her frequent sighs and nervous finger tapping, Sylvester threw out another riddle. "What was Jeffrey Dahmer's favorite bean?"

"Bean?" PS asked half listening and half watching the front door of the police station, picking at a thread that was teasing her from just beneath the hem of her brand new blazer.

PS had run out of clean clothes and had managed to eek out some time to buy three new blazers to get her through the rest of the week.

"Yeah. You know. Bean. String bean, lima bean? Bean. What was Jeffrey Dahmer's favorite bean?"

"I don't know. You tell me, Sylvester," the reporter said, trying not get too distracted from the entrance of the Pixley cop shop.

"Human being!" Laughed Sylvester. "Get it? Bean, like green bean, or string bean. Human being. Okay, okay, one more. What did Jeffrey Dahmer say to his victims when they got angry with him?"

"This is sick, you know," PS replied.

"Yeah I know," Sylvester panted with pleasure. "But what did Jeffrey Dahmer say to his victims when they got angry with him?"

"I don't know."

"Hey man. Don't lose your head. Get it? Don't lose your head? I just made that one up."

"You don't say." She replied with a dry chuckle, and squinted toward the front door of the police station.

The two sat in front of the Pixley police station for two and a half hours. It was already 2:30 and PS was starting to get more than a little nervous. She'd be on deadline in another hour and a half. She'd made it clear that she would be able to turn a story, probably the lead at five, and they still hadn't shot a frame of tape.

The sun was high and the car's windshield conducted heat like a solar panel. The TV crew was burning up and didn't have anything to drink or to nibble on. Sylvester had run out of morbid crime scene jokes and riddles and hadn't brought anything to read, and neither had PS.

She rummaged around her reporter's bag for a stray mint, cracker or something, but Sylvester had polished off the last candy bar an hour before.

"Think we oughta order a pizza?" Sylvester asked as he gnawed at a stubborn hangnail.

"Give me a break!" PS said, annoyed that they hadn't thought of it earlier, and now it was too late to be a viable option. "What address will we give? The white unmarked Mercury Marquise in the parking lot of the Pixley police station? Besides, if we don't get some tape soon we're gonna have to blow."

Sylvester began studying the second hand on the dashboard clock and continued to fight with that hangnail. PS stared at the front door of the police station, fighting sleep as her head bobbed heavily and helplessly to her chest.

She was staring at a bright sunburst on the inside of her eyelid, when her head bobbed up and her breath labored into a snort. She shook her head about to regain her senses, and that's when she saw him. The tall, white male with dark hair, glasses and a beard and mustache walking down the stairs of the police station.

He was about six feet five, and extremely slender, almost emaciated—just like the Chief described.

PS snapped out of her fog and jumped out of the car and trotted up to the steps to catch him on his way to his vehicle—her mind racing to catch up with her feet with each step.

Sylvester instinctively hung back a bit, but kept the camera rolling, not wanting to intimidate the man before getting any video.

The reporter was carrying a wireless microphone tucked casually beneath her newspad so it wouldn't be obvious as she approached the stranger.

"Good afternoon, Sir. I'm PS Garrett from Channel Six. Do you mind if I talk to you for a moment?"

And then she said quietly, almost as a whisper, "I'm carrying a microphone and you're being recorded."

The old timer looked startled at first. But as he began to recognize the reporter from TV, he relaxed and even became a little intrigued.

"Yeah, I seen you before. You're what, that young gal on the TV screen. Am I going to be on TV?"

"I'd like you to be, Sir. If you don't mind," PS answered, beckoning Sylvester to come closer.

He did, with the camera still rolling. He walked up and extended his left hand, as his right hand remained on the camera as he held it steady on his shoulder.

The man was excited that he might actually become the celebrity witness who helped police crack the Pixley murder case, not to mention he was obviously excited that a reward had crept up to sixty-thousand dollars for anyone with information that would lead to the arrest and conviction of whoever was responsible.

PS sighed relief for the first time that day. She couldn't afford to bear the blame for keeping the 5 o'clock beast hungry, yet again. And this was going to be easier than she thought.

She unwrapped her newspad from around the mic, and held it up toward the star witness. "Sir, can you recount what you saw at the Pixley Gas 'N Go three days ago?"

The man dropped his head, so that his mouth was almost on top of the microphone. PS subtly moved it down so he wouldn't choke on the thing as he spoke. "I was getting gas when this green SUV pulled up. I looked up because I could feel the truck coming because the bass in the music was so loud everything began vibrating on my car as the truck came to a stop behind me.

"As soon as it pulled up behind me, I got a bad feeling, like something was about to happen."

PS looked back to make sure the cameraman was rolling, and when she was satisfied that no gremlins were keeping the tape spools from going round and round on their rollers, she turned her head and nodded to the stranger so he could continue his story.

"I remember seeing two men, thugs, get out of the vehicle. I couldn't really see their faces, and they kind of looked alike, like they could be brothers or something."

This was great stuff. PS could feel exclusive all over her body.

Eat dirt and die Channel Three. Eat dirt and die.

On he went. "All I can remember was they had dark skin, and dark colored clothing. One of them may have been wearing a cap of some sort. Anyway, the driver of the vehicle got out and began pumping gas while the other one went inside. I stood there watching the two, when the driver looked at me and sneered, 'Is there a problem, Sir?' It was real nasty, his eyes got real big and his nose flared like he wanted a piece of me or something."

The interview was totally re-living the night. He started to sweat a little, and he began to get emotional.

PS salivated.

He went on. "I just didn't like the way that boy said, Sir. He kind of spat it out like he was being a wise-ass or something. I didn't say nothin' back. I just got in my car and drove around to the side of the gas station, and made believe to put air in my tires. That's when I saw the license plate. It had a 2, a B, an A, a D, and then the number 4 and a letter U. Kind of hard to miss that one wouldn't you say?" The man nodded his head at the reporter with a slight smile. He was sure of what he had seen, and proud of it.

PS politely nodded and returned the smile, and put the microphone in her left hand to give her right arm a break. The gentleman grabbed the microphone and tried to pull it closer to his mouth. But PS held onto it tightly, and gently pulled it away.

A reporter never relinquishes control of her mic. Never. That would mean she's lost control of the interview.

He got the message, reluctantly took his hands

off the mic, dropped them to his side and continued. "Well, that one boy was in there in that store for a long time, and the other one just kind of leaned on the car, like he was waiting or something. Well, I just couldn't stand there forever so I left. Yesterday when I heard about the shootings on the radio, I called the police and told them everything I saw.

"That's it. But I know those kind of people. I see 'em on the TV all the time. They did it. That's for sure. I just hope they haven't gotten too far away for police to catch 'em, dirty black son-offa-bitches. I'm sorry, I didn't mean nothin by that."

PS began to notice a sinking feeling in the pit of her stomach. The license plate stuff was good, but some thing in the tenor of his voice sounded the alarms in her built in bullshit detector. "Sir," she said. "Do you have any better description than two dark-skinned Black men in dark clothing? After all that could be the description of half the men in the Detroit area."

The interview rolled the question around in his mind for a few seconds, thought about it and said, "I really can't think of any other description, I didn't get that close a look at them. But they did it. I'm sure of it. I can just feel it, right here," the stranger balled his fist and slammed it into his gut, then returned his hands to the inside of his right pocket.

PS felt something on the inside of her gut too. She just wished it was as harmless as a fist.

He continued. "Like I said, I know those kinds of boys when I see them, and they're dirty. All them nnnnnn..." The interview caught himself and paused. "I didn't mean nothin by that."

133

"Yeah right," PS retorted, struggling not to purse her lips in disgust.

"One went into the shop and I could see from the side window he was loading up on pop and chips, and they didn't look like the kind of guys who would be buying pop and chips. It wasn't right. They were casing the joint. That's for sure. They were up to no good!"

"Sir," PS interrupted, her left clavicle pounding as her exclusive lead story was barreling toward the crapper. No doubt, the cops would want to track down these guys as potential witnesses, but she still wasn't getting the sense that this man had actually come face to face with the murderers. "What wasn't right about it? Couldn't it have been just two guys buying soda and chips?"

"No, nope. That's not it," insisted the man getting defensive. "Now, if they were buying malt liquor or something, maybe, cause you know, well..." He paused, obviously hearing himself and feeling at least, a modicum of embarrassment as he stood in front of this particular reporter. But then true to his nature, her forged on. "Nope. Not pop and chips. They just weren't the type for pop and chips. I know. Like I told you, I know how those kind of people are."

"Sir, what the heck do guys look like who buy pop and chips?"

"Are you trying to be smart or something? What do you mean, what do guys look like who buy pop and chips? I can tell you they don't look like those two boys, I can tell you that."

PS persisted. "Mr., I'm sorry, I didn't get your name."

"Smith, John Smith," he snapped—his lips pursed and his chin tilted up in righteous indignation revealing the bright red beneath his chin.

"Are you serious?" The reporter asked with a half-hearted chuckle.

That's all the name you need to know right now, girl."

"Okay," she said, with a slight sigh of frustration. "Mr. Smith. Help me out here. Did they say or do anything specific that made you think they were about to commit a crime?"

Mr. Smith got very annoyed and said, "You trying to be wise or something? Obviously you're not listening to me. I told you they were two colored guys, playing that kill whitey rap music stuff. If those weren't two boys bent on doing murder..."

"Mr. Smith, we really don't like to be called colored anymore."

"What? Scuse you!" He shouted. "You came tottling up to me askin' if you could talk. I don't need no lip from the likes of you. I don't need no lip at all. Now, I told you what I seen. I'm goin' home to wait for my reeee-ward money."

With that, Mr. Smith stormed off muttering under his breath about how he couldn't stand the bunch of them—damn media and their snooty democrat ways.

It was obvious that PS had just wasted a whole lot of time on an everyday, garden variety bigot.

"Mr.!" She yelled out after him. "Do you have any African American neighbors by chance? Do you know any blacks personally?"

He didn't answer, he just got in his little Ford Fiesta and drove off churning up gravel and dust in the old parking lot in his wake.

"Fucker!" The reporter spat. She turned to her photographer and sighed. Sylvester gave her a sympathetic smile and then quipped, "There's one vote for Trent."

"Enough with the morbid jokes," she snapped as she kicked at the gravel beneath her dark blue leather pumps. "Crap! There goes the five o'clock lead."

PS Garrett was a dead woman and Salina Kingsley was holding the noose.

CHAPTER SIX

Chief Grainger walked down the steps of the cop shop and walked over to the TV crew. He had been watching the interview for several minutes.

"So what do you think?" PS asked, hoping against hope that she could still wrangle some sort of story out this interview.

"Not much. Sorry to drag you all the way out here on this one. He sounded pretty convincing on the phone. But once we got him in here for the details, it kind of went down hill from there."

"Is it even remotely possible this guy is on to something?"

"Well, I think we need to track these guys down. Maybe they saw something. But the timeline is all wrong. The story just doesn't fit. We'll track 'em down anyway, for propriety."

This was bad.

PS called the five o'clock producer. She explained the circumstances. But Salina wouldn't hear of it. She had the news ethics of Geraldo Rivera and all she cared about was keeping commercials from bumping into each other. "I don't care if you have to rub two sticks together and send up smoke signals. I already have you in my rundown, and I don't have anything else to fill the slot with."

"But," PS protested. "There's no real story here."

"Sounds like one to me. Cops talked to a witness didn't they?"

"Well yeah, but..."

"Then you've got yourself a story," Salina continued in her shitty, I hate all reporters, especially women, voice.

"This is irresponsible, you know. You want me to go on the air and tell people that police are bird-dogging a hot tip and that's just not true. Salina, there's nothing here, I'm telling you."

"Are police looking into it?" She asked impatiently.

"Well they're going to check it out, but they don't believe there's much merit to what this guy is telling them."

She persisted in a condescending voice. "Again, I say, the police are looking into it?"

"Technically, I guess you could say they are."

"Then that advances the story. Is anybody else out there with you?"

"No. We're the only ones chasing."

"Then I'll couch it a bit, say that police have received some information they think is worth looking into."

"But it's not..."

"Look!" Salina yelled. "I can't believe you don't know a story when it bites you on the ass. If police are looking into it, we have a story. Period. I'm on deadline here. Now your live truck should be arriving any minute. You put together a quick package and we'll talk about this with Bob Tucker when you get back." And she hung up the phone.

"I swear!" PS said. "That woman is capable of eating her young."

"It never gets that far," returned Sylvester. "She eats the eggs before they become young."

An hour later, as PS Garrett stood on the sidewalk with the Pixley Police Station sign framed properly over her right shoulder, she was not surprised to hear the anchors leading into her live shot with, "Our top story, a Channel Six exclusive. Pixley police have a major break in the case of the two teen-agers murdered at a small convenience store earlier this week, with two possible suspects in their cross-hairs. Let's go live to our reporter who's standing by at the police station with this breaking story. PS, what can you tell us?"

The following day the police checked out the bigot's story—they had to. It was the first quasi lead they'd gotten in the now, four days since the murders — even with its obvious holes their hope was that these guys had seen something other than a pumpkin-head bigot pumping gas. Police had hopes these fellows might have seen something before or after that might lead to a real suspect.

They ran a search on the plate and the vehicle. It was pretty easy to track down. And sure enough, the Pixley authorities found the deep green sports utility vehicle with the Michigan license plates, 2BAD4U.

The car was parked in the driveway of a mini-mansion in a suburb just south of Pixley, about twenty five miles from the murder scene.

The vehicle belonged to Nathan Small, a tall, brown skinned black man in his early twenties, who'd been on his way home to see his family. He had stopped at the Gas 'N Go with his college roommate from Dartmouth.

Nathan was a sophomore there, studying economics. He'd been away at school and this was his first visit home since the semester started in January.

Police found him lounging by the household's swimming pool wearing a FUBU sweater and a knit cap playing cards with a couple of buddies in the unseasonably warm February air.

Young Nathan told police he did remember stopping at the Gas 'N Go to top off his tank before getting home. He and his roommate had been driving for thirteen hours, and they were a little hungry, so they jumped off the interstate to the little convenience store.

And yes, he had heard about the murders. He'd seen the report on television the day after the murders, and his father had been talking about them at the dinner table. It was a big deal in the Small household, since Nathan's dad would ultimately be responsible for assigning a prosecutor to convict a suspect if one was ever found.

Nathan was a very cooperative young man, who—instead of being angry about the interrogation, was amused that he had been fingered by some hay seed pumping gas at the same time he was.

But Nathan, understanding the gravity of his *informal* interview with Pixley police, did say that he would be more comfortable calling his father at his of-

140

fice near the county courthouse, and having him come over to continue talking to police—his father, being none other than the Oakland County prosecutor, Nathan Small, Senior.

Grainger walked out to the waiting news crew and filled in the blanks.

PS had been sitting outside the Small mansion with the photographer, Brad, and shot video of police moving in and out of the home quietly and calmly. But she'd heard enough. She called the studio and asked to speak to Salina, and once again suggested that they drop the story and look for another lead. Given the circumstances, this time Salina agreed.

PS thought about the low-rent bigot she'd met the day before. Mr. Smith, or whatever his name was, had obviously watched too much television. If she could have called him, she would have informed him that not all black males wear handcuffs as everyday attire. It just looks that way on the news.

And when she saw that kid, Nathan Small, as he wandered out of his father's mini mansion, she had to admit, he seemed exactly the type to eat potato chips and drink pop.

It was the highest level of sucktivity as the news crew pulled off and headed back toward Detroit.

Desperate for a lead story, the assignment editor diverted them to the scene of a natural gas explosion—which took them forty miles away to the west side of Macomb county.

It turned out to be a construction accident, in which a piece of heavy equipment punctured an underground pipe. No injuries, no evacuations. Translation—no story.

They were called downtown on a five-hour-old report of an attempted schoolgirl abduction. Only, when they got to the police department, PS discovered the sixteen-year-old tenth grader had made the story up to cover her tracks after being late for school. She'd actually been with her twenty-five-year-old truck driver boyfriend. Because she was of the age of consent, PS didn't even have a statutory rape story to squeeze out of it.

It was close to two in the afternoon. The weary reporter hadn't won a story in three days, and could feel the heavy pressure of failure on her record. There was a small window in her contract and it would be coming up for review soon, and these weren't the kinds of impressions she wanted fresh on her news director's mind. Especially with Salina harping in the background.

PS Garrett had to turn something. Anything.

"Base to unit six, come in unit six."

"This is unit six, go ahead," PS said into the mic and then turned to Brad. "Great, they won't be satisfied until they send us to Bum Screw Bizaro World, as if it's our fault we can't turn a story today."

She then re-keyed the mic. "What can we do for you, base?"

"We need you to swing by the cemetery on Mt. Elliot. We're getting word of a disturbance there."

"Sure, no prob."

Brad sighed, and swung out into the far left lane to make an illegal U-turn. "Great, what kind of disturbance can possibly be going on at a cemetery. Dead people rolling over in their graves over the crap we put on the air?"

"I don' know," PS chuckled. "But it's a living. Hey, isn't that the cemetery near the airport where they've been talking about relocating graves, so they can put in a new runway?"

"I don't know."

"Yeah, I think it is. That is without question, spooky stuff. Can you imagine someone saying we're going to dig up your loved one and move them to someplace you have no say in, and tough shit about it?"

"No, I can't imagine," Brad answered. "Some people work really hard to find their final resting place. I think when it comes to progress it should stop at gravesites."

"You know, this could be a big deal. The Mayor has been trying to sweep this story under the rug for weeks. I did the original story a couple of months ago. They said they were going to condemn the cemetery as soon as the ground softened up. Can you imagine? How in the Hell do you condemn a cemetery? What are you going to say? It's not safe to live here?"

Brad pressed a little harder on the accelerator, and the TV crew reached the entrance of the cemetery in fifteen minutes when it should have taken them twenty-five.

It wasn't pandemonium, but there was definitely a story beginning to play out.

It started with about a dozen people standing

in small clusters at the gates of the cemetery. They were talking loudly amongst themselves and complaining about how the cemetery people were trying to pull a fast one.

As more people started arriving, the pitch elevated.

PS and Brad sat in the vehicle just observing quietly.

By the time the crowd swelled to about 40, the reporter sensed an eminent flashpoint. She could see from her car window that some of the gravesites inside the locked gates had been disturbed. It looked like some sort of construction was going on.

The swell of people became more agitated, leaning up against the fragile, aging iron fencing—jostling it, and then pushing, and then pushing harder.

She nodded to Brad and the two piled out of the car.

As soon as Brad pulled out the camera and pointed it toward the crowd, something in the wind shifted. The murmurs became louder, and louder still, and then the jostling of the fence became more intense.

A huge microwave live truck screeched to a halt several hundred yards away, closer to the front entrance of the cemetery. It had the words *Channel 3, Live at 5*, emblazoned on the sides. The passenger side door swung open, and the spit-shined Johnston and Murphy, smooth leather loafers of Sherman Hall hit the pavement.

That was just the catalyst needed to push the crowd into a mob.

People started yelling and screaming. Some

started trying to climb over the wrought iron fence, others were pressing hard against a large gate at the entrance trying to break a chain that looked too old to remain reliable much longer.

Brad and PS immediately made a run for the action. As they ran up to a set of fences, PS passed a man in his late sixties, pounding hard on the decorative poles that wrapped and winded into an ornate fence. The reporter paused long enough to grab the mic from Brad and shove it in the man's face. "What's going on here?"

"Those bastards, they've taken it upon themselves to just move these graves. I don't give a crap about the city's plans, my grandfather is buried here, and I don't want him moved so the airport can make a few extra bucks."

"Sir, how did you find out they where actually moving bodies? Do you know how many bodies they've moved?"

"My sister called me an hour ago. She said she drove by and noticed the backhoe. There hasn't been a new burial here in fifteen years, so she knew what was up. They've already moved about eight sites. Look, you can see the holes. They haven't even filled them yet."

"How in the heck did authorities think this would go un-noticed?"

"I don't know, but..."

The man stopped talking, squinted past PS and broke out into a hobbled run. Further up the street, she could see more commotion where some people had successfully breached a gate and were pouring into the cemetery at the far end. The TV crew also sprinted in that direction, sliding through the slit in the gate with the rest of the desperadoes, including the man they had just interviewed a few minutes earlier.

PS's reporter's antenna zeroed in on an elderly woman who had fallen to the ground and wrapped her arms around a headstone several hundred yards away. She was sobbing uncontrollably.

The Channel Six crew made a run toward her.

Several dozen yards into their jaunt, they noticed there was another crew, also making a beeline toward their interview. It was Dirk Danbury with Sherman Hall just a few paces behind.

This was a direct threat. PS needed this interview, and she didn't want to share. It was personal. She didn't want him asking a million and one questions, gumming up the works and slowing down the process. She had to get to that woman first. Brad sped up, and PS was right behind him, struggling to keep her heels from digging too deeply into the soft soil. As they passed the other crew, Brad yelled, "What the Hell do you think you're doing?"

"What do you mean, what the Hell am I doing? What the Hell are **you** doing?" Dirk shot back, laboring to keep his camera on his shoulder with one hand, the other scratching desperately at his testicles. "Sheeeet! Flick," he blurted. "Screech, nithhhhhh," he chirped as he struggled to keep up, each muscle twitch slowing him down as he hiccupped and scratched.

"We're doing our job. Why don't you find some-one else? That one belongs to us," PS screamed, equally

146

as desperate, minus the physical spasms that for the first time, as near as she could tell were giving her an edge to a story.

"The Hell she belongs to you. We have just as much right to her as you do," Sherman panted.

"Look, I'm on a deadline. If you grab her, there won't be enough to go around," PS yelled back, finding it difficult to keep up with her taller, stronger counterpart.

"Go to Hell!" Yelled Dirk. "You think you're the only one who counts. Who the Hell anointed you a news God? Get the Hell out of my way, fliiick, weeeeek!"

"No, you get the Hell out of my way!"

Sherman held his hand out to balance himself, as he stumbled on the loose mud and it caught PS on the shoulder. She faltered and stumbled as well, but was able to regain her footing and catch back up. Thinking it had been a deliberate attack, she grabbed Sherman's overcoat and tugged. She could hear a rip in the Burberry lining.

She didn't care.

The two of them started to tussle, he in self defense, she in anger, as they ran for the distraught woman.

It's not clear who shoved who first, but in a matter of steps, the two of them were running and wrestling as the cameramen continued to sprint toward the sobbing, desperate woman who was clearly going to be the defining interview of the day.

"Stop it!" PS shrieked.

"No, you stop it!" The other reporter yelled.

Adrenaline was coursing through their veins.

Desperate times like this lowered the bar of acceptable behavior and clouded all reason and judgment. Both reporters were frantic for the lead story. Both were desperate for something the other didn't have.

The two continued to push and shove and argue, while running.

The Channel Three photographer then pushed PS hard from behind. She tumbled to her knees. Brad, who somehow had gotten behind her ran up and, never missing a step, lifted his partner back to her feet.

"That bastard," PS yelled, thinking that it was Sherman who'd shoved her. "You bastard! You're screwing it up for everybody!"

PS lurched forward and threw herself into Sherman Hall. It was more of a trip as her heel snagged a twig that had been mired stubbornly in the mud, but the momentum tossed her full thrust into her rival who staggered sideways and then stumbled several feet before disappearing from sight as though he had tumbled off the face of the planet.

"Oh, Jesus!" PS screamed as she regained her footing and continued to run. "Did you see that?"

"Yeah, but to Hell with him," Brad yelled. "That'll teach him to grapple with us."

PS slowed and retreated to see what had happened to her adversary.

"Forget him!" Brad yelled. "We've got a story to do."

PS turned away and re-focused on the interview that would save her life that day.

As the TV crew approached her, the woman

hugging the worn tomb stone started sobbing even louder. "No, no. Please don't. Please don't take my picture. I'm not supposed to be here, I'm supposed to be at work. I'll lose my job."

"Then what are you doing here?" PS asked as she made certain that her mic was turned on before thrusting it into her face

"No, please don't. Please. My great-grand-mother is buried here, and I had to come to make sure they didn't move her. They put a little, teeny notice in the paper, thinking we wouldn't see it. And to think I voted for that mayor. They are defiling graves. They are stealing our loved ones, without our permission. Please, I beg of you. Please I beg of you. Don't take my picture, I'll lose my job, but I had to come here to protect my Nanny."

"Ma'am it'll be all right, certainly your employer is going to understand you protecting the gravesite of your loved one," PS insisted.

"No, I'm telling you. I don't want to be on tele-vision. I can't. Turn off the camera," the woman sobbed.

PS could see with her peripheral vision, Brad, who was standing behind her had dropped the camera to his side.

The reporter turned around and looked up at him. "What are you doing?"

"The woman said she doesn't want to be on cam-era."

"She'll be alright, Brad. Roll."

"She said she doesn't want to do an interview, PS."

PS could see, not so far from where she was standing, Dirk was trying to pull his partner out of the deep hole he had tumbled into.

"I don't care," she hissed. "I need this. Now, roll it, please."

"We can't do this. These people are in grief."

"People are always in grief. That's what we do. Grief. Now, we have to do this," she whispered harshly. I haven't had a story in three days. We're on deadline. Now pick up that camera and turn it on. I need this woman to talk to me and I need it to be good."

Brad gave her a nasty look. And didn't budge.

"Brad, we need this. You need it as much as I do. Do you want to explain to Salina Kingsley why Sherman Hall has this interview and we don't? Now please," she pleaded.

Brad looked at her with the same measure of disdain that she knew she would see herself when she looked into the mirror that night.

He slowly raised the camera to his shoulder, and PS heard the familiar click that made her comfortable in knowing that the camera was rolling and recording.

"When did you realize that they were moving your great-grandmother's grave?" She pressed.

"I told you. I can't afford to be on camera. I'll talk to you off camera, but I don't want my face on TV."

"I'm trying to help ma'am, but I can't do it without your assistance. You have to talk to me."

"Can't you talk to anybody else? Please. I can't be on camera," the woman started gasping and sobbing.

PS glanced quickly around and sized up the situ-

150

ation. No one else that she could see had draped themselves around a tombstone. Yes, people were angry, but none was as emotional as this one woman, who was clearly over the edge.

She could see that Sherman had returned to the living and was brushing mud off his slacks, and scraping muck off his shoes. She didn't want to still be standing there when he got around to making it over to where she was.

She and Brad had dawdled away enough time with those earlier non-stories, and time was a wastin'. This woman had to do the interview and at the moment, anything else she had going on in her life just couldn't matter.

"Ma'am, they are going to dig up the bones of your Nanny and cart them away if you don't talk to me. I don't have time to look for another interview, and I'm trying to help as best I can. When did you realize that they were going to dig up the graves? Do you feel like you got proper notification? Have you been compensated in anyway?"

The woman continued to heave and sob as she tried to wave away the camera and hide her face.

"This is wrong," Brad sighed behind her. "This woman doesn't want to be on television."

PS glanced back. "Do you want to tell it to Salina Kingsley? Stop fighting me and roll! Zoom in. Zoom in and get me those tears on tape. Set the shot up. Got it?"

"I got it," Brad hissed. "You're the one who doesn't get it."

"Oh, I get it all right. You have no idea how

well I get it."

She turned back to the woman and knelt down with desperation mounting so quickly it manifested itself as a dry lump in her throat that threatened to block her airway. "Ma'am?" She choked. "What if I block out your face so no one will recognize you. Will you talk to me on camera then? I'm really trying to help you."

"Can you do that? Can you make it so no one knows who I am?"

The reporter squinted to get a look at the woman's watch. It was already four o'clock. There was no way an editor would have time to disguise this woman's face. She could ask, but at that hour it just wasn't likely. "I can try. If we have enough time, I can try to."

"But what if you don't have enough time?"

"I'll do what I can. Okay? Now, where are they going to move the remains of your Nanny? Have they told you yet?"

That day PS Garrett would win the battle, triumph the fight, bring home the bacon, lead the show. Yes, she would redeem herself for the perceived ills she had committed, by coming home empty handed for the last few days in a row. Her news director would forget that she had been beaten on the Pixley murders. She would survive another day.

Sherman Hall would probably report his nemesis to his boss, who would report her to hers and she would be pseudo-reprimanded for accidentally pushing the competition into an open grave.

The two would be greater adversaries, and Willina's hope that they would mend their squabbles and find their way to each other's pillows would become flotsam and jetsam on the wind.

Everybody would have a laugh. Except, Sherman Hall and that weird Dirk Danbury.

Down the road, PS might get a letter or an e-mail from an angry interview who lost her job because she cut work to save the grave site of a loved one.

The graves would ultimately be moved. The city would win.

It was all part of the dirty little business called television news. So what?

But as PS Garrett looked in the mirror at herself that night, all she could see was the reflection of someone who hated her life that day and no doubt many more days to come.

It wasn't even that she had reached a new level of sucktivity. It was the ease in which she had climbed to that level and perched a little too comfortably there on the ledge.

She was so distracted, when she returned home that evening she didn't even notice that a fresh bouquet of wild flowers had been laid at her door-stoop, this time with a note attached.

Early the next morning, before PS even rose, the property custodian was doing his customary sweep of the complex breezeways. He saw the dried and crumpled bundle just off to the side of the front of the doorway and thought it was just garbage that had blown into the breezeway on a gust of wind. He didn't even bend over for closer inspection. He continued whistling his song and collecting debris in the bristles of his long rectangular push broom.

The next day, PS received a phone call from Tammy Moore's mother, Virginia. She wanted to do a sit down interview. She was upset that five days after her youngest daughter was murdered, police still didn't have a suspect.

This was just the break PS had been looking for. None of the other television stations had talked to the parents of the female victim. And in fact, she had yet to get any parents on tape at all.

"Mrs. Moore, thank you for calling me," she said, measuring her voice.

"Well, I know you were the only one who didn't mistreat Stan, Dan's dad. He said the other stations just ambushed him that night, and then twisted a lot of what he said."

"I'm sure they didn't mean any harm Ma'am," PS said, knowing that had she had the opportunity she would have grabbed an interview with the boy's father like everyone else.

"What kind of person just attacks a grieving man like that? I don't know. I just know, that my husband and I know you've been covering the story, and we were talking to the Chief and he suggested we give you a call. If he can trust you, we can trust you."

"Mrs. Moore, I appreciate that very much."

"I'm packing up my daughter's belongings today."

There was a long pause, and PS could hear gentle

sobbing in the background. The reporter wanted to ask if the woman was alright for lack of anything else to ask. But she knew that answer and bit her tongue to wait out the emotion.

"I'm sorry…" The voice on the other end wept. "This is so hard."

"I know it is. I am so sorry for your loss. You'll never know how much I understand how you're feeling."

"I believe you. Thank you. Anyway, I'm packing up my daughter's things today and if you were able to stop by, I thought I might like to talk to you."

"I'd love to. Thank you. But I need to see about getting a photographer. May I have your number and call you back?"

PS ran to the back room where all of the managers had gathered for the morning planning meeting. She was very excited. "I have your lead story today," she sang.

"Oh, and how many times have I heard that from you this week?" Salina Kingsley spat.

PS ignored her and turned her attention to the other producers and the news director who were discussing the morning's assignments.

"I just got a call from Tammy Moore's mother and she's willing to do an interview."

"What's she going to talk about?" Larry Pink, the assignment editor asked.

"Well, she's busy packing up her daughter's things, great visuals—and she just wants to talk about the lack of progress the police are making. It would be a great way to advance the story."

"I like it," the six o'clock producer said. "But my show is stacked, I don't have anywhere to put it. I've got that five minute investigation piece on the Mayor of Warren's ethnic intimidation charge."

"Well, we could put it in the 5:30 show," Bob Tucker, the news director said.

"Nope, can't do that. Got too much Pistons," the producer of that show said. "Wish I could use it though, that could be a great story. And it seems to me, we haven't talked to any of the parents yet."

PS shrugged and tried to make herself smaller. She didn't really want any reminders that she hadn't been able to serve up any of the parents of the victims. But at least, with this interview she could redeem herself.

"Oh, wait a minute, George got that interview with the boy's mother over in Marine City," Larry said.

"Yeah, but she hadn't seen him since he was an infant. She didn't even know the kid, and if I remember correctly didn't really have much to offer," Bob Tucker countered.

"That's still a parent," Salina said in the most saccharine sweet voice she could muster. After all, this time she was talking to the boss of the newsroom.

"Well, that may be, but this could be pretty decent. Can you use it, Salina?" Bob asked.

"Well, if she does the Tammy Moore story, who's going to follow up on the cemetery story from yesterday," she answered smugly. "I think that affects more people right now. Besides, Pixley is way the Hell out there. I don't think we can afford to send another reporter out of town today."

"By the way," Bob Tucker broke in, "PS, that was great sound you got with that woman in the cemetery yesterday. Great. You owned that story. Good job!"

Everybody, except Salina Kingsley nodded their heads in agreement.

"Well Salina, we do have a rogue murderer running around one of our suburbs. I think that story affects a lot of people," PS disputed. "I mean the cemetery story is a natural follow up for sure, but those people are already dead. Who knows how many more people will die at the hands of this nut case?"

"Oh please," Salina said as she sucked her teeth. "Cool the over-dramatics. All I'm saying is that we have a story in which we've caught the mayor of a major metropolitan city, sneaking off with the corpses of his constituent's loved-ones so he can extend an airport runway. This is a national story, happening in our own back yard, and I need it followed up today.

"Now we have three reporters on vacation which means we need to pick and choose what we get covered today. And the murder story, sans a suspect feels old to me."

"Old? Salina, I told that woman we'd be happy to talk to her today. And on any other day this would lead a newscast!" PS said getting extremely frustrated.

"I'm not saying it's not a good story. I'm just saying it's not a good story today with everything we have going on," Salina said.

"Salina's right," Larry Pink interjected with a sigh.

It was a bad day when he had to agree with

Salina Kingsley. "I don't think we have the people-power to get both done. And that cemetery story is going to be big. The Today show called about it this morning."

"So you're picking and choosing between own-ership of two big stories?" PS protested.

"We just don't have the staff." Bob said. "It's a great story, you're right. But we can't get it done to-day. You know we're forced to do more with less these days, we just don't have the reporting staff and we have too much other stuff on our plate."

"Can't you send a photographer to grab a soundbite with the mayor?" PS whined, digging in her splintering fingernails for some way to get the Virginia Moore story done before it disappeared forever. "I'll put both together, just send Terry or Tom to tail the mayor and get some sound."

"PS, you know better than that." Bob chided. "The union would have our heads if we asked a photographer to get a soundbite without a reporter."

"You tell Mrs. Moore we'll have to get back to her," Salina Kingsley said as she waived the reporter off as though she had been dismissed from Her Majesty's presence.

"Are you kidding me?" PS protested.

"It is, what it is. PS, get over yourself. We need you to follow the cemetery story today." Salina dic-tated.

PS was furious.

She looked around at the faces of the other man-agers sitting around. Each one seemed to be mesmerized by something on their shoe, or the table, or a newspad. Nobody else helped her fight for the story. And without the news director's okay, it was as good as dead.

"You know what, Bob?" PS said, setting her jaw. "Doing more with less is a phrase that gives employers undue license to take unreasonable advantage of otherwise dedicated workers.

"If the phrase could be washed from the hearts and minds of managers, it would likely do away with the need for unions which, at least, in the TV news business force employers to pay more for less. This is Bullshit, you know it, I know it, and you know I know it." And then under her breath as she walked by, she whispered, "Fuck you Salina."

She then stormed out of the back room where the generals were plotting the battles of the foot soldiers in the way of the dreaded morning editorial meeting.

"Are you going to let her get away with that insubordination?" Salina scowled.

"Let it rest, Salina." Larry Pink said.

As the assignment editor, he was the one who was forced to juggle crews and stories to meet the growing news demand with fewer resources. "Do my job for a day, or shut up," he continued.

And then under his breath he muttered, "We're not doing more with less, we're doing less with less."

Salina popped a mint in her mouth to sate the sudden need for a cigarette.

PS went back to her desk and called Tammy

Moore's mother. She explained that she wouldn't be able to get out to talk to her that day, but she would try very hard to do an interview with her in the coming days.

But rather than rush the poor woman off the phone, the reporter took an extra fifteen minutes to chat with her and console her. She told her that she too had lost a loved one in a violent crime and that she still hadn't come to terms with it.

Mrs. Moore thanked the reporter for her genuine concern, and said that she and her husband and two other daughters would be leaving town right after Tammy's funeral to get away for a while. She promised she would call PS if she heard of any new developments and the two said their goodbyes, just as Salina screamed across the room that PS would have to get out the door if she was going to catch the mayor between appointments.

Hours slipped into days, days faded into weeks and one month later, anyone else in the newsroom would have been hard-pressed to even remember the names Tammy Moore and Danny Weinstein.

That's how it is in the TV news business. For better or worse, every day there's a new story to cover. And the old ones just seem to disappear.

CHAPTER SEVEN

By mid-March, the Pixley murders had been relegated to an archives reel that would eventually be tucked away in the tape library. The entry would be scribbled into a logbook somewhere so that the video would be next to impossible to find within the year. No one was bird-dogging the parents anymore, the news cameras were no longer there when they went to church to pray that police find a suspect, even the assignment desk had stopped calling the police for updates. The story just seemed to disappear.

That March, PS Garrett also met a guy. The first real prospect since the only man she'd ever loved broke her heart three years ago.

She met him at Barbara Bennett's annual soiree.

Every year, Barbara Bennett, the Channel Six main anchor, gave an incredible bash at her equally incredible home in the suburban countryside.

Her palatial home was in a very exclusive part of Bingham Farms about twenty-six miles due north of Detroit. The spread was tucked behind a copse of thirty-foot evergreens that stood at attention along a nondescript little road. There was no mailbox or newspaper caddie. If you didn't know what you were looking for, you'd probably pass the entrance without ever realizing there was an opening in the trees.

As you pulled into the driveway, you were welcomed by open meadows on either side of the drive. A good quarter mile from the entrance stood a huge fieldstone Tudor mansion complete with faux turrets and a carriage house. It had been an unusually warm winter, so Barbara decided to have her yearly event early, since the crocuses had already started to bloom and she didn't want them wasted.

The unseasonably warm late March air also brought out a bumper crop of yellow and red tulips, which grew in luxurious patches all around the sides of the house.

It was incredibly warm out, and for the last week, Michiganders had even put away their heavy winter coats. Some had even ventured out in short sleeves.

To the west, a slender fieldstone arch beckoned you to the inner courtyard and its perfectly manicured grass.

It was obviously a home built for entertaining, having once belonged to one of the big three auto barons a generation ago. And Channel Six's long-time anchor was famous for taking full advantage of all the trappings that went along with being moderately wealthy, starting with throwing really clever parties that revolved around some sort of theme.

Last year's theme was Roman Holiday.

The city's movers, shakers and news-makers showed up in togas made of sheets, their nubby bare legs barely covered with their roll-down socks.

The station's general manager arrived draped

in a blanket and wearing thong sandals. Of course, his wife was wearing the latest chic in sheets, a Laura Ashley toga, tailored of course, and Liz Claiborne sandals.

The year before that, Barb's bash centered around a sixties theme, Make Love, Not War. She had her servers hand out love beads at the door and she even burned incense in the inner courtyard. The caterers wore daisy laurels and wild flower leis. At first, everyone from the media was afraid to eat the brownies, since the studio did have a random drug testing policy and no one ever knew who was going to be called to pee in a cup, or when.

But after thinking it through very carefully the skeptics and cynics all felt foolish for even considering the brownies might be loaded—that's not how Barbara Bennett did things. She was a class act. Smart, pretty, well-married, well connected and well paid. She'd worked her way up the ranks as a grade 'A' reporter, was lucky enough to land in the anchor chair and had earned her right to do less work for more money, unlike her co-anchor who had the right look, the right voice and the wrong sized ego to be likable or good at what he did.

That spring after the Pixley murders, the party's theme was, A Day At The Circus.

All of the bigwigs from the station were at the party, as well as most of the producers, on-air staff and some of the more popular photographers. The mayor of Detroit, some city council people and even the police Chief accepted invitations to that party. It was just that kind of high-profile affair. To miss it meant missing a major schmooz opportunity. To not be invited was devastating.

Just as PS had for the last three years, she took a girlfriend as her date.

She had hoped to take a really cute doctor she'd just met. He was tall, and handsome and smart, and PS was impressed with herself that he had shown more than a modicum of interest since, recently, most men treated her as though she were coated with invisible ink.

The Wednesday after she'd met the doctor on a story, they made plans to meet at an exclusive restaurant for dinner the following weekend. PS had laid out her outfit by Thursday, had a really expensive manicure scheduled Saturday afternoon in anticipation of some much needed hand holding. And by then, couldn't wait for seven o'clock to come so she could wow this new guy with all that was her.

She sat in the manicurist's chair musing about the date. She hadn't been on a real date in almost six months, and Dr. Cutie Pie was so handsome. What a way to break a drought! If things worked out she'd hoped to ask him to Barbara Bennett's party the following weekend.

The manicurist instructed PS to step into the back room to wash the almond oil off her fresh new acrylic nail tips. As she sat back down the small framed Asian woman said with a heavy accent that her cell phone had rung.

PS rummaged in her purse, grabbed the phone and saw the customary digital envelope blinking, indicating that she had a message waiting.

"You know, I could sit here all day and the phone won't ring. But the minute I walk away, Voila!"

The friendly manicurist laughed. "Shame here, shame here. Never fails, eh?"

"Nevah."

PS punched in her security code and listened to the message. It was Dr. Cutie Pie. But to her utter shock and dismay, he was saying that he decided he didn't want to go out with her after all. He just didn't feel comfortable going out with a local celebrity. He said he hoped she wouldn't be too disappointed.

He couldn't possibly know how disappointed PS was. "Is he kidding?" She exclaimed.

"Careful there!" The manicurist said trying to steady the bottle of bright red nail polish that was disturbed by PS's sudden jolt.

"I don't believe this!" She said, a pit forming in the middle of her stomach as her Saturday night dream date began sliding down the customary Black hole all of her Saturday nights seemed to go.

She tried several times to reach him on his cell phone, but kept getting his voice mail, even though his message had come in less than two minutes prior. "I can't believe it!" She exclaimed.

"Wassa matter?" Her manicurist asked. "Evewy sing okay?"

PS felt humiliated. Her forehead was hot and she looked around thinking that every woman in the salon must be able to read her disappointment. She was embarrassed and angry.

That prick! She thought to herself. *What a*

coward. I wasn't going to ask the guy to marry me, just buy me dinner. WHAT A BASTARD!

She placed her hands back on the small manicurist table so that Ria could continue painting her nails, all for naught.

At least the creep had the decency to call and inform me of his sudden shift rather than leave word with the restaurant valet. She thought to herself, her lips pursed in bitter disappointment. It was the last straw in a long line of male domesticus disappointments.

She had only been on three dates in as many years. It seemed as though no man had so much as taken her to the movies or the corner Baskin Robbins for ice cream since Danny's abrupt departure. She had gotten used to hanging out with girlfriends. It had even gotten comfortable.

When PS stumbled over the cute physician, she felt like she'd been given a sip of cold water to soothe her parched lips. It would have been fun to take him to the station party so he could see all of her co-workers and equally important they could see her with him. Especially that bitch, Salina Kingsley. She couldn't wait for her to catch a gander of the cutie pie on her arm. When he canceled, she felt in her heart that no man would ever look her way again. Correction—no suitable man. The only people who seemed to show any romantic interest in her at all were married men, criminals in shackles and lesbians. It was devastating.

So PS forced herself to not mind going to Barbara Bennett's party dressed as a roadie with one of her favorite work colleagues, Zoe, the underpaid, underappreciated writer who would be blowing that lowly gig the minute she got a little extra confidence — since Wil had gone out of town with her lover.

PS and Zoe smudged their faces with dark brown Ben Nye stage make-up, Blackened some of their teeth and rolled boxes of Lucky Strikes into their T-shirt sleeves. They wore baggy, raggedy Levis' and their nastiest sneakers. And set out in hopes that there would be some cute single guys on Barb Bennett's guest list this year.

Once again, Barb went all out. A giant banner in the front foyer announced the Ringling Brothers and Barbara Bennett Circus. Knowing Barbara, she probably commissioned the banner from the printers of the Ringling Brothers Circus.

A small white Shetland pony with a braided mane and sequined bridle noshed painfully close to the tulips, just before the entrance of the courtyard. Two llamas, a brown one and a Black one, were tethered to ornamental trees taking full advantage of the young premature blooms on the ends of the branches—their feathered red and blue headdresses bobbing up and down as they strained for the fresh shoots.

The butler who took the invitation at the door was dressed like a freak show barker, complete with a top hat, a bow tie, long Black tails on his jacket with matching striped knickers and a thick, waxed handlebar mustache.

Inside—no expense had been spared. There were cotton candy and popcorn vendors. The parlor and library had live entertainment—jugglers and magicians and dancing women. Two of the servers were dressed like Siamese twins, joined at the side by their clothing. One had a silver tray of hors d'oeuvres, the other a silver tray of champagne.

PS and Zoe grabbed some champagne and meandered through the crowd to check out the local dignitaries dressed like hobos and carnival acts. Of course, Barbara herself was dressed as the ringmaster, her husband, a clown. PS wondered if there might be anything Freudian in that. But then after enough champagne, everything seems Freudian.

The two women walked up to one of the striped tents toward the end of the courtyard. Inside there were two palm readers and a fortune-teller. The line was building for the fortune-teller and since there were two palm readers with very little waiting, the choice was easy.

PS and Zoe walked into the tent and the palm reader welcomed them. "Halloo, My name ees, Gladeez ze Great. Velcome to jour future."

The woman was very mysterious, and spoke in a thick European accent of some sort. PS didn't know if it was a real accent or a put on, and it didn't matter.

The woman was olive skinned and wore a shiny gold scarf around her head that had been wrapped like a turban. Her foundation was entirely too thick, even for a costume party. "She could use a long consultation with the Channel Six make-up guy," PS whispered to Zoe, who started laughing uncontrollably with a hint of too-much-to-drink-already, holding her stomach to contain the ache. Obviously Zoe's tolerance for alcohol was not as high as PS's.

The two sobered a bit when the Gypsy spoke

again. "I know vhat jhu are saying. Gladeez knows all."

Gladys had an extremely pronounced brow and big deep eyes lined in Black eyeliner. Her entire eyelid had been painted a shocking metallic peacock blue, and she had glued glitter under the arches of her painted brows. Her lip liner extended over the natural lines of her lips, and she had colored between the lines in a vibrant fire engine red lipstick.

She coaxed the women closer.

Gladys the Great took Zoe's left hand into her own and looked it over carefully. With her right hand, she ran her fingers across Zoe's right hand, tracing the lines and brushing over the valleys. Zoe looked up with wide eyes, as though she were impressed. The palm reader continued to pour over Zoe's palm as if it were an intricate work of art and she didn't want to miss any of it. When she finally spoke, her voice was low and mysterious.

With champagne bubbles prancing in her head, PS stifled a snicker and tried to pay close attention to what the palm reader was saying to Zoe.

"You are a very preety girl, yes?"

"Is that a question or a statement?" PS smirked.

"Ssshhhhh!" Zoe commanded. "Yes, go on."

"Yees, I see zat jhu are not happy wiv vhat jhu do. Yes?"

"Yes," Zoe said, nodding as though she were in a trance.

"I see zhat it eez time zhat jhu move on. But jhu must be very careful wiv timing. Yes? Timing eez very important right now. Jhu understand?"

"I think so."

"Jhu are a very smart girl. Yes? In jour heart, jhu already know zat it eez time to move on, but vait abouts a veek before you start looking for a bigger position. But don't jump at ze feers opera-tunity. No? Jhu jes see vas eet is out zhere for jhu, but vait a bit longer before jhu make your move. Yes?"

Gladys then turned Zoe's hand over and scoured it once more. "I also see zat jhu must vatch jour diet right now. Yes? Zat vill be very impordant right now. Jhu trust Gladeez. Gladeez knows all."

That was all a little uncanny because Zoe did have a big job interview with one of the networks coming up on Wednesday, and she had been pretty torn about what a possible change could mean to her future. Zoe was also known to start the day off with a candy bar and can of Pepsi.

Zoe was sold. She pressed Gladys the Great for more details. Would she make more money in the long run, even if she had to take a pay cut now? Zoe wanted to know how Gladys the Great knew she didn't eat well, and wanted to know if you're born with the gift of predicting the future, or was there some sort of training she, herself, could employ? She thought this might make a great feature story.

Gladys the Great informed her that although the current position was not the right one for her at this time, nor would the opportunity that seemed to be on the horizon be suitable, that she still had things to learn at Channel Six. But just after the first of the year a real opportunity would present itself and she should begin preparing herself for greatness.

Gladys informed Zoe not to worry and assured her she would make the right decision. She then ended her prediction with, "And don't forget to call your mother."

Zoe felt a great sense of relief. She thanked Gladys, tipped her twenty dollars and stood up with a broad grin on her face.

PS had been watching the ridiculous display with some amusement. Indeed, Gladys seemed to know things about Zoe that she shouldn't have. But then if you considered it rationally, talking about someone who is under-employed and doesn't eat well would likely apply to 90 percent of the American population. It wasn't even a crap shoot to get those details right, presented just broadly enough to just the right gullible soul. It was a well-orchestrated act as near as PS could tell.

"If I had known you were passing out twenty dollar bills, I would have told you to call your mother," PS said snidely.

Zoe looked flushed, and a little embarrassed.

"PS, cut it out. She was good."

"Come on now, this is for fun, it's all a joke," PS whispered. "You're not taking this woman seriously are you? That stuff she said could fit anybody, even me. I don't remember the last time I started the morning off with orange juice and oatmeal. It's all part of the joke. It's a party, for crying out loud," PS said having to remind herself that this was all just part of the elaborate entertainment courtesy of Barbara Bennett.

But when Gladys the Great asked for PS's hand, the reporter felt a little uneasy.

Gladys studied her hand carefully, more thoughtfully, than she had studied Zoe's hand. She was intent, following the lines and cracks with her fingers. She ran her index finger across her palm and followed it to her outstretched ring finger with her own, circled it and looked up into the reporter's suddenly frightened eyes. The old woman then looked down and continued to trace PS's palm. Her finger skittered across her open hand like an insect on hot asphalt, it made PS grit her teeth. Gladys furrowed her brow a bit, and PS, who first though this was supposed to be amusing, felt a chill go down her spine.

When the fortune-teller finally spoke, her words sounded more like a puzzle than party advice.

"Bevare ze angry vint?" She said with a heavy accent.

"I'm sorry?" PS broke in with a nervous chuckle. "I don't understand."

"Silence!" She commanded. "I tell you, Bevare ze angry vint."

"Vint? What's a Vint?" PS asked growing uneasy.

"Shhhh! Listen carefully," she warned. She had the reporter's attention, and PS could feel Zoe quaking a bit as she leaned over from behind her chair, the fun wearing off the event.

"Bevare, something bad comes jour vay." Gladys the Great seemed bothered by what she saw in PS's palm. Genuinely bothered. Her thick brow furrowed and the air in the tent became cool and thick.

"Vint, what the heck is vint. I don't understand," PS commanded, fighting a mounting nervousness.

Gladys looked her in her eye, and what passed between the two made PS shiver. She didn't know what she was seeing in those deep set eyes that seemed to have no pupils, but indeed, it appeared that this was not a joke, nor mere entertainment. The two of them sat there for a moment, engaged in an unusual staring match in which it felt like Gladys was trying to convey some sort of message with her eyes. But, having left her powers of telepathy at home for the day, PS was at a loss. She stared at her, trying to understand her silent message, but couldn't.

This was not fun. And as far as PS Garrett was concerned, that was against the law. The law is, at a party you're supposed to have fun. *Where are the party police?* PS thought to herself. *I want this woman arrested!*

Almost as if she had been reading PS's thoughts, the expression on Gladys' face changed, softened as she cupped her hand in hers smiling gently, almost motherly.

Gladys shook off her serious tenor, and within a nanosecond, she relaxed, forced a broader smile and un-cupped the reporter's hands to peer back into her right palm. "Vatch vhat jhu eat and accept no invitations from strange men for the next month. Yes?" She said with an enveloping smile that revealed several gold teeth.

"No problem there," Zoe chimed in, trying to break the ice. "I know about a dozen men standing in line to not ask her out."

PS looked up at Zoe and forced some of the stress to melt. Her friend's smart-ass comment made her feel a little better, but Gladys the Great didn't get the joke. Her face became stern again, and like a fast moving roller coaster she was back to being serious.

"Quiet!" She cracked. "I say thees is werdy impordantant," her voice was stern and she was a little agitated, almost as if these stupid gringos had unwittingly stepped on a holy alter of some kind. "I tell you these things von more time. Leesten to these things. I know jhu, I know jhu. Bevare an angry vint that comes jour vay and accept no invitations from strange men for zee next month. Von man can be jour undoing. Jhu understand? Vatch! Vatch!"

Another chill ran down PS's chest. "What did you say?"

"Vatch, Vatch. Jhu know vhat I am saying. Vatch, Vatch! One man vill be your undoing. Gladeez have spoken. I am now through!"

Gladys the Great put the stunned woman's hand palm down on the table, gently picked up her left hand and laid it on the right. She then patted them with her own and quickly stood. She then shuffled the two women quickly out of her tent and closed the curtain behind them.

"What, whoa!" PS protested. But the two were already standing out on the courtyard lawn when the striped curtain was pulled shut on their noses.

"I guess she went out to get a smoke or something." PS said with an uneasy smile. "What did you think?"

"I think she was very good. I liked her. What about you?"

"I think she was full of crap. But I do wonder

what the Hell is a Vint?"

"Maybe she means wind. Beware an evil wind."

"Bullshit!" PS protested. "We live in Detroit, not Kansas. Bullshit!"

As the two women wandered back to the main house, they managed to scoop up two more glasses of champagne each before meandering back into the house and into a sitting room where the mayor, Chief of police, Barbara Bennett and several dozen of her closest friends were being entertained by two opera singers.

"I am not listening to this caterwauling shit," Zoe said in a giggly voice that hinted at inebriation as she tugged at PS's shirt. "Besides, look. Salina Kingsley is in there and I'm not going to let that she-devil ruin my buzz and turn my weekend into one of indentured bitchtitude."

"Indentured bitchtitude. That's very clever. Well done, Zoe, well-done!" She said, clapping gently.

"Cut it out, I'm not kidding, I'm not going in there. I hate that crap."

"Wait a minute, will you? Not so fast. Look, over there. Hottie alert."

Standing in the corner near the fireplace was the most beautiful specimen of the male domesticus species PS Garret had ever seen.

PS hurriedly began picking at her teeth with her index finger to remove the wax she had used earlier to Blacken them.

"What?" Zoe protested. "That short guy with the funny nose dressed like a carnival strong man?"

"No, you ignoramus. Not him. The guy next to

him. The tall one in the tux, dressed like a waiter. The one with sparkling green eyes."

PS continued to stare in the direction of the fireplace in hopes the tall stranger would glance her way and catch her smiling at him. He did, and she gently nodded her head in what she hoped would be an inviting, approachable manner. The tall, dark and stunning creature began walking her way, and PS felt butterflies flutter along the front of her chest.

"Ya see. Lookie there!"

"You're pathetic. You know that?" Zoe huffed.

"Why, because I see a cute, successful looking guy and managed to get his attention?"

"No, because you're making googly eyes at a waiter."

"You're full of shit, Zoe. That's not a waiter—shhh! Here he comes."

"Madam?" The gentleman said as he looked deeply into the reporter's eyes.

"That's Mademoiselle," she corrected coyly.

"Very well then. Mademoiselle, would you like a libretto?"

"Excuse me?"

"A libretto. The words. We are listening to Tosca this afternoon. I'm afraid I became most engrossed in the music and didn't see you standing here. I apologize. Here you go. Please enjoy the rest of your afternoon."

"Thanks Lurch," Zoe said with a triumphant laugh and then whispered in PS's ear, "Okay so he's not a waiter, he's an usher. Oh, and he's gay."

She continued to do her Cheshire cat impersonation in spite of PS's glower. "I'm afraid I became engrossed in the music... What hetero man talks like that?"

Zoe looked up at the usher and continued to talk in hushed tones, so as not to disturb the caterwauling. "And do you mind showing me the way to the restroom? And please make it one furthest away from this noise."

PS was steaming. She had the worst luck in the world when it came to picking men.

She settled down on a bench just inside the door well. The music was full and beautiful, but PS was frustrated because she couldn't find the words in the little booklet the usher had handed her.

There was a man singing to a woman. He dropped to one knee and put his hand to his heart and began singing to the heavens. PS was so moved by his voice, she gasped as she felt tears rolling down her cheek. "It's so beautiful," she said quietly as she looked around for a cocktail napkin or something to dry her eyes before anyone turned around. "I wonder what he's singing to her?"

"You make me forget God," a voice whispered behind her, and then a hand reached over PS's shoulder holding a colorful paper napkin.

"I beg your pardon?"

"That's what he's saying. You make me forget God. May I join you?"

PS looked up and it was the strong man with the funny nose who'd been standing near the cute, but now obviously gay usher earlier.

Before she had time to answer, the strong man

177

was sitting next to her. "You see, Tosca is the most beautiful woman in the land," he said, as he made himself cozy next to the reporter, sitting closer than she was comfortable with. "And Baron Scarpia, the Chief of police in the village will be her ruin. He doesn't love her, he just wants to have her because he's obsessed with her beauty. Here's the part right here in your libretto."

The stranger pointed out the column of English translations to the right of the Italian column in the little booklet PS was holding. She struggled to follow along as the man now seated painfully close began whispering in her ear.

"By having her he will increase his status and stroke his ego. But he has no intention of falling in love, he just wants to use her for what he can get out of her. And he wants her so badly he's saying that he has forgotten everything except what it will take to get her into his bed. He's even denounced God."

"How could this guy, Geo-como Puccini write such beautiful music to go with such evil words? And how is it that you know all of this?" PS asked, scooching a little to the right so as to put a comfortable space between herself and the strong man.

"That's Gwa-como Puccini, and I know because it's my favorite opera." He said moving his leg so that once again, it was touching PS's. "And Scarpia is the most dastardly man in opera. He's my favorite character. Hi. My name is Allen. Allen George."

"I'm..."

"I know who you are. I watch you on television all the time. It's a pleasure to meet you."

"Thank you. You too," PS said, once again scootching to the edge of the bench as far as she could go without tumbling off. This time the stranger held his own ground.

The introduction was interrupted by heavy applause as the two singers at the front of the room took their bows.

"Well, show's over. Care to join me in the courtyard for a drink? I think there's also a hotdog out there calling my name."

"Uhhm, well," PS looked around and didn't see Zoe anywhere so, what the Hell?

Allen extended his arm and led PS out of the room and toward a food vendor in the courtyard.

PS was curious about this man. She looked at Allen closely and studied his face. He wasn't anything special to look at, in fact, he was strange to look at. He wasn't bad looking, exactly, just odd. She cocked her head as she studied his profile while he talked to another party guest who had wandered over to investigate the cotton candy at a nearby vending station.

Nothing seemed to match on his face. His narrow dark eyes seemed out of place with the freckles on his nose, a nose which just seemed too small for his face. He had a cookie duster mustache that kind of looked like it was fashioned after Adolph Hitler's, but his lips were round and full.

But every time he spoke directly to her, his appearance seemed to softened, it was as though his voice melted the stifled air that surrounded him. He was so witty and confident, but not cocky. He seemed to make friends instantly with everyone he came in contact

179

with. He talked with impressive ease, and his laugh was generous and loud.

"So you seem like you have a tough job," Allen said, stepping uncomfortably back into PS's space.

She stepped back gingerly to give herself a little extra breathing room. She was a master at taking control of stranger interactions, but she couldn't seem to maneuver to a comfortable space around Allen George. Every time she gained control, he seemed to take it back. "It's an interesting job, I'll give you that," she said, re-maneuvering to his maneuvering.

"Well, you certainly seem to do very well."

"Why, thank you, Mr. George," PS said modestly.

"Well, that too. But I mean financially. Those gold bracelets are stunning."

PS cupped her hand around the bracelets thinking what an unusual thing that was to say.

Allen George immediately picked up on the tension and stepped back a few inches.

PS breathed a sigh of relief. All of a sudden she didn't feel as overwhelmed or trapped.

"You probably meet a lot of interesting people," Allen George shifted quickly.

"Uhm, well, yeah. I guess if you call criminals and cops interesting people."

Allen George began to laugh. It was infectious, and it made PS laugh too.

"I also noticed that you're not wearing a wedding ring. That's a little surprising to me too," Allen George said.

PS immediately began feeling trapped again.

There was something about the way he insinuated himself into her personal space that made her uneasy. But he seemed to know just what to say to evoke response, create heat and then step away before being scorched.

"Well, I don't really talk much about my private life to people I don't know," PS said defensively.

"Then how do you meet men?"

PS was dumfounded. It was a realistic question, though it made her feel very uncomfortable. It was as though this Allen George fellow could read that she was having problems meeting suitable men.

Allen George walked a few feet away to investigate a box of popcorn. PS watched him carefully. She wondered what Willina would say about his walk. In fact she wished that Wil had been there with her, but her best friend had been increasingly scarce. She said she'd gotten a sexy job at a movie studio, was meeting lots of celebrities and all of a sudden Wil was seemingly living on the west coast with only a few weekend trips back to her Michigan townhouse. Wil had far more experience dealing with men. And it had been so long since a seemingly single man had engaged PS in social conversation, she wasn't even sure how to respond. She didn't even know what was appropriate conversation for males and females just meeting. She had hoped to find out with Dr. Cutie Pie, but that didn't go any further than a cell phone call and a false invitation to dinner.

Allen walked back with a small bag of popcorn, and offered some to PS.

She politely declined. "So, your job must be very

interesting," he said, picking the conversation back up.

"Yes, it is actually."

"Exciting, too. I bet you lead a really exciting life."

"Sometimes I do."

"Man, how do you do those sad stories? I mean, I saw one you did last month about two kids who got killed at a little gas station. I mean, how on earth do you stand there and do those stories and not let them affect you? You must have nerves of steel."

PS knew that she was anything but steel. That story had affected her deeply and in fact, still haunted her. Police still hadn't found a suspect. And there were barely perceptible changes in PS's life since covering that grisly scene. She was haunted by the bloody words scribbled on that plate glass window. More than a few times, she fished the video tape from the bottom of her file cabinet, when no one was around and looked at it, trying to figure out what the culprit meant by the words, 'Watch, Watch'.

She would go for days on end feeling as though someone were watching her, observing her from a far. The feeling would disappear from time to time, only to return. Her reporter's sense made her feel as though the story lingered, though there was no way to advance it in the news without a suspect. It was like a ghost pestering her to do something, do something, DO SOMETHING!

She was sorry Allen had said anything. It had been days since she'd had that creepy feeling that sent her left shoulder into a tremble. Now it was back.

She turned her attention back to Allen, he was

smiling at her and she was grateful for the friendly face. "Yeah, I remember that story. That was a tough one."

"Did they ever catch anybody?"

"No. Not yet," PS said finding her feet more interesting to look at, at the moment.

"Well, I bet when they do find the bastard who did it, you'll be right on it. You seem to be everywhere news is happening."

PS smiled and relaxed a bit for the first time since Allen George had joined her on her bench and coaxed her out into the courtyard.

"You know, we kind of teach ourselves to brush off emotion," PS offered generously feeling like she had regained control of dynamics between the two, knowing that what she said about brushing off emotions was a complete fabrication. But it made her feel better to say it. "If we let every story get to us, we'd be raving loons."

"Is that why you've talked yourself into believing that it's okay to not have a boyfriend?" Allen asked. "You've trained yourself not to have basic human emotions? I'm not saying that reporters are necessarily sub human, but it certainly appears that way on TV sometimes."

PS bristled.

"I don't mean anything by it, I'm just saying a beautiful woman like you should have men dripping from her shoulders. You're obviously smart, you have an exciting job. I've been watching you throughout this entire party, and I noticed you seemed to be hanging out with a female buddy. And it just kind of surprised me, that's all."

"Well, Mr. George, it was nice meeting you. I guess I better see where Zoe has been off to," PS said as she began to extricate herself from the area.

PS was trying desperately to mask her emotions. "I should probably find my ride," she said searching the crowd for Zoe.

"Don't go. Don't go angry," Allen pleaded. "I'm an idiot sometimes that's all. I'm really sorry. Just call me socially retarded. I guess I don't have much experience with women. I'm so sorry.

"I'm sorry if I offended you. I guess I'm just not very smooth. I apologize. I just didn't know any other way of asking you out," Allen George said seeming sincerely embarrassed by his behavior. "I don't mean to be a groupie or anything, I just always wanted to meet you. And when I saw you sitting in the corner, I just thought it would be the perfect opportunity to say hello. I guess I screwed this one up, I'm so sorry."

PS paused. Something told her to accept his apology and keep going. But something stronger told her to stay. Loneliness.

He had brought up that ghastly Gas 'N Go murder in Pixley. It reminded her that someone had killed two kids, sixteen year old Danny Weinstein, and fifteen year old Tammy Moore. They had slaughtered those kids and then scribbled a taunt for police with their blood.

Every time PS thought of the name Danny Weinstein, it conjured up the name and image of Danny Rierson. She missed him—had told herself a million times that he was gone and never coming back. But she missed him. She missed his gentle kisses, the way he always stroked her disobedient bang from her face, the way she felt knowing that no matter what story she was doing, or how long she was working there was someone at home waiting for her—missing her—loving her.

She felt her spirits sink, but quickly forced herself to snap out of it and re-focus on the present. In the background she could hear Allen George continuing his apology. "I'm not a stalker. I promise. I just wanted to get to know you better. Maybe take you out for dinner or a drink. That's all."

Feeling as though she had gained firm control over the interaction, PS re-entered her comfort zone. "Well, Allen George, why don't you tell me about you," PS said as she lifted another champagne off a silver tray that had nearly floated past her and took a deep swig to render invisible the grief that was welling up inside her chest.

Allen dove in, obviously very comfortable with the present topic of conversation—him. He said he was a stockbroker who also owned half interest in a health club. He said he was Ivy League educated and had just broken up with a woman, who didn't appreciate his talents.

PS asked him what talents, and he said, with a wink, that he didn't know her well enough to disclose them. But she could change that, if she so chose.

He lost her again, and PS sucked her teeth in boredom, hoping he would notice her disdain for his role as tour guide to Smutsville.

He did notice and quickly shifted the line of conversation, almost seamlessly.

He told her that he knew the mayor and was doing financial consulting with some city commissioners. He was pretty matter-of-fact about the whole thing, so PS thought he must be a pretty important fellow, though, she did wonder how it was that the two hadn't crossed paths professionally, with his credentials.

At second glance, and her third or fourth flute of champagne later, she'd lost count, he seemed to be a pretty complete package.

Three more champagnes later and no sign of Zoe and PS was feeling very comfortable with Allen. It was almost as though they had known each other for years. Her lips loosened with spirits, she found herself confessing to him, "What a lot of people don't understand is, it can be very difficult finding companionship when you're on the air, especially if you're female."

PS emptied her champagne glass, and Allen motioned to a server who walked up and poured more from the carafe on a silver tray.

PS took a sip and continued her thoughtful dissertation marveling at how well she thought her speech was holding up in spite of the fact that even she could tell now that she was impaired. "Half the available men out there are intimidated by you and what you do for a living. You know the whole pseudo celebrity thing. A fourth of the men think you're stuck up or snooty. You must be because, after all, you're on television. Those guys aren't even going to attempt to ask you out. The others think you must already be with someone."

Allen listened intently. He was very interested in what the reporter was saying and prodded her on gently seeing how she was so easily intimidated. It was clear to him that it was important to her to be in control.

She continued, "Of those groups of men I mentioned, I believe half are totally aware of how much money you make, or at least have some sort of inflated idea and are trying to figure out how they can grease their palms with your loot."

"Hmmmm," Allen hummed thoughtfully. "I can see why it's so tough on you."

"I didn't say me in particular," PS corrected. "I said in general."

"Ah, I see," Allen said softly as he gently brushed imaginary ants off PS's forehand.

A pang of sadness struck her. Danny used to stroke her hand as if he were chasing imaginary ants. PS felt flush and warm. She sneaked a peak at Allen, but he seemed to have looked away just before she started turning pink. She sighed relief. She glanced around to see if anyone was laughing. But no one else was paying attention. So she relaxed.

She started doing the math in her head. He seemed genuinely interested in what she was saying, but his responses were cool and non-committal. She didn't quite know what he thought about what she was saying or the kind of person she was putting on to be, but she was surprised at how curious she'd become of what he thought of her. He wasn't handsome, but he wasn't Shrek.

PS was sizing him up, just like she did with a news story she'd been sent out to cover. She listened carefully to what he said, and how he said it, and though she was struggling with a reoccurring feeling of uneasiness, she felt glued to the spot.

The two sat on that courtyard bench engaged in unusual conversation, a tennis match. No one was competing, but the ball kept skimming the net.

After more than one hour, PS felt as though she had been too judgmental about Allen in the beginning. She was out of practice talking to members of the male domesticus species. She'd been alone for some time. Danny had been gone three years, and she hadn't the heart to go out in search of another to love. Instead, she plunged herself into work. She didn't have the heart to start over again. It cost too much time, too much energy, took too many resources to fall in love. Love made women embarrassing. And when it ended badly, and it always seemed to end badly, it stuck to you like skunk stink — the nagging odor of disappointment always just beneath the surface of the skin.

How long have I been without sex? She mused. She thought back, and tried to remember the last time Danny and she had made love. She was struck that she could no longer picture the act, taste the flavor, savor the thought. It just was not there anymore.

She looked at Allen George again. His mustache wiggled when he chewed. His nose was too small for his face. His words were clever enough, but they didn't seem to fit the face of the man speaking them.

A breeze blew through and PS grabbed her left shoulder and began to rub away a creeping ache.

Bevare an evil Vind. She thought to herself.

"You're very beautiful," Allen said. His words slicing through the noise that was building in PS's head.

"I can't believe you came to a party like this without an escort."

"I came with a girlfriend."

"Yes, but a buddy is hardly and escort for an affair like this. You deserve better."

"Well, Zoe is no slouch. She's a good pal."

"I'm not saying anything bad about her. I guess what I'm really saying is, would you like to have dinner with me tomorrow evening?"

PS cleared her throat and looked at Allen George, prepared to decline. But instead, "Yes," is what tumbled uncontrollably from her lips.

The word came out so quickly, PS had scarce time to catch it before it fell. She reared back and looked at him again, as some high city dignitary stopped to speak to him. She thought, *So what if his eyes dart quickly about. So what if his life seems too perfect. So what if I don't really know him. He is an acquaintance of Barbara Bennett's, so he must check out.*

Why do I always have to be a reporter? Allen is obviously interested in me. He made it clear with his body language. He looked me deeply in the eyes as we talked. He reached up from time to time to brush my bangs out of my face. I missed those things. I deserved to have those things.

She wondered if work had possibly been her lover long enough. Perhaps it was time to try a new companion. This man was as good a start as any. She brushed off any trepidation she had and chalked it up to nervousness. "Yes. Tomorrow night is fine. Thank you."

After their meeting at Barbara Bennett's best

party ever, Allen George, and PS Garrett went out every single evening the following week.

Had she known then what she knows now, she would have walked away from Allen George at first hello, and never looked back.

CHAPTER EIGHT

The first child of Doug and Dorothy Williams was a big boy. After a long and difficult labor, he finally had to be taken by Cesarean section.

For the Detroit couple, this was a miracle baby.

Doug and Dorothy had been married eleven years. Nine of those years had been spent trying to have a baby. They didn't have the kind of money it took to go to a fertility specialist. As a teacher and a sales associate at a local department store, the couple struggled just to meet their bills. But they desperately wanted a family so they worked on it the old fashioned way, threw in a fair amount of prayer for good measure and were finally blessed.

After the delivery, Dorothy was in bad shape, needing heavy pain killers just to get through the days just after Billy's birth. She was nearly unconscious when a nurse came to take the baby from her arms. Even through her fog, Dorothy knew she hadn't met that particular nurse before, and she wanted to ask her name, but fell into a deep sleep before she could open her mouth. The nurse gently removed the baby from his mother's arms, and quickly disappeared down the corridor.

Baby Williams was gone.

When the hospital realized the baby was missing, it did all it could do to keep from calling the media. This would be an embarrassing breach of security, and would likely prove costly after a pack of hungry attorneys got through with it all. But, finally, for the sake of the infant, the media had to be called in.

The hospital needed its help.

At the hastily called news conference, the director of the hospital answered questions and passed out a snapshot of the newborn. He described him as a ten pound, African American male with dark curly hair and a birth mark under his left nipple the size of a half dollar—and he'd just been circumcised.

As PS Garrett sat in the briefing room considering the merits of a good Mohel, there was a commotion at the side door next to the podium. A hospital orderly was wheeling in the mother. She was still heavily sedated. Her eyes were wide and glassy behind her thick eyeglasses. She looked dazed and vacant. Doug Williams walked in behind the young orderly piloting his wife's wheelchair—his eyes red and sunken.

There was panicked commotion in the small meeting room that had been turned into a briefing room for the media.

Of course, every reporter had put in a request to talk to the parents of the missing child. Of course, everyone had made the argument that the parents would probably be more effective in making a plea for the safe return of their child. Of course, it was explained to the hospital management that the producers of the various news shows were more interested in hearing from someone in the family. Of course, the hospital administrators said, "Nothing doing."

So when the hospital brass refused to be coerced into approaching the family, the reporters expected to air some *talking head* facility official who would glibly give them the facts, delivered with the emotion of a ceramic door knob.

When representatives from TV, radio, print and cable from both sides of the US and Canadian border saw Dorothy Williams being wheeled in, the reporters in the room flew into high gear. Cell phones were clicked on as reporters checked in with producers and editors to tell them of the pending interview. News cameramen popped out cassettes from their cameras so as to reload fresh tape. Print photographers snapped furiously, capturing each frame as the fragile woman was wheeled gingerly to the podium.

Flash, flash, flash, flash, flash.

Each reporter in the room screamed out questions and jockeyed to have a question heard and answered by the grieving couple. It was a scene reminiscent of a pack of carnivores squabbling over the meager remains of some unfortunate animal that had been too slow or too weak to get out of the way before becoming carrion to a ruthless predator.

It was horrible and unfair. But none of the journalists gathered could think about that. They had a hot story to get on the air, and at the moment that mattered more than this couple's personal and emotional pain. This was going to be one Hell of a lead story on the 5 o'clock news. The monster would have more than enough leftovers to fill its belly for the 11 o'clock news, and refills for the morning shows.

"Mrs. Williams, when did you first realize your infant had been kidnapped?" A reporter yelled from the crowd as the spent young woman was wheeled up to the microphones perched on the podium.

Dorothy Williams struggled to answer the question. Her voice quaked. "I was supposed to feed him at lunch time. I called for the nurse because she hadn't come down with the baby yet. I kept being told to wait, and finally..." her voice trailed off and her husband picked up the baton.

"Apparently the hospital staff had realized for some time the baby was missing, but it took them more than an hour to come to us with the news."

Before he could finish his sentence, another reporter yelled out, "Mr. Williams..."

"Hey!" Sherman Hall, interrupted. "Stop stepping on my soundbite, man. Let the guy finish his sentence."

"Screw you," the print reporter hissed and continued, "Mr. Williams, have you contacted an attorney? What I mean to ask is, are you planning on suing the hospital?"

"I think the only concern I have right now is finding my son," Mr. Williams answered as he patted his wife's shoulder for support. "I know the hospital is doing all it can to help in that matter."

"Mrs. Williams, did you have any idea the hospital had this kind of sloppy security?" Called out a reporter from the 'All News All The Time' radio station.

"No. Of course not," Mrs. Williams shook her head in confusion.

The reporter from the associated press chimed in. "So you mean to tell us that your baby had been missing for more than two hours before you were even notified? Don't you think that's a little irresponsible?"

The hospital's director chimed in at that point. "We weren't sure, I mean to say that we notified the Williams' as soon as we were sure. As you know it had been a difficult birth, and we were unclear if the baby had been taken to another part of the hospital for tests," he paused and cleared his throat. "As soon as we realized the child was no longer in the hospital, we notified the parents and the police."

He then turned back to the podium where the Williams' were perched and addressed them personally. He spoke earnestly, with what looked like a genuine tear in his eye. "We can't express how sorry we are this happened. We are, of course, reviewing all of our security procedures, and we will leave no stone unturned in effecting the safe return of your baby."

He then turned back to the hordes of reporters waiting to pick apart his bare bones.

The room erupted with questions. There was an explosion of noise. Reporters from every news service within a two hundred mile radius were vying to ask the big question, the most important question, the one question that everyone else would have to use on the air or in print because of its clever profoundness. It was pandemonium as Dorothy, Doug and the hospital administrator took turns, frantically trying to answer all of the questions.

"Have you taken a look at your personnel records?"

"Have you found a ransom note?"

"What would you like to say to the kidnappers if they're watching?"

"Do either of you know of anyone with some sort of grudge against you?"

"How long will the hospital search? And have you contacted FBI? What about the Network For Missing and Exploited Children?"

And then in the cacophony of voices and inquiries, one question stood out and hung in the air like the stink of a sushi fart, "How do you feel?"

The room fell silent. Each reporter looked at each other reporter trying to figure out who asked it.

How could someone ask such a stupid question?

There was a murmur of unrest in the noisy crowd of journalists. Hushing each other and squabbling amongst each other like Hyenas over the remains of some day old carcass.

Doug Williams composed himself. He held his wife's hand tightly in his and he stared at the cameras poised on their tripods and the flashes of bright light from the still cameras, and he faced an army of reporters struck dumb by the ignorance of one of their own, and he answered the question. "How do you think we feel?"

He then wheeled his heartbroken wife out of the room so the two could pray and grieve in private.

"Good work, Einstein. How do you feel?" A voice mocked out loud in the crowd of cameras and reporters.

"Fuck you." someone yelled from the back.

And the news conference was over.

If PS Garrett had to bet, she'd say that question came from a Channel Three reporter. Probably Sherman Hall.

The night after the Williams' baby's kidnapping, PS found herself in Detroit's most prestigious restaurant, serving up the events of the last 24 hours to Allen George who was rapt with attention. He had missed the original story because of a business meeting he had to attend, so he wanted every detail, *don't skip anything!*

So over chicken fettuccine and a glass of white wine, PS recounted the day's events for him, and he listened with great interest.

His ability to listen was one of the things that was starting to grow on PS. He was a good listener, seemingly hanging onto every word she uttered.

But when he was listening, instead of talking, PS couldn't help but be nagged about him. There was something about Allen George that made her uncomfortable and she couldn't shake it. But neither could she directly put a finger on it. It wasn't just his looks and the fact that they just didn't fit. Nothing about the way this guy's face was put together seemed to fit.

It always hit her like a ton of bricks when she first saw him. Even after practically two weeks of going out almost every evening, she was still struck nearly dumb by his appearance. That is, until he started talking. That's when all the incongruity seemed to melt away. By the time the check came, or as they polished off their ice-cream cones, she'd forgotten about those narrow darting eyes, that freckled nose and that stingy

197

mustache. Until next time.

Without question though, there was something else about Allen George. There was something about the air around him that always made PS Garret intimidated, almost afraid.

But since there hadn't been any other men banging down her door, PS arranged her usually impossibly high standards on a Bell curve for Allen George.

PS wanted Willina to meet him, but she had been out of town and wasn't expected to return for yet another week. Her married boyfriend had taken her to the Caribbean, and even though he had to leave she talked him into letting her stay a bit longer. On his dime, of course.

With a slight lull in conversation PS turned her attention to her surroundings. She marveled at the Regal Restaurant. It was everything she had imagined and more. She had driven by it on lower Woodward Avenue many times, but had never eaten there. Too expensive.

The carpet was rich and intricate. The crystal chandeliers were lit and sparkling. The waiters wore real tuxedo jackets, with pearl studs as buttons.

"Mmmm, the food is really good here," PS said as she finished off the fettuccine and continued to survey the room.

Allen said he ate there often and it was a crime that Detroit's top police reporter hadn't so much as graced the steps.

"I guess they haven't had a murder here at the Regal," PS said sipping her perfectly cooled late harvest Riesling. "Had they had a murder here, I would have been here measuring the length of the chalk drawing."

Allen laughed. "Oh, come on, it's not that bad is it?"

"Allen, I'm telling you. If it's not dead, dying, burning or decomposing, they don't send me out of the studio."

"That's gotta be tough, lonely work," Allen said as he poured the last of the wine into PS's glass and turned the bottle upside down in the bucket.

Allen held his hand up, and the waiter responded immediately by collecting the empty bottle and running off to retrieve a second.

"This is really good wine," PS said, tipping her glass toward Allen who responded with a smile and a wink.

"PS, do you have family here?"

"I have a roommate."

"Oh?" Allen said, setting his shoulders back a bit. He didn't know there was roommate in the picture.

"Well, sort of. Here's a picture."

"You keep a picture of your roommate in your purse?"

"Just look," PS said with an amused chuckle.

"What is this?" Allen said, studying the photo.

"That's Fido. My roommate."

"You have a cat?"

"Yup. Do you have any pets?"

"No," Allen said, his skin crawling. He hated cats. He hated all animals. He had no use for them, whatsoever. "So how do you take care of a cat, what are your hours like?" He asked, not reacting at all to the news that this was a woman who liked cats.

"Crazy. Sometimes, I don't know if I'm coming or going."

"Yeah? Give me an example."

"Okay," PS rolled it around in her head for a second, but it didn't take long to come up with an example. "Take yesterday, for instance. I covered that kidnapping. That's going to be a hot story. And I'm the primary reporter."

"What does that mean, primary reporter?"

"It means that I'm the one who does the main story. It's up to me to dig up the nuts and bolts information for the newscast. There may be one or two other reporters on the story, but I'm the one responsible for being able to connect all the dots. The others do what we call sidebars, or companion pieces."

"Okay, got it," Allen said as he fished around on her plate, looking for any stray garnishes.

"So yesterday, I got in to the studio at around nine in the morning, and I didn't leave until well after the eleven o'clock broadcast. Sometimes, I think it's a waste to even have a condo. I'm never there."

"You have your own condo?"

"Yup. Northern burbs."

"No roomies or anything like that?"

"Well, sort of. I have a cat."

"Hmmm, a single woman with a cat. How cliché is that?" Allen said.

Once again, PS started getting that feeling of discomfort. "What's that supposed to mean?"

200

"Nothing. It just seems like such a waste."

"What's a waste?"

"A beautiful woman, with her own place and no one to share it with."

"It didn't start off that way."

"Oh?" Allen asked with great interest. "This sounds interesting."

PS wasn't sure why she was compelled to explain anything to Allen. But it was as though he had a magic power of coaxing information out of people. She recognized it immediately.

She paused and began to tell the story of Danny Rierson, but then thought better of it. Danny had been her own personal gift, and she wasn't up for sharing the story.

"That was a lifetime ago. Change of subject," PS said emphatically. "What was your day like?"

The two sat and talked for a few moments more when Allen started. It was nearly 9:45 and he had to get going. For the first time since their meeting, he seemed flustered and unsure. "I've got to get going!"

"Why?" PS asked. "Do you turn into a pumpkin or something?"

"Sort of. Actually my sister's the culprit. Um... her car is in the shop, and I promised to pick her up at work and take her home. I hope you don't mind."

"Wasn't her car in the shop last week?" PS asked, extremely puzzled.

"Foreign car. What can you say? But, I gotta go. I'm so sorry."

"Well, I guess I don't mind. I should get going too. Thank you for dinner."

The two had met at the Regal after work on a whim. The original plan was to meet at a small, quaint little Mexican restaurant further up the street. But Allen had called PS after her last live shot to tell her there had been a change in plans.

"It was my complete pleasure. May I see you later in the week?"

"Well, let's see what the News Gods dictate."

"The News Gods?" Allen asked with interest.

"Yeah, that's what we call the open ended air that surrounds anything that's not a newscast. We control nothing as mere mortals. Everything is up to the News Gods and the monster they've created to rule the world," PS laughed.

Allen chuckled a bit too, and then moved toward PS to give her a kiss.

She saw him coming and considered allowing him to kiss her, but at the last moment diverted in order to catch the peck on the cheek. She looked up and smiled coyly.

It wasn't that she was being shy, and it wasn't that she was that out of practice with men. At least that's what she told herself. There was just something about this particular man.

"Can I walk you out?" Allen said, as he reached down to grab PS's blazer and placed it gently around her shoulders.

"No. I'm fine. Thanks. I'll talk to you a later in the week."

"Great, Honey. I'm looking forward to it."

As PS walked out of the restaurant, she realized that walking into such a place with a man on her arms had been luxury. The food was good, the wine was good, the evening was good. Perhaps she had been too judgmental about Allen George. He was a perfect gentleman. He was refined and sweet and attentive. He was obviously successful and he seemed to be genuinely interested in her. No doubt, he had just dropped a bundle on dinner.

She walked out into the open air of the Regal restaurant with Allen watching her leave. He then motioned for the waiter, who walked over with the bill. Allen looked at it. As he had expected, it was three-hundred dollars and some change. He reached into his pocket slowly to retrieve his billfold as he spoke sternly to the waiter. "This was my first time here. The same for the lady. Do you know who she is?"

"Why yes, Sir. I do. Isn't that PS Garrett from Channel Six?"

"That's right."

"Did the two of you enjoy your evening?" The waiter asked in eager anticipation of the answer.

"Well, we did up until the point PS found that at the bottom of her plate."

The waiter looked down and there, mired in what was left of the cream sauce was a long blonde strand of hair.

"Oh my Goodness," the waiter exclaimed. "That's awful. Sir, I'm so sorry. I'll be right back, I need to go apologize to Ms. Garrett."

"No, don't bother," Allen said hastily. "She's already gone. But I can tell you that neither of us are very happy about this."

"I completely understand, Sir. Will you excuse me, I'll go and get the manager."

"No. Don't bother," Allen said. "I'm sure it's an accident, I suppose you just don't expect this sort of thing from a restaurant like this."

"Sir, I assure you. I have never seen anything like this before. In fact, I don't even know where it came from. None of our chefs or wait staff even have hair that long. I'm so embarrassed, and to think we had a local celebrity in here. Sir, I insist. Please let me retrieve the manager. I know that there is no way in the world he's going to have you pay for this meal. I assure you, this has never happened before. I assure you. Please, let me speak to the manager."

"Okay. If you insist," Allen said magnanimously, glad that he had noticed the strand of hair while traveling in a friend's vehicle earlier that day and had thought enough to stick it in his coat pocket.

Friday morning, when PS walked into the studio around 10 o'clock, Bill Thorn, the managing editor, was frantic.

The assignment desk was made up of a team of people. Bill Thorn, the managing editor who ultimately made the final decisions on what should and what should not be covered as it came across the scanner. Larry Pink, the assignment editor, who gets the blame when Bill Thorn misses something. And assistants—a host of low paid, minimally experienced recent college grads, desperate to get their feet wet in the news business in any way they can while putting resume tapes together to try and get jobs on the air.

The desk assistants were the most dangerous to field news crews.

"We've got to get you out the door," Bill said excitedly. "You have twenty minutes to get to the FBI building. An agent there has put together a character profile of the Williams' baby's kidnapper and we want the story for the noon show."

Terry, the photographer was standing at the door dressed in the usual Terry attire—baggy jeans, hooded sweatshirt, dark glasses. Terry was one of those rare photographers whose video was so extraordinary, you could ignore the odd personality quirks that popped up from time to time—starting with a propensity to look like a bank robber. When Terry was your partner you could be assured the story would not only get on the air, but with minimal fuss and quality video.

That's half the battle of teamwork. A great cameraman could shoot a grain of sand, and rack focus the camera to make that grain melt into a wave of water at the beach. A great photographer could shoot a sunset so brilliantly it takes the viewer to the very gates of heaven and back in the 29 frames of video that make up a second. A great photographer anticipates the mood of a story and the reporter—and has the shot two minutes before you ask for it. When a reporter turns to run on a breaking news story, a great photographer is right behind her, or already in front. But if that photographer's attitude sucks, it doesn't matter how close to God his or her video takes you, the day is going to suck. It's going to take twice as long to get the work done. It's going to take twice the energy to get through the day.

That's what made Terry such a choice shooter. Good eye, good attitude, good partner. Even with this late start, with Terry as PS's partner they could still get the story done in grand style, with plenty of time to spare to feed the monster.

The TV crew got to the FBI building a few minutes late, but it didn't seem to matter much. The assignment editor neglected to mention this would be an exclusive story. It was already fully set up, and all PS had to do was conduct the interview. No-one else was chasing it, because none of the other stations were aware the story even existed. Yet.

Of course that would also change a few minutes after noon. Then everyone would be clamoring for the details. But for now The Channel Six reporter had the leisure of talking to this FBI guy about his criminal character profile knowing that she wouldn't have to sift through a pack of useless questions from other reporters in order to get the story on the air.

That's how it worked. Sometimes you got the goods, sometimes the other guy got the goods. That day it was PS Garrett's turn to be on top. She loved it when it happened like that.

The TV crew walked into the special agent's office. Terry set up the camera and lights. Before PS could pull out her pen and newspad, the special agent in charge began to explain the importance of a character profile.

"A character profile," he began, "is just what it sounds like. It gives us an idea of who we're looking for."

PS hustled to pull out her pen, and started taking notes. The agent was a little nervous but continued. "If we know how our suspect thinks, we have a better chance of catching him, or in the case of the Williams' baby's disappearance, we have a better chance of catching her.

"Based on specific details in the case, how the crime was committed, what was said during the commission of the crime, how the crime was planned out, we're able to put together clues and piece together a picture of who we're looking for. I guess you could say we kind of get into our criminal's mind," the special agent stopped to chuckle a bit at that last line.

This is great shit, PS thought to herself. *What a story. The inner workings of a criminal kidnapper's mind. It's so high tech, it's so mysterious. It's so exciting, and at least for the noon show, it's so exclusive.*

PS Garrett loved the word exclusive. That was her favorite word in the English vocabulary, just before the words sale and clearance. It had such a nice ring to it. Especially on the days she was competing against Sherman Hall.

"Go on," PS said. "This is just fascinating."

The special agent obviously felt stroked by her interest. He visibly puffed out his chest and continued, suddenly sounding a bit pompous and condescending.

"What we believe is, we're looking for a woman with a tenth grade education. We don't believe she's originally from this area, rather somewhere further south. She's divorced and possibly has had a string of miscarriages, including one within the last three weeks of the kidnapping. She's obviously had some experience working in a hospital. Probably as a nurse's aide or maybe an orderly.

"We believe she's living alone with the child and will move from state to state as the child gets older and she finds it difficult to explain his existence. She's a loner, who moves around at night and stays out of public places."

"And inspector," PS broke in. "How is it that you're able to surmise all of this?"

The agent cleared his throat and answered. "Well you see, we consulted with an expert psychologist who deals with this kind of crime who suggested the type of people who are likely to do this kind of offense. He said the type of people who generally commit crimes like this are usually poorly educated and have no family ties.

"We know she doesn't intend to sell the baby, because there really isn't a market for African American infants. If she were dealing with a black market baby broker, she'd have kidnapped a healthy white infant. So this baby is obviously one she intends to keep for herself."

"Okay inspector, I'll buy that the baby is probably not up for sale, but how do you pull out that she's living alone, and operating only at night? How do you know she's moving from state to state? How do you know she's not from around here? How do you know she's not the cousin of the janitor who works in the maternity ward? I'm not trying to shoot down your theories, or even play the devil's advocate. But I'm just not following you here."

The special agent looked at the reporter, his eyes glazed over, as if he were stumped. "This is the profile we put together to give us something to follow. We don't know if it's completely accurate. We don't know if it's accurate at all. You could call it educated guessing, but at least it gives us something to go on, a few places to start looking. Is that camera still on?"

PS pressed on. "Inspector, in fact, all we really know for sure is the suspect is a light-brown-skinned black woman or Middle-Easterner with braids. We got that based on the recollections of Billy's mother who was heavily sedated when she saw the suspect. Isn't that right, Sir? I've talked to Mrs. Williams several times since the kidnapping and I happen to know the kidnapper never even spoke. So how do you know the suspect is a southerner?"

"Well again, this is just the profile we've put together. Yes, we do have a composite drawing of the suspect, but we're also confident our character profile will produce some leads. The director talked to your managing editor this morning and was under the impression you were interested in this story."

PS was puzzled and continued. "I'm not saying we're not interested. But Sir, your profile doesn't seem to be based on any facts in particular. It's all speculation. How can you look for a suspect with information based on pure speculation? It seems like if we put this stuff on the air, somebody might actually overlook a bona fide suspect who doesn't necessarily fit this profile. Inspector, can you tell me how often your character profiles are successful in ferreting out suspects in various crimes?"

"I don't believe we have any statistics handy on that," he answered with great agitation. "I'm sure we can dig some up." The FBI agent gestured to a woman standing in the doorway, whispered something in her ear and she promptly disappeared.

PS had heard enough. It was eleven o'clock and she was on deadline. She stood up, and politely extended her right hand to the inspector who reciprocated tentatively. "Thank you, Sir, we appreciate your time. I'll see you on the noon news. Here's my card. Will you please give me a call as your investigation progresses?"

The young FBI agent looked a little dazed. He shook her hand, straightened his tie and accepted her business card. As she walked out the door he filed it away—in the circular file.

Terry and PS walked to the elevator in silence, got on and headed down to the waiting live truck. As they stepped out of the building and walked down the sidewalk toward the remote truck that already had its mast fully extended, PS said to Terry—feeling safe that they were out of earshot of any electronic bugs that might have been in the hallway or elevator of the FBI building, "Ter, have you ever heard so much psycho babble in your life?"

"Nope."

"Now I gotta make a story out of this crap and treat it like it has some sort of credibility. This is shit, pure and simple. Boy, do I hate this crap."

It was close to noon, and there was no way the

producers were going to give up the lead slot in the newscast that would carry the exclusive banner on the top left hand corner of the screen. There was absolutely no use in calling the station to let them know the story was total, complete and unadulterated garbage.

PS Garrett would have to turn chicken shit into chicken salad—again.

The noon news went on without a hitch. Channel Six flashed the big exclusive in the upper left hand corner of the screen for the entire story. And PS made a proper big deal out of it. She talked about how the FBI was primed to crack the case of the Williams' baby's kidnapping by using a sophisticated criminal character profile.

Neighbors, shop-keeps, and everyone on the street, keep your eyes peeled for a woman who might look like this composite sketch, she probably didn't finish high school, is living alone, and speaks with a twang. Armed with this high tech tool, the FBI could be closing in, and Doug and Dorothy Williams could have their baby back in their arms in a matter of days.

By the time PS Garrett got off the air, the other stations crews had, no doubt, been rolled out the door and toward the FBI building at top speed.

Why should I care that it was crap, pure supposition on the part of a few overzealous, albeit desperate FBI stiff necks in dark clothing and mirrored sunglasses? PS thought to herself as she stood on the sidewalk near the live van waiting to get the all clear from A-control. *Who cared if there wasn't a shred of hard evidence to back up any of that silly profile? The FBI said it, I aired it, the monster ate it, and that settled it. At least we were able to get that baby's picture back on the news and we flashed that composite of the suspect again. That was information the public could use to really help crack the case.*

Her photographer cued her and PS began to speak, with authority, with conviction and with full knowledge that, this time she was not doing a public service, but paying her bills.

CHAPTER NINE

Allen picked PS up after work so the two could have drinks. But at 9:45 Allen had to leave. His sister, Janet, needed another ride home from work and Allen was the designated driver.

PS was annoyed, because she'd had a good day, and she wanted to talk about it, but this had become an unpopular routine. No matter where the two were or what they were doing, Allen had to meet a deadline, which meant he had to break things up in order to get to whereever it was he had to go to pick up his sister by 10:30.

This time, they were too far away from the studio for PS to retrieve her car first, so Allen insisted that she ride along to meet his sister.

Much to her surprise, when they got to the hospital where Janet George worked, Allen jumped in the backseat and Janet, who barely said hello, took over the driver's seat.

Janet was annoyed when Allen announced that they needed to drop PS off at her car at the studio all the way across town. PS tried to lighten the moment by offering Janet a tour of the TV station when they got there but she curtly declined.

When the happy threesome pulled into the garage, PS said good night with the usual, nice-to-meet-you verbiage. Janet just kind of nodded her head.

PS said good night to Allen and walked to her car without looking back. As she turned the key to her ignition, she was startled by Allen who was knocking on her window. "Janet asked if she could borrow my car this evening, so I told her you would drop me off at my apartment. You don't mind, do you?"

Even if she did mind, it was certainly too late to do anything about it now as Janet's rear lights disappeared down the garage ramp with a red flare. PS pushed the automatic unlock so that Allen could get in on the passenger side, but he insisted that he drive.

"Do you know how to drive stick shift?" PS asked trying to mask her great annoyance.

"Of course I do. Now let me drive, you've had a long day, and besides, you don't know the way to my place, yet," Allen said with a lascivious chuckle.

PS pursed her lips, reluctantly stepped out of her vehicle and walked to the passenger side of the car. She decided that would be the last time she saw that man. All of a sudden, even lonely Saturday nights seemed more attractive than Allen George. He just had too many question marks. And the 10:30 routine had become a strain.

When they got to his apartment complex, Allen invited PS in. She politely declined. When she returned to the driver's side of her vehicle, she plopped in and Allen reached down to try to kiss her, but she turned her face.

"Is everything okay?" He asked innocently.

"Yeah, everything is fine."

PS didn't know how to break things off with a guy. She was customarily the dumpee and this was new territory for her. On the way to Allen's she had decided that she would just stop answering and returning his calls so that things would burn out naturally.

As PS said a final good night and began to roll up the window, he held on to the top of the glass with one hand, and with his other cupped her chin. He pulled her face to his and whispered, "I better be careful, I think I'm starting to fall in love."

He then gave PS a gentle kiss, pulling each of her lips into his mouth one by one.

It felt warm and good, and she felt a tinge of excitement. *Did this guy just tell me he loved me?* She wondered to herself. It was as though she were in suspended animation as she mulled his words over in her mind. She was shocked at how much that phrase touched her heart.

As Allen turned and walked into his apartment he yelled over his shoulder, "Don't forget about my nephew's christening Sunday."

By Sunday, much of PS Garrett's uneasiness about Allen George had melted away. The two had only spoken briefly by phone on Saturday to tighten up details for the christening. And a one day break seemed to give PS a chance to forget how disturbing Allen felt in-person.

She was actually excited.

She put on a pale yellow summer suit.

Having not been raised in church, she didn't know much about organized religion, so she didn't know if she'd need to wear a hat. She pulled one down from her top shelf that kind of reminded her of the top tier of a wedding cake. It was pale and pretty, with a single ribbon and a cascade of sugary silk flowers. Danny Rierson, the only man she'd ever really loved had purchased it for her the weekend they consummated their feelings for one another. PS was surprised at how quickly three years had slipped by. She'd almost forgotten the hat was there but stumbled over it while looking for something to wear to the christening.

She wasn't sure if the flowers went in the back or the front, but it was pretty either way, and it matched her suit. She decided to figure out where the flowers went later if she needed.

Fido strolled confidently into PS's bedroom as she was primping and posing in the mirror and gave her customary greeting of a mew and a bow.

"Hey, beautiful," PS said with a smile and reached down to pick the cat up. "Have I been neglecting you?"

The large orange and white cat began to purr and placed her damp pink nose just beneath her owner's. "Whoever says cats aren't affectionate are idiots," PS said as she delighted in the cool kiss her cat had just planted on her.

She sat down on the bed and allowed the cat to make herself comfortable on the pale suit she had just slipped on. "How's my girl?" She asked as the cat continued to circle until she found just the right crevice to situate herself in. "So what do you think of all this? Huh? Do you think I'm doing the right thing?"

PS began scritching the feline beneath the neck in just the proper spot to elicit a louder purr. This cat had become a part of her—a constant and reliable companion. Wil was often out of town or out of touch. PS's parents and sibling lived out-of-state. And men came and went, mostly went, but Fido the cat had always been there. "You miss him too, don't you?" PS whispered as the cat began to close her eyes.

The kitten had been a joint venture between PS and the love of her life. Danny Rierson loved that cat as though she were a daughter, instead of a pet. And Fido loved him, would follow him everywhere. She liked PS too, but Danny was the love of her life. It wasn't until he left that the feline and the reporter took solace in each other and now they were inseparable.

"Are you hungry, sweetie?" PS said as she tried to gently maneuver the cat from her lap onto the bed. "I have to go. I have a date."

The words struck PS.

She had a date. Other than Allen George, it had been so long since she had uttered those words, they seemed almost foreign to her. She felt a tinge of excitement and worry as she stepped over a pile of dirty laundry to get to the door and go into the kitchen to fetch the cat a saucer of rice milk. Rice milk lasted longer than regular cow's milk in the fridge. And Fido loved it.

PS was excited to be getting out of the house and seeing something as new as a christening. But she also realized that she must seem awfully desperate. After all, she didn't really think a lot of this guy. She had yet to truly nail down any redeeming qualities other than he seemed to be pretty interested in striking up something with her.

Was this the best to be offered her? She wondered. Perhaps there would be an answer in church.

She reached up into the cabinet and pulled down an elegant, but plain bone china saucer. She set it aside, and stood on her tippy toes to reach in and fish out a different one. When she finally pulled out one of the saucers with the 18 karat gold lining, she went into the fridge and poured a liberal serving of rice milk. She then placed it on the counter.

By then, Fido was rubbing up against PS's leg and marking her generously with the glands on the side of her mouth, mewing in delight over the early morning treat. PS reached down, hoisted the large tabby to the counter and continued to stroke her fur as she lapped up the milk.

Her heart began to beat heavily. All the love she'd had for Danny had been transferred to this cat. "I love you," she said as the phone rang.

PS walked away from the feline and grabbed her cordless. It was her mother calling to check in. PS absent-mindedly walked over to the balcony door, cracked it open and stuck out her toe to gauge the temperature. It was warm but brisk and as PS chatted aimlessly, she wandered back into her bedroom to grab a spring overcoat.

She looked at the clock and realized that she was running late. She explained to her mother that she had a date and she would have to call her back. She then put down the phone and ran out the door.

As soon as the front door shut, Fido jumped down from the counter and wandered over to the slightly opened door. She knew she wasn't supposed to be on the balcony, but it was a rare treat that her owner would allow her out. The balcony was too low to the ground and PS feared that Fido might jump down and disappear to visit her other cat friends and get lost along the way. And PS didn't believe she could survive the loss of her cat.

More than a few times, the cat had made a great escape, but had always managed to find her way back to the breezeway and her owner's front door. But since Danny left, PS had gotten overly protective and rarely let the cat venture out at all anymore.

It was a great adventure for the curious feline. Not only had she gotten an extra helping of rice milk, but she was able to sit on the balcony for a while to enjoy a sunny spring day and watch the birds up close.

PS was at Allen's apartment by 10. He looked very dapper in his dark suit and crisp white shirt. She'd seen him wear that suit before and always thought he looked really nice in it. She tried on what it felt like to be a couple. Even though she knew she didn't love him, or anything even close to it, it was fun to be invited to the party. She hadn't been a part of a couple in such a long time and it was nice to pretend.

Allen opened her door and gently pulled her to her feet, escorting her to the passenger side of her car. "Where's your car?" PS asked, the whole idea of being a couple crashing like the sound of splintering glass.

"In the shop," Allen said nonchalantly as he pecked PS on the forehead and shut the door before hopping into the driver's side, clumsily putting the car into first gear and pulling off with a jerk.

The two arrived at Straight Line To Heaven, Church of God in Christ on Detroit's East side by 10:30.

PS didn't know exactly what religion it was, and somehow hadn't pegged Allen George with being rooted in any faith. Not being a church-goer, herself this was all new.

PS noticed that only the older ladies going into the church were wearing hats so she decided to leave hers in the back seat.

After Allen parallel parked at the sidewalk, he got out and quickly walked to the passenger side of the car to open the passenger door. He extended his hand to help PS out, and planted a light kiss on her cheek as she stepped out of the car and up to him. She almost felt like Cinderella, after all, she was with a pumpkin.

She chuckled to herself at the charade. What did she have to do on a Sunday, anyway?

As she stepped to the sidewalk, a man approached them. He had a broad grin on his face and immediately offered a warm hug and handshake to Allen, never taking his eyes off of PS. He looked at her car, quickly sized her up and said, "Al, my man. I see you're finally moving up in the world," he patted Al on the shoulder and laughed.

Allen returned the chuckle by throwing the car

keys in the air, catching them and then putting them in his pocket.

He just pee'd on me! PS thought to herself. *I just got marked as his personal territory.*

PS was annoyed. She'd seen this behavior before, but it was usually women who did the Tom Cat thing on men. PS could think of a dozen times or more, while engaged in conversation with a man, a woman would come over, hold his hand, kiss his cheek, or otherwise *pee* on him to mark him as hers. And she resented the fact that Allen George had just backed his ass up to her and sprayed with that key tossing stunt.

He then turned to PS and introduced her as his girl.

His friend looked at the reporter squarely in the face and then his eyes focused in recognition in a way PS had seen a million times.

"Hey, don't I see you on the news?" He asked.

"Yes, yes you do," PS answered sheepishly, casting her eyes coyly to the sidewalk.

"Channel Three right? No Channel Six."

"That's right," she said. "Channel Six."

She smiled her usual obligatory smile when someone recognized her. Allen's friend's eyes narrowed and he looked at PS in a way she thought both inappropriate and lascivious. Allen picked up on the gesture immediately and put his arm around her and broadly smiled back at his friend, once again *peeing* on PS.

"Well," the grinning man said as he turned to re-address his friend, stepping back a bit having lost the pissing match. "You are moving up in the world. Don't forget where you came from or your friends when you get to the top."

Allen's friend then strolled away quickly with a smile on his face, slowing down once to glance back in their direction before disappearing into the crowd.

The whole exchange was a little odd, but PS didn't have time to process it because within seconds Allen spied his sisters and two aunts and was hurrying her into the church to catch up with them.

There was a brief service with some muttering and chanting PS didn't understand. Some ushers dressed in white robes escorted five women up to the alter. Each woman was carrying a baby, dressed in a long white gown. You couldn't really see the infants for all the blankets and swaddling but you could hear the cooing and murmuring of the proud mothers, and a few cries from a couple of the babies.

The priest announced that today's christening was unusual in that all the babies were boys.

The crowded church erupted in cheer.

Each woman took turns stepping up to the priest, as she did, she was joined by the child's father.

Allen's sister was the last in line. In front of her, a woman who stood hunched over, her face buried deep in her baby's swaddling.

When she walked up to the priest, she didn't seem to have a father or any Godparents standing proudly to the side. She stood alone and silent in rapt attention to her child never once looking up.

PS tried to pay close attention to what was going on, but was distracted by the noise in the congregation behind her. Allen and his family were eager in anticipation of the nephew who was to be received next. And for all they cared, he was the main attraction.

When Allen's sister stepped up, her little boy was already boasting his healthy lungs. Allen looked over at PS and beamed, "That's my boy, that's my boy."

He stuck out his chest as though those were his chromosomes coursing through the body of that little boy. Indeed, little Gregory made the biggest spectacle and put on quite a show. By the end of the service that's all anyone in the group was talking about, the loud, healthy cries of Allen's nephew.

Outside the chapel, the chatter turned from little Gregory's performance to the fact that a TV news personality was visiting the congregation. People made a point to come over and speak to the Allen George clan.

His sisters and aunts were the belles of the ball, and lapping up all the attention like hungry poodles. There were lots of pats on shoulders, air kisses from elderly ladies with too much cologne and big hats, and everyone who approached the family managed to meander over to PS to speak and shake her hand.

The George family loved it.

Allen was chatting with a Mrs. Jackson, who apparently hadn't said a word to the bunch of them in more than a decade, but managed to find plenty to talk about that day, when an older man strolled up and took PS by the hand.

He gently pulled her away from all the hubbub.

She thought he was pretty presumptuous, and she was very annoyed until the older fellow introduced himself. "I'm Virgil Williams. I met you a couple of weeks ago. Do you remember?"

"Um, no Sir, I'm sorry I don't."

"My nephew is Doug Williams. His baby was kidnapped at the hospital. I was at the hospital a week or so ago when you dropped by to talk to his wife Dorothy about the kidnapping."

"Oh, yes, Sir, I do remember. How are you doing?" PS asked.

"Not so well. We had planned today as Billy's christening. Dottie's distraught. We all are. They even postponed her release from the hospital. I guess you know she had another emotional set back."

"Oh, Mr. Williams," PS offered. "I'm so sorry."

She gently propped her left hand on his shoulder for support.

"God bless you, girl. God bless you."

The two talked for a few minutes more. He told her that she had done a fine job reporting on the disappearance of his great-nephew, and that the whole family was really pleased with the sensitive way she handled matters. He said that of all the reporters in the city, his family felt most comfortable with her.

He told her Doug should be taking Dorothy home from the hospital in a couple of days and he might be able to talk them into doing an exclusive interview with Channel Six, provided they send PS.

Now that would be a good story. Parents returning home to a nursery with no baby in their arms.

PS thought to herself. People would definitely tune in to watch that. *I could get them walking through the door of their tiny home. I would show the baby's crib, and even get them to crank up the musical mobile. Certainly there would be a musical mobile, and tears, and of course that all important word at the top left hand corner of the screen. **Exclusive**.*

"That would be great, Mr. Williams. It would be another opportunity to show little Billy's picture on the air. We might even be able to lead the evening news with it. Then we can give the story extra attention."

The young reporter looked at Virgil Williams' face. He had lost his great-nephew to God only knew what fate, and here she was planning a newscast around his misery. She could have kicked herself. How could she have been so insensitive? "I'm sorry, Sir. I didn't mean to sound like that. It's just that's how the news business is. The truth of it is, Mr. Williams, it is a good story. And a good story gets air time. And the more times I can get that baby's picture on the air, and the more times I can show the composite of that suspect and go over the details of the kidnapping, the more times people are going to see it. Just maybe it'll jog someone's memory."

Her heart definitely ached for that family, even in her excitement at getting a good story. Dorothy Williams should have been standing in that Christening procession, cradling her little boy in her arms.

Ummmmm. She thought to herself. *This is a good tidbit to add to the story when Dorothy goes home next week.*

225

"I understand," Virgil Williams said. "And I appreciate everything you've done for my family. I know you're just doing your job, but you do a good job. And I can tell you really care."

Virgil Williams was right. PS Garrett was just doing her job. No matter where she was, or what she was doing, she was always on the job. That's the kind of job it was. But he got another thing right. Deep down, PS Garrett really did care.

A day with the Allen George clan was like being caught in a tornado. Never had PS Garrett met so many kinfolk with such big personalities all swirling around her wildly. At the celebration after little Gregory's christening, even Janet treated PS as though they were old friends.

The family members danced with each other, sang, and told wild stories about each other. One outrageously funny game was called Tall Tales, in which family members drew names out of a hat and then had thirty seconds to weave an outrageous Paul Bunyon sized yarn about the person whose name was drawn.

Allen George won and everyone congratulated him for his stellar ability to lie on demand.

It was the best time PS had had in years. She was sorry Willina couldn't have been there. No doubt, she would have beaten Allen George hands down.

That night when Allen invited PS into his apartment, she agreed. He kissed her neck and nibbled her ear all the way through the breezeway and into the door.

It had been a long time since she'd made love, and she was hoping that the encounter would break the spell Danny Rierson seemed to hold on her life.

Once she got inside his dimly lit apartment, though, she was struck by its austerity. It certainly wasn't as she'd pictured it. Allen had such good taste. He always had on a neat suit, and his little mustache was well-groomed. Everything about the man said taste and refinement, but his apartment didn't reflect any of that.

There were no pictures on the walls. His television and stereo were nice enough, PS had seen similar models at an electronics store, and they were top of the line. But they sat on a cheap particle-board shelf along with a couple of books and a dusty backgammon board. There was almost no furniture to speak of.

As she stood there, kind of surveying the room, Allen chimed in. "I've been really busy building a life outside of my apartment, I haven't had much of an opportunity to build a home. All the place really needs is a woman's touch."

Allen kissed her on the back of her neck. The hairs on her body stood at attention. He turned her around and kissed her deeply on the mouth. She began to thaw.

As he led her to the bedroom, PS told him she had to go to the bathroom. He pointed down the hall and disappeared into the nearest bedroom.

She stood still for a moment and continued to look around feeling uneasy. After three years of celibacy, she most certainly felt as though she re-qualified as a virgin. She found her way to the bathroom, took stock one more time and decided, Allen was right. All the place really needed was a woman's touch.

By contrast, his bathroom was fully decorated. Every nook and cranny had some sort of detail. Not an inch was untouched by a human hand. The entire bathroom was awash in the worst shade of maroon PS Garrett had ever seen in her entire life. It was like three tons of Merlot wine grapes had exploded and landed on everything in the room. There was a maroon, two tiered shower curtain, with a maroon liner. There were wicker shelves—can you believe it? Wicker shelves that were maroon. The toilet was covered with that furry crap you get at K-mart that covers the toilet seat and the water tank of the commode. And guess what color they were? The same horrible shade of maroon. He even had the matching rugs on the floor. The stuff was dreadful and as PS looked around, she felt herself getting dizzy. She even started getting an upset stomach.

It had to be more than nerves, perhaps an omen of some sort.

She ran some cool water into the sink, and washed her face, and thought about the day. She'd had so much fun with Allen's family. They were off-beat, fun-loving and fearless. Allen had been extremely attentive, rarely leaving her side, giving her encouraging hugs and kisses when it was her turn to tell a tall tale.

She'd weaved a yarn about Allen and Janet's 10:30 routine in which Allen was actually a pimp, who kept his furry pink Stetson in the trunk along with matching cowboy boots and a feather boa for Janet. And that Janet had a standing date with a John, whom she hated because he was missing his front teeth on both the top and the bottom, and he smelled like stale towels that had been forgotten in the washing machine for several days. The reason Allen had to pick her up at work each night was because this John was their largest account and Allen felt like he had to personally escort Janet, who wasn't really his sister, but his favorite hooker in his stable of eighteen girls.

PS had gotten a standing ovation that included Allen's old aunt Millie and Janet.

As she looked in the mirror in Allen's bathroom, she started laughing aloud. She'd had so much fun that day.

She rinsed her mouth out and began to feel better. She opened the medicine cabinet to look for any signs of psychotropic drugs or Valtrex. She didn't see any, but did see a box of condoms. With a sigh of relief, she grabbed two.

She stiffened her lip, and resolved to herself that she was going to have sex that night. She wasn't going to let a case of the jitters get in the way. She took a deep breath and then found her way to Allen's bedroom.

There was a night light on in the corner, and she could see Allen sitting on the bed. He was already naked. She started feeling uneasy again, but pushed herself forward. He seized her hand and pulled her to him tenderly kissing her letting up only to gently brush his lips over her eye lashes and then to her ears, the back of her neck and down to her lips again.

It felt good and her nerves started settling down as she warmed up. It was wonderful to be in the arms of a man again. Her body ached for the attention. Allen continued to touch and kiss her. The thaw turned into melt as PS began returning the kiss, their tongues moistly finding each other and pulsating gently.

Allen started unbuttoning her blouse. Instinctively, PS reached up and grabbed his hands to delay her disrobing. She just wasn't there yet. Allen's hands then moved to her shoulders and then ran down her back in a light tickling motion that made PS shiver with pleasure. His hands then ran back up her front side, stopping to circle her breasts and then back up to the buttons of her blouse. He successfully unfastened one, before his hands traced back up her neck and cupped her head on either side.

Then he whispered "There's someone I want you to meet."

With her head firmly, but gently gripped he began to coax her head toward his crotch. "This is Sylvester," he announced.

Then with his right hand, he lifted his penis with forefinger and thumb—with his pinkie standing at attention, and aimed it toward her mouth.

STOP HERE FOR A MOMENT! PS gasped to herself. *Why is it that every man I know has named his prick? Do men really see that part of their anatomy as a separate entity from themselves? I know there have been legends about penises having minds of their own, but this is just plain ridiculous.*

PS put the breaks on her neck and struggled to shift her face away from the approaching new member of the party.

Danny's member was named Alvin. A boy she'd screwed just out of college had named his little buddy, Frank. She lost her virginity to Jacob, had an affair with Avery and Jake. Same guy—Jake was the one with the little head. There was Bob, who'd cleverly named his dick, Bob. And now she was being formally introduced to Sylvester.

She strained to lift her head and said softly to Allen and Sylvester and whoever else might be listening, "I'm sorry, but I don't do that."

Allen pushed her head back to his crotch and said, "Of course you do. I need you to kiss him so he'll get hard. You don't have to put Sylvester in your mouth, just kiss him."

Even as she strained against Allen's strength, her head was barreling toward his crotch. It had barely grazed her tightly pursed lips when she found the strength to stop the inertia. Even in the dim light, she could see that Allen's flaccid alter ego was uncircumcised.

She bolted up in revulsion. *EEEEEEGADS!!!!* She thought to herself. *What have I gotten into?*

Her entire female system was going into automatic shutdown.

"I'm sorry Allen," she said. "I don't do that and I mean it."

She began to remove herself from the bed that had become the dragon's lair, sure she'd spoiled the mood for him and would be sent packing.

Thank goodness, she'd be spared. She chastised herself for not listening to her instincts when she first hit the door. When was the last time she agreed to sleep with a man because he and his entire family were clever liars? But at least now it would be over. No harm done. No dirty deed consummated. She could get the Hell out of there.

Her whole opinion of this man had changed at the sight of his uncircumcised Sylvester. She was completely grossed out. She didn't care how witty he was, she didn't care if he owned 200 businesses. He could broker stocks 'til the cows came home, she didn't give a hot hooey. He had ugly furry maroon shit in his bathroom, and a fully clothed dick, and she was getting out of there.

She started backing away realizing that somehow her panties had already been pulled down below her mid thigh. She began pulling them up, when Allen caught her by the elbow and firmly pulled her back to him.

PS became startled at first, but then Allen began talking to her. Coaxing her. "You told me you haven't been involved with a man since that Danny fellow left. Aren't you lonely?" He asked in a gentle, soothing tone as he gently rubbed her arms and shoulders with one hand while pulling her back to him with the other.

She resisted and started pulling away. He let her retreat, but then grabbed her right hand and moved it to his mouth gentle kissing her on the inside of her palm and then the tips of her fingers continuing to talk and coo all the while. "Don't you miss being kissed by a man? Feel this," he insisted as he sucked her middle finger into his mouth and began to felate the tip erotically and irresistibly. "Do you like this? I can do this anywhere you want," he said, creating a rhythm and heat PS couldn't ignore

"I don't do oral sex," she said firmly.

"You don't have to. I do," Allen cooed.

"Allen, I don't know. I think I should leave," PS said still feeling very uneasy about the encounter.

"No, you don't want to leave," Allen cajoled. "This is all good. I promise. I won't do anything you don't want me to do. Aren't you lonely? Don't you want to be with a man who loves you?"

Allen had taken PS's throbbing finger out of his mouth and had gently placed her arm around his neck. He then maneuvered her effortlessly back toward him, by placing his hands around her buttocks and gliding them to his torso, working his hands down to her panties.

She sat on his lap straddling him as he pulsated his body to hers as he continued to kiss her, his penis rubbing her crotch gently through her underwear. "It's okay." He announced magnanimously. "You've come too far to be denied, just wait a minute."

He then gently pushed her back from his body just a bit and reached down to grab his penis with his right hand. And for the first time, PS understood the dynamics of spectators who crane their necks to look at a fatal car accident. She understood the hypnotic fixation of standing on the corner waiting for the medical examiner to pull back the sheet of the shooting victim so you can get a good look at the corpse. She finally understand the morbid compulsion to look, even though you're disgusted and sickened by what you see, because that's how she felt as she sat there inches away, watching Allen George masturbate until his penis got hard and that icky piece of skin that covered it disappeared exposing a ghastly shiny, pinkish pointy head.

PS was mortified but couldn't move. It was as though she was glued in place.

Allen pulled her back to him, and she was paralyzed. He began rubbing his hardening prick on her hands. He'd somehow maneuvered PS to a near standing position, though he kept his left hand firmly on her buttocks as he worked his penis down her body to rub Sylvester on her feet as his head paused at her crotch. He circled her pubic hair with his tongue. The hand that had gripped her buttock had now worked its way to the mouth of her vagina. He opened the lip on the left side and whipped his tongue inside for several quick, precisely aimed jabs that made PS arch her back and grab his shoulder to hold on.

Allen began to stand. He had complete control of his body and never even bobbled as he made sure Sylvester rubbed every portion of PS's body on the way up. He laid himself backwards on the bed, pulling PS on top of him.

"Stop!" She said. "Finally getting a hold of some of her senses. "We need a condom."

"No we don't," Allen insisted. "I want to feel you," he growled. "I want to feel all of you."

"No, Allen. We need a condom."

He moved PS off of him and to the side of the bed. But before she could seize the opportunity to roll off to the side and make a break for it, he had spit in his hand, rubbed his penis violently to create friction, and then as Sylvester became SYLVESTER, he deftly slipped a condom on that he had quickly retrieved from a bedside table, and unwrapped in a nano second.

He then quickly pulled PS back on top of him.

It was as though he had become an animal once inside of her, squealing and writhing and thrashing about with PS looking down in horror— frozen with horror.

"Fuck me baby," he screamed. "Fuck my brains out!"

Then he'd thrash and writhe and holler some more.

She was mortified as she watched this scene as though it were an out-of-body experience. She found herself emotionally perched at the ceiling looking down on this thing as though it were some sick porno flick. She watched the same way people watch a grisly smash up between a car and a train, and they can't wait to see what the body looks like when it's cut from the wreck- age.

The bed started shaking, and Allen's face started contorting wildly. He scowled as though he were Lu- cifer himself. He started screaming and writhing— shivering at the knees as he pushed PS up and down on top of him.

She wasn't sure at first, but thought she saw

235

plumes of smoke rise from his sweaty body and thought, *Jesus Christ, this man is actually on fire.*

She began smelling smoke and thought the friction of the bedposts hitting the floor must have caught the hardwood on fire.

At first, she thought it was her imagination. Her mind was playing tricks on her. It happened all the time. She had little brain apneas that would take her out of real time and send her to a world on the other side of the looking glass. She thought watching this man turn into Satan himself was just another trick being played on her by her own mind as a defense mechanism.

S   he tried to contain herself, when she began to cough. She started gasping for air, and felt dinner snaking its way toward her esophagus.

This was no hallucination. That man's apartment was on fire. His room was filling up with smoke. Real smoke. *Oh my God*, she thought to herself, *I've gone to Hell. I've literally gone to Hell!*

It took her a few more seconds to pull her faculties together and realize she was in real danger. That's when she saw flames licking their way up the Venetian blinds.

She bolted up. "Fire!" She screamed. "Fire!"

Allen was still writhing beneath her as she extracted herself from him, instinctively grabbing at the panties that had been worked down to her ankles.

She slid off the bed, and dropped to her knees on the floor, feeling around for her skirt. When she found it, she rolled over on the floor to slip it on, buttoning it at the waistband, but neglecting the zipper.

She didn't know where her blazer was and didn't care. To Hell with the jacket. She thought. *The Devil can have it.*

She bolted upright again, but became dizzy as the smoke started competing with her for air, and she dropped back down to her knees loosing sight of Allen altogether on the bed. For all she knew, he was still where she'd left him, finishing his orgasm by himself. She didn't care to stick around for the finale.

As she crawled to the door, her hand grazed the bottom of her skirt, and she thought she felt fire. She felt herself begin to panic. "I'm on fire, I'm on fire!" She screamed and bolted back up to run blindly for the door. But she tripped over her shoes in the doorway and stumbled to the floor with a thud, the wind knocked out of her momentarily.

She caught her breath and began to cry out, "This kind of thing doesn't happen to me. It happens to other people and I do reports on it. That's how it's worked for years," she began trying to scramble back to her feet so she could run.

"STOP, DROP AND ROLL." Allen yelled from somewhere behind her. "Remember what they taught you in elementary school. STOP, DROP, AND ROLL!"

PS dropped to her belly and began rolling herself out into the hallway with Allen yelling out after her. "When you get through the hall, crawl beneath the smoke until you get to the front doorway."

With that, Allen George disappeared into the smoke.

237

PS's faculties began returning. He was right. She'd just seen a special report three nights ago on Channel Three on how to get out alive in a fire. One of the big segments was on how parents can teach their children to survive a fire. The narrator was saying how most people who die in fires don't die because they burn to death, they die from smoke inhalation. The smoke gets them before the flames. Because the smoke tends to rise, the cleaner air will be closer to the floor.

The reporter had done dozens of stories on burning buildings. She'd watched weeping firemen run from the flames, cradling the lifeless bodies of innocent children. The medical examiner would almost always declare the cause of death as smoke inhalation and she never understood before that moment how, if they could smell the smoke, they just didn't get out of the building.

The narrator explained how the smoke cuts off your oxygen and you suffocated. That's why you tell your children to drop to the floor and crawl, so they can escape the rising smoke.

The apartment was completely filled with Black smoke, and PS was blinded by it. She snaked her way toward where she believed the front door was a shoe in each hand.

Somehow she found her way out of the apartment and on to the landing. The front hall of the entry way was filled with smoke, but it wasn't as black and sooty. As she stumbled to her feet and opened the front door to exit the burning building, she could hear Allen's voice behind her.

Allen! She had completely forgotten about him in her panic to save her own hide. "Allen!" She screamed, but it was too late. He couldn't hear her. Somehow, he had already made it to the top landing, and he was banging on the doors of all the neighbors, screaming and yelling for them to get out.

As PS began to run toward a fire truck, she didn't know how Allen George had managed to get out of that apartment before her, but he had, and instead of saving himself first, he chose to warn the neighbors.

Outside the night sky was orange. The angry blaze had communicated to three buildings to the right and the fire was beginning to engulf Allen's unit. The smoke was the calling card, snaking its way through vents and heating ducts.

It was a major blaze, and firefighters from several different companies were battling the beast. And as it was with all big fires, you have people standing outside, wrapped in blankets, eyes transfixed on what used to be home.

There were mothers who'd been reunited with their children. There were children weeping for their pets. "Fluffy, where's Fluffy?"

There was the usual storm of flashing lights, spraying water, and stubborn flames licking up out of windows and doors.

And when you have all of that going on, you have news crews capturing it all on tape.

Of course every television station was there,

covering the four alarm fire at Allen George's apartment complex.

PS wove her way through the maze of displaced people, puddles of water and fire lines, buttoning her blouse and slipping on her shoes. She saw the News 6 live truck and headed in its direction. She didn't have a spare set of car keys with her. She just hoped someone from work would be more than happy to get her home eventually. She would just curl up in the back of the live truck and catch a nap until a member of the crew could break free to get her home to get her spare keys.

She ambled up to the truck, opened the passenger side door and hopped in. The technician who was already feeding tape back to the station, and the photographer who was changing batteries on his camera didn't seem terribly surprised to see her.

"It's about time you got here," Steve the cameraman was annoyed. "I called 'em twenty minutes ago and told them to send a reporter, and they said they didn't have anyone to send. When I told 'em Channel Three had a full crew, they said they'd see what they could do. But I didn't believe them. Who'd you piss off to get sent in?" He asked.

"God," PS answered. She didn't bother correcting Steve. She didn't want to explain how she had gotten there in the first place. She just grabbed a pen and a pad of paper from the glove compartment, picked up the microphone and went to work.

She interviewed three brave souls who'd broken a window to rescue an old man and his cat.

The fire Chief told her it appeared the blaze had

gotten started in the rental office hours ago, but no one noticed because it was a weekend and the office had closed early.

A woman broke her leg when she jumped from a third floor balcony and hit the pavement. Steve got video as she was being scraped up off the sidewalk and loaded onto a hospital gurney.

Five elderly people were sent to the hospital with smoke inhalation. PS could certainly relate to that.

But the best video and sound of the night was that of an elaborate aerial ladder rescue.

High upon the fourth floor, firefighters were spraying water to beat back the flames. Thick black smoke billowed from the balcony door wall which had been broken. A young firefighter leaped from the ladder onto the balcony and then disappeared into the smoke. The building's floor crackled as the boots of the fireman hit the hardwood.

The surrounding crowd gasped.

There was a great deal of alarm and yelling from his colleagues until the brave young firefighter appeared from the smoke and back onto the balcony cradling a jet black mutt in his arms.

On lookers broke out into spontaneous applause, and a child's voice squealed from the crowd, "Fluffy, that's Fluffy!"

Talk about a true Kodak moment. When that firefighter handed that little girl her dog and patted her on the head, even PS Garrett felt tears well up in her eyes.

She couldn't have scripted it any better. The

only thing missing was a fifty piece orchestra with a strong section of violins. She half expected someone to cry out, "See Billie, now we really are a family again."

The crescendo of violins would fade up from the background and the words, *The End*, would appear out of nowhere.

PS Garrett went live from the scene at 11 that night, and again for the early Monday edition of the news. By then the billowy black smoke had been replaced by clean white steam that hissed as firefighters sprayed water on the remaining hot spots.

After her last live shot, PS was spent, only continuing to function with adrenalin as fuel. She turned her back to the camera to face the building she had escaped. The entire complex had been gutted. Very little would be salvageable. *How do people survive this kind of tragedy?* She thought to herself. For her, the very idea was almost unimaginable. But people did survive these kinds of experiences and worst. Not only did PS have first hand knowledge, but she reported on it, every day of her life.

After the morning news signed off, the live truck technician drove PS home. She told him she must have dropped her keys somewhere in the complex in her rush to get the story. What really happened would remain her own dirty little secret. She was embarrassed and ashamed.

Once she got to the safety of her complex, she jumped out of the truck, asked Jerry to wait a few minutes while she retrieved her spare key from the manager's office.

She knocked on the condo manager's door, covered with soot. The condo manager didn't ask any questions. She didn't have to. PS could hear the Channel Six morning game show blaring in the background. She thanked Frida for keeping the spare key to her apartment for just such an occasion. PS had lost keys to her place several times so she worked out a deal with the manager who also doubled as a pet sitter when PS was sent out of town unexpectedly.

"I saw you on the news this morning," Frida, the condo manager said. "Girl, they have you out there at all hours, don't they?"

"Well, you know..." PS said trying to decide whether or not she wanted to tell her the whole story. She decided to save it for Willina. "Wherever there's news. I'm there to give it to you fast, first and accurately."

Frida accommodated PS with a laugh. "Maybe you could see about doing a story around here."

"Why, Frida? What's going on around here?"

"Well, I'm not sure, but for the last week or so, the maintenance man has been finding dead animals."

"Frida, what kind of dead animals?"

"Birds, squirrels, a rabbit. They're always found on the other side of the complex near your place."

"What?" PS exclaimed. "What do you think it is, some sort of rabid animal? A fox maybe?"

"That's what he thought at first. But these animals aren't being eaten up. They're being caught and cut up. We brought animal control out here to inspect one of the carcasses and bring a trap, but he said you can't set a trap for whatever's killing these animals. We think it might be some bad ass neighborhood boys or something. Whoever's doing this stuff is sick and cruel, I can tell you that."

"Oh, my goodness, Frida. This is scary."

"Yeah. We thought it might be some devil worshipers or something. Whoever it is, they like to draw pictures on the walls with the blood. Pretty grisly stuff. Jones has been pretty good about washing it down before folks around her get home for the day and catch wind of it.

"We're thinking about putting something in the monthly newsletter to let everybody know. We don't know what to make of it, but think it's probably some kids."

"Frida, this is ghastly!" PS said in horror.

"Yeah it is. Maybe you could do a report on it, so parents can keep a closer eye on their bad ass kids."

"Frida, I'll look into it. Thanks. Hey, I gotta get going. I've got a photographer waiting for me to take me back to my car. I'll swing by to return this key when I get a moment."

"Don't wait too long. You'll forget and I'll have no way to get in to feed your cat in an emergency."

"I won't forget. Thanks. I appreciate it," PS said as she ran back out to the front of the building and jumped in the truck, so that Steve could drive her to other end of the complex.

As PS got to her door, she saw Fido laying on the front mat. "Fido?" What on earth are you doing out here?" She yelped.

She opened her door and immediately saw that her balcony door was cracked open on the other side of the living room. "Oh my God! I can't believe I did that. I'm so sorry!" PS said as she reached down to give the cat a grateful hug.

The cat wrestled to get free and ran into the kitchen and perched herself by the refrigerator.

"You poor baby. You must be starving," PS rummaged around her china cabinet for another saucer, filled it with rice milk and placed it on the counter. She then picked Fido up and placed her in front of her breakfast. "I'll give you some food when I get back, okay? Steve is waiting for me outside and I've got to get my car," she said as she reached over to give the cat an affectionate hug and kiss on the top of the head. "I love you, sweetie. I'm so sorry. Bad mama, bad mama."

PS opened her junk drawer and rummaged around to retrieve the spare keys to her car. Once in her hand she bolted out the door so as not to keep the photographer waiting much longer.

When Fido had her fill of milk, she jumped down from the counter and wandered into the living room. There she saw that the balcony door was still left open.

The large red tabby flattened herself like a rodent and squeezed back through the slender opening, just as she had the previous Sunday morning.

CHAPTER TEN

Embarrassed and exhausted, PS returned to her condo apartment. She had just lived through One-hundred and eighty-two hours in about twenty-eight hours. She was so sore and spent, her nerve endings felt like sand sifting through needles.

She just plain ached.

It seemed like mid morning, but PS didn't feel like walking into her bedroom to look at the clock. Her philosophy on clocks was the same as it was for watches. She owned one—to wake her in the morning. Other than that, she had even disabled the LED read-out on her microwave oven. For all other time matters she relied on her inner clock. At the moment, that was screaming, "Wake up and smell the coffee!"

What had she been thinking? Having sex with Allen George had been a colossal mistake. It would have been laughable had the deed not been so fresh in her mind.

It would be laughable by the time she finished telling her sordid tale to Willina.

As she walked to her bathroom, she mused about how she would re-tell the story. She was a master at embellishment, but this needed none. It was sufficiently gruesome on its own merit.

She dropped her skirt at the entrance of the hallway. Her shoes came off at the door of the guest bedroom. She hopped over a pile of blues in the middle of the floor, and deposited her panties. By the time she got to the door of her bathroom, she was clad only in her bra. She unsnapped it in the front and left it on the bathroom door as she moved in to turn the hot water on in the shower.

The steam immediately started filling the room. She closed the door so none would escape and it could envelop her. She was grateful that it had clouded the mirror because she still wasn't strong enough to look at herself. It was just too embarrassing and she hadn't worked out all of the angles in her head to rationalize her complete and abject stupidity, yet.

By the time she stepped out of the steaming shower, she was able to laugh, a little. But she still cringed when she caught a glimpse of herself in the mirror. She decided to study her face, to see if there were any changes, any tell-tale signs of her complete stupidity.

She had thought that sleeping with Allen George would erase the spell Danny had cast on her. Then she became angry because it hadn't. *That bastard!* she thought to herself. *How could he leave me like that? How could God let him?*

As she gazed into the mirror, looking at the small imperfections in her face, turning to the side and sucking in her belly, judging her hair far too harshly, she didn't need a clock to tell her what time it was. She knew. It was time to get over Danny Rierson, so she wouldn't continue to make stupid judgment calls.

"Loneliness kills!" She said out loud. And walked out of the bathroom.

She called the studio and told the assignment

247

desk that she wouldn't be in. To her surprise there was no fuss about it.

It was rare she had a weekday off, so she decided to use the time wisely. It had been weeks since she'd looked at the pile of bills that had stacked up on her kitchen table. She marveled that she even still had electricity. She went to her phone and picked up the receiver. She still had a dial tone, but noticed that it had been days since she had received caller ID. She pulled out her checkbook and spent the next forty minutes writing out bills. She then decided she may as well handle a few loads of laundry. Even though she was exhausted, she was too tired to sleep.

As she reached down into the pile of whites, she pulled out one of Danny's old shirts. She slipped it on over her bra and panties and continued to widdle down the piles.

It was lunch-time before she noticed that Fido hadn't sought her out. A bolt of panic ran down her chest. Fido always greeted her. How was it she hadn't seen the cat for nearly two hours?

She dropped the load of Blues that were bundled in her arms and headed toward the bedroom. If Fido had been in the house, surely she would have come out to lick the water off her legs after her shower. Perhaps she was sick, or incapacitated under the bed. The condo only had two bedrooms so it would only take a few minutes to scour the place.

She fell to her knees and checked under the bed. Nothing. She ran to the hamper in the bathroom. Once she'd found the feline hiding inside the hamper. She hadn't gotten that far in her laundry yet, so it was possible the cat was hiding inside the large wicker basket. She was not. Nor was she in the guest room. She ran to the kitchen, to see if the cat was waiting impatiently by the refrigerator, or on the counter. But as she ran through the living room, her feet stopped as, in her peripheral vision, she saw that the balcony door was cracked open. Her blood ran cold.

She ran to the bedroom and threw on a pair of blue jeans that she had just taken out of the dryer and had thrown on the bed. She had thought about running outside with just Danny's shirt on, but she was wearing tattered underwear. Every other pair had just been thrown into the dryer. All 56 pairs.

Without claws, Fido had no way of defending herself. If a dog was chasing her, she couldn't escape up a tree. She had to find her cat fast.

As she opened her door and sprinted out into the breezeway, she was startled as she ran headlong into a tall lean figure who had been standing at her door, hand poised to ring the bell.

"Ouch!" She yelped, rubbing her head that had connected to a broad chest with a thud. She stumbled and stuttered a little until she regained her balance and was able to focus up on the face that was standing in front of her.

It was Allen George.

"Allen!" She said. "What, what, what..."

Those were the only words she could manage to squeeze out.

"I don't have any place to go," he answered with a smile.

"What are you talking about? You have three sisters. You have plenty of places to go."

"Let me rephrase that," he said smugly. "I don't have any place else I want to go other then here."

"Allen, I can't talk about it right now. I can't find my cat. She slipped outside sometime yesterday and I have to find her."

PS slipped by Allen George and ran out into the courtyard. "Let me help you!" He yelled out after her. He threw his large green garbage bag of belongings into her front hallway and ran out after her.

Three hours later, after searching the entire grounds with Allen George, PS returned to her condo heart-broken.

"Don't worry," Allen said as he put his arms around the sobbing woman. "She'll turn up."

PS was so distraught she couldn't answer. She numbly walked into her bedroom and fell onto the mattress face first, coughing and wheezing through her pain and deep sobs.

She didn't even realize that her body had released. She didn't know that it was possible to fall asleep when she was so filled with grief and anxiety. And she didn't realize that Allen George had unpacked his belongings, walked into the kitchen to fix himself a sandwich, watched the afternoon talk shows and then crawled into bed beside her to cradle her into his arms.

She had a faint, almost unconscious awareness of being held, but in the fog of desperate sleep it felt like Danny had returned. And somehow she managed to fall deep with the comfort of knowing she was not alone.

As PS stirred, sat up and rubbed the sleep from her eyes, she was startled by the presence of someone in her room. At first, fear shot through her body, she thought it was an intruder. But as she lay with her cheek scrunched on the pillow, looking up with her left eye, she slowly realized that it was Allen George sitting up reading on the other side of the bed.

Just as she blinked to clear the apparition from her view, he looked over and smiled. "Hi, are you feeling better?"

Pain shot from her head to her toes, as she remembered that her cat was still on the missing and endangered list. But still exhausted, she didn't have the immediate strength to move her body, only her lips. "Allen, what are you doing here?"

"I'm waiting for you to wake up so that we can go back out and look for Fido," he said with a sympathetic smile. "I've already contacted the condo manager and let her know that we're missing a cat."

Did he say, 'we're?' PS thought to herself in her haze.

"Everybody's out looking for him. Is it a him or a her? I'm assuming it's a him."

PS continued to gaze up at Allen in a yet-to-clear-up fog. Nothing on his face matched. His eyes were too small, and his freckled nose looked more like a bird's beak than a nose. And she didn't like that

Hitler-styled mustache. These things had bothered her before, but now she was outraged at the sight of them.

"Allen," she said again. "What are you doing here?"

"Well, as you know, my apartment complex went up in a blaze of glory, and I didn't have anywhere else to go."

"Allen, you have sisters and aunts, why didn't you go to them? I just don't think this is a good idea."

"Just for a couple of weeks."

PS raised her head and began to protest.

"Days. A couple of days."

"I just don't think this is appropriate, I'm sorry." PS said as she raised herself on her elbows only to feel a new wave of exhaustion.

But before she could make further protest, she fell back to her pillow on her face, and was asleep in a matter of moments.

Allen George bent over to kiss her on her forehead. He was used to women protesting at first. But he was always able to win them over. He prided himself on knowing who to pick. The woman laying next to him would be easy prey. He didn't fear for a moment that she would put him out, especially as long as her beloved cat was missing.

Allen quietly got up off the bed, and went to the kitchen to see what he could find to eat.

The pickings were slim. Some ginger ale, moldy bread and lots of wine.

This would be easier than he thought.

He grabbed his keys and went to his car to head to the grocery store he had seen on his way to PS's apartment. He knew exactly what this woman needed to win her over. That was his greatest gift. He could read women like a clairvoyant. He always knew what women needed and more importantly, he knew what he needed from women.

When PS finally woke up, it was to the smell of food cooking. The scent drove her groggily into the kitchen where Allen was in a button down shirt, gym shorts and sweat socks. From behind, he looked adorable, every bit the doting boyfriend at home in his girlfriend's kitchen.

And then he turned around.

PS was taken aback. He looked different then she remembered. His beak more pronounced, his eyes more narrow. His entire presence was vague and un comfortable.

She grabbed her stomach as much out of distress that he was making himself at home in her home, as from hunger.

"Where did the food come from?" PS asked, salivating.

"Well, we didn't have any food in the house, so I went out and got some groceries. Are you hungry?"

"Allen, don't say 'we'. We are not a we. I'm a me, and this is my house, and you can't stay here."

"I know, honey. It'll just be for a little while. I don't need to stay forever," Allen said as he reached up into the cabinet and grabbed some paprika for the chicken that was simmering in the frying pan.

PS didn't know whether to be more shocked that she had paprika in the house, or that he had already familiarized himself with what was and was not in her cabinets.

"Allen, I don't want to be a bitch about this, but the answer is, no. Now, I appreciate your going out and getting groceries, and I appreciate your cooking dinner. But after dinner, you really need to leave. I'm not kidding, and I'm not being coy. You can't stay here."

"Well, I don't plan on staying here forever, but surely you're not going to deny a man a place to lay his head after saving your life."

"Saving my life?"

"Tsk, tsk. What a short memory you have. Did I or did I not get you out of that burning apartment?"

"Allen, I appreciate that, but I'm telling you, I'm not interested in living with anyone."

"You're not living with anyone, you're helping a friend out. Now sit down and get something to eat and we can go out and look for your cat."

"I'm not hungry," PS said as she slipped on a pair of sneakers at the back of her sofa and headed to the door. "I don't want to be ungracious, but please don't be here when I get back."

Just as she reached the door, the bell rang. She opened the door to find the condo maintenance man standing there with a grave look on his face.

"Mr. Chuck!" PS said with surprise. "Good evening."

"Miss Garrett, you doing okay?" The maintenance man asked in a somber voice.

"Mr. Chuck, what is it?" PS said, a shiver and a throb suddenly speaking up in her left shoulder.

Allen George came out of the kitchen and walked toward PS.

"Miss Garrett, we found your cat."

"Thank goodness. Where is she?" PS asked as she tried to push her way past the kind old southerner. "Where is she?"

Mr. Chuck didn't move to let her past. Instead gently grabbed her arm. "Miss Garrett, don't."

"Don't what?" PS asked indignantly, understanding what was being said by his looks and his tone. Her eyes began to tear up, and her voice started to quake. "Where is she? Is she okay?"

"Miss Garrett, is this her collar?"

Mr. Chuck held up the bright purple collar with the little bell. The front was embroidered with gold lettering that spelled, FIDO in capital letters.

"Where did you get that, Mr. Chuck? Is she okay?" PS asked, starting to cry.

"What's going on here?" Allen asked as he stepped up behind PS and placed his hands on her shoulders.

"Mr. George, we found the cat near the woods and it ain't good. I'm so sorry."

"What do you mean it ain't good? And how do you know Allen's name? What is this?" PS insisted through her stifled sobs.

"Well, ma'am, he was out there with us for quite some time helping us look for your cat. He said he's a friend of yours and he'd be staying here for a while. If you don't mind my saying so ma'am, I'm glad you have a friend like him right now."

"Mr. Chuck, let me see the cat. What happened

to her?" Allen insisted.

"I don't know what you're talking about, but I need to see Fido. Where the Hell is Fido? What happened here?" PS said in a wild panic, her reporter sense answering everything she was asking.

"Ma'am, I think some of those bad kids got a hol' of her. We've been having a problem with small animals turning up, you know, kind of mutilated. I don't think you want to see what they did to her. Just let it be.

"I've dug a hole in the back. I just want your permission to bury her. I'll take you to her when I get through burying her. You don't need to see this, and you don't need to hear no more about it. Trust me on that ma'am."

PS felt her knees buckle beneath her. The ceiling started whirling and then fading. The last thing she saw was Allen's face as he caught her in mid swoon and swept her into his arms to carry her back to her bedroom.

When PS awoke, the room was dark and she was lying on Allen's chest, his arms cradled tightly around her.

As she stirred, he opened his eyes and kissed her on her forehead. He then found her lips and gently kissed them.

She allowed it. She allowed him to kiss her, undress her, and make love to her. She barely even noticed it was happening. She was almost numb, and whatever he was doing on top of her, it blocked what little she could feel—pain.

When she got up the next morning, she walked out into the living room to find Allen perched in front of the television.

"Good morning, Sunshine," he announced cheerfully wearing only PS's favorite, fluffy white bathrobe with the pink rose on the lapel that she had just laundered the day before.

She blinked hard but when she opened her eyes he was still there. She stood for a moment, trying to digest this dreadful scene, and decided a shower would help. Without saying a word, she walked into the bathroom and almost fainted.

It looked like a grape had exploded. Everything in her bathroom—her pale peach shower curtain and the matching trashcan, her woven cotton bath mat she'd gotten while on a story in Cherokee, North Carolina, her vase of pastel silk roses that looked like the real thing, everything had been replaced with that awful maroon crap that had been hanging in Allen's bathroom seventy-two hours before. The faint stink of smoke, obviously from the fire hung in the air.

This was some sort of cruel joke that would have to be dealt with later, at the moment she was running late for work.

As she started getting dressed, the uneasy feeling that this guy had completely moved in started to haunt her. She looked in her medicine cabinet for lipstick and there were his toiletries. She looked in the cabinet under the sink, more toiletries!

She walked back into the living room and Allen hadn't stirred. He was totally engrossed in one of those talk shows in which two homosexuals were fighting for the affections of a third and the audience was cheering.

"Aren't you going to work, Allen?"

"Uh no," he barely shifted his attention from the tube. "Not today. I'm just going to make some calls from home."

Your home burned down you fuck, PS thought to herself. *This is my home.*

"Oh, and I'll need a key. Love ya." Allen waived his hand from the sofa almost as if he were dismissing her while saying good-bye. Without ever looking up at her, he re-focused on the television and tuned her out.

PS walked to the kitchen and saw Fido's collar sitting on the counter. A fresh wave of pain hit her, and she had to hold on to a bar stool to steady herself. She sucked up her grief as she had done so many times before, grabbed her reporter's bag and walked out of her condo.

Five minutes after PS left, her phone rang. At first Allen ignored it. The talk show he'd been watching was getting good. Two of the homosexuals who were fighting over the affections of the third had already come to blows, and they were moving toward another altercation and Allen didn't want to miss any of it. But after the sixth ring, Allen wandered over and picked up the phone. "Hello."

"Oh, I must have the wrong number," the voice on the other end said. "I'm so sorry."

"No problem," Allen said, as he hung up, barely taking his eyes of the television set. He strolled back over to the sofa, when the phone began to ring again. He was annoyed, but walked back over to pick up the receiver. "Hello."

"Hello," the voice on the other end said. "I thought I had dialed the wrong number, but I don't think I did."

"Well, what number are you trying to reach?" Allen asked, bothered by the disruption in his favorite morning talk show.

"I'm trying to reach PS Garrett."

"She's not here, right now."

"Well, where is she and who the Hell is this?" Willina asked alarmed.

"Who the Hell is this?"

"This is Willina Johns, her best friend."

"This is Allen George, her boyfriend."

"Her boyfriend?" Willina asked in a confused huff. "She doesn't have a boyfriend."

"Well, I guess you're not her best friend if you didn't know she had a boyfriend."

As soon as the words tumbled from his lips, he was sorry he had said them. He knew exactly who Willina Johns was. PS had talked about her numerous times. And he couldn't afford to start things off with her badly.

He stammered for a nanosecond, but quickly recovered and was about to make amends when Willina screeched into the phone, "Is that so?"

She hung up her phone and raced over to PS's condo.

When she got to the door and rang the bell,

she was startled that Allen George opened the door. He had changed into a pair of blue jeans and a large T-shirt he'd found on the top of a clean clothes pile in the guest room. He had a feeling she was coming over, and not having anything at the ready to put on that didn't smell like smoke, he grabbed the first shirt of PS's that fit.

He and Willina locked eyes immediately and sized each other up. He could see at once that this woman spelled trouble for him. And Wil could see instantaneously that Allen George spelled trouble for PS.

"And who are you again?" Willina asked.

"Oh, you're the one I just talked to. Sorry that I got smart with you, you just kind of threw me off guard a little."

"Oh, is that so? And what did you say your name is?"

"I'm Allen. Allen George. You must be Willina. How was your trip? To the islands, was it?"

"Well, you certainly seem to know enough about me, why is it that I don't know anything about you?" Willina said as she pushed past Allen who had been blocking the entrance to the apartment.

He dropped his arm that had been barring the door, glared behind Wil and then walked in after her, closing the door behind him, measuring his temper.

"Well, I guess you've been off on your vacation. A lot can happen in three weeks."

"Not that much. Where's P.?"

"She went to work. She's had a rough couple of days. Fido died."

"What?" Willina spat, startled as she spun around. "Is PS okay? What happened?"

"He apparently slipped outside and we think some kids got a hold of him."

"Her," Wil corrected sternly.

"I beg your pardon?"

"Fido is a she, not a he. And how long have you known PS? She's never mentioned you, not even when I talked to her last week."

"We met at Barbara Bennett's party. I admit things happened a little quickly between us."

"That's an interesting shirt you have on. Where did you get that?"

"Uhm..." Allen stuttered as he looked down to get a good look at the shirt he had grabbed.

It had silk screen writing that read, 'My best friend went to London and all I got was this stupid shirt.'

"So you've moved into her closet, too? Do you not have any clothing of your own, Mr. George? That is what you said your name is, isn't it? I gave PS that shirt several years ago. You seem to have made yourself mighty comfy in it."

"Yeah, that's right. Uhm, my place got a little burned out a couple of days ago and PS is letting me stay here for a few days until I get back on my feet. It's not a big deal."

"It feels like one."

There was an uncomfortable silence. Allen had tried to *pee* on PS but on this one, Willina was the alpha tomcat. Nothing Allen could say could remove the power the woman standing in front of him had over the situation.

The two continued to stare at each other, each pacing slightly around the other to get an advantage and a closer look. But each one knew what the other was dealing with. And they knew the threat each posed to their position with PS Garrett.

Allen understood that he was the underdog, and that he didn't have a prayer to win Willina over. All he could do is mitigate her damage, and hold on as long as he could. Had he met Willina at Barbara's party instead of Zoe, he would have immediately set his sights on a different target. This woman was for-midable.

"Allen, do you work?"

"Well, I own a couple of business interests. I guess you could say that I'm an entrepreneur."

"Is that so? And does that mean you work?"

"I work very hard, in fact."

"Then why is it that you're sitting around your girlfriend's house wearing her clothing? Why aren't you out working?"

"As I said, there was a fire at my place and I'm just taking a couple of days off while I get back on my feet."

"Is that so?" Willina scowled. *Lies, all lies.* She thought to herself. She could see it in his eyes, hear it in his voice and see it in his walk.

"And what about you. Do you work Willina?"

"What's it to you?"

"Nothing, I'm just making conversation."

"Well, don't. I don't like you, Allen George.

There's something about you that makes me very uncomfortable. And I'm not so much a pushover as my buddy is. It might take me a minute to figure your angle, but I've already figured you've got one. And that's half the battle."

"Well, I don't see why you don't like me," Allen said, trying to reposition himself so that he wouldn't lose this fight on the first round. He knew he would lose the battle over PS eventually as long as Willina had a finger in the pie. But he also knew he had to find some way to neutralize this woman or he wouldn't get what he needed out the allegiance he'd formed with PS. She could possibly be his best conquest yet.

Thus far things had gone very well. The death of a beloved cat was a bonus, it had given him firm footing in the door and he wasn't willing to let that edge slip away by some globe-trotting bitch. "I'm a nice guy and I love your friend. I think very highly of her. And I'd venture to guess she thinks a lot of me, too."

"Love! Is that what you told her? You don't love her. You might love her position. I guess you get a little glow from the spotlight she stands in, but you don't love her. You don't even know her, other than biblically I'm sure."

"You can't say that, and you don't know me. You have me all wrong. What I do know is that your friend is lonely, and her cat just died. And you were nowhere around. I was.

"You have your life. You have your adventure. Why are you trying to keep her from hers? It's

263

been so long since that girl's been held by a man, she doesn't remember how to respond. Let her have some companionship. I don't know what's going to happen, but let us work out our own thing."

Willina pushed pause. Just before she'd left town, she had advised Willina to seek out some physical companionship. She had hoped it would be with Sherman Hall. The two were naturals for each other, just enough competition and admiration to create bedroom bang.

Even with this guy, she didn't mind PS screwing him, as long as he was a good lay. But she was uncomfortable with him living in her house, calculating her worth. There was so much more damage he could do with keys. And this guy wasn't capable of loving anyone other than himself. In fact , as near as Willina could tell, he loved himself so much there wasn't room for anyone else. PS was the exact opposite. She didn't love herself enough.

Willina was surprised that he'd made such a convincing argument. He was even more clever than she initially thought. She gave him points for creativity, but that was all.

"Look, Allen George…" She started.

"Wil, leave her alone. Leave us alone. You're wrong about me. I swear it," Allen said in what he hoped would be a capitulating voice.

Willina was the Alpha dog here, so he tucked his tail and showed his belly. "What do you want? You want her to be alone for the rest of her life?"

"I don't think I am wrong about you, Allen George," Willina said as she walked toward the door, changed her mind and instead headed for the phone.

Allen's first inclination was to race her to the phone and stop her. But he managed to hold on to his anger. Any physical contact with this woman would be a fatal mistake.

Wil dialed out PS's cell phone, with Allen nervously watching. She looked at her watch. It was noon. News time. She'd be lucky to reach her.

The phone rang three, four, five times before PS's quaking voice answered.

"Hello?"

With Fido gone, Wil knew that she was vulnerable, and nothing eased grief like a man around the house or at least a woman's arms around a man. Wil just wished it had been another man.

"Girl, what the Hell is going on here? I'm at your place," Wil asked as gently as she could muster under the circumstances.

PS began to sob. She stuttered and stammered and choked as the river of tears blocked her breathing and flooded her. Wil could barely make out any of the words she was saying with the exception that PS had to go, she was on deadline.

Willina didn't get a moment to find out what happened to Fido, or protest the presence of Allen George in her home. She couldn't. Not now, with PS on deadline. She would have to wait him out, watch him carefully, and make sure she minimized the damage she was sure he would try to do. But to criticize PS right now while she was mourning the death of her cat would have been cruel.

Allen George would luck out this time. At that

moment, Willina Johns missed Danny almost as much as PS did.

Sitting outside the condo in the parking lot in a freshly hijacked white Toyota, a brooding figure of a man remained transfixed on the apartment of PS Garrett.

Nothing had gone as planned. It seemed that none of his messages had gotten through, no matter where he placed them.

PS Garrett seemed to be surrounded by people who watched her carefully and protected her and it gave the criminally disturbed man absolutely no chance to make contact and make her, his woman.

And now some asshole had moved into her place. Now it would be almost impossible to get her attention.

He was afraid of the man who'd moved in. There was something about him that made the lone figure very nervous about approaching. He was too observant to be surprised. He would be hard to dispose of.

The stalker had *accidentally* brushed by him after following him into the grocery store the day before. Allen George bristled and shot him a chilling look. The disturbed man tucked his tail beneath his legs, apologized and went back out to his beat up vehicle and drove back to PS's apartment to wait and watch.

Getting the reporter to come to him was more difficult than he had imagined.

He'd left clues of his love for his favorite reporter. Bouquets of freshly picked flowers, notes scribbled in dew on her windshield, small notes at her stoop.

Why wasn't she answering his notes?

He knew that he and the reporter were meant to be together. When she talked on television, he could tell that she was talking directly to him—sending him messages telepathically that only he could receive.

He could tell PS Garrett admired him. At first he thought it might be his imagination, but when she showed up at his crime scene in Pixley a few months before, when she waved to him the night he rubbed out those two kids, it was an acknowledgement.

He'd been one of the on-lookers at the scene, milling around the parking lot to see if anyone would notice him. PS had walked by casually and smiled. That was his first clue she loved him too.

He was glad he killed those two kids at the Gas 'N Go. He hated them. He hated their youth, and their happiness. They seemed so much in love. He knew it was all an act—a plot to make him feel inferior.

The first time he'd wandered into the gas station, the teenagers were chuckling at a television tucked discreetly beneath the cash register, but he thought they were laughing at him behind his back because he didn't have enough money to pay.

When he returned, he showed them a thing or two.

The tormented man, sat in his car and twirled a long braid around his fingers as he thought about the way those kids had died.

He shot the boy straight away, the moment he walked into the gas station, BANG! He loved the sound of gunshot.

Gunpowder in the afternoon. He thought to himself. *Man's aphrodisiac.*

In his own twisted logic, he believed killing those two kids was the smartest thing he ever did. Little did he know that it would plop his favorite reporter right there in his lap. They would exchange a smile, and he'd have an opportunity to see her home safely.

He felt himself get excited, and moved his hand down to his crotch to cool the rise in his trousers. He rubbed and grasped as he thought about the way that chubby little chick cowered and begged and pleaded for her life. That made it even more fun to shoot her in the face. He liked the way her brains went *pop*, as they splattered on the glass window behind her. He liked the way the blood looked in the dim back light of the streetlamps in front of the store.

As he remembered the blood hitting the window in an explosion, he too exploded and rested his head on the steering wheel to pant his satisfaction, his hand continuing to rub and tug gently so as to exhaust the last few throes of his ejaculation.

Blood, he mused. *It's so beautiful and artistic. Cavemen painted memorable murals in the blood of victims. And they've been remembered in the history books.*

That's what had given him the idea to leave the message painted in blood.

He liked the power he had to end the lives of

those teenagers. He was proud of his handiwork. Maybe in the end there would be a spectacular shoot out between him and the pigs. He hated cops and hoped to take a few out when he went. He would go out in a blaze of glory. His name would be legendary and he would never be a nobody again.

Meeting his favorite reporter had been the icing. If he could make her his, all of his problems would be solved. People would stand up and take notice. He would be somebody special. And he knew she would love him and put him on a pedestal. She was just like him. He could tell.

Maybe someone would make a movie about him and his lady love. It would be like that Bonnie and Clyde movie he'd seen last month on cable television at his Ma's house.

He had to make PS Garrett his own. He had to.

But now she was surrounded by people. She was being watched, and he couldn't get close enough to her to re-introduce himself, to remind her that she had acknowledged him on the night of those murders by waving at him as he sat behind her in his car, willing her to be his very own.

Now he had to do something else to get her attention. Something bigger.

Willina Johns walked out of PS's condo, into the breezeway and out toward her Beemer. She opened her car door but stopped, just short of getting in, and looked over at the small white car that had been sitting there when she screeched into the parking lot.

The position of the sun made it difficult to see if there was anyone inside the vehicle. There was something odd about the way it was parked. It seemed out of place.

Willina moved toward the car to look inside.

The stalker behind the wheel held perfectly still, trying to make himself invisible to the woman who was now cautiously approaching him. His right hand inched over to the passenger seat where his pistol was hidden beneath some newspapers and debris. This was that nosey bitch who was always hanging around his beloved, PS Garrett. He'd hoped she would disappear and she had for a few weeks making him feel his powers of want were stronger than even he had realized.

But now she was back and he was furious.

Killing her would be easy. There was no one around to see him.

Willina moved slowly toward the car, the sun moving in and out amongst the clouds threw strange shadows on the windshield, and she wasn't sure, but she thought someone was sitting inside.

If someone was inside, why wasn't he moving? How come he hadn't stepped out? Why had he been sitting in that spot for more than thirty minutes.

As the sun burst back out through the cloud cover, the glare on the windshield made the car look empty again. Still, Willina felt as though she needed to investigate, so she inched closer but stopped when she heard her cell phone chiming from her purse in her own vehicle. She wanted to ignore it, but thought it might be PS so she backed back to her open door and retrieved her phone, her eyes still focused on the small white vehicle parked just beneath the low hanging branches of a freshly blooming Dogwood tree.

"Hello?"

It was PS. She was sobbing uncontrollably.

"Oh, don't worry, honey. Cry it out. Where are you? I'll come to you right now," Wil said as she hastily jumped into her vehicle, turned the ignition and headed away from the condo.

The stalker, exhaled and took his hand away from his pistol. "That bitch!" He gasped aloud.

Yup, it was time for him to do something big to get PS's attention once and for all.

But first, he'd need a new car. In his mind, the one he was in was starting to draw too much attention. And he wasn't ready for that kind of attention, yet. He had a lot more he had to do.

He had to have PS Garrett. Dead or alive, he had to own her. He thought about what her blood might feel like, and taste like. He thought how good it would be for him to be inside her. She would like it. And if she didn't, it wouldn't matter. He would like it.

He grabbed the key to start the ignition of his stolen broken up white Toyota, and drove away from PS Garret's condo, a new plan beginning to formulate.

CHAPTER ELEVEN

Once PS had gotten over the initial shock, the first month Allen lived in her apartment wasn't so bad. There was a great deal of acrimony between Allen and Willina, but since Wil hadn't advised her to move him out, she just assumed that the two just had a personality conflict. Surely if Wil had seen anything malignant about him, she would have spoken up immediately.

Sometimes having Allen around was actually fun. PS had company, he was intelligent and he made her laugh.

She was, however, deeply bothered by two persisting routines. Several times a week, Allen would disappear in the mornings. He didn't offer or give any explanation. PS would wake up, and Allen would be gone. He'd generally return to the condo before PS left for work, he'd have a paper and a coffee and nothing else to say about the matter. He also continued the musical car routine with his sister, Janet. No matter what was on the agenda the two couldn't do anything that would interfere with his picking up his sister from work. There was also this thing about giving her his car on the weekends, which had just gotten ridiculous. There had been times Janet didn't want to give it back, and Allen had to borrow PS's car to drop her at work and pick her up.

When Janet was ready to give the car back, PS would have to drop him off at his sister's to pick up his car.

The whole arrangement struck her as being very low rent, not the kind of behavior you'd expect from an upwardly mobile professional.

The sweater really began to unravel when, one week, Janet decided she wanted to keep his car for the entire week.

"No problem," Allen said to PS. "I told her you wouldn't mind being chauffeured around in your own car. You're probably sick of driving in rush hour traffic. I'll get you to work and you can catch up on your reading and some sleep. It's a perfect arrangement."

"Abbbbbb-soooo-loooot-ly not," PS said angrily. "I am not going to stand around at the station and wait to be picked up with my own vehicle. Besides, you're not even insured to drive my car."

"I can't get my businesses off the ground without wheels of my own," Allen argued.

"I thought you said your business ventures were already off the ground? And this wouldn't be your own car, this would be my own car." PS countered..

"No business is completely off the ground." Allen defended. "I mean, you know, uh, er…"

"Enough is enough," PS screamed. "If Janet wants continuous access to a car, she'll have to tighten her belt and get her own."

"Who do you think you are?" Allen screamed back. "Not everybody makes top dollar like you. Not everybody can afford a nice apartment, and a nice car.

273

She makes minimum wage. Do you know how hard it is to get around on minimum wage or less?"

"Stop right there. First of all, you have no idea what I make. Second of all, you are arguing with me about the use of my vehicle, lest I remind you. And you are staying in my apartment for free. So perhaps the question should be, who the Hell do you think you are, Allen George?"

"Now wait a minute..."

"No, you wait a minute. You were only supposed to be here for a couple of days, it's been more than a month, and I haven't seen so much as a penny to help out with bills or food."

Allen looked stunned. "I lost everything in that fire. Everything. I am having to rebuild my life. I thought you appreciated the fact that I was here."

"Allen, this is a real problem," PS continued with a long, drawn out sigh. "I'm going to have to ask you to leave."

"I have something to tell you," Allen said after a pregnant pause.

"This should be good. Go ahead, I'm all ears."

"I haven't exactly been completely honest with you about something."

"Oh, and how is that pray tell?"

"Well, the reason I can't argue with Janet about the car is because it's her car."

"Why on earth would you need Janet's car? I don't understand. Where is your car?" PS asked, confused and dazed—an ache that had taken up residence in her left shoulder, began to throb.

"It's been in the shop," Allen answered as his eyes darted from side to side.

"You were driving her car when we met? So you mean your car has been in the shop for several months? Give me a break!"

"Well it's a foreign car—um, an Alpha, and um, the mechanic says he's having trouble finding a part for it."

PS looked at Allen. "I could see having to wait a couple of days. I could even see waiting a week for a part. But months? I didn't think so. Allen, that's not true. What's the real story?"

"No, that's the truth, I swear it on my mother's grave."

"You know Allen George, your mother's going to be mighty pissed at you when she sees you in Hell. You're lying to me, and I've had enough. Let's go pack your belongings. I've had it."

"No, wait a minute," Allen changed his tenor. He was a chameleon, a man of many disguises. "Well I didn't want to tell you this, because I thought you would lose respect for me, but you're right. It's not that they can't find a part for it, it's um... well because of my business holdings, all of my capital is tied up and well, I just haven't had the money to get it out."

"What? You mean to tell me some mechanic has been holding on to your car because you don't have the money to get it out? Why didn't you tell me in the first place? Why have you been putting your sister through this musical cars business? This is ridiculous. How much is it? I'll get it out, and I'll add it to your tab. And make no bones about it buddy, I'm running a tab."

"No way, I'm not taking any money from you. I won't have it. I will not have a woman subsidize me like that."

"Oh, but you can put me and your sister out so you can have free use of a vehicle? It's ridiculous. If you're going to get back on your feet and find your own place to stay you need your own vehicle."

"Actually," Allen interrupted. He took her hand and put it in his. "I was hoping that you and I were getting close and maybe you'd want me to stay here." He rubbed her hand and gently kissed it.

PS looked at Allen in disbelief. She was helping him out. She hadn't planned on his staying there forever. "Allen, I'm sorry if I've given you the impression..."

Allen cut her off. "Well I noticed you don't have a lot of men banging down the door to take you out. That kind of surprised me. I mean you're on TV and all, and I figured your dance card would be kind of full. But now that I see that it's not, I thought maybe I was filling some sort of void. You never talk about any other boyfriends or anything like that. I thought you kind of liked not being all alone. But of course, if you're tired of having a sure date on the weekends, and if you're tired of being invited to parties... I can dig it. But I've been watching you. You're not the kind of girl who wants others to think she can't get a date. And then when Fido was murdered..."

Allen paused for a moment to size up the effect of his words. He knew they were cruel. He knew they would hurt her. But he had a big meeting coming up that would guarantee a big cash advance. And he needed this woman on his arm for credibility. It was too close to closing the deal.

He would be happy to take off as soon as he got his cash. This woman had turned out to be more trouble than she was worth to him, especially with that nosey Willina Johns always snooping about.

Allen reached over and kissed PS gently on the cheek. It burned a bit. What he said stung, and it was also true. Men weren't lined up to take her out. And she was frightened to come home alone since her cat had been sliced up just outside her door. PS did feel a little safer with Allen George about.

She opened her mouth to speak, but only a gasped choke escaped from her throat. She felt a deep ache in her heart, and blinked back a tear. She turned her back. She hadn't felt so alone since Danny left.

Allen had chased away that horrible loneliness she'd been feeling for so long. And even though his very presence made her feel dirty and used, at least she wasn't alone. She had some measure of safety with a man in the house.

"Allen, how much do you owe on the car? I'll bail you out and you can just pay me back when you get the money. I can't afford for you to keep running around in my car, and it's pretty clear Janet is getting tired of the charade too, so let's just get your car out of hock."

Deep down, PS knew that to hand this man money directly would set a whole new dangerous precedent. She knew she was sliding down a slippery slope.

But she also realized that she wasn't sure if she was ready to kick him out yet. For whatever reasons, she just didn't feel safe enough. A nagging still small voice told her, this situation was the lesser of the evils. She just wasn't sure what evil.

"Allen, how much is the car?" She insisted. "This is ridiculous. I'll get the car out so you can leave tomorrow."

"I can't leave tomorrow."

"You have to leave tomorrow."

"You don't really want me to leave tomorrow. You need me here. You're being stubborn. You're safer with me here. Even Willina thinks I should stay."

Allen grabbed PS and held her so tightly she gasped to breathe. He stroked her hair, and rubbed her shoulders. She pulled away abruptly.

"It doesn't work Allen. That doesn't work on me anymore. Tomorrow, you're gone. It's that simple."

Pathetically Sad, PS thought to herself. That's what my initials stand for, Pathetically Sad.

Allen watched PS as she stormed into her bedroom. His blood boiled as she slammed the door and he heard it latch.

"That bitch," he said under his breath. "No one kicks out Allen George. No one."

His jaw clenched and his fists balled, he walked to her door and gently tried the knob anyway. He then settled for a night on the uncomfortable bed of the second bedroom.

When PS rose in the morning, she felt a resolve she hadn't in weeks. Today would be the day. Today she would reclaimed her life. Today would be Allen George's last as her unwelcome guest.

She walked out of her bedroom.

Allen was no where in sight. So what, she thought. He would be asked to vacate the moment she got home from work that evening.

PS walked into the bathroom and turned on the shower. She stood outside the stall waiting for the steam to fill the bathroom.

In a spark of panic she ran to the kitchen. Her car keys. Both sets were still on the table. She ran back to the shower and stepped in and tried to wash the previous night down the drain. "He's looooooooooong gone," She sang quietly to herself. "loooooooooong gone."

As she stepped out of the shower, she could hear the familiar beacon of her electronic tether.

Beep beep, beep, beep, beep!

Draping her towel around her torso, she walked into the kitchen and grabbed her pager off the dinner table and read the display. All reporters call in ASAP!

"Great!" She said aloud. "Now what?"

She grabbed the phone and dialed the TV studio. Larry Pink answered the phone. "Where are you?" He asked, breathing rapidly. "It's PS, I have PS on the phone." He yelled out into the news room. "PS, where are you right now?"

"Larry, it's 7:30 in the morning, where do you think I am?"

"Hey, I have a breaking story and I need to get a reporter to the scene as fast as possible. Our morningsider is out of pocket. You live in the northern sub-urbs, don't you?"

"Yes..." PS said impatiently.

"How fast can you get on the road?"

"With or without makeup?"

"PS, we're hurting here. Can you be on the road in five minutes? I already have a photog in route."

"Sure, put the directions in my pager. I'm out the door. Do you mind if I take a moment to slip on some panties?"

From her house, Crystal Lake Estates was only a seven minute drive. PS had traveled that route dozens of times but had never before noticed the trailer park tucked off North Road, one mile west of the grocery store she often shopped.

As she approached the trailer home park, she could see the tell-tale activity of disaster—flashing lights, emergency vehicles entering and exiting the property, and the cars of the curious pulled over on the side of the road no doubt hoping to see the horror for themselves.

She slowed down, past the entrance of the Su-permarket, inching past the spectators, looking for a place to enter the trailer park and situate herself as close as possible to the action without jeopardizing the emer-gency work or the finish of her sports car.

She reached down and pulled her press creden-tial placard from the side pocket of her door and slipped it underneath her windshield so that anyone guarding the front of the trailer park would allow her access with few questions.

She reached up and rubbed her right shoulder which began aching, driving slowly, taking notice of the faces of the people entering and exiting Crystal Lake Estates, trying to judge the magnitude of what she was about to see by their expressions and demeanor. A woman cradling a baby in her arms, hurried along the embankment of the trailer home park, sobbing. Her curiosity likely satisfied by what she had seen. Most people ran from the mobile home park to their cars on the side of the road with shocked and saddened faces.

"Whaddaya expect?" PS murmured to herself sarcastically. "It's a trailer park fire, people."

As she moved to the mouth of the trailer park, she was startled by a man who stepped into the street and in front of her car. She hit the breaks hard and the jolt bounced her head from the headrest to the steering wheel.

"Ouch!" PS touched her forehead and felt a slight bump. "Great, now I'll have a big bruise on my face."

She composed herself.

The man who'd stepped in front of her was now at the hood of her car in the middle of the street glaring at her.

PS assumed he was angry because she'd almost nailed him. She looked up and gave a sheepish smile and a courtesy wave. The man raised his hand automatronically and waved back. He parted his lips in a strange jagged leer as his whole manner seemed to be suddenly buoyed. He pointed to the trailer park, as if pointing her in the right direction and trotted off.

"What an A-S-S", PS said to herself. "Get a real life."

She pulled into the mouth of the mobile home park. There was a cop stopping cars going in and commanding detours of others. Standing just behind the traffic cop nearby on an embankment was the idiot who had just forced the near vehicle/pedestrian confrontation. He was olive skinned and lean with a strange pock-marked face and a long pony tail. He was clearly trying to get her attention, forcing eye contact. He didn't look anxious or frightened. Instead, he was smiling and waving and clapping his hands excitedly.

PS was used to people being excited to see her, but for some reason the man seemed out of place, and his behavior was disturbing.

She pulled forward into the entrance of the mobile home park and paused to wait for the cop to clear the car ahead of her, still watching the strange man on the hill from the corner of her eye.

She startled a bit from a tap on her window and turned her head to see a police officer at the passenger side of her car. She rolled down her window and greeted him with a smile, "Channel Six, I'm PS Garrett, can I get through?"

"You bet. No problem," he said as he waved to the cop in front of her. "John, let her through. It's that Channel Six woman. The one the captain told us about."

"Huh?"

"You know, Grainger from Pixley asked us to look out for this one. The Captain told us about it a while ago."

"Yeah. Okay, I know the one. Miss Garrett, you doin' okay?" The officer conducting traffic said waiving enthusiastically.

PS nodded and waived back.

The original cop who stopped her then stooped back down, "Your photographer was here five minutes ago and said you were on your way. It's good to see you in person, Miss Garrett. We appreciate everything you do for us."

"Oh yeah? You're welcome. I'll be sure to tell Chief Grainger you helped me out. Did you say my photographer told you I was coming? Hmmmm, that's interesting. I didn't know I'd be here five minutes ago, but, whatever. Where should I park?"

"Why don't you go down that road toward the end of the complex, if you don't mind. That's Sunflower Court. We've got a lot of equipment coming through. You should be out of the way there."

"Hey, are there any fatalities? Can you tell me what's going on?"

"Big fire. That's all I can say, Ms. Garrett," the officer answered politely. "I'd tell you more if I knew it, but I've been fighting with the public all morning. I haven't had time to find out for myself. Sorry."

And then the officer turned his attention to the car behind her. "Sir, Sir. I've told you ten times you can't come in here. Now, next time I'm going to arrest you. Turn your car around and stop blocking traffic. She's a reporter and it's none of your business, now get out of here!"

As PS got into the subdivision the most horrific scene she'd ever witnessed was unraveling. Crystal Lake Estates was on fire.

On Hummingbird Lane, an entire stretch of mobile homes was ablaze. It looked as though a cluster bomb had been dropped decimating everything below. But in fact, a perfect storm of circumstances had gathered to create human disaster.

The fire started from the southwest section of the fairly rundown trailer park and was eating its way through several other units. And though the fire department had responded within minutes, little could be done to contain the fire or the desperate residents whose panic actually impeded the firefighting efforts.

PS could see that already, four trailers had been destroyed and fire had spread to a fifth unit upwind.

The blaze was scorching hot, and from where PS was watching she could tell there was very little water pressure coming from a hose being held by two firefighters while three others were kneeling down at a hydrant that appeared to have very little left to give.

PS backed her car up to a concrete divider that seemed to separate that particular mobile home park from a decidedly Jerry Springer-like trailer park one street over on Jacobee and Sunflower Court and jumped out of the vehicle to look for the photographer she had been told had gotten to the scene before her. That's when she saw the man with the long braid. He was standing on the opposite side of the street on Hummingbird Lane. He was watching her and smiling, which was odd in itself considering the frantic activity that surrounded him.

PS walked toward the man. Though he seemed detached she thought perhaps he was a family member or neighbor and wanted to do an interview. Maybe she'd met him in the past. Or perhaps he was just an idiot who didn't understand that people's lives were being ruined around him and rather than grabbing a bucket and pitching in, he wanted to shake her hand and tell her to make sure Barbara Bennett knows he said hello. Either way, PS was compelled to walk in his direction.

Just as she was about to cross the street, she was side-swiped by a rushing man with a soup-pot filled with spilling water, racing toward yet another trailer that had just burst into flames moments ago. She fell to *all fours*, as her eyes followed him down the street and she was shocked as she watched the flames lick up from the ramshackle roof and the embers curl as a wisp of wind whisked them onto the roof of the trailer next door where they seemed to sit and burn for a moment before a new plume of smoke rose, and curled before turning into yet a new fire.

Nearby neighbors ran from their homes with their own garden hoses, first trying to douse the flames of the burning unit, and then realizing what was happening, turning their hoses onto their own homes in hopes to wet them down and save them. Five minutes later, three more trailers were on fire.

By her count there were at least eight trailer homes fast ablaze.

A passing police officer hefted PS to her feet. "You okay?"

"Um, yeah," PS answered, brushing dirt and gravel from the knees of her blue jeans. "Thanks."

But she deflated when she saw her photographer trotting up.

"Hey Sylvester," PS groaned.

Why did it have to be Sylvester? He was slow and sloppy. If three people were getting shot on the corner, he wouldn't think to lift the camera and roll unless the reporter told him what to shoot. Add to that, his name was SYLVESTER!

PS began rubbing her shoulder vigorously.

"Are you okay?" He asked.

"Yeah. Thanks. Where'd you come from? Why aren't you shooting?"

"I just pulled in. I saw you pulling in on North, but there was a back up at the entrance so I had to find my own way in. Sorry I'm late." He said excitedly. "It looks like Armageddon in here!"

"Late?" PS asked. "The studio told me they sent you here long before they called me. That cop over there said you'd already checked in."

"Um, I kinda got lost. Sorry."

"Lost!! Why didn't you call the studio and ask directions? Why didn't you call me?"

"Oh, um, well. I forgot to put the phone on charge last night. I stopped a couple of times to look for a pay phone on the way up, but did you know pay phones don't exist anymore?"

"You haven't shot any video?" PS said, measuring her temper as best she could.

"I'm just getting here. I swear, I saw you pull in, but couldn't follow you."

"We've been diverting traffic offa' North Avenue, Miss Garrett. Too many gawkers and spectators," the police office said. "Sorry about that man," he said to Sylvester.

"No problem man, I know you guys are just doing your job. Thanks for getting me in that other entrance."

"Hey," the cop continued. "You're my favorite station. I'll help you any way I can. I gotta go, I just got radioed to get to the main entrance, it's getting backed up again. Miss Garrett, you're sure you're okay? Do you want me to call a paramedic over here to look at your knee?"

"No, officer...," PS looked at his badge. "Randallson. I appreciate it, but I'm fine."

"Okay, ma'am. You be careful. It's dangerous in here."

The officer walked across the street toward the main entrance.

"That's the first guy to try to pick you up in months isn't it?" Sylvester said laughing.

"Screw you SYLVESTER!" PS spat. "Let's get going, we have some catching up to do."

That's just what she needed was to spend the day with another dick named Sylvester.

"Why do we have catching up to do?" Sylvester asked. "There's no other media here, yet. The world is our oyster."

"You're kidding. You haven't seen any other stations here? Not even print?" PS asked. "Where'd you park?"

"Over there on West Boulevard. Good thing, easy in, easy out. Oh, and the cop on the corner told me they can't contain this thing. The hydrants aren't working. They can't control the fire. This is a Hell of a story, come on!"

Sylvester dashed down the road, his camera perched on his shoulder. He stopped, lowered it and peered inside the window on the side of the camera's canister and ran back to PS. "Hey, watch this for me, please."

"What are you doing? We have a fire here to cover."

"I forgot to put in a tape."

"You are effing kidding me, right? PS screamed out loud as she pulled out her cell phone and dialed the studio. Larry Pink picked up the phone.

"I can't believe you sent that idiot!" She hollered.

"PS, we didn't have anybody else. We needed to get someone to the fire fast."

"Larry, this guy is just getting here. He forgot to put a tape in the camera. He wouldn't know what to shoot if it tapped him on the shoulder."

"Com' on, PS. You're being over dramatic. He's not that bad. I've seen some of his stuff."

"LARRY!" PS screamed. "You people are killing me. I'm behind my deadline and I haven't even gotten started, yet."

"I can help you. I just talked to the sheriff's department."

"Okay. And...?"

Sylvester ran up huffing and puffing. He shoved the video cartridge into the waiting chamber.

It jammed.

He took it out and turned the cassette around in the proper direction, and it slid cooperatively into place. He lifted the camera to his shoulder and began to run toward the action.

"Sylvester!" PS yelled after him. "Turn on the camera. Roll as you run."

"Oh, good idea. Thanks. See you in the mix."

Sylvester dashed away toward the burning trailer.

"Don't say anything, PS. I know. We didn't have anybody else to send. I swear it. " Larry said on the other end of the line.

"Why does the union protect this guy? Wouldn't it be stronger if they didn't protect incompetence?"

"PS, I know you're frustrated, but this just isn't the time to get into a philosophical discussion."

"Larry, if I was that incompetent, you guys would fire me on the spot. Hell, you scream at me if I don't turn in my Chyrons!"

"PS, I'm not saying you're wrong. Just do the best you can."

"Larry, I never do the best I can. Ever."

"PS, lemme' give you some information. It might help you."

"Are there any fatalities, are there any injuries?"

She asked, taking note of a departing ambulance.

"I think so." Larry said. "But they're being a little cagey here. I know some people have been transported, I don't know what condition they're in. But I get the sense it's pretty bad."

PS trotted hurriedly toward the action, balancing her phone to her ear while also taking notes.. "Okay, now tell me something I can't see for myself."

Larry punched up his own notes on his computer screen. "I made some calls to some addresses nearby. Some of the neighbors tell me the trailer park is known as Little Mexico. A whole group of families are living down there, like they're own little commune. Obviously they're immigrants. Migrant workers. Aunts, uncles, cousins, the whole nine. I'm trying to call the hospital to get some conditions."

PS watched as Sylvester disappeared behind a throng of desperate firefighters, sweating, sooty, and nearly defeated.

She watched as another trailer caught fire, and then another. "Larry, this thing is really bad. I think you're going to have to send me another crew."

"I don't have anyone PS. You're it. I gotta live truck coming your way, but that's it. You're going to have to do the best you can do."

"Larry, I never do my best. Ever." PS said as she hung up.

And then PS heard a high pitched scream from the row of trailers behind the fire line on the other side of the concrete barrier.

She ran through the closest yard, climbing over the concrete divider.

A new fire had popped up, seemingly out of no where, in an entirely different trailer park.

As she ran toward the new flames, her heart raced. "Oh my God," she said out loud. "That's near my car!"

She ran even faster, but was overtaken by several firefighters who were sprinting in the direction of the fire.

This time the residents were still trapped inside.

Three firemen pulled a hose as far as they could and tried to coax more water from the nozzle. Another firefighter ran to the fire hydrant across the street from the burning unit on Sunflower. Two others were close behind with fresh hoses. They tried to attach them to the hydrant, and PS could see them struggling with the coupling . It was futile, and the firemen knew it. The tell-tale signs of sticks and an old tire iron told them that children had gotten to the hydrant first and broken the connection, likely on a hot day to open it up for fun. Today that cool summer shower would prove fatal, but the firefighters still struggled trying any way they could to screw that hose on.

Sylvester ran over to PS, damp with sweat and excitement. "Oh my God, this is bad. You won't believe the video I just shot!" He said.

"Of what?"

Sylvester began to speak but his words got caught in his throat with a tearful gurgle. "I can't say it right now. I don't even think we can use it. But I know you have at least one fatality."

"What?" PS said with a bit of a whine. "Nooooo."

"PS, I don't have any sound. We need to get some sound. I've been shooting nothing but video, but I don't have a single soundbite."

PS instinctively grabbed the microphone and headed for the first sobbing neighbor she could find. The live truck would be on the scene shortly and she knew that the studio would want to do break-in-programming coverage, since they were in sweeps.

PS ran up to the woman who was sobbing uncontrollably, sitting at the bottom of her wooden stairs on the side of a pale blue trailer. "What did you see? What did you see?" PS asked breathlessly keeping an eye on the burning trailer knowing that she couldn't afford to miss any action, but needing an interview just as badly. Sylvester too, kept an eye on the burning trailer behind him as he pressed the record button on the camera.

The woman's face was ashen. She was almost catatonic, but somehow managed to squeeze out the words, "His skin. His skin," she cried and then her eyes rolled back and she began to seize.

"Ma'am, are you okay?" PS asked dropping her microphone to steady the woman by the shoulders. She looked around for a paramedic to wave over realizing the woman needed medical attention more than Channel Six needed an interview.

The woman fixated on the sky with utterly unseeing eyes, and all she could gurgle was, "His skin. His skin."

An older man walked out of the trailer seemingly in shock, "Nanny, Nanny you okay?"

He ran to the woman and elbowed PS away as

he grabbed his wife. "I promise you, you don't want to show what we just seen. I promise you that," he said wiping tears from his eyes as he cradled his wife. She stopped shaking and the two held each other as they sobbed, overcome with emotion.

"What happened, Sir? Can you tell me?"

"Hernendez was a good man. He was a hard worker. I can't believe what I seen this morning, I can't believe it."

The man just stared off in the direction of the still burning trailer, unable to speak. He held his hands to his mouth and watched in horror.

PS realized that she had dropped the microphone on the ground and reached down to retrieve it so that she could do a quick interview while the couple seemed able to talk. As she raised the mic to the old man's face, she heard a loud shrill scream that trilled and hung in the air like a fog. It was followed by several other screams as neighbors started yelling, "They're still in there. The girls are still in there."

PS and her photographer leapt off the stoop and ran down the gravel road to the perimeter of the fire as firefighters were struggling to keep several neighbors from approaching the trailer which had now become a fireball.

Yet another shrill scream pierced the air, and PS held her hands to her ears. The screams were garbled and desperate and pitched so high, PS's brain could barely process the sound.

Two young girls were trapped in the back of the burning trailer.

The screams poured out of the mobile home in

Spanish, chilling the air against a fire so hot even the bravest firefighters couldn't force themselves to move any closer.

PS looked away, unable to watch. But instead her eyes fell upon emergency crews feverishly working on the stationary body of a man who was bloodied and blistered. At first, PS didn't even realize it was a human being. It resembled charred roof debris until she saw it, saw him, saw it thrashing a bit on the ground.

The trailer behind the man was smeared red with blood. The father of the two girls trapped in the burning trailer, lay at the foot of his neighbor's stairs, blood and more blood was coated on everything he'd touched. His skin, or what was left of it was still smoking as were the tips of his socks.

"What happened?" PS cried out in shock forgetting to turn her microphone on.

"He tried to get to his daughters," another neighbor cried as she ran up to hand the paramedics a clean white towel.

From somewhere very near death, the man on the ground heard the howls of his daughters and tried to get up.

The monstrous figure of what was left of a desperate father, actually got up off the concrete platform at the bottom of the trailer's stairs and hurled himself in the direction of the nearby flames.

PS screamed, and the emergency medical workers looked up, but couldn't catch him before he landed face down on the ground in a HARRUMPH. He raised his head in agony and looked toward his home that was now almost entirely engulfed in flames. He knew it was his eldest daughter, Marnia, who continued crying out as the flames licked closer to the corner she huddled in with her sister.

She yelled, "Dios Mio Salvanos, Dios Mio Salvanos." Dear God save us!

From out of nowhere, PS heard a screaming voice. "STOP DROP AND ROLL, STOP DROP AND ROLL!"

To her surprise the voice was hers, she didn't even realize at first her lips were moving. They had gone on autopilot as the reporter became a horrified participant instead of a journalist.

Neighbors were running up to the trailer with buckets and coffee pots of water, tossing them on to the flames to no avail. The firefighters had brought in a tanker truck filled with water, but couldn't get it down the street, because several curious on-lookers had blocked the road with their vehicles. The three firefighters who were first trying to activate the closest hydrant were now yelling and kicking at it.

It was pandemonium.

The fire became hungrier, and the flames licked high in the air as they consumed the roof and then continued to approach the two screaming young women inside. As the flames lapped at their skin, the screams became more shrill and desperate, as Marnia began begging, "Dios Mio Naslo pronto!" Dear God, make it quick.

A large burly man in boxer shorts and a torn T-shirt, managed to break past the brigade of firefighters and police officers who were holding the yelling neighbors at bay. He had a rake in his hand and he was heading for what was left of the back of the trailer.

A firefighter standing at the front of the unit saw him out of the corner of his eye and raced toward the neighbor yelling, "No, don't!" But his sprint was broken by debris laying on the ground and the firefighter fell—the wind knocked out of him as he shielded his head and helmet instinctively with his arms, knowing what would happen next.

It was too late.

With one throw of the rake javelin, the neighbor, desperate to give the young girls inside a way out, broke the back window of the mobile home. In a flash he was thrown back when a wall of flames, whooshed through the trailer—consuming what was left of the mobile home and the small remaining living space of Marnia and her sister. The flames, starved for oxygen had found the fuel they needed and licked angrily out the, now, broken window. The back-draft was swift and deadly. And in a flash the screaming ceased.

The tanker finally made it down to the burning trailer, and firefighters immediately started spraying water to douse the flames.

There was silence for a moment, but then another loud shrill scream came from the other side of the trailer, as the only surviving member of the immigrant family began to wail.

An old woman, with deep lines in her olive face was inconsolable as she screamed in Spanish. The paramedics had just thrown a sheet over her husband's body as it lay feet away from the burning trailer. She knew her daughters were gone. She'd listened to them die. A bilingual police officer walked up and embraced the woman from behind to steady her for the news that her son, had died on his way to the hospital.

The woman's knees buckled and she fell to the ground with deep throaty sobs that filled the air.

"I bet they just told her Hernendez is dead," a man's voice said hoarsely from behind PS.

"Hernendez?" She asked as she turned around and saw that she was facing the man she had been talking to earlier, several trailers down. "Who's Hernendez?"

"Their son. He tried to get into the trailer to save his sisters. He tried three times. The third time, he was burned so badly, my wife and I tried to hold him back."

The man held out his hands. They were recently scrubbed rough and raw. "His skin came off in our hands," the man said as he placed his outstretched hands to his face and began to sob.

"Sir, I know this is a bad time to ask, and please accept my apologies, but it's my job. Do you mind if I do an interview with you?"

"I can't. I can't right now. Come back tomorrow and ask. But not now. I just seen stuff that no one should see," he said as he walked away crying.

PS walked around trying to get people to talk about what they had just witnessed, but what few English speaking residents who were there either didn't want to talk or were too traumatized.

She approached several immigrants to try to get something—anything. Even in their shock and grief, they were gracious. But not one of them spoke a word of English.

PS wandered the scene for another five minutes, looking for someone who could say anything about this family. In bits and pieces from camera shy neighbors with broken English, she gathered that the family had come to Michigan from Mexico and worked as migrant cherry pickers, gardeners, and kitchen help in various golf clubs around town.

It was a hard working, tight knit family who were ideal neighbors in every way.

PS continued to wander the scene with her cameraman, trying to be sensitive, herself in shock, but on autopilot working to get anybody who saw anything to say something on camera.

As more immigrants arrived in broken-down cars and rusty trucks, PS's frustration mounted. She needed soundbites, but she couldn't communicate with anyone. "Sylvester?" She asked. "You don't speak any Spanish?"

"Just bon jour," he said.

"Sylvester, that's French."

"Well, if we get a truck load of French cherry pickers in here, we're in business."

The Channel Three live van sped up to the scene, and screeched to a halt behind the tanker truck. A Ford Explorer with big red and blue writing that said, Channel 3, Live at 5, came to a fast halt, just behind the van.

Out stepped Sherman Hall and his cameraman, Manuel. They had missed everything. They missed the fire, the frantic race to try to save the two young girls, the screaming and the pandemonium.

With a slim sense of relief, even though PS had

no interviews, she was gratified in knowing that Channel Three would have even less.

The only thing Sherman Hall would have was aftermath video, and steam as it rose from the skeletal remains of the mobile home that had finally and futilely been doused with water.

But to her surprise, Sherman and his photographer walked over to the grieving widow who was surrounded by a wall of fellow Mexican immigrants. Manuel spoke to a large Hispanic man who had been bent over the sobbing woman. The two shook hands, and Manuel patted him on the shoulder. And then, to PS's horror—with his camera on his shoulder and a microphone in his hand, Manuel began speaking to the woman in Spanish.

Sherman leaned over his cameraman's shoulder and fed him questions, which Manuel repeated in Spanish, and then translated into the microphone.

PS and Sylvester walked quickly over to where the Channel Three crew was, but weren't allowed to approach them. At Manuel's request, several very large immigrant workers had been quickly dispatched to stop the Channel Six crew.

This was the heat of battle. Reporters lived and died by the interviews they scored. It was, at the end of the day, a competition. And all PS could do was stand there and watch the other station get the story, from the mouth of the only surviving victim of the fire.

That night, Channel Three had a riveting news story to air. The sobbing widow spoke in Spanish, and told how she had been watching the other fires from her back window and walked away to tell her children to get out. Within moments her own trailer was on fire.

Another neighbor from one of the first units to catch fire explained in Spanish that he smelled gasoline and had walked outside to investigate, only to see the corner of his trailer ablaze. Manuel's voice translated the entire interview.

The woman described how she and her husband tried to save their daughters. They didn't even know their eldest son, Hernendez had come home. He must have arrived sometime after the fire had already started.

The men in the family died trying to save the women. And now all was lost, because she had lost everything, her family, her home, her green cards and documentation, along with what little money the family had that was tucked beneath a mattress in the front room.

The woman talked about wanting to bury her family back in Mexico, but she didn't know how she would find the money.

PS watched the Channel Three story on the monitor in the back of her own microwave truck. It was poignant, and moving and well written. Sherman had done a good job mixing facts and details in with the voice of his photographer who translated each word with great emotion.

PS sat in the back of the truck and cried. She cried because she had nothing on tape to tell the personal story of a family that had suffered an immeasurable loss. The only interview she had was a sterile police-speak dissertation from the fire inspector who said the fires were likely arson. She cried because she couldn't use three quarters of the video Sylvester had shot, because it was too graphic and violent to be shown on commercial television. She cried because almost an entire family had been wiped out. Eleven other families had lost their homes and everything they owned. They had come to this country for a better life, and this is what they got. She cried because she ached for the woman who would first, have to beg for money and then accompany the bodies of her three children and her husband across the country to be buried in their homeland.

She cried because just a few short weeks ago, the fate of that poor immigrant family could have been her own fate as she fought to escape Allen George's burning apartment.

And she cried because she had seen things that day that no one should ever see.

When PS Garrett got home that evening, kicking Allen George out of her home was the last thing on her mind.

Several weeks after the fire at Crystal Lake Estates, the car issue with Allen George had still gone unresolved. He'd given up using his sister's car, and instead was now tooling around town in PS's full time.

The two had slipped into a new routine. He would insist on driving her to work, disappear in her car and pick her up at the end of the day.

More than once he was late picking her up. The

first time he was late it was only by about fifteen minutes. The second time it was by more than forty minutes.

And then there was another uncomfortable routine that had developed. PS had become paper and Allen was her glue. Outside of work, he went everywhere with her. It was as if he couldn't bear to have her out of his direct sight.

One hot mid-June Saturday the two went shopping—actually PS went shopping and Allen tagged along.

Even though Allen went to work every morning, he never seemed to have any real money on hand. It was always tied up in some sort of business venture, or someone in his family had run into financial difficulty and needed a few bucks to tide them over.

Paydays would come and go, Allen had been in PS's home for a month and a half, and he never offered to help with the mortgage, never offered to buy any groceries, and never seemed to have more than a twenty dollar bill on him.

The few times Allen convinced PS to go out, he no longer bothered with the charade of pulling out his wallet. He just didn't pay. PS hadn't seen him pull out a credit card in weeks.

On that hot June Saturday, the reporter needed something to buoy her spirits so she decided to go shopping. A new dress and apartment fumigation was just what the doctor ordered. The new dress, of course, being the immediate solution.

She had planned to go out alone. What a shift!

It was Saturday and PS Garrett actually wanted to be alone.

As she walked out the door, Allen ran out of the guest room, pulling a crisp white knit tee over his head and hastily tucking it into his slacks. He sat on her sofa slipping on lambskin loafers, and said that he was thinking about getting out early himself.

It had gotten impossible to go anywhere outside of work without Allen George by her side. If she raised her voice or gave a stern look, Allen would always sweet talk her out of her anger. He was a master conversationalist. Always seemed to know what angle to play and when. And he had become the woman's goddamned shadow.

They went to the mall. PS tried on a few dresses, and settled on a little black and white number with ultra thin vertical stripes. She liked it when she looked in the mirror—it made her look thinner. She hoped it would look as nice on television.

She paid for the dress, and joined Allen who was waiting for her outside the store in the mall.

When she walked up to him, he gave her a half hearted peck on the cheek and hurried ahead.

PS slowed down and allowed him to get some distance ahead of her, and for the first time she took a good look at how he walked.

He had a wide gait. His legs shot out from his hips with each step. His body shifted deeply from side to side, and he swung his arms swiftly as he walked. It was almost as if his arms were his ballast and if he didn't use them he would topple over.

He disappeared into a men's store for a few min-

303

utes, and by the time she made it to the shop's entrance he bobbed out, and darted in front of her again. This time when he walked—he walked erect. His gait was smooth and easy, and casual. His steps were measured. He had his hands stashed in his pockets and he barely shifted from side to side as he had just a few minutes before.

Had Willina seen the man in front of her at that moment, she would have likely said he's a successful business man with a lot on his mind and cash in his pocket. PS chuckled at that idea and kept observing.

Allen's walk had already melted into a jaunt. He was on the balls of his feet, and with each step— sprung up from his knees. He looked like a punk, looking for a purse to grab.

PS followed him into a picture store, where he began sizing up paintings.

He sifted through a couple of pre-framed pieces of art, and settled on a rather large painting of flowers. It had a beautiful gold leaf frame, but it didn't look like something he'd be interested in, and it didn't match anything in her condo.

"Ummmmm. This is the one," he said as he gently licked his lips in approval. "What do you think?"

"I think it's okay," PS answered.

"Look at those flowers, look how they just pop right out at you. It almost looks as if they're real doesn't it?" Allen continued.

Without question, that painting was not something she'd buy for herself. But this was the first time Allen was offering to contribute something to the household. She didn't want to discourage him so she agreed, "Yeah, it's a pretty picture."

"Yeah, I think so too. And it's only twenty-eight dollars. Perfect."

Allen put the picture down, and pulled out his wallet.

PS was stunned. She didn't really know if he owned a wallet anymore, it had been so long since she'd seen it.

He flipped around a few bills, there was his customary twenty, she could see a five and some ones. He pulled out what he had and looked at PS "I'm going to be a few dollars short."

"Well then I guess you'll have to buy a less expensive gift for the apartment," she replied in a condescending way.

"Apartment?" He exclaimed. "This isn't for the apartment. A friend of mine just bought her first house, and I thought it would be nice to give her a house warming present."

PS fell dumb. This man who'd been living in her home for almost two months, hadn't raised a finger to pay for so much as a gallon of milk—was standing in front of her asking for a few dollars so he could buy some other woman a present. And what's more, he saw nothing wrong with it.

PS looked at him as though he had grown a third eye on his forehead and said, "Have you lost your mind?"

She then turned on her heels and walked out of the store. Allen followed behind her. Without the picture of course.

PS had nothing to say to Allen George the remainder of the weekend. She spent the time asking herself over and over again, *What the Hell is wrong with you? Why is this man still in your house?*

The answer was on the mantle of her gas fireplace. Two pictures. One of Fido, and one of Danny.

For his part, Allen tried his best to ease the palpable tension with PS. He cooked dinner, asked what she wanted to watch on television, and was very careful to pick up after himself—for a change. He sat close to her on the sofa, pretending to brush imaginary ants off her hands, but that hadn't worked in weeks.

PS simply turned off the television, walked into her bedroom, closed the door and locked it.

She had become a prisoner in her own home.

The following Monday, before she could protest, Allen said he had a very important meeting so he'd have to drop her off at work early. When she raised her voice to protest he quickly included that he was about to close a really big account that would mean a hefty cash bonus that could mean a deposit on an apartment of his own.

Since PS was in favor of anything that would put money in his pocket and expedite his departure, once again she bit her tongue.

She put on her new cotton dress, slid on her Black pumps grabbed a blazer and walked out into the breezeway to get into her car that was waiting for her at the stoop with Allen in the driver's seat.

When they got downtown, PS opened her own door and hurried into the studio without looking back. "Reptile!" She spat as she disappeared into the studio.

She sat down at her desk, but Bill Thorn the managing editor was waiting for her and motioned her to walk over to the assignment desk. "We've got a real weird story for you today," he said.

"No weirder than the one I could tell," she muttered under her breath.

Bill continued. "It seems some farmer lost his herd of one-hundred-eighty-three prize Guernsey's three days ago."

"Are you kidding me?" The reporter asked Bill in disbelief.

"No seriously. And we're real high on this story."

"What the Hell do we care if a farmer has lost his cows? What news market do you think this is? Amarillo, Texas?"

"No!" A voice blurted out from behind her. "It's Detroit, Michigan."

It was Salina Kingsley.

"And in this market we cover news," she continued. "And news is whatever we say it is."

"You know, Salina," PS replied turning around so that she was nearly nose to nose with the only person in the newsroom who wasn't taller than she. "You're wrong. News isn't what you say it is. Or do you not subscribe to the philosophy of Edward R. Murrow? In fact do you even know who Murrow was? That's Murrow, not Marlboro."

Salina moved her face even closer so that the two women were now within breathing space of each other. She was so close, as she spoke, PS could taste the faint smell of stale coffee, a thirty-minute-ago smoke and a ten-seconds-old peppermint candy on her breath. "You know what your problem is?"

"Yeah, I do," PS interrupted. "It's you. Now back up, Salina. You're barking up the wrong tree today. If you get any closer, this will get personal instead of professional."

"Ladies, ladies," Bill said in a voice the two had heard many times before as he'd broken up the squabbles between them. "Lighten up, girls. The truth of the matter is, it's a slow news day. And we can either go to Southwest Detroit to cover the cat that got hit by a car last night, or we can go check out this cow story."

"Bill, I told you guys that I wanted to work on the story at my apartment complex. I think we might have some kids out there doing animal sacrifices. It's really creepy stuff, and I think it will lead the newscast."

"Not my newscast," Salina said.

Are you kidding me? You love this kind of shit, Salina. Had anyone else suggested the story, you'd be all over it."

"Well, that's besides the point. I'm not interested in a few rabbits and squirrels turning up dead. It's probably a fox. You live in the boonies anyway. I think you just want to be close to home for your evening live shots."

"PS," Bill jumped in. "We'll call Animal Control and check out your story, but we need you to get going on this one. It's not nearby at all. Besides, I think it's a real unusual human interest story and we want it for the 5 o'clock news.

"Now I know you keep spare clothes in your car, you have a few minutes to change. Get going will ya?"

Salina jumped in. "No Bill, maybe we should send her to the story where the cat got ran over by the car."

"Run, Salina."

"Excuse me?"

"Run!" PS shouted.

"Are you threatening me?"

"No Salina," the reporter sighed in contempt. "I'm correcting you. It's, 'let's send her to the story where the cat was **run** over, not **ran** over.' If you're going to produce a newscast, learn to speak English properly would you?"

PS turned and walked out of the newsroom and muttered beneath her breath, "And get a better breath mint while you're at it."

Salina made her life miserable. But she made hers miserable too, so they were even. Dead even.

PS never knew what her assignment was going to be from one day to the next, so she always kept a pair of blue jeans, hiking boots, and a T-shirt in her trunk.

That practice had saved her on more than one occasion. There was nothing worse than being sent out on an assignment that you weren't dressed for. A flood in a mini-skirt would be a no no. Being choppered to a manhunt in a crepe suit—garment suicide. And since she was on her way to Old McDonald's Farm to investigate the missing cow caper, she preferred not to do it in her brand new dress and black pumps.

PS was still steaming when she got to the third level where she'd parked her car in the same place for years. She meandered on auto-pilot to the designated space, and it wasn't there. She looked around in confusion. Who in the heck could get into a private garage to take a car? She felt a surge of panic, as she backed up to the elevator to ride down to the guard shack to report her car missing. She decided to walk down instead, just in case she had mistakenly parked it on a different level. She slowly walked passed her empty parking space and was halfway to the next lower level when it hit her. She didn't have her car that day. She hadn't had her car in days. Allen George had her car, and her spare clothes, too.

She stood in the garage for a few extra seconds to compose herself before returning to the newsroom in her brand new black and white, vertical striped dress to tell the assignment editor and Simone Lagree that she'd have to cover the story as she was.

She went back to assignment desk. Bill Thorn was not happy to see her standing there in her *church* clothes. "Is that what you're wearing?"

"Yes. I forgot, I loaned my car to a friend, so this is it. Either you send another reporter, or I go out like this."

Larry Pink who'd been working the scanners most of the morning chimed in. "I don't have another reporter to send," he said. "I'm sorry kid, you're it."

Salina smirked from her perch not far from the assignment desk, snorted a snooty sniff and walked pompously back to her chair.

"Okay, fine." It couldn't get any worse than this. "Larry, who's my cameraman?" PS asked.

"Brett. He's gearing up now."

Correction. It could get worse. It just did.

Brett was one of those photographers, who likes you one day and loathes the very air you breathe the next. There's no reason for his rollercoastering disdain, it all seems to be a matter of which way the wind was blowing. Or maybe it was hormones. That's it! PS thought to herself. Maybe Brett is going through the change—kind of a male menopause.

Whatever the reason, reporters never knew whether this particular crew member liked them or disliked them until they stepped into his microwave truck.

As PS climbed into the van, sat down and pulled the door shut, Brett sucked his teeth.

"What?" PS sneered.

"Nothing," Brett sneered back.

"All I did was get into the van. Why is that something to get an attitude about?"

"I didn't say anything," Brett defended.

"No, you did say something. You huffed, like a spoiled brat, because I deign to get into your van to do my fucking job!" PS screamed.

The other thing about this particular photographer was, if you out-bitched him, you stood a chance of having a better day.

When PS looked over at him, to return the sigh, she saw Allen's face.

Her eyes narrowed, and her heart rate quickened with the disgust of what she was seeing. If Brett wanted a quarrel, he'd get a war.

The designation of power had been completed for the day. Whatever it is that gives someone an edge over people one day, and makes them emotional minions the next had been cast. PS was the victor. She was too pissed off not to be.

"You got something else to say, or do I need to make your day extra miserable, buddy?"

Instead of dragging the shenanigans farther, Brett just engaged the ignition and pulled out of his parking space—burning rubber.

A crappy crew person could make the difference between being competitive and simply keeping the commercials from bumping into each other—with garbage. The partnership in news is just that fragile and important.

"But then, who has to be friends? Why unite in the common goal of beating the competition when you can be a shit-head. Right?" PS said, under her breath.

Brett just ignored her.

CHAPTER TWELVE

On their way to Vernon, a small farming community just outside the State capital, PS was suffering. It was barely summer and it had already been long and hot. It was unusually warm for a Michigan June day. The thermometer on a bank building the live van whizzed by said eighty-seven degrees—and the humidity had to be right up there, too.

PS was hungry, parched, and she could feel her pantyhose sweating in the crotch.

"Brett," she finally said after languishing for about twenty-five miles. "We have to stop. I need something to eat, please."

"Why didn't you eat at home like the rest of us?" Brett said in his usual wise-guy tone of voice.

"Does it really matter?" PS snapped impatiently and in agony. Her fuel light had been flashing for more than two dozen miles. "Damn it to Hell! Come on, give me a break would you?" Then she gasped slightly under her breath, "What an asshole. What-an-asshole!"

A deep sigh escaped her chest like a semi truck blowing out exhaust. She looked up to the heavens to make a silent prayer for strength, and decided if Brett didn't stop this crap, the cops would be wise to meet them in Vernon with handcuffs so that she could be rightfully hauled away for murder. She then slowly turned her head toward Brett and spat in a low, slow, laboring, take-no-crap-voice, "Let's just pull off this exit,

I'll run into a fast food place and grab something quick. Why do you always have to be such a creep?"

Brett recoiled as if he'd been struck. He actually seemed genuinely hurt. "I'm sorry. I didn't know I was being a creep. I just asked a question. I don't think there's a fast food place between here and Vernon. If we were going to stop, we should have done it closer to town that's all," Brett paused for a moment and then added, "But I think I know where there's a mom and pop grocery not far from here, we can hit that."

"Fine," PS huffed.

As they pulled off the exit, about thirty-five miles from Vernon, her heart stopped. Surely Brett wasn't going where she thought he was going.

The reporter wrapped her fingers tightly around the van arm rest, and held on so tightly her knuckles ached. In her headachy fog, she looked around to try and confute her surroundings. But she couldn't. It was obvious. They were in Pixley, and the only mom and pop grocery PS Garrett knew about was the Gas 'N Go where two kids had been murdered more than five months ago.

Sure enough, Brett pulled into the parking lot of the Gas 'N Go, only it was no longer called the Gas 'N Go. Now it was called Aunt Millie's Deli and Quick Stop.

PS turned to Brett, green with hunger sickness. He couldn't possibly have been this cruel deliberately. This kind of evil wasn't planned, it was stumbled over.

As they pulled into the parking lot, Brett commented, "Oh, they changed the name. I wonder if there are new owners?"

PS didn't say anything. Hunger and whatever else was ailing her pushed her out of the van and toward the front door. If she wanted to eat—and she needed to, this was it.

It was agony, on top of agony, on top of agony.

The young woman pushed open the door of the little shop, and metal bells attached to the springs announced her arrival. She felt butterflies in her stomach as she crossed the threshold, searching for traces of blood or bone on the floor as she walked. She surveyed the store and tried to visualize where that poor fifteen-year-old girl, Tammy, had lain in a pool of blood—a bullet hole in her head and a defense wound on her wrist. She squinted her eyes and thought she could see where the girl's sixteen-year-old boyfriend, Danny had fallen behind the counter. She looked up at the plate glass window. Of course those bloody letters that said *Watch, Watch* had long since been scrubbed away.

This was the first time she'd been in the shop.

The place gave her the creeps, but she was going into hunger shock and her will for survival propelled her further into the store toward the deli counter. As she walked cautiously and haltingly, she wondered who would reopen this shop. Surely Aunt Millie, or whoever she is, knew the history. PS wondered if she was serving cold cuts where the police chalk drawings had been. She looked over at the plate glass window. Had it been replaced or just scrubbed clean when the man with the new stick on letters showed up?

She stopped at the snack section. It was dusty

315

and unkept. She reached for a box of Fig Newtons and tiny dust bunnies jumped up out of their burrows and floated gently back down like delicate angels to hide in the crap piled high upon the shelf.

PS decided she wasn't in the mood for cookies after all, and kept going.

As she got to the counter, she could see that it, too, looked a little unsanitary. She veered away and headed for the refrigerated section instead. There was very little to choose from, so she opted for a single serving of macaroni salad and a Mountain Dew. It was hardly a healthy breakfast, but it would have to do in a pinch.

She paid for her purchases without even a hello or goodbye and left that awful place, she hoped, forever.

She got back in the van and was so hungry she inhaled the food and quickly washed it down with the soda. She'd eaten so fast, she developed a little heartburn that started as a lump in her chest. She continued pounding the Mountain Dew in hopes that somehow she would dislodge whatever was burning a hole in her esophagus.

That went on for forty more minutes, as they zipped up the highway toward Vernon.

As the News Six truck pulled into the farmyard of the man with the missing cows, PS had run out of soda and her heartburn had turned to wildfire. She tried to squeeze out a few belches before jumping out of the live truck, but only managed a few gurgles.

An ulcer, she thought to herself. I must have developed an ulcer.

She pulled a newspad out of her reporter's bag and pretended it didn't hurt. She paused for a few seconds more. Brett didn't bother waiting or inquiring about whether she was alright. He walked around to the passenger side of the remote truck, and opened the sliding door just behind her. He reached for his camera, cradled in its protective box, mumbled something to the reporter about watching her step when she stepped out of the van, shut the door and walked a few feet away from the vehicle and stood.

As PS stepped out of the van—there on the ground was the biggest, thickest, widest pile of dog shit she'd ever seen in her adult life.

She tried to stop her foot in mid-stride, but it was already spiraling toward the water-logged mound.

Divert, divert! Danger Will Robinson!

The jerky motion made her lose her balance and she felt herself tumbling out of the van, face first—heading toward a fresh pile of poop.

It was Hell incarnate!

"Uhhhhg! I'm gonna hurl! I'm gonna hurl! Oh my God."

"Huh? You say something?" A voice piped in from just beyond the van.

PS snapped out of it.

"You say something to me?" A voice mumbled again.

"Uh, no Brett, I was just thinking out loud."

She shook her head and checked behind her. She was still in the vehicle, her hind quarters still planted firmly on the seat. Her imagination and illness were playing vertigo on her. *Thank God*, she thought to herself, grateful she'd heard Brett's half-hearted warning in the recesses of her mind. "Eww, Yuck!" She squealed, as she jumped gingerly out of the van, clearing the pile of poop.

" I told you to watch your step," Brett muttered from where he stood near the van.

Thank goodness, PS thought to herself. *Today he really does like me.*

She needed a drink. She needed a lot of drinks.

Also waiting for her exit was a hayseed appropriately clad in denim coveralls, a plaid short-sleeved shirt, and a baseball cap advertising some sort of cattle feed.

"It's a scorcher, ain't it?" He greeted.

As the reporter stepped to the soft farm soil and sank a half inch in her pumps, the humidity slapped her hard in the face. She felt a little woozy, but talked herself out of swooning, and extended her hand to the young farmer and introduced herself.

"Yeah, I know who you are. I watch you guys all the time. Hey, didn't they tell you you was coming out here? You're hardly dressed for the occasion," he snickered good naturedly.

PS ignored the comment, still smarting over the fact that Allen George had her car with the sneakers and blue jeans in the back. "So what's this about you missing some cows?" She asked as professionally as she could, feigning great interest.

"Well, actually they're my uncle's cows. They disappeared three days ago during that big electrical storm. When those thunder-boomers moved in, it wasn't time to milk them so they was still out to pasture. I guess they got spooked and ran off when the storm hit.

"We haven't seen them since."

Brett had pulled out the camera and handed PS the microphone. She instructed the cameraman to go ahead and start rolling and urged the young farmer on. "Aren't you worried?" She asked.

"Oh very worried. Those ain't just any cows. Those are blue ribbon Guernseys who've won top honors at the state fair the last five years in a row."

"Yeah?" PS asked, forgetting her own pain, and becoming mildly interested in the story. "What makes 'em such great cows?"

"They've been bred special. They're beautiful animals. Ever see a cow up close?"

"Of course," she answered with a little indignation. "I'm not a complete city slicker."

The farmhand chuckled, sizing the reporter up in her pinstriped dress and shiny black high heeled shoes. "Of course you have, I didn't mean nothing by that. I just meant to say, I bet you've never seen a cow like these. They're big, extra big. And you know what udders are, don't you?"

PS nodded her head.

"The udders are this big," the young farmer cupped his hands and held them out far beyond either side of his head.

"Well, how the heck do you lose one hundred eighty-three prize Guernseys?" PS asked.

"Good question. It's a big place. We have several pastures that stretch for miles..."

The farmhand's explanation was cut short by

the sound of an approaching tractor and screaming and yelling. The young man turned and ran in the direction of the noise. Instinctively, Brett and the reporter ran after him.

As they caught up to the tractor which had stopped, they could see an older man with tan leathered skin gesturing wildly. Tears streamed down his face and he was yelling something indistinct about his herd.

Within minutes, Brett and PS found themselves on a flat bed trailer of the tractor for a bumpy four mile ride in the hot sun to a pasture far, far away.

The sun was beating down on them, and PS could feel herself sweating beneath her cotton dress. As the tractor negotiated bumps, bends and craters— she could feel her stomach starting to churn again.

Beads of sweat began to form behind her ears and she could feel the curl in her hair starting to sag and swell. She swatted at some sort of buzzing insect that she couldn't see but could hear as it serenaded her. She would swat at it, it would disappear—only to return.

She would swat it again.

Brett was soaked, and several times pulled out a cloth handkerchief from his back pocket to wipe his brow, face and neck. A few droplets of sweat rained down on his camera, and he wiped those away with his hand. He pulled at the short-sleeved shirt that was clinging embarrassingly to his body.

Finally the tractor came to a halt at a clearing. The news crew could hear the growl of another farm vehicle coming through the woods not far behind them.

And about five-hundred feet away she could see another large tractor-like vehicle hard at work.

It was some sort of large earth moving machine furiously digging at a long dried up creek bed. She could only see the top of the bucket, with its large teeth scooping up earth and piling it along the edges of the natural trench.

The work crew, with their heavy equipment were neighboring farmers who had come quickly after a call from Farmer Sabring when he discovered his herd.

PS prepared to climb down from the flat bed, careful not to snag her pantyhose in the process. The old farmer had already jumped off his tractor and was there to help her to the ground. "I am James Sabring. That's my nephew, Dave," the farmer gestured to the young farmhand PS had been speaking to earlier.

"Mr. Sabring, this is my partner Brett. Thanks for calling us this morning, can you tell me what's going on?"

Mr. Sabring began to talk but his words tumbled out of his mouth in deep sobs. "My cows. My cows."

Farmer Sabring tried to composed himself, and then led them to the top of the hill the other tractors had disappeared behind.

When they got to the top of the berm they could see a trench that looked to be about a hundred feet long, and it was already as deep as the deep end of a swimming pool.

The farmer pointed to another hill five hundred feet or so from the newly dug trench. There was a large tree, or rather, what was left of it.

From where the news crew was standing, PS could see the fresh white bark of the tree that had obviously been sliced in half. Judging by the telltale black singes around the edges of the tree it was clear it had been the victim of a lightning strike.

Beneath the tree, the vague outlines of what appeared to be one hundred eighty-three prize Guernsey cows.

"Are they dead?" The reporter asked. She knew the answer, but the sight was just so stunning she regressed to a three-year-old.

"You can't tell because you're upwind of this breeze. But they're dead," the farmer whimpered as he wiped his face with his shirt and stared off in the direction of his decimated herd. "They must have gathered around that tree when the storm hit three days ago. They would do that when it rained or got chilly. Just huddle together for safety.

"It looks to me as though the lightning hit the tree and electrocuted them all."

"How's this?" A voice yelled up from the ever deepening pit. They barely heard it over the noise of the machinery chewing up the ground.

"Why don't you get started on the far west end, and let Adams keep working on the other end," Mr. Sabring yelled back, pulling himself together a bit.

Dave, flashed the A-OK sign with his right hand, gave his emotional uncle a reassuring hug and then chomped up the trench toward the herd.

Mr. Sabring then moved the crew closer to the

edge of the trench. Brett lifted his camera to his shoulder and began rolling tape. Now this was a worthwhile story.

They stood at the edge of the deep crater that had been dug, and watched as Dave used the front end loader to cart the first member of the herd to the edge of the open pit.

With a nudge, the animal's carcass fell to the bottom of the hole with an incredibly disturbing thud. He then backed up his farm vehicle to return for another.

"Isn't there anything you can do with them?" PS asked.

"No. They're fried. They've been laying out here in ninety degree plus weather for three days."

Again, Dave hauled a carcass to join its herd mate. Again, an unearthly thud rang out as the cow fell into the trench and on top of the remains of the cow already at peace at the bottom of the pit.

The next cow brought down the hill wasn't rolled or pushed. Dave had scooped it up in the bucket of his backhoe.

The animal was so large that only its mid-section fit in the bucket. Its front legs stuck straight up in the air with the stiffness of advanced rigor mortis. Its head bobbed lifelessly as the vehicle bumped down the hill. Its mouth hung open and its tongue, which licked up on the side of the dead animal's bobbing head, was green.

Dave dumped the cow onto the other two that were at the bottom of the pit, and this time when she fell atop them, her udder—which had swollen and bloated in the sun for three days—popped. Instead of curdled milk, a thick yellow pus oozed on top of the other cows.

That's when the macaroni salad in PS Garrett's stomach from breakfast began to speak up again.

She didn't remember when, but the two men in the pit had been joined by three others. She had been standing at the edge of the trench in a foggy stupor for some time. All of the workers wore bandannas around their faces to cover their noses. She could see that even Brett had wrapped his handkerchief around his face as he shot video from the far west end of the trench.

All of a sudden the breeze shifted. And the young woman was standing downwind of the carnage. The smell of one hundred eighty-three prize Guernsey's decomposing in the hot sun, slapped her in the face like a Mack truck. It caught her in mid inhale.

It was sickening sweet and foul. The air was thick with insects and stench. She felt her consciousness slipping, and the hot blue sky suddenly started turning black. She could feel her knees buckling under the weight of her body, and the macaroni salad she had for breakfast began scorching its way up her esophagus.

As her body swayed, and her knees gave way beneath her, she felt herself falling in the cow pasture. She began thinking to herself, *Oh my God I'm going to fall face first in bullshit.*

Not fully understanding the forces of good that swooped down to save her, without any deliberate effort on her part, she felt her body snap up straight.

When she realized that her new dress would be spared, she decided she'd seen enough.

She limped back to the flatbed of the tractor she'd rode in on, pulled her knees up to her chest and buried her head in her hands, and waited for the farmer and the photographer to return.

The story turned out to be the lead story on the 5 and 6 o'clock news. And PS Garrett never ate macaroni salad again. In fact the mere smell of it makes her stomach boil.

The one speck of good news for the day was, the live truck was out of range in Vernon, and the Satellite truck had been committed to a sports story on the other side of the state. So at least, PS could deliver her story from the comfort of an air conditioned newsroom with a clean bathroom nearby.

She was still queasy as she walked away from the newsroom camera and saw Peter heading her way.

She felt so close to death at that point she feared any conversation with him might push her over the edge. Besides, it was already 6:15 and Allen would be waiting for her in front of the station.

She ducked out the back of the newsroom, and walked the corridor to re-enter from the front. She still had to grab her reporter's bag from her desk otherwise she would have just kept on walking toward the front door.

As she rounded the corner and walked into the newsroom, she bumped head on into Peter, Peter the hour eater—the man most likely to make you want to slit your wrist with a rusty razor blade—and of course he wanted to discuss the story she'd just finished.

325

Her head was spinning, and she was in a stomach-ache induced daze. She wanted to throw up, but didn't think there was anything left to vomit. Peter's voice was ringing, and ringing, and ringing in her ear. It sounded like the gong of a tug boat at close range. Lights were flickering, and the failing young reporter could see dots before her eyes. Finally she couldn't take it anymore. "Stop!" She shouted. "Staaaaaaaaaaaaahhhhhhhhhhp! Pete, I guess you didn't notice, but I've had a pretty rough day. Can you imagine what it was like looking at those dead animals, and hearing them go thud at the bottom of a pit?"

She place great emphasis on the word, thud so it was spat, more than spoken. "I know you can't imagine the smell because you don't leave the building. I only wish we had smellavision so you, too, could experience it.

"Pete, I wanted to die. I wish I could have, particularly when I got back to the studio and vomited up everything I'd eaten in the last two days.

"You don't know this, Pete, because you haven't let me get a word in edgewise. Well, Pete, I have a ride waiting for me outside the studio. I'm already thirty minutes late. Fifteen minutes ago, I was only fifteen minutes late, but you've been yapping at me for fifteen minutes, so now I'm thirty minutes late.

"Geez Pete, I hate to be rude, but did it ever occur to you that I might want to get the Hell out of here?"

She didn't wait for an answer. She didn't care to hear one. She snatched her arm loose from Peter's grip and stormed over to her desk. She grabbed her reporter's bag and walked to the back of the newsroom, and down the hallway to the front of the station.

She knew she had probably hurt Peter's feelings. But at that moment, she didn't care. She just didn't want to have to see the stung look on his face. He was a nice guy—a great guy. At that precise moment, however, he was the devil.

She moved quickly to the front door of the television station and her heart sank when she looked across the front lawn to the street and her car nor Allen was there.

Surely he didn't leave.

She went to the reception desk. "Betty, did you see my car pull up in front? Did anyone come in asking for me?"

"Sorry, Miss Garret," the receptionist answered and shook her head, no.

PS went to the phone in the front lobby and called home. Her home. No answer.

She called Willina's cell phone. "Wil, where are you?"

"Are you okay?"

"That mother fucker didn't pick me up from work. I've been waiting almost forty minutes and there's no sight of him."

"Are you serious? That prick. He has to go. I'm telling you girl, I've been biting my tongue, but he's a snake. He's evil and must be destroyed. I had planned to talk to you about it this week. That prick."

"Where are you, Wil?"

"I'm stuck at the border. I just went into Windsor to do some shopping. We're at some sort of high alert leaving Ontario, and I've been stuck at the Ambassador Bridge for more than an hour. They're stopping every car up there at customs. I've already cleared the toll and I'm just sitting here trying to figure out how to dump these Cuban cigars I picked up for Henry before they get to my car. I hope the customs guy is a man, or I'm screwed."

"Shit! Okay I'll talk to you later."

What are you going to do?" Willina asked, suffering because the crap was going to hit the fan and she was going to miss it, barely even mildly concerned about her current pickle with four boxes of illegal contraband in the trunk of her car.

"I'll call you back."

PS stood at that front door for more than an hour before finally calling a cab.

That night when she finally did get home, the light on her fuse had finally hit the stick of dynamite.

When she walked through her front door, there was Allen, perched on his favorite spot on the sofa watching television. And it wasn't even Channel Six, it was Channel Three.

Her first words to Allen George were not spoken, they were screamed with all the strength she could muster. "Allen, YOU'RE DONE! I waited at that station for an hour and a half for you to pick me up, and ended up having to take a cab. Now why is that? Why do I have to wait for a ride, when I have a Godamned car? I took you in for a couple of days. A couple of days when your place burned down, Allen George. A couple of days. You've been here for weeks, sopping up every pint of everything I own. And I'm done. You're done! You're out!"

She walked into the dining room and grabbed his keys off the dining room table, and removed her car key.

She saw that he'd actually had the un-mitigating gall to have a spare made, and numbly took that one too. Just as she was removing the apartment key which was stubbornly hanging on to its home on Allen's keychain, he grabbed her hands and stopped her. "I'm sorry, I forgot."

"You forgot!" PS snatched her hands away and continued to fight with her house key on his chain. "You forgot to pick me up at work with my own car?"

PS felt like one of those cartoon characters who's faces turn red and then steam blows out from their ears with the sound of whistles blowing. "That's it, brother."

She continued to struggle to get the teeth of the key-ring to open up and flinched as the nail on her index finger splintered. "Shit!" She screamed, getting more frustrated by the second. She went to the kitchen drawer and grabbed a butter knife, slid it between the rings and feverishly fought to maneuver the key off his keychain, to no avail.

"No, I don't mean I forgot exactly," Allen chimed in trying to mitigate what he'd just admitted. "What I mean is, I was busy at a meeting and time slipped away."

"Time slipped away, or you forgot? Which is it?"

"The truth is..."

"Do you know what truth is? Would you know the truth if it reached up and bit you on the ass?"

"Please wait, I gotta tell you something. Please don't kick a man when he's down"

"What do you mean down? You have everything. A free house, the use of a car. Meals, anytime you want. My bathrobe, my bed. You bastard, you have everything. How on earth can you feel like you're down? Let me tell you about my day, let me tell you what I saw today and let's compare notes over who's down here."

She would have never had this conversation with Danny Rierson. She would never have called him a name. She knew you don't call people you love bad names. Danny Rierson always put her welfare before his own and it was reciprocated till the end. Even when he walked out her door for the last time, she couldn't think of a time she and he had said cruel words to one another.

Allen was struggling. He had to move fast or this whole thing would blow. He knew he had been on thin ice for some time but just hadn't worked out a new angle, yet. This would take work to piece back together. He had to get to the back bedroom. What he had tucked away in the back bedroom would stop her tirade. He started inching backwards to the hallway as PS continued to rant.

"Don't you walk away from me, if you go anywhere it's to the front door and ass-out!"

"Wait a minute, please hear me out on this," Allen pleaded ,concerned that he couldn't get to the back room. What he had there could turn this thing around, but it had to be properly executed. He didn't dare cross her at the moment, though. He was a pro at reading women, and he knew that this was delicate ground for him. "I mean," he stammered. "I mean, I've had some really bad luck and I wouldn't have been able to make it had it not been for you. You are an exceptional person. You've opened your home to me, you've been helpful and supportive..."

"Great. Then I'll loan you the money and you can get your car out of hock. And you can get the Hell out of my apartment. Let's start there."

"There's more to it then that."

"What else can there possibly be to it?"

"The car's not at the shop."

"What do you mean the car is not at the shop?" PS asked numbly, desperately needing an Alka Seltzer and a backhoe to clear his shit out of her home.

"The car was never in the shop."

PS was floored. She stumbled backwards as if the wind had been knocked out of her, the key ring dropping to the floor.

"What are you talking about? If your car isn't in the shop, where is it?"

PS looked at Allen as though she were looking at an alien. She looked at his narrow eyes, and that beak-like nose. She hated that Hitleresque mustache and she hated Allen George.

"I know you're a good woman. And I know that you're kind and like to help people. Well, I need your help. I need a place to stay. I'm going to be rich one day, and I'll pay back every thing I owe you and more. You'll never have to work again if you don't want to. I'll share. I'll share it all. But the truth is, right now, I don't have very much. If it wasn't for my job and this business I'm struggling to get off the ground, I would have nothing.

"But in order for you to trust me, I need to re-build this relationship. I need to be honest with you, so you'll know you can trust me, and you can decide if you want to help a man who is in desperate need of your help."

"Oh yeah?" PS asked, regaining her composure and turning to reach under the sink to grab a green garbage bag to pack his belongings.

Allen moved toward PS, but caught himself before he put his hands on her. If he touched her, she could get angrier and strike him. And he felt cornered. He didn't think he could stop himself if she struck him. So he stepped back, took a deep breath and composed himself. This bitch had been more trouble than she was worth. He had misjudged her. Had he realized in the beginning, he would have gone after her buddy, Zoe. She had been his original target, but then he saw PS Garrett at that party at Barbara Bennett's and changed his mind. He always liked PS Garrett on TV, thought she was friendly, approachable, vulnerable and a little dented. He had been right about most of it, but she was a lot stronger than he had anticipated. And a little more clever. He was exhausted trying to stay ahead of her and wanted to leave as much as she wanted him to. But he was in now. And in deep. He had to save this thing. He wasn't ready to leave, yet. Wasn't able to leave, yet. He needed a little more time.

Allen struggled on, clearing his throat several times. "Because some of my business holdings and my money are tied up in so many places, I couldn't meet my note."

"You couldn't meet your note? What does that mean?" PS asked, pulling the bag from beneath the counter.

"I couldn't meet my car note. My car was re-possessed five months ago."

PS looked at Allen in utter shock. She recoiled as if she had been struck in the face. Her head was spinning. The macaroni salad's ghost was haunting the lining of her stomach. She felt herself burp, as a bit of vomit re-entered the staging area, but then changed its mind.

"Your car was what?"

"It was repossessed."

"And you didn't tell me?"

"But I've got some money coming to the apart-ment tonight. That's why I was late picking you up. I was waiting for it. An associate of mine is on his way here to pay me. And then I can give you everything I owe. Rent, food, money you loaned me here and there. This guy just called and is on his way. I wanted to surprise you."

"Allen, you're a liar. I want you out of here by tonight. As soon as you get that money, you leave here."

PS grabbed her car keys and opened the front door. She stopped, walked over to the dining room table and grabbed the two spare car keys Allen had made. She put them in her pocket and continued out the door. With Willina stuck at the border, and not within reach, PS didn't know where she was going and didn't care. She knew she just had to go somewhere to collect her thoughts.

As the door slammed, Allen strolled calmly toward the sink, whistling gently. He bent down and picked up the key chain PS had dropped. His house key was still on it. He tossed it gently in the air, caught it and stuck it in his pocket as he continued to whistle his merry tune. He strolled confidently back toward the bedroom where he was hiding his secret weapon.

He'd been saved.

When PS returned an hour later, Allen was still there, and not one ounce of his belongings had been packed.

"What are you doing here, Allen?"

"That bastard didn't come."

Which bastard is this, Allen?"

"The guy who owes me money. He called and said he's going to be delayed a couple of weeks. I'm sorry."

"Allen, that's not my problem," PS said as she walked over to her phone, and noticed on the caller ID that no phone calls had come in. She turned and looked at Allen. "You have to go. Tonight. I'll pack up your things and when the cab gets here, you and your belongings are out. Go to your sister's, or your aunt's, or whoever the Hell. But you have to get out of here tonight."

"I can't. I don't have any place to go. Just let me stay another two weeks. That's it. My money's coming in, I swear it, and then I can pay you back everything. Everything and then some."

"Allen, no."

"Besides," Allen was talking fast. "You left so

334

fast, you didn't have time to see the surprise I got for you."

"Allen, I've been surprised enough today. You need to get out, before I call the police."

"We don't need to go there. Besides, the police won't remove me. I've been here long enough, they'll see that I've been living here. They'll just chalk it up to a domestic squabble, and you don't want the cops around town talking about you having domestic squabbles with your lover. Let me show you what I got you."

PS cringed at the word lover. And he was right. She didn't want talk around town talking about her man trouble.

Allen didn't wait for an answer, he just got up from the sofa and ran into the back room where he'd been sleeping.

PS grabbed the garbage bag that was still on the floor, and went to the foot of the sofa to grab Allen's shoes to toss them in. When she looked up, Allen was standing on the other side of the sofa with a small orange ball of fur.

"What the Hell is that?" She asked.

"I saw a sign on somebody's lawn today that said free kittens. I don't know what made me stop, but I did. They had about five of 'em. All different colors. This one reminded me of Fido, and so I got it."

"Allen, you had no right!" PS said, starting to cry.

"I just thought it might cheer you up. You've been in such a bad mood lately. I know you've been grieving the loss of your cat. I thought it might cheer you up.

"The people I got him from were pretty poor. I told them, I might have to bring him back. They said they couldn't take him. I was the first to stop and ask about the kittens in more than three weeks. They were going to take the others to the pound."

Allen cuddled the kitten and kissed it on the forehead. "I'm sorry little fella, I guess you'll have to go to the pound with your brothers and sisters.

"I'm sorry PS, I thought this would make you happy. I can see that I've misjudged you in every way."

Allen put the small kitten on the floor and walked back to the guest room. The ball of fur raised up on it's toes, curled its tail and looked at PS as it began to wander over.

PS fell to her knees to welcome the little critter to her lap. He was precious.

She scooped him into her arms, and his light paw reached out and touched her on her chin. He then gently clawed his way up to her shoulder and walked across to the other side as though her clavicle were a plank. He was so light, PS could barely feel him, except for the pads of his feet that massaged her soul as he walked.

She slowly got to her feet so that her little passenger wouldn't lose his balance, and walked to the kitchen.

She pulled down a bone china saucer, went to the fridge to get rice milk, and poured it into the saucer. Without hesitation, the kitten jumped agilely down to the counter and began purring loudly as he lapped up the milk.

"I'm going to name you Guernsey," PS said as the cat lapped the last of the milk, and willingly returned to her arms.

The two went to her bedroom and PS locked the door behind her.

CHAPTER THIRTEEN

Allen was allowed to stay a little longer, but it was a business arrangement only.

But the arrangement grated on PS. It didn't feel good, and she knew that she was being used. But she was desperate to recoup some of the money he owed her.

A week later as she sat at her kitchen table with Guernsey playing at her feet she put her head in her hands and wondered how she had gotten into this situation.

Allen wasn't a business partner, he was a crook. And he was abusing her home, with her permission. There were so many things that bothered her since he'd come to be a squatter in her home. There were phone hang-ups when she picked up the receiver. She would check the receiver and the read-out would say, unavailable or restricted number.

There were small lies, insignificant lies that Allen would tell just for the sake of lying. It was as if he lied for sport. He never seemed to have any money, yet new belongings popped up in the apartment.

Several weeks ago he'd purchased a beautiful plasma television set, and a state of the art DVD surround sound system. He had a couple of new suits, and a snappy pair of calfskin loafers.

Indeed, she had been desperately lonely since Danny left. But this man wasn't half the man that he was. And PS suddenly realized that her life alone had been better than her life with Allen George. The only good thing that had come out of the relationship that she could point to was the furry ball of energy that had just discovered her toes, and was pretending that they were mice to be stalked.

PS grabbed a piece of paper and a pen, and started doodling out a time line. She wanted to see if she could plot on a grid, exactly where she had started going wrong.

It was not like her to allow herself to be taken in by a con artist. Even though she was lonely, she had the best poker face in town. No matter what was going on in her heart, she always prided herself on being able to rationally size up her situation and decide on the best long term course of action.

This time she'd fallen down on the job. Desperately fallen down on the job.

She'd had met Allen in late March. Within a month, there was a man she barely knew, whose sexual performance repulsed her, living in her house, his maroon shit strewn throughout her bathroom.

There was that incident last week when he'd forgotten to pick her up at work. The cat saved him that night. And now, here it was, the second week of June and Allen George was still stinking up her apartment.

Her life wasn't her own anymore. She wasn't herself. Frankly, she didn't know who she was anymore.

"Why have I let that man into my life? How is it that I couldn't see how dangerous he was? He is robbing me, yet I let him stay," PS said aloud.

No, she didn't think he was actually going into her purse and stealing money. He didn't have to. She was supplying him with everything he needed. "But why? What diabolical hold did this man have on me?"

Guernsey didn't answer. The small kitten had just discovered the fringe on an afghan that was slung over the sofa in the living room. And it had become his new prey.

It was almost time to go to work. Allen had lost car privileges, and had hitched a ride to God knew where with some anonymous stranger.

PS decided to call her mother to tell her what was going on. She hadn't talked to her in weeks, and when she did she omitted the part about having a man living in her apartment.

Allen had been instructed to check the caller ID before answering the phone. If he even accidentally picked up when PS's mother was calling, he would be removed immediately, no questions asked. Allen never made that mistake.

The two weren't particularly close, but PS thought that maybe, just maybe her mother might be up for lending a sympathetic ear, though she had been fairly nonchalant about PS losing Danny—she said she couldn't support the relationship to begin with.

PS had no idea what she would say about her inviting a viper into her house. She suspected she'd be angry.

She picked up the phone, and dialed the area code to Houston. She then hit the hang up button and put the phone to her chest, to think about it for a few minutes.

Maybe it wasn't such a good idea to call her after all. She stared at the phone as if the keypad would offer her some sort of solution. It didn't.

She picked up the headset again, and forced her fingers to dial. Butterflies pounded on her chest as she waited for the connection, but on the first ring she slammed the phone down again.

Finally, she decided that perhaps she just needed to call and say hello. Maybe something in the sound of her mother's voice would coax her forward to bare her troubles. Perhaps she could offer some advice.

PS picked up the phone again, and quickly dialed before she could change her mind. This time when the line connected, it was busy.

"Dammit!" She yelled in frustration.

She walked to the guest room to make certain the door was open, and the kitten had access to its litter box. She went to the kitchen to check the water saucer. It was full. She grabbed her keys off the counter and headed out the door toward work.

It was close to six o'clock in the evening, and PS was in no hurry to get home. She sat at her desk reading email, when Salina Kingsley came sauntering up. "Hi, how ya' doing?"

PS looked up suspiciously. "What is it, Salina? What do you want?"

"Well, it pains me to ask you for a favor, but I must."

"Well, I think that's a great way to start when you need something from me. Whatever it is, I'm sure the answer is no."

"I'll ask anyway."

"Alright," PS said, returning her attention to the last few unread emails on her terminal screen.

"Will you work a double shift today?"

"No," PS said, almost before Salina could finish the question.

"Please?"

"No," PS answered just as abruptly.

"Oh, come on. Susan called in sick again, and we really don't have anyone else to ask."

"And whose problem is that?"

"Listen here, you…" Salina barked.

PS turned her attention back to Salina and just looked at her. "I don't have to do this. So don't get bitchy with me, Salina."

"I'm not getting bitchy, I'm producing tonight, and I really need a strong reporter on the street. We don't have much going on, and I need someone who can dig."

"You're producing tonight?"

"Yes. Unfortunately," Salina said with her customary dissatisfaction.

"Then dig this," PS retorted. "No."

"Well, I thought you might be this difficult, so I am authorized to give you an extra comp day for working tonight."

"An extra day. That means two days for working just tonight."

"No that's one day," Salina answered.

342

"If I work a double, Salina, you will already owe me a day. An extra comp day means that's two days. Get your math right, when you're trying to negotiate."

"Oh, I guess you're right," Salina said with a smirk. "That's right, you'll get two comp days if you stay and work nightside."

"No," PS said cruelly, and turned back around to her computer terminal. "Oh, look at the time. I need to get out of here."

"Wait a minute. How about we give you two extra days for staying. We really need you to stay. So that will be three days for working tonight."

"Salina, are you authorized to give me those days?"

"Actually… yes."

"Then why didn't you come to me and offer that in first place. You tried to low ball me and get me to do a sixteen hour day for damn near nothing."

"That's why it's called negotiation."

"Well, negotiate this," PS flicked her middle digit in the air, and bent over to collect her reporter's bag. "The answer is still no. Go manipulate someone else."

"PS that's the best I can do. I swear it. Bob Tucker only authorized me to give you a total of three days. I swear it. And even you have to admit that's a pretty good deal. Three full comp days for staying an extra five or six hours."

"Salina, I don't believe you. You have Bob Tucker call me and if he authorizes it, I'll stay."

"Deal," Salina said triumphantly as she trotted

off to the news director's office. "Thanks so much," she said sarcastically.

"Don't mention it, bitch," PS said under her breath. "I would have done it for free. I don't want to go home any way."

There was nothing really going on that night so the desk put PS in a live truck with Steve and asked the crew to go on a news cruise.

A news cruise is done when there isn't any real news going on and the station needs to have something to keep those commercials from bumping into each other. Anything found is probably going to be junk, but TV people are always mindful of the monster that they're charged with feeding so they go trolling for tidbits.

All the crew does is ride around town in the worst neighborhoods and look for something to happen. There were the rare occasions when they stumbled over a great story, other times they were grateful to be able to package grass growing.

It was all a crap shoot.

Steve was a great cameraman to go on a news cruise with. He was kind of a character who knew all of the rotten spots in town. He could tell you where the crack houses were, he could tell you where the underground gambling was going on, but his favorite spot was on Cass Avenue where the hookers were. He said he could pick out a hooker a mile a way. And honest to God he could. He even knew several by name.

Steve also had a great sense of humor and air of fun about him. Even if they didn't find a story, it was going to be an interesting night. It always was with Steve.

He affectionately called himself PS Garrett's video lover. He had decided that because they made such a good team, and he knew how to give her exactly what she wanted and needed, their working relationship was like a love affair.

"You always get your jollies when you work with the video lover," he'd say proudly.

"Whatever, Steve."

By six, the news crew had cruised up Woodward to the Silver Spur. They took in their portable scanner and sat around to chew the fat with Mack.

PS hadn't seen Mack since Allen had moved in. She really hadn't told anyone, other than Wil what was going on because of her embarrassment. She hadn't realized it 'till then, but she'd also gotten into the habit of shunning her own friends.

The only people Allen and she managed to go out with anymore were his friends. And even that had stopped in the last few weeks.

Even as PS sat in the Spur talking to Mack and one of her all-time favorite photographers, she felt isolated. She was uncomfortable with herself and the excuses she had been making to herself for Allen.

She was painfully lonely. And it was hard for her to admit that to herself, let alone others.

Mack was genuinely glad to see her. And he talked a mile a minute. He told PS he was worried because she hadn't been around. He thought maybe she found somewhere else to eat, perhaps a place that always had the TV tuned to Channel Six.

PS laughed out loud for the first time in weeks. It was a hearty, healthy laugh and it felt good and cleansing. She gave Mack a hug and told him she would never hang out at some other dive. "I know I said I would," she confessed. "But those where just idle threats. Of course Mack, it would be nice if you turned to my station every once in a while."

Mack smiled, lifted the reporter to her feet by the arm and led her to the front of the bar. "Come here, I want to show you something."

While still holding her beneath her arm, Mack led her to the bar and parked her on a stool facing the big screen television that sat dark in the corner.

To her surprise, Mack took out the remote control and flipped the TV on. It was to her utter shock to see the video read out in bright neon green letters in the upper right hand corner of the screen, that said Ch 6.

"This is a trick, right? A ploy, isn't it?"

"No," Mack said earnestly. "I missed you. I thought you were mad at me. I missed you," Mack bowed his head and his shoulders started to heave. He was genuinely moved by the return of the prodigal daughter. "I thought the only way I would see you again would be to watch you on television."

PS bowed her head and fought to control her own emotions. For the last two months she had been through Hell and she didn't feel like she had any place to go.

She bit her bottom lip to stifle a whimper and turned to Mack to lift his face to hers.

It was the first time she had ever looked closely at Mack. He had a large round face, a nose as red as Rudolph's and dull, dark brown eyes. He was balding, and his hair was graying and he had a deep scar just below his receding hairline. She could also see the tiny dots that had once been stitches, puckering on either side of the gash. His face was wrinkled and worn, and there was an unnatural cast in the pallor of his skin.

It was the most beautiful face she'd seen in months. The most beautiful face she'd seen in years.

She had always considered Mack a pal, but up until that point never realized he was a friend. A true friend—family.

She looked him deep in his eyes. The flood gates opened. After she stingily squeezed out the first tear, the others followed quickly and obediently. She swallowed deep and reached over to give her friend a hug.

She cried because she'd lost a pet that had been so dear to her. She cried because she'd lost the only man she had ever loved, and her attempts to replace him had been disastrous. She cried because she was tired, and wanted to go home to see Guernsey, but couldn't because Allen George might be there. And she cried because as she sobbed in the arms of Mack, she felt loved.

She held him lightly in her arms, but that wasn't enough for Mack. He grabbed her by the shoulders and pulled her to him in a bear hug that took her breath away.

PS could feel his body quaking in her arms.

347

But PS was actually happy for the first time in ages. She was home.

Crying with Mack was cathartic. When the two finally let go of each other, she sniffed up the last of her tears, wiped her eyes with her blouse and smiled at him. He smiled back. Then she got off the bar stool and headed back to her usual table where Steve was sitting there shaking his head. "You two are sick," he said.

Mack walked back to the table, his eyes still red and a bit swollen. PS ordered her usual broasted barbecued chicken with spicy lo mein noodles and drank a Pepsi instead of a Brown Cow. After all, she was still on the clock.

Steve, PS and Mack sat in the back of the restaurant and made small talk until Steve finally came out and asked PS what was really on his mind. "So what's going on with you?"

"Nothing really," PS answered and took a deep swig of her soda.

"You've been preoccupied lately. Not quite yourself. I know because I'm your video lover, and the video lover knows."

"Steve, it's nothing I really care to talk about."

"Well I don't mean to pry, but I thought you might be thinking about your man, Danny. I mean it was this time of year..."

"Stop it," she cut him off abruptly before he could finish. She had already had enough displays of emotion for the day. "Steve don't, I just can't take it," she commanded continuing to stifle a sob. "I just can't take it tonight."

Steve apologized and went on to another topic. But he peered up from time to time with a look of concern, and a few times PS even thought she saw pity in his eyes.

But he was polite enough to not broach the subject any further.

Mack came over with food and started talking about this Romanian gang he'd been hearing about over on Tuxedo Street. Apparently some things were heating up between rival factions and he thought that since the news crew obviously didn't have anything better to do, they might want to drive over there and poke around after finishing their chicken wings.

PS asked Steve if he was game and he informed her the video lover was always game.

"I'll even make a bet with you," PS announced. "I say we get a story no later than eight-thirty tonight. If I'm right, you owe me dinner the next time we work together."

"Ain't gonna happen, I'm telling you. The video lover knows. Things don't start to cook in this town until ten," Steve said with bravado.

After all, he should know. He was a regular nightside photographer and he had a nose for news and an internal antenna to match.

"Okay, fine, Mr. Know It All. So, if we get a story before eight- thirty, I get dinner out of you. If we get a story any time after eight thirty, Grub's on me. Deal?"

"Deal."

The two got up to leave the Spur, PS gave Mack a big hug and told him she'd see him in a couple of days after she cleaned up a big mess at her place and she and the video lover walked out of the restaurant, hopped in the van and cruised over toward Tuxedo for some news.

"Hey, hey, put me on the news," a tall wiry boy yelled from the sidewalk as the van slid to a stop at a light, five blocks from Tuxedo Street. The video lover and the reporter just ignored him. This was something they were accustomed to. The logo on the side of the live van was a beacon for attention. The young boy, probably around fourteen-years-old, based on the prepubescent pimples on the side of his face, took advantage of the red light and trotted up to the van.

"Hey what are you guys doing around here?" He asked excitedly.

"Oh we're just doing a story. No big deal," PS answered.

"Hey, are you Barbara Bennett?" He asked.

"Nope," PS answered patiently. "She's probably back at the station getting ready for the news."

"Oh yeah?" The kid replied, obviously not really listening to the answers. "So where's Barbara Bennett?"

"She ain't here already," Steve chimed in curtly.

"Oh yeah? Well will you put me on the news?" The kid persisted.

"Why should we put you on the news, man? What have you done to be on the news?" Steve barked.

"I ain't done nothing."

"Well then you can't be on the news."

"Oh yeah? Well, what if I shoot somebody, can I be on the news then?"

Steve sucked his teeth in disgust and began rolling up his window. "Yeah, that'll get you on the news."

"Okay, then I'm gonna go shoot somebody. Bye," the kid announced as he ran back across the street.

"Good riddance, prick," Steve scowled.

"Steve, why would you tell somebody that?" PS asked, annoyed.

"Because it's true. If the little son of a bitch shoots somebody he'll get on the Goddamned news. If he shoots somebody near a school yard, guaranteed, he'll lead the show."

"Don't do that shit, Steve. Like we need to give any kids around here ideas on why to use guns."

"He ain't gonna shoot nobody. He's just a little prick," Steve said as he re-engaged the accelerator and continued heading south toward Tuxedo Street.

As the crew approached their destination and slowed down to a cruising speed looking for trouble, a bunch of little kids came out from a back ally to greet them. "Are you Barbara Bennett? Are you Barbara Bennett?"

" 'Fraid not kids, she's probably at the studio," PS said with a smile starting to feel better about things.

"Can I have your autograph?" One of the kids asked. He couldn't have been older than eight.

"Sorry kids, I don't give autographs. But can I have yours?"

"Why do you want my autograph?" Another little boy asked.

PS wondered why he was running the streets at that hour, rather than doing homework. "I want your autograph because you're the special one, and I want to tell all my friends that I met you. And if I don't have your autograph no one is going to believe me."

"Really?" The little boy asked with genuine excitement. "You want my autograph for real?"

"You betcha. Here's a pen and some paper, okay?"

The little boy gleefully grabbed the newspad and pen and carefully wrote his name on the paper. He then proudly handed over his autograph. His handwriting was neat and measured. The reporter looked at the tiny signature. "Jumandi?" She asked.

"Uh huh," the little boy said proudly with a big grin. When he turned his head up and smiled, PS could see a fresh crop of boogers in his nose.

"Thanks, I appreciate it," she said with a smile. "So what are you going to be when you grow up to make me proud, Jumandi?"

"I'm gonna be Michael Jordan!" He announced excitedly.

"Hmmm, I would think only Michael Jordan can be Michael Jordan. Do you mean you want to be a basketball player?"

"Yup," he said with a giggle.

"Well how about you go to college and study business, or pre-med, just in case you don't grow tall enough to be like Michael Jordan?"

"Nope, I'm gonna be a basketball player. I don't need no school for that."

"I'm gonna be a doctor!" A little girl announced from the crowd of children who'd gathered around the van.

"You are? That's great. We need more women

doctors," PS said waving to the little girl. "When you graduate from med-school, you give me a call at the studio so I can be your first patient. Okay?"

The little girl nodded her head in excitement.

"I'm gonna be President of the United States," another little girl cried out as a dozen or so children huddled around the van and began yelling out their future professions.

No, you won't!" A tall, wiry, scruffy little boy said. His face dry with ashy white streaks, and his clothes tattered. "Girls can't be President."

"They can too," the neatly dressed child with matching hair ties defended. "My daddy said I can be anything I want and I want to be President."

"You're dreaming girl. You ain't gonna do nothing 'cept stay around up in here and have babies."

"I will not, Lexus!" The girl screamed angrily. "What did your daddy tell you?"

"Girl, you know I ain't got no daddy. Got lots of uncles though," he laughed.

All of the other kids laughed too.

"Steve, that kid's mother named him after a car!" PS said with disgust. "Why did she do that? He'll be lucky if he can get a job cleaning toilets at a Willie Wickie's Big Burger. Why would someone handicap a child like that?"

"Ignorance," Steve said. "PS, if my mother named me some stupid shit like, Lexus, I'd change my name to Lester or something that would give my resume a fighting chance."

More kids gathered around the live van to join the game of shout.

353

"I'm going to be a math teacher."

"I'm going to be an astronaut."

"I want to be a famous actress."

"I'm gonna be a drug dealer!" A voice yelled out from the crowd.

"Then you're gonna be dead," the little girl with the matching hair bows chided.

"No I won't, I'm gonna be rich. I'm gonna be a drug dealer and if you don't shut up I might shoot you."

Wow!

PS was snapped back into reality, remembering what kind of neighborhood she was in. For a moment, she was enchanted with the faces of smiling inquisitive, imaginative children, all of whom should have been off the street at that time of the night. But violence and drugs were as common here as a jogger was in the burbs. That's what these kids saw, and the child who wanted to be a drug dealer wasn't being a smart alec or a wise guy, he wanted to be what he saw as successful. And in this neighborhood, that meant peddling drugs on the street.

PS looked at the children she'd been holding court with as she hung out of the window of the live van and wondered which ones would really become the doctors or the President. She looked at each face and wondered which ones would even make it out of this mean neighborhood.

Anywhere near Tuxedo, these children stood a better chance of being caught in the cross fire of some shoot-out than going on to college.

She looked at their smiling happy faces, and hoped some of them would make it out, but knew—

most would not.

BANG! BANG! BANG!

The sound of gunshots rang out from around the corner. All of the children standing around the van screamed and scattered. Steve revved up the truck and the crew was off in the direction of the gunfire.

They drove up to a horrible scene, three blocks away.

A young man was lying on the grass, a bullet had gone straight through the front of his head and had exited out the back. A steady stream of people had already come out to investigate the commotion.

Steve jumped out of the van and grabbed his camera. PS grabbed her newspad and jumped out as well and began to move into the crowd and among the on-lookers. "Did anyone see anything? Did anyone see anything?" She asked.

A few on-lookers shook their heads no, but for the most part people looked at her as though she was speaking some sort of foreign language. The curious stepped back to let her pass through the crowd, but no one said anything.

All of a sudden a piercing scream came from the back of the crowd which had quickly swelled to about fifty. A girl, barely a woman ran up yelling and crying, pushing and elbowing her way through the crush of spectators with one hand, grasping her swollen belly with the other.

"Ziggy, they got Ziggy?"

She ran forward and dropped herself on top of the figure that lay on the ground laboring to breathe. "Why'd they do this? He didn't bother nobody. They got Ziggy," she cried.

Finally the sound of sirens could be heard rounding the corner. Two police cars pulled up, and within five minutes an ambulance came roaring to a stop several feet away from the dying teenager. Paramedics jumped out of the vehicle and ran toward the young man on the ground whose body began to convulse.

He was obviously slipping away.

One technician carried an oxygen tank and mask, the other had a big orange tool box. They fell down beside the young man and went to work.

Someone from the crowd lifted the sobbing young woman from the teenager's side and cradled her. She was very young, probably not more than fifteen, but PS could see that bulge in her stomach quivering as she stood there crying, pounding and praying.

Steve had the camera rolling on it all.

This would be intense video. The news crew had gotten to the scene well before the medical technicians. Usually when the TV cameras pulled up to a scene like this, there was either a sheet on the ground and a chalk drawing being made, or the body had already been spirited off to the hospital.

But this time, they were the first on the scene. And this time the reporter took great interest in the dynamics that surrounded a neighborhood shooting, since technically it was the first she was covering from almost the moment the bullet left the chamber and found its mark.

Some of the little kids PS had just been talking to a few minutes before, who had scattered at the sound of gunfire three blocks away, had found their way to this horrible scene.

They were no longer afraid—the gun shots had ceased.

Now they danced and played mere feet away from the man surrounded by paramedics—gurgling, eyes fixed and dilating. A few of the kids played chicken, as they dared each other to get close enough to see the blood pouring out of the entry wound. The brave would venture close enough to yell, "Ewww", and then titter off to laugh and joke with the others.

The little boy named Jumandi ran up to touch the feet of the young man who lay on the grass with blood spewing from his forehead in spite of the best efforts of emergency technicians. It was a joke for the young boy. A game.

PS wondered where his mother was.

If she had heard shots fired in her neighborhood, she was sure that she would have gathered her children quickly and hurried them into safety behind closed doors, calling a realtor on the way.

But this shooting didn't seem to be anything more than the usual spectacle here. People milled about and talked. Some watched the paramedics with their hands over their mouths.

One man walked up to a young girl in short, short shorts, with her hair pasted to her head like a tower, and asked for a cigarette.

"Do I look like your personal vending machine?" She fussed.

"Ah, com'on girl. Why don't you ease up offa one a them smokes?" He cajoled.

She did, he bummed a light, and then kept on going, leaving her to count what was left in her crumpled pack of generic cigarettes without even a thank you.

PS marveled at how casual people seemed to take the shooting. She half expected to see popcorn and pizza vendors, and almost wasn't surprised when an ice cream man rode by on a cooler, hooked up to a tricycle-like contraption that was blaring loud, obnoxious music.

Several of the kids and one or two of the adults, meandered over to him and conducted Häagen-Dazs business, a few feet away from the dying man.

There were some shocked and saddened faces, and obviously that one young pregnant woman who'd run through the crowd was distraught, but other than her, no one seemed to be particularly moved.

PS walked around and looked at the blank empty faces as they watched those paramedics work on that teenager. "Does anyone know this young man?" She asked.

"Yeah, I know him," a voice answered from the crowd. "But I don't want to be on TV."

"That's fine. You don't have to be. Who is he?"

"His name is Lathan. But we call him, Ziggy. I just saw him around the corner at his girl's house."

"Why would someone want to shoot him? Was he in a gang, was he selling dope?"

"Naw, not this one. He was a nice kid. Everyone in the neighborhood liked him. You didn't see him around too much. He caught a bus out of here to go to some private school, somewhere I don't know. But he was a good kid. He didn't get mixed up in this shit 'round here."

"So why was he shot?" PS persisted.

"Don't know," the fellow in the dark, loose clothing answered with a shrug. "In the wrong place at the wrong time I guess. We've had some trouble around here, guess he just got caught in the middle of it. He lives in that house over there. I guess he was walking home, coming from his girl's house, you know? That's all I know."

The stranger with dark eyes melted into the crowd, and within seconds PS couldn't distinguish him from anyone else.

The number of people standing around staring had doubled. There had to be a hundred people crowding the corner of Tuxedo and Peerless. She could feel the growing hordes pressing against her, tugging at her clothing to get her attention, touching her hair.

PS got a deep sense of foreboding. A realization that she wasn't safe, even around all of these people. Perhaps the shooter was milling around in this crowd. Maybe he came back to take a look at his handiwork. The reporter looked carefully at the people standing around. Several of the young men had on dark clothing, baggy sweat pants and hoods. They kept their hands sequestered in their pockets and their eyes darted from side to side.

For all she knew she had been standing next to the murderer, asking him questions. She didn't know. All she knew was she didn't belong here.

She inched her way toward Steve who was shooting the paramedics as they lifted the young man on to a gurney and into the ambulance. They were still working on keeping him alive. One would pump and pound on the young man's chest, never even stopping to clear the sweat off of his forehead. Even after the back doors were closed, PS could still observe through the window the desperation in the movements of the medical technicians. As one would throw up his hands in exhaustion and despair, another one would slide into place, never missing a beat, pushing and pounding and coaxing the dying young man's heart to beat again.

The crowd parted again as an older woman was escorted to the scene by two neighborhood men. She was wearing a tattered housecoat, and slippers. She'd obviously just pulled curlers out of her hair, as you could see the neat sections of tightly curled gray hair all over her head. She had great difficulty walking, possibly because of her weight and age, and she limped painfully as quickly as she could on big, fat, swollen ankles and feet.

"Where's my grandson?" She cried. "I want to see my grandson. Lathan!" She screamed as she made her way into the clearing. Her cry was shrill and hung in the air, almost like a high pitched chime.

It made PS wince.

"Lathan!" The woman wept as she made a spry sprint toward the ambulance.

A police officer stepped in to intercept her before she got to the vehicle, which was still stationary, its flashing lights darting about the darkness. "They're doing all they can for him ma'am. I need you to come with me so I can talk to you."

"Lathan!" The old woman gasped as she put her hand to her mouth, and blinked back tears, unable to tear her eyes away from the back windows of the ambulance.

The young officer held her as her arms flailed, lifting her housecoat to reveal a tattered white slip and control top pantyhose.

After whispering gently in her ear, the officer gently led the woman away. Several times she looked back toward the ambulance where the paramedics were still feverishly working to re-start the dying young man's heart.

The boy's grandmother had a face with deep wrinkles in it. Her eyes were swollen and tearful. "Oh God, no," she wept as she was slowly led away. "Not this one, not my Lathan, please Lord."

All the while she was escorted away, PS sensed this was not the first taste of tragedy in the aging woman's life. She had a way about her that revealed a painful existence.

The reporter struggled to stifle her own ache that began creeping into her heart. "How do they stand it?" She said aloud. "How do you live through this kind of grief?"

Asked and answered. PS knew exactly how. She'd seen it up close in ways she never thought she could imagine.

Somehow your lungs keep filling with air, even when it hurts to breathe. Somehow each foot continues to take one step at a time, even though in your heart you're crippled. Somehow the fabric of a person's soul becomes the most enduring garment a human can wear.

And PS grieved, knowing that the fate of Lathan and his grandmother, and his unborn child, would likely be the fate of many of the children she had just been talking to around the corner.

And indeed, as long as humans continued to prey on other humans, this reporter would eat.

The cycle was vicious and strong.

The reporter turned her attention back to the rear window of the ambulance where a technician had stopped pumping on the young man's heart. She saw his head drop in despair, as his partner patted him on the back. They took a sheet off a top shelf and laid it over Lathan's body.

PS had seen a lot of things as a reporter. But she had never actually watched a man die.

She stood on the sidewalk, watching the paramedics open the door and step out from the ambulance. She stood there surrounded by people, but felt all alone. The reporter felt a deep pang of grief, and touched her hand to her heart to steady herself. And then she looked to the sky and silently asked God, Why? If this was a good kid, like everyone said, if he was just walking home from seeing his girlfriend, why? Why not take all the die-hard killers on the corner, the punks peddling junk to desperate people, the guys recruiting seven-year-olds to run heroine from dealer to dealer? Why allow that bastard who slaughtered those two kids in Pixley to live. Why wasn't he killed before he could murder others? Why, God? Why?

She knew those guys did get shot up on the streets. She'd rolled up on similar crime scenes dozens of times. If it looked like a drug hit, the photographer didn't even bother taking the camera out anymore.

But this was different. This was apparently a good kid, someone's son, grandson, brother, lover—a father-to-be. This one apparently wanted a future, had a future, offered promise. He wasn't going to grow up and perpetuate the misery he was born into. From what PS could tell he had no aspirations to become a drug dealer, or a druggie. He might have been a doctor or President of the United States.

But this guy was not going to wake up the next day and see the sunshine or the flowers bloom. He would never again know the taste of a cool drink on a hot summer day. He wouldn't hear children laughing, or make love again. He had no promise of the future. His life ended on a concrete slab near Tuxedo Street, and for the life of her, PS couldn't understand why God chose to take out the good ones along with the trash.

And then, it happened again. Something she thought she had trained herself to steer clear of. In fact, it had been happening more and more in the last six months—she was truly saddened by a story.

She turned her face back to the moon and fought to hold back the tears. "How many, God? How many more young black men will you take like this?" She said to the sky.

The video lover walked up to her, with his camera still perched on his shoulder and touched PS on the arm. "You ready to go?" He asked. "We're about done here, unless you want to do some interviews. I think that girl over there might talk to you, I think that's the kid's girlfriend."

"She," PS said sadly.

"Huh?" Steve asked, genuinely confused.

"She. You said, I think that's the kid's girlfriend, and you should have said, she's the kid's girlfriend. Not 'that', she's a 'she', not a 'that'."

"Huh?" Steve persisted.

"Never mind." PS dropped her head and glanced at Steve's watch. She wiped away the tear that had meandered down her cheek. It was eight twenty-five. As usual, with its own twisted sense of irony—life and time went on despite the things that make no sense at all.

Steve would owe her dinner after all.

PS woke up trembling.

At first she thought the heat had gone off in her apartment, or the covers had been snatched from her feet.

It was pitch dark, and for a moment she forgot where she was. In her fog, she thought she was back near Tuxedo Street, watching paramedics pull the sheet over Lathan's face.

She shuddered and trembled at the thought.

But as she sat up and got her bearings, and heard the slow rhythmic breathing from the other side of the bed, the realization slammed into her like an angry storm that battered and bruised.

She was in her bedroom, on her bed, and Allen George had crawled in beside her.

She wasn't trembling because she was cold, she was trembling because she had been crying in her sleep, dreaming about her beloved Danny Rierson.

She missed her Danny. She missed the solid gaze of his beautiful eyes. She missed the touch of his long fingers on the inside of her thigh. She missed his cool, fresh breath brushing across her ear as they made love together. She missed the man who first gave her the world, and then crumbled it without ever realizing the destruction his leaving had done.

For the last three years she had been struggling to not think about Danny. She thought she had trained herself to shut him out when he crept into her thoughts. But as she sat there on her bed, quietly weeping and shaking, it was clear that Danny was back and she would have to deal with what happened.

Even now, his spell remained. It had been cast on her the moment the two locked eyes.

CHAPTER FOURTEEN

Danny Rierson had been the new special projects producer at the station.

A special projects producer does absolutely everything in a newsroom—kind of a glorified Chief cook and bottle washer. They do research for stories. They write newscasts. If, for some reason, a line producer can't oversee a newscast, the special projects producer steps up to the plate to fill the need.

When they're good, they do as much, actually more, than most reporters. And they only get a fraction of the credit and the salary. When they're good, they're a Godsend.

When they are bad, they are Salina Kingsley.

Danny was the prince of producers. The very best—professionally, personally, the best in every way.

The first week Daniel D. Rierson worked at Channel Six, PS didn't see him, she only heard his voice. She had been out in the field, working on a story forty-five miles from the station. Since the story was close to her apartment, she just drove to the location every day from home rather than tracking all the way downtown to the station and having a photographer courier her out to the scene.

PS hadn't actually set foot in the studio for two whole weeks.

She had been covering a story in which a big stink was being made over the closing of a nursing home for mentally retarded people. Because of budget cuts in State funding, this home was going to close its doors in a matter of weeks. The big question was, where were all of the residents going to go?

A dozen or so of the profoundly retarded were going to be shuffled into another home almost two hundred miles away. Some of the autistics were being scattered to smaller group homes around the state.

For many, who'd spent their entire lives at the institution, it would be a horrible change in routine and surroundings. Many had never been on a real car trip, so just the transportation created huge problems of its own.

These were the throw-away-people. No one really wanted to see them or even know they existed. That's why they had been locked away at South Haven Center.

With the shutdown of the Center, the children and adults with severe Downs Syndrome and the hydrocephals—their large heads bobbing around disturbingly on their pencil thin necks, were facing eviction.

So the people who loved and cared for them were forced to show them on television—parade them like circus animals. They needed the public to get angry and frightened. They needed to show these unfortunate souls—the children born of alcoholic mothers, the ones who came into this world with their legs facing in the wrong direction, the violent autistics. The public needed to know that these human cast-offs could end up in group homes in a neighborhood coming near you!

The Center needed sympathy from bleeding heart suburbanites who wouldn't want them to show up next door, or be sent to some God-awful place where they might be strapped in a chair and left alone or out of sight, out of mind.

The lives of the South Haven residents depended on the public's knowing and seeing. So the facility opened its doors and let the media in to do what it did best—exploit the matter.

For a full two weeks, PS chronicled the mini-dramas, day by day, story by story.

The Monday of the second week PS had been banished to South Haven, a huge group of more than a hundred people showed up an hour before news time with signs and posters imploring legislators to restore funding for the center.

All of the media types had previously figured it would be a quiet day. There was supposed to be a lot of legal wrangling behind the scenes—some injunctions filed at a court, a few motions to be heard in the closed chambers of a judge. At least that's what reporters had been told. Most hadn't even made any preparation for a story in the regular newscast.

Everyone had to stay put, though, until the end of the newscasts, just in case something happened.

Something almost never happened in situations like this.

PS did observe a radio reporter doing a live remote from his car. But for the most part it was like a lazy afternoon in the Serengeti on the African plains and the pride of lions were lazing about beneath a Baobab tree.

PS was told the day's events would be a reader. So she propped her bare feet up on the dash of the live van and settled into what she thought would be an easy-peasy day on the beat.

She looked in the mirror and noticed that her bangs were tangled and stringy. She didn't have anything better to do, so she grabbed her hair spray from her reporter's bag, two large hairpins, a lipstick and a tube of lip gloss and fashioned hair rollers out of them.

Steve, the video lover stepped into the van as she was rolling the top half of her bangs onto the tube of lip gloss and holding it into place with the hair pin.

"What the Hell are you doing?" He laughed.

"I'm curling my hair."

"With make-up?"

"I don't have any hair rollers. Do you have a better idea? Besides, my mother would kill me if she caught me outside with rollers in my hair."

"And she wouldn't shoot you dead if you had a tube of lipstick pasted to your forehead?"

"Shut up, Steve. What's the big deal? I'm not going on the air."

"Well, you look scary. That's all I'm saying. And you look silly."

"At least I need lipstick in my hair to look silly. What's you're excuse on a daily basis?"

"Oh!" Steve laughed. "It's gonna be like that. Uh, huh… okay , sistah! Let's play the dozens."

"What the heck are the dozens, Steve?"

"Oh, your video lover is gonna take you to school. Hold on to your hair rollers, we 'bout to get crazy up in here," he laughed.

But all of that changed with the arrival of the picketers. And with all the commotion, came a new urgency. All of a sudden, the news crew was plunged into a breaking news story, complete with emotional video and sound.

The protesters were loud and angry. They showed up at the Center because they knew that's where the cameras would be. And being media savvy, they wanted to make certain that their message was going to be televised.

They chanted a well-rehearsed, "Hey, hey, ho, ho save the center or you've got to go! Hey, hey, ho, ho, you vote yes, or we'll vote no! "

And inside the Center, the surprise picket created chaos with the residents.

PS flew into high gear, slipping her shoes back on and jumping out of the live van, microphone in hand. The story had gotten so hot, so fast, it burned.

She grabbed the cell phone and called the station to let them know what was going on. There had been quite a bit of news that day, a robbery at the mayor's residence, a missing girl in town, but the change in her story with the arrival of the protesters made it the big story of the day, and with less then an hour before news time, that meant lots to do.

The rundown had to be changed, editors had to be corralled to cut the video quickly once it had been sent back. There was drama playing out and it needed to be televised.

There was so much being done back at the station to get the story turned around quickly to make air, everyone at the studio forgot about the poor little reporter at the scene, who desperately needed support. So after her initial instructions had been cast over the phone, she was put on hold—eternal hold.

That happened a lot.

There had been a commotion on the upper level of the Center's main building as the residents had become startled by the noise the protestors were making below.

It was EMMY award winning stuff, but only if it made the air.

PS was getting desperate. She needed some background information on the legislator who was spearheading the Center's shut down. She needed file tape pulled on the story she had done on one of the residents the week before. She needed to know how many centers like this one had been closed in the last five years. And she needed it in ten minutes or less.

From where she sat in the remote live vehicle, she was helpless. All she could do was write a script and feed in tape, everything else had to be done back at home base. She wasn't worried about her taped package, that was a home run. But she knew this would turn into continuing coverage. It was a breaking story, happening during the news hole. The anchors would want her to talk and give commentary and know facts and numbers and dates.

PS kept calling the station—and kept being put on hold. She called back and got put on hold again. No one there seemed to remember the vital link to getting this story on the air was the reporter!

Finally her frustration reached the boiling point and she picked up the two-way radio. She was screaming.

It was forty minutes to news time, and no one at the station seemed to notice there was a story floating around somewhere in the hinter lands.

"What the Hell is going on back there?" She yelled, not caring one iota if the FCC was monitoring. They could snatch their license to broadcast if they wanted, she needed attention, and she needed it pronto!

"I warn you," she screamed. "Unless I have someone address some of the logistics issues I have here in the field, all that running around you are doing back at the station isn't going to make a damn bit a difference. Now who's on the desk? Does anybody hear me back there? Hello."

There was no answer.

"I'm not kidding, if someone doesn't give me a call right now, I'm not going to stand out there and look like a fool. You'll have a black hole at the top of your newscast. Commercials will come hurling in from space and knocking into each other. Are you listening?"

Still no answer.

Just as she was about to re-key the mic, a voice crackled over the two-way. It was a voice PS had never heard before. It was calm and reassuring.

"I'm sorry you've been getting the run around, it's like a Chinese fire drill here. My name is Danny, I'm the new producer here. You've been doing fine work out there all week. What can I do to help you?"

"Well the first thing I need you to do is stop talking on this frequency." she barked. "The other stations monitor it, and I'd just as soon they do their own damn work than have me draw them a map. I'll call you on the phone. And could you not put me on hold, please?"

"Understood," the voice replied, unruffled by the curtness. "Give me a call. I'm standing by."

PS didn't know who this guy was, but he certainly seemed to have an understanding of the urgency of the situation, and he seemed perfectly in charge.

Had the station made a mistake and actually hired someone competent? She didn't know. She'd have to investigate further—after her story got on the air.

She called the studio and the stranger picked up the phone and introduced himself again.

PS brushed passed the niceties. She told Danny, or whoever he was, exactly what she needed. She told him where to find file tape. She asked him to call the local ambulance service to see if they'd gotten any calls to make a run to South Haven. She told Danny she needed him to contact a psychologist, with actual experience with profoundly retarded citizens to explain how the noise and commotion outside could be harming the vulnerable people inside. It was a lot of work to do in a short amount of time, but she needed the help. And this Danny guy's performance that day would set the tone of their relationship for his tenure at Channel Six.

He delivered.

At the top of the hour, PS Garrett stood in front

of South Haven listening to Barbara Bennett read the lead-in to her story.

Just before the camera cut to PS, a voice crackled in her ear. "Hey, your hair! What the Hell is that in your hair?"

It was the voice of that new producer.

PS reached up and realized that she hadn't taken out her makeshift hair rollers.

She snatched at them and tossed them to the ground, and the usually disobedient spray of hair dangled gently to her face in a perfect curl.

Geez, what does PS stand for? She thought to herself. Pretty Stupid.

She could hear in her ear, Barbara Bennett already reading her lead-in. "There's trouble at the South Haven nursing center tonight as people protesting the scheduled closing of the home unwittingly do more harm than good. We have this live update from the scene."

PS picked up the piece from there. "Thank you, Barbara. This was supposed to be a quiet day at the center. Most of the activity was behind the scenes and on paper as concerned citizens went head-to-head with their government to save this facility. The meetings for the last four days have all been conducted behind closed doors. No media allowed, so very little information about progress, or the lack of progress as the case may be, is available. But then someone decided a little more noise would be needed. A public showing of sympathy for the residents here. So eleven van loads of protesters showed up to make a ruckus, and make a ruckus they did."

The reporter stopped talking, and turned her head to the portable monitor that had been placed at her feet. That was her cue to the director back at the studio to roll the pre-taped piece that had been hurriedly edited back at the station.

This part of the act was out of her hands, all she could do was watch, and hope and pray that her instructions had been followed, and that where she may have failed to give proper guidance, would be handled by a competent editor and producer—right video with right audio, soundbite here, soundbite there, etc.

She watched the monitor with butterflies in her chest. The first video and sound were of a faint banging at an upper window of the South Haven nursing facility. Then shards of glass and blood rained down on the heads of picketers who at first didn't even realize what was happening. Then the reporter's audio track came up under the video as she reintroduced John, the young autistic man she had profiled the previous week.

"John is twenty eight years old, though you wouldn't know it to look at him. He's lived a difficult life in a tortured soul. John is severely mentally retarded and diagnosed as autistic. He wears a helmet and thick padded gloves to keep from hurting himself. But late this afternoon, all the protection in the world couldn't help John."

The video then faded into the ring of protesters outside the front doors of South Haven. The editor brought the sound up full of the angry mob chanting, "Hey, hey, ho, ho save the center, or you will go!."

The editor then brought the reporter voice track,

back up full.

"Late this afternoon, a group of protesters be-gan a loud, angry demonstration just beneath John's bedroom window. They were trying to be helpful."

Next came a soundbite with one of the protest-ers.

"We want lawmakers to feel our anger. They need to vote yes to keep South Haven open or know that when it comes to election time next fall we'll re-member who voted for what. Hey, hey, ho, ho you vote yes or we'll vote no!"

So far, so good, PS thought to herself.

Next the editor cut to video of the residents who could be seen running in confusion on the upper level of the facility. Through the plate glass window you could see counselors and staff members scurrying to hug and coddle the frightened residents. One of the counselors ran outside and tried desperately to quiet the protesters, but they were oblivious to it all, until that gloved hand came through the window and pieces of glass and drops of blood sprayed their signs and their faces red.

The tape faded back to the reporter as she stood in front of the facility where the unfortunate protest had ended less than thirty minutes before. Now there were scattered protestors, police officers and ambu-lances on the property creating the perfect backdrop for the story.

PS Garrett couldn't have scripted it any better herself.

She continued to look sternly and confidently into the camera, ready to convey the information the new producer had relayed to her by cell phone four minutes before the broadcast began.

"We talked to a psychologist about the impact the protest had on the residents here. Dr. Rita Bravard tells News Six that any kind of disruption can have a detrimental effect on the people here. These are people with special needs, who've been tucked quietly away where they can get the kind of attention and care they need. They're not used to outsiders. Everything in their environment is controlled—regimented. These residents live on routines, and the least bit of change can send these special needs people into a panic.

Of course the folks protesting really were acting in what they thought was the best interest of the people at the facility, but I guess we all know that even the best laid plans of mice and men, oft times go astray."

Barbara Bennett picked up her cue and continued with a scripted response. "That's true, and well said, PS. Tell me, any idea what happens next?"

PS answered. "Everything depends on what's being decided at the legislators closed door sessions this week."

Barbara continued with the next question Daniel D. Rierson had scripted for her to ask PS, "Do you know if any of the lawmakers are even aware of what happened at South Haven this afternoon?"

PS, too, had been given a hasty script by that wiz kid on the other side of the cell phone, who'd written it to sound like a natural ad lib. "We have no way of knowing for certain if word has gotten through that closed door session. We did contact State Senator Warren Smith's office a few minutes ago, and his assistant said that the legislators are all still in a closed door session. But she did confirm that there is a television set in that conference room and I can say, based on conversations I've had with several lawmakers in the last few days, the indication was they made it a point to watch the news coverage of this story as we followed it. I can only guess, if they didn't know before, they certainly know now having seen this newscast. Reporting live, PS Garrett, Channel Six news. Now back to you in the studio."

"Okay, thanks very much and keep us posted." Barbara Bennett said, then turned to a different camera to read the lead-in to the next news story about the break-in at the mayor's residence.

PS sighed deeply and snatched her IFB out of her ear. She turned to the video lover and gave him a high five. He had done everything he could in the crunch—shooting video, acting as van tech to feed it back to the station. It was a Herculean task done with class and aplomb.

PS Garrett then went to the cell phone to call this new producer. He had been an integral part of getting the story on the air, and it looked good and crisp. It clicked, and it moved.

They looked good. And she was sure she had beaten the competition.

Sherman Hall had already wrapped up his live shot and was on the cell phone in the van. When he looked over in the direction of PS Garrett, he wasn't smiling. His pager went off while he was on the phone, he pulled it off his belt, read the display and then rolled his eyes.

Channel Six had won this one. PS was sure of it.

When she called the studio, that Danny fellow answered the phone. "PS is that you? Excellent job. Excellent. You beat the pants off the other guys.

"Now that's what I call teamwork. It all flowed together to make a perfectly coherent story. The audience was able to see and hear for themselves the chaos of closing down this center. Your package was perfection. Great job. Really."

"No. Thank you." PS countered. "You were wonderful. Where did you find that psychologist on such short notice?"

"She's a friend of my cousin's. I remembered her telling me how this buddy of hers worked with disabled kids, so I gave it a shot. It was a shot in the dark, but a lucky one."

"I'll say," PS grinned.

"But you, you were awesome. You put the elements together so quickly. Did you write that script in thirty seconds? I've never seen anyone who could put something together like that in no time flat."

The truth was PS did this kind of magic act on a weekly basis. The nature of the beast is changeable, unpredictable, and ignorant of deadlines. Never before had a member of management conveyed to her that he got it. Never before had someone given her so much credit for a job well done.

It felt good. Really good.

PS liked this new guy. She could tell he was a great hire. She smiled at her small victory and sat down in the truck and put her feet up to revel.

She and the new producer continued to chat on the phone, comparing notes and complimenting one another. She looked into the front seat of the Channel Three van. Sherman Hall was scowling.

It had been a good day.

What does PS stand for? She thought to herself. *Pretty Sweet.*

PS Garrett and Danny Rierson didn't meet face to face until the following weekend. It was the Saturday of Barbara Bennett's big summer soiree.

That year the theme was Water Wonderland.

The servers had on sailors' uniforms. Barbara was dressed as the captain, her husband—first mate. The Police Commissioner of Detroit had a clever costume made of light foam and pantyhose. He had eight long octopus tentacles. The joke was on him. The following year he was indicted for fondling a female cadet.

In Barbara's courtyard—a buffet was laid out with some of the most incredible seafood ever seen. The shrimp and Alaskan king crab were as bright and crisp looking as they are in commercials. The table was decorated with large seashells and sea weed. And the two bartenders in the corner were dressed as boy and girl mermaids, which was weird since PS had never seen a boy mermaid before.

Leave it to Barbara to be original.

No one knows how she did it, but Barbara had borrowed what looked like half a papier mache ship from a local parade company and it sat near her pool, where people were floating and playing spirited games of Marco Polo.

The Police Commissioner won every time he played.

The entire time, PS kept her distance from the festivities. She was in a grumpy mood and had even thought about blowing off the party that year. But she didn't want to risk being erased from the guest list.

She called Willina, but she already had another engagement and couldn't possibly change her plans. So PS ventured out alone in hopes that her mood would improve.

It didn't.

Since PS wasn't much of a swimmer, she just kind of stood at the edge of the pool sticking her big toe in from time to time. The pool was obviously heated because the water was so warm, she could barely feel it.

She decided to bundle her hair up on top of her head and use a coated rubber band she usually kept on her wrist where a watch should be.

Using the ladder, she eased herself in, and began to float on her stomach while holding on to the edge of the pool. She went back and forth between floating on her stomach and floating on her back and letting the warm water wash over her.

Marco Polo had apparently grown old, and most everybody piled out of the pool to go over to the far court for a clambake. PS wasn't a huge fan of clams so she contented herself with keeping the swimming pool company.

She'd had three or four seafoam martinis and was feeling light headed, almost drunk. She was completely enjoying the solitude when someone swam up beside her. She felt a little annoyed that someone was invading her space, but it wasn't her house or her pool so she just floated with her face to the sky and didn't even bother opening her eyes.

After a few minutes her solitude returned, when she no longer felt anyone bobbing up and down beside her.

"I'm Danny. Danny Rierson. The new guy at the station. You really do a great job," a voice suddenly blurted from beside her

PS was startled and jumped a bit. She was embarrassed that she hadn't noticed him beside her and decided that if she pretended to be preoccupied, he might swim away.

When he didn't she decided to answer, her eyes still closed and her face still facing the sun. "Thanks," she answered desperately hoping he was just being polite and would swim on and leave her in peace.

He didn't so she added, "By the way, thanks again for your help the other day. I really appreciate it."

"My pleasure," he answered. And then seemed to quietly disappear.

PS rolled over onto her stomach for a moment, and then allowed herself to float back to her gently paddling her feet in the warm water.

"Were you happy with the editing of the story?"

What? This guy is still here? She thought. "Yeah, it looked great. Thanks again."

And finally silence.

She never heard Danny swim away, but it got

so quiet she assumed he did. She floated for a few more minutes and then felt an incredible urge to pee. The warm water started getting to her, and the martinis she'd had twenty minutes before was knocking at her bladder. It was a big pool and PS doubted anyone would notice. Besides, she was sure it was well chlorinated, so rather than risk catching a chill as she exited the pool and made a run for the main house, she decided to sink herself a little further down into the water and go.

She opened her eyes to scan the area and make sure there was no one standing above her to see the yellow stream, and as she looked to her right, that Danny guy was floating quietly next to her.

Her face turned flush with embarrassment. That embarrassment turned to annoyance as she turned to angrily address him. He was floating lazily beside her with a stupid grin on his face as it faced the sun.

"Danny," she said. "I didn't realize you were still here."

He rolled over on his side, turned his face to her and opened his eyes.

PS Garrett's heart stopped.

His eyes were the most gorgeous shade of green she'd ever seen in her life. It was as if behind his lids, slept the entire Amazon. They were vibrant, and intelligent, and deep and beautiful. She was paralyzed, and couldn't break the stare.

Beneath her honey brown skin, her face turned eighteen shades of red as she realized she was dreamily staring into the eyes of a complete stranger.

Danny obviously sensed the embarrassment and turned a little red in the face too. Then he flashed a smile that was so bright, and perfect and dazzling, PS's heart stopped again.

This was an extraordinary being. He was so handsome, with that little cleft in the middle of his chin. His eyes almost seemed to twinkle. His skin was starting to bronze and the drops of water that danced about his bobbing shoulders sparkled in the sunlight.

PS Garrett was hooked.

Danny and PS became a formidable team in the newsroom. They seemed to have an innate rhythm and understanding of each other that made them hard to beat.

Every time the two were assigned to work together, other reporters took notice, and Salina Kingsley became more bitter.

She'd had her eye on Danny when he first walked in the door.

On his second day on the job, she invited him out for a drink. He politely declined, saying that he had some research to do for an upcoming assignment and then he still was going to drive around to check out some apartment listings.

On his fourth day, he was discussing his search for an apartment with some other co-workers. Salina Kingsley offered to show him around. He politely declined, saying that he had some research to do for an upcoming project.

The Tuesday after Barbara Bennett's party, as PS was leaving for the day, Salina Kingsley overheard Danny asking her if she'd like to grab a quick bite.

Salina Kingsley had always been cool to PS. There was just something about her that rubbed the producer the wrong way. She had subtly and capriciously tried on several occasions to sabotage some of her work, by not turning in Chyrons , or making misstatements in her lead-ins. But PS Garrett was like Teflon. Nothing bad ever seemed to stick.

Salina Kingsley finally decided to just leave the reporter alone.

But when she heard PS Garrett agree to think about it, Salina went silently berserk. At that moment, she swore that PS was her mortal enemy. And she vowed to destroy her.

Up until then, that was the only time Danny and the reporter went out after work. Their relationship was strictly professional, though Salina always managed to interpret their behavior as something more.

If Danny and PS were standing in a corner talking quietly, Salina saw it as them nuzzling and cooing at one another. If PS bent over his shoulder as he sat at his computer terminal to work on script changes, Salina was sure she was just rubbing her impressive breasts on his shoulders. When they went out on stories together, Salina imagined they stole kisses in the news vehicle when the photog's back was turned. Even though the date for drinks never materialized, Salina was sure that an elicit affair had already started.

Two weeks after the big Barbara Bennett soiree Salina was rounding the corner toward the coffee machine. It was evening and Salina was the nightside producer.

As she neared the vending machine Salina overheard PS talking to another co-worker who was vacillating between a Snickers bar and an Almond Joy.

"I have a hot date tonight. I'm excited but kind of nervous," PS confided.

Zoe, the writer at the station was a close friend and confidant of PS's and was all ears. "With who?"

"This guy I met."

"Well, I figured that. Where'd you meet him? Not at the producer's table, I don't suppose?"

PS was genuinely perplexed by the question. "What are you talking about?"

"I see the way the new guy is always goo-goo eying you?"

Salina couldn't stand to hear anymore and she stormed down the hall in the other direction. She had noticed the way Danny looked at that freak-show, too. And it infuriated her. Now the two were going out on an official date. It was almost more than Salina could bear. Why didn't Bob Tucker stop these shenanigans? There should be strict rules about fraternizing and management dating subordinates, though PS Garrett never seemed to get that she was subordinate to anyone. *The Bitch!* Salina thought to herself.

"Zoe, you have lost it. Of course I'm not going out with him. He can look at me any way he wants to. I'm not interested," PS insisted.

The truth of the matter was, PS was interested. Every time she saw Danny, her stomach jumped. She'd had a great deal of trouble concealing her interest, so she had gone on a mad dating binge to try to douse the fire she felt every time he was within a few inches of her. Even if she couldn't see him, her body knew every time he was near.

But she didn't want any scandal from dipping her pen in the company ink well, and since things tended to go badly between her and men, she didn't want anything to get in the way of a stellar work relationship with the first competent producer the station had hired in the five years she'd worked at the station. "No, it is not with Danny. It's with this gorgeous V.P. at my bank. We had been kind of making polite talk to each other for a while, and last week he asked me out."

"And..." Zoe asked impatiently.

"And we've gone out four times since then."

"And..." Zoe continued.

"Aaaaannnnd..." PS taunted. "Let's just say I shaved my legs this morning."

"You dog!" Zoe exclaimed. "You are so lucky. I haven't had sex in about six months and it's driving me crazy."

"Well, I'll tell you how it was. That is if I get lucky tonight."

"What do you mean? What guy is not going to let you get lucky with him?"

"Who knows?" PS laughed. "You know, he could be on his period."

At the assignment desk, the scanners were going crazy. There was loud excited chatter from several municipal police departments and a lot of communication with fire departments and emergency units.

"What's going on?" Salina asked as she walked up to the assignment desk window?

"Looks like we have a severe weather front moving through the western suburbs. It sounds bad. I think some people are trapped in a damaged house," Larry Pink, the assignment editor answered.

He was sitting in the elevated cubicle, surrounded by glass, with one ear to the scanners, and the other ear to the phone receiver as he hurriedly tried to pin down the what and where.

It was quitting time, and he already had his trench coat on, but the elevated chatter on the scanner had drawn him back into the assignment booth.

Salina stopped to listen too. "Yeah it sounds pretty bad out there. Do you have anyone on the way?"

"I sent my last two available photographers out the door about fifteen minutes ago and asked them to call me when they get there, but I think this is a big deal. I think we need to get a reporter in gear to go."

"That's a problem. Everybody's gone. My two nightsiders are already out of pocket." Salina said, formulating a plan.

"I'm thinking about pulling Susan Michaels. She's the closest, and could probably get to the scene in about forty minutes." Larry said looking at the night's assignment sheet.

"What's she on?" Salina asked, the plan brewing in her head.

"Nothing big. Something totally dumpable. I'm gonna give her a call."

"No, don't. Keep her where she is. I think I saw PS Garrett around the corner. Pull her. It will save you some time."

"But I don't have a photographer to courier her out to the scene. I'm gonna call Susan's crew."

"No, don't," Salina snapped. "We're going to need some other stories in the mix tonight. Call a cab for PS. It'll be fine. I'll authorize the petty cash."

"Are you sure, Salina? That's gonna cost a pretty penny to get her out past Novi?"

"Oh yeah," Salina smiled triumphantly. "I'm positive. Send PS. That's our best bet."

Salina Kingsley walked around the corner to the vending machine where she had spotted PS and Zoe a few minutes before.

The two women were already strolling down the hall toward the back door that led to the garage.

"Oh, PS," Salina sang gleefully.

"Can't stop right now, Salina. I'm already running late for something."

"Well, you're going to have to run a lot late. We need you."

PS swung around and faced Salina who was quickly approaching her. "Oh, no you don't Salina Kingsley. I have plans tonight. I can't do a double."

"You have to. We have breaking news, some bad weather is moving through the area and you're the only one in the studio. You have to go."

"No I don't. Find someone with less seniority to cancel their plans. I can't help you."

Just then, Bob Tucker, the news director walked up behind PS.

"Are you refusing an assignment?" Salina asked loudly, so as to catch the boss's attention.

"No, I'm telling you I'm unavailable. I'm off the clock. You don't own me, Salina. I have a life and tonight, that life has plans."

"More important than helping us out in a crunch?" Bob said as he walked by PS and stood next to Salina.

"Hi Bob. I'm sorry you guys are in a crunch, but I have really important plans tonight."

"I can appreciate that, PS, and you're right. You are allowed to have a life. I just walked by the desk and Larry's in a real pickle. Is it possible at all to reschedule your plans? I'm not going to force you, but I would really appreciate it. We need our top reporter to check this weather thing out."

"Bob..." PS sighed. "No fair."

"Completely unfair. I agree. And I wouldn't ask if it wasn't urgent. For some reason, I don't understand, Larry's uncomfortable pulling Susan. Fisher is too far out of town to get to scene. We could really use you.

"How about I sweeten the pot. I'll give you an extra comp day. That's two days off for helping me out tonight."

"Bob..." PS whined.

"Please. We'd really appreciate it."

Salina listened to the conversation, struggling to conceal a broad smile that kept creeping across her lips.

PS looked at Zoe, who shrugged her shoulders. "Two comp days ain't a bad deal girl. Go ahead.

Your friend will understand. If he doesn't I'll keep the date for you."

"Yeah, right," PS scowled. "Big help you are. Okay, Bob. Give me a minute to make a phone call and another to grab some blue jeans and sneakers out of my car."

"Thanks, PS. You're a trooper. I appreciate it. And I'm sorry if we screwed up anything important."

Don't mention it, Bob. PS thought to herself. *No matter how I cut it, I'm getting screwed tonight.*

As PS jogged up to the assignment desk, her change of clothes bundled under her arm, she walked up to a heated discussion between Bob Tucker and Salina Kingsley at the assignment desk.

"It's going to cost how much to cab her to the western suburbs?"

"About a hundred and fifty dollars, Bob. But I just don't see any other way unless she's willing to take her own car."

"And why is it that you couldn't pull Susan from a catfish eating contest in Monroe?"

"Well, Bob I thought she was too far out of the way. And I knew we'd need some balance in tonight's show," Salina said defensively.

"Salina, we're going to have to talk about this one later..."

Danny Rierson had been sitting at the producer's table listening to the interchange at the assignment desk. He had gotten up to approach the argument as PS rounded the corner. "I'll take her," he announced.

"What?" Salina asked angrily.

"I didn't have any plans tonight anyway, I was just going to finish some research and check some apartment listings. Besides, if she's going to be reporting, she shouldn't have to think about getting there. I'll take her. Do we have any extra news cars? I don't think I want to drive my own vehicle into the danger zone if I don't have to."

"Yeah, we sure do," Larry Pink chimed in from behind the assignment desk. "We have unit 22. It's the white Ford explorer on the first level. Here are the keys."

Salina spun around and glared at Larry, who innocently shrugged his shoulders in confusion at her obvious anger.

Larry didn't like to make Salina Kingsley angry.

"Great. No problem," Danny sang.

"Danny, you don't have to do this," Salina said frantically, the gravity of the situation setting in. "Maybe we can pull Susan."

"Don't bother. I want to. PS shouldn't have to report and drive. It's a breaking story. You don't have to wait for a cab, you don't have to pay a hundred-fifty bucks. I can shuttle her. It'll give me a chance to see our intrepid reporter at work, as well as learn my way around town. Maybe I'll even see an apartment for rent on the way."

"Or you could pull Susan," PS said, hoping she still had time to salvage her date.

"She's probably too far away by now. It would take an hour and a half just to turn her around." Larry said. "If we'd pulled her twenty minutes ago that would

392

have worked. I'm sorry, lady. Tonight's your lucky night," Larry said with a sympathetic smile of appreciation.

Danny looked at PS as she stood at the desk understanding her fate. "Giddy up, little lady. We're officially on deadline," he said smiling.

"Thanks, Danny. We'll make it work, huh?" PS said, putting on her game face.

The two trotted out to the garage, with Salina Kingsley glaring off after them.

CHAPTER FIFTEEN

PS hadn't had anything to eat and was starving. She rummaged around her reporter's bag and dug out a candy bar and inhaled it. She found a couple of pieces of gum, and shoved them in, too.

Then she turned her attention to getting ready to cover the bad weather story.

She took off her suit blazer and pulled her shirt over her head, quickly replacing it with a T-shirt that had been bundled on her lap.

"You better not be looking," she said curtly to Danny, who was having trouble keeping his eyes on the road as he zipped up the expressway at eighty miles per hour.

"It's hard not to look."

"This isn't a peep show, buddy. You drive while I change clothes, and no peeking. I'm not kidding."

"I'm a gentleman," he insisted, as he tried to garner peeks with his peripheral vision.

PS unzipped her skirt and then pulled it down below her bottom. As she worked it down pass her ankles, careful not to let the delicate silk touch the filthy floor, her T-shirt rode up revealing her thin lace panties.

The car swerved to the right in a jolt, and then righted itself back on the road.

"Very funny, Danny. I'm not kidding, keep your

eyes on the road," said PS, feeling her own excitement rising.

She was glad she had on pretty underwear. And she found that having to strip in front of the gorgeous hunk of producer extremely titillating.

"I'm trying to," Danny answered, gripping the steering wheel with both hands and struggling not to turn to his right to steal another peek. "Do you always wear underwear like that?"

"What's it to you?" PS asked defiantly—glad he'd noticed. "Did you want to take a picture, I think it will last longer."

"I'd love to but I'm driving. I'm sorry. I didn't mean to embarrass you. You look very nice, that's all."

"Oh yeah? Well how about I drive the return trip back to the station and you be the quick change artist on the way back?"

"Deal," Danny said as he looked at her and flashed that sparkling smile.

Her toes tingled. It felt like a little tractor was running up and down the inside of her stomach. She was very attracted to this man. Very.

She quickly slipped on the blue jeans that had fallen to the floor but couldn't find her sneakers.

She unbuckled her seatbelt and turned around to check her reporter's bag in the back seat. She leaned over to retrieve them, and once again the car swerved sharply to the right.

"You're a real wise guy," she laughed.

Had PS Garrett known that covering breaking news could be this much fun, she would volunteer more often. She made a mental note to thank Salina later.

When the two pulled up to the story scene, PS could barely wait to get out the car. This story was so hot, it burned. Camera crews were all over the place recording every tragic detail, including the Channel Six nightsider who'd already been on the scene for an hour or more.

The damage was absolutely horrific. People stood around in shock, with their mouths open—some with a few possessions in their hands.

Their loss. The monster's gain. PS thought to herself.

She did eight live updates that evening.

Danny could have gone home earlier since he had been off the clock since six that evening, but instead he stayed to field produce. He went around with the second photographer finding compelling interviews. He turned the tape around quickly and kept his reporter hopping on the air.

With his help PS looked great. Her work was crisp and smart, and it looked like they had all the bases covered, even with only one full roving crew, since the other one was tethered to the camera.

In hindsight, she couldn't have done it without him. He worked so fast and was so creative.

The other stations only had a single reporter and photographer crew on the scene, and were handicapped since they couldn't go live and gather new tape at the same time.

But Danny, working as a field producer allowed the News 6 crew the flexibility of gathering new information fast, first and accurately, just like the commercial said.

At the end of the evening, as the photographers rolled up their cable and packed away their gear, one of them asked if he could drop PS back at the station.

"Damn," she said. "It's almost faster if I just get home from here. I guess I can catch a cab into the studio in the morning. Do you mind taking me home? I know it's out of your way, but you'll get overtime?"

"Nope," Danny said as he walked up behind the cameraman. "We're on an overtime freeze. I'll get you home."

"Is that so?" PS asked, having not been aware of any freeze on photographer overtime.

"That's so," Danny said firmly.

"Okay. I'll ride with you," PS smiled coyly.

"Nope," Danny said.

"Nope?"

"That's right, nope," Danny said walking the reporter away from the photographer who had turned his attention back to lowering the mast on the live van and packing up the gear.

"Nope to what?" PS asked.

"You don't get to ride."

"I thought you just said you were going to take me home?"

"You have a short memory. It's your turn to drive," Danny said, as he looked back at the reporter and smiled.

"I'm bushed," PS said, those little tractors started running up and down the inside of her stomach again.

Danny smiled, resisted the urge to brush the dangling strand of hair away from her beautiful brown eyes, and took the wheel.

He had barely pulled away from the carnage before PS was fast asleep on the passenger side, with the ambient sound of jazz drifting in and out of her consciousness.

She could see Danny's eyes in her dreams. She could hear his voice. In her subconscious she wanted this man with intensity of the red hot sun.

She was startled when the car stopped bobbing and she was being gently shaken.

"Sleepy head. We're home. I mean, you're home," Danny said with a broad smile. "You give good directions."

"Thanks. And thanks for the lift," PS said as she began to gather her clothing and belongings before tumbling out of the car.

Danny jumped out of the car and raced around to the passenger side to meet PS at the door.

"Wow, you mean chivalry isn't dead?"

"Nope," he said. "It is on resuscitation, though." He said as he grabbed her hand and held on. "Let's go for a walk," he insisted. "It'll help you wind down."

"This time of night?"

"I can't think of a better time," he said, tugging at her arm.

The two walked passed PS's apartment to a small park down the road. Danny held her hand in his, and they walked and talked about the evening. They compared notes and tried to figure out how likely it was that they had beaten the pants off the competition on the storm story.

They decided that not only was it likely, but probable.

As they walked past a large tree, Danny pulled PS to a stop and turned her to him. "You know I have a thing for you, don't you?" He said, his sparkling eyes gazing into hers in the moonlight.

The two were almost eye to eye and it was hard for PS to breathe, her heart was racing so.

She wanted to be clever and answer with some snappy retort, but couldn't think of one with her head spinning. "Yeah, I know." Is all she managed to blurt.

"And you like me too, I can feel it," he said.

As he spoke, Danny raised PS's hands, which were still clasped in his, and clutched them to his heart. He stared at her, and even with the bashful moon that darted in and out between the clouds, she could see it was a deep searching look.

He was a good bit taller than she, but still somehow their noses seemed only inches away from each other.

She could feel his breath on her mouth. In fact, she was standing so close she felt as though she was breathing what he was exhaling, and she was utterly intoxicated by the pheromones.

He gently pulled her to him, then masterfully positioned them beside the tree as their noses touched.

Their lips touched, gently at first, tentatively—cautiously. And then he pressed his lips firmly to hers.

His tongue slipped into her mouth and probed as he gently pulled, first her top lip and then her bottom into his own mouth.

He was a craftsman.

This man knew how to kiss, and it was driving PS Garrett wild.

Before she even noticed, they were horizontal on the ground. Several blades of grass brushed passed her right ear, and the faint aroma of pine tickled her nostrils as the branches from a nearby tree reached out to sweep their bodies as they moved rhythmically with each other, barely touching at first but with each second more of probing kissing he became a magnet to her metal.

The ground felt hard at first. Bumpy and uncomfortable. But again, with each kiss, with each caress of his strong square fingers upon her shoulder, across her throat and down her chest, the ground became a feather pillow, first warm and supportive and then invisible.

PS was on a blanket of air.

She was faintly aware of traffic lights off in the distance, but they were fleeting beams unable to find and unaware of the two people who laid beneath the row of trees on the far side of the park.

Danny's body lay partially atop PS's.

She didn't feel pinned. But she was breathless, totally and completely in rapture. She could feel her heart pounding, she could hear it in her head and sense the throbbing at the tip of her pelvic bone. Her breasts brushed his chest as her own heaved quickly up and down.

He slowly moved his lips from hers, and worked his way down the side of her neck.

She gasped. She could still smell the fragrance of his breath as it lingered in the air above her. She could still taste his kiss. She ran her tongue along her upper lip to savor the flavor, to capture each drop of Danny Rierson.

It was magic.

Her fingers tightened on the back of his shoulders. His muscles twitched. His skin shivered beneath her fingertips and he lifted his head for a nanosecond to express a barely audible giggle.

But to PS, it was surround sound. Everything was amplified. Each breath was a roar, every shudder an earthquake and she gasped again. And again, she could smell the fragrance of his breath as it lingered in the air above her. She could still taste his kiss.

PS felt dizzy, and warm, and wonderful. If they had made love right there and cameras had been rolling, she knew she wouldn't have cared. That's how much she wanted him at that moment. That's how much she ached for him.

Danny and PS lay on the ground and kissed and caressed for more than an hour. Their bodies found a rhythm and moved together, touching and grinding, as they explored each other with their mouths and hands.

Sometimes Danny would stop kissing her and would just look down on her and smile. His eyes would shift from her mouth to her forehead. He seemed to inspect her hairline as he caressed her hair, brushing the damp curls away from her face.

He would stare, and smile and lift a lock of hair and press it, first to his nose and then to his lips. And then gently plunge back into her mouth, and she took him gladly.

As he grinded closer, PS could feel he was hard. Rock hard, and she wondered how long they could keep this up without taking it all the way. But Danny had complete control, he seemed perfectly comfortable being aroused and not letting it control him.

"You know I've been falling in love with you for some time," Danny spoke softly and kissed her forehead, her cheek and her nose between each word.

"Oh yeah?" PS spoke as casually as she could, understanding this was not the time to lose complete control of her senses.

She wasn't used to losing control. She mastered all she surveyed, except when it came to Danny Rierson. She had loved him since the first time their eyes met in Barbara Bennett's swimming pool.

But they did have to work together. They had tomorrow to think about. And while she wasn't exactly cooling down from the make-out session, the thought of tomorrow was sobering and PS wasn't as gripped by the fever that had been carrying her away for the last hour.

Her ability to think rationally was returning.

And then she did something she had never done before in her entire life. She relinquished control. She made a conscious decision to step away from the driver's seat and let whatever was meant to happen, happen.

She put her arms around Danny's neck and pulled him back to her for a long deep, satisfying kiss that seemed to last forever and still wasn't nearly long enough.

Danny brushed another imaginary ant off her forehead and swept away a wisp of hair that had gotten plastered to PS's forehead by sweat.

He was leaning on his elbow. He leaned down to lightly kiss her on her eyebrow and whispered, seemingly painfully, "Yeah. But I'm also aware that we have to maintain a professional relationship. And since I haven't figured out how to do that and still make love with you, I think I'll walk you back to your apartment."

Danny focused on her forehead and kissed it gently. He stood up, took her hands and helped her up then dove in to help himself to one more kiss. He then walked PS to her front door and said good night.

PS knew he was right. But she also knew that she wanted him to come into her apartment and into her bed. She was ready for him. Her legs had even been shaved.

Reluctantly she bade him goodnight, as a slight throb began knocking at her right shoulder.

That night as she lay on her bed, his words kept repeating themselves in her head. *He said he wanted to make love with me, not to me. With me, as if in a partnership. I was his for the taking, yet he chose to wait.* He wasn't typical at all.

As sleep began to coerce PS to close her eyes, she played his kisses over and over in her mind. Her toes tingled. Her head felt hot. She wondered how she would face him in the morning.

She couldn't wait!

The next day at work, Danny was very professional toward PS but there was a warmth in the way he spoke to her. He smiled more, and looked her directly in he eyes as he spoke. He held his gazes a little longer than he needed to. He was letting her know, that what happened the night before was not lost on him, but it was no one else's at the station's business.

When Salina Kingsley got to work that afternoon, though, she noticed it.

PS went through the day, finding reasons to walk past him or speak. She was floating at least a dozen inches off the ground. She wanted to tell everyone she saw about them, but didn't dare—not even Zoe.

The truth of the matter was, she didn't exactly know what was really going on between them.

She began to wonder if this wasn't a casual flirtation with a man who was new in town and lonely.

She didn't know if what she was feeling was love or lust.

On twenty-second thought, she didn't know what was really on his mind. She found herself staring, and daydreaming of the night before as he rolled on top of her, and blanketed her with his body. And his slow rhythmic kisses, she couldn't forget those slow rhythmic kisses.

She felt herself getting warm again. She was definitely in heat.

But she was slapped back to reality at the sound of Salina Kingsley's voice. "So how'd it go last night?" She asked, trying to probe.

"How'd what go?"

"You know, working the story. You two did a bang up job out there."

PS looked up at Salina suspiciously.

Salina Kingsley passing out kudos?

She was standing just behind the file cabinet at the reporter's desk.

"Salina, didn't you produce last night's show?" PS asked annoyed that once again Salina had spoiled a wonderful moment.

"Yeah."

"Did you see the show?"

"Yeah," Salina answered embarrassed.

"Then you know how it went out there. We kicked ass."

PS turned to her computer terminal and pretended that she had been focused on it all along. Salina continued to stand at her desk, trying to think of another way to find out if anything had happened between PS and Danny.

PS looked up. "Salina, in there something else you wanted?"

"No," she answered looking defeated as she walked slowly back to her desk.

All her life, Salina Kingsley had been invisible to men. It made her bitter and desperate. But that seemed to change when Danny Rierson showed up at the station. He was so friendly. He always smiled, always engaged her by staring into her eyes.

The truth is, that's how Danny was with everyone. He was a pure spirit. A genuinely nice person, who allowed everyone their own space and had a way of conveying their value to him as a living being, without having to say anything.

Salina, took it for romance.

But Danny was just being human.

After a fairly uneventful news day, PS Garrett packed up her belongings and started walking out of the studio. She looked around casually to see if Danny was around. He wasn't.

She was reluctant to leave, but didn't have any obvious reason to stay, so she slowly meandered out of the newsroom hoping to bump into him.

She paused at the mouth of the newsroom.

"Forget something?" Salina asked as she walked up behind her on her way to the control room for a live update with the anchors.

"Um, yeah. I did," PS answered as she walked back into the newsroom, looked through her Rolodex and feigned a few phone calls.

Still, Danny was nowhere in sight. His briefcase was still at his desk, so she knew he was still somewhere in the building. But rather than risk being sent out on another breaking story, PS decided he was busy and if he really wanted to talk to her, he could always call.

She took one more cursory look around, and then walked out to the garage with her ears down, and her tail between her legs.

As she stepped off the elevator, she heard a car horn beeping. She looked over, and saw Danny sitting in his white Honda, he rolled down the window. "I thought you were never getting out of there. What took you so long?" He said in a loud whisper.

PS began to grin inside. She didn't want to tell him, she had been puttering around for the last twenty minutes, waiting to see him, so instead she just said, "I had some stuff to do. What's up?"

"What's up? Come here, I want to tell you something."

PS walked over to the passenger side of his car and got in. He reached over and pulled her face to his, and gave her a light kiss on her lips, gently tugging the lower one into his mouth. "I missed you today."

PS couldn't stop smiling. She knew it had to be one of those stupid puppy love grins, but she couldn't help herself. This guy made her smile from deep down in her soul. "What are you talking about, you saw me all day."

"Yeah, but I couldn't do this."

Danny pulled her back to him and kissed her ear. He ran his finger down her neck and toward her chest, stopping just above her left breast. He stared for a moment, and then his eyes returned to hers before he nuzzled her with his nose and kissed her chin. "I missed you. I couldn't take my eyes off of you. I kept thinking about last night."

"So what do you think?" PS asked, once again relinquishing any control she might have of the situation.

"I think we should go to dinner. I'll drive you back to your car later if you want."

What did he mean, if I want? Why wouldn't I want to come back to my car? PS thought to herself. *Maybe tonight we'll make love together.*

PS searched her mind to remember, and then sighed relief that she had re-shaved her legs that morning and slipped on another pair of pretty underwear.

Allen George rolled over and flopped his arm around PS's stomach. She angrily moved it, and he

407

flopped it back over.

She nudged him. He wouldn't budge. So she shoved. "Wake up. Allen, wake up. What are you doing in my room?"

Allen muttered something inaudible, but didn't respond even though he'd actually been awake for sometime. He'd snuck into her room, because for the first time in weeks, she had forgotten to lock her door after coming in late.

He knew what story she had been working on, because he'd watched the news. He thought she might be vulnerable and he might be able to coax her into making love, thus extending his stay.

He only needed to stay a little while longer, but even Allen George knew he was running out angles and out of time.

He knew if he left her bed that night, he would never have another opportunity to woo her. So he continued to feign deep sleep in hopes that he could catch her later at a groggy moment.

PS continued to nudge and push, to no avail. "Bastard!" She said spat.

She threw her feet over the side of the bed. Guernsey had been underneath and felt the motion on the mattress above him, and wandered from beneath the bed skirt to investigate.

As PS placed her feet on the floor, she nearly stepped on him. "Come here you," she said affectionately as she picked up the small kitten, snatched the comforter off the bed with a yank, and went out to the sofa in the living room to sleep.

Even though her eyes closed, she couldn't make herself sleep. She still had Danny on her mind.

After dinner Danny and PS went for a stroll along the waterfront. They held hands and looked out across the Detroit River and the moon that danced off the wake of a barge that was heading for Lake Saint Claire. They did very little talking, and almost no kissing. They were just *there*. That's all.

PS was getting sleepy and couldn't stifle a yawn. Danny pulled her head to his lips and lightly kissed her on the lashes, and then the forehead. "I better get you home," he said.

"Are you okay to drive?" She whispered.

"Yeah, I think so," Danny said, stifling a yawn of his own. "You know I can take you home, and pick you up in the morning if you like. It's no trouble at all."

"Oh no," PS said with another wide yawn. "I wouldn't think of putting you through the trouble."

"What trouble, I want to take you home. I wanna do a lot of things for you. Come on let's go."

Danny led the drowsy reporter to his car, opened the door and jumped in on the driver's side. He looked her squarely in the eye in a deep searching fashion, but saw very little as her droopy lids had become mere slits.

He started the engine.

When PS opened her eyes, he was standing at the passenger side, holding the door open. He pulled her to her feet and walked her to her apartment with his arm around her shoulder and her head resting on his.

She handed him her keys, and he opened the door and led her in.

It was dark inside, all PS could see was his outline with the help of the moon that was streaming through the open blinds.

"Do you have any pets?" Danny asked.

"No. Why?" PS yawned.

"This place needs a pet."

"Why is that?"

"Everybody needs someone or something to love unconditionally."

"Okay, Dr. Spock, I'll take that under advisement." PS said sarcastically.

Danny pulled her into his arms for a few moments and then began kissing her gently starting at her forehead and working his way down to her neck.

She came back to life immediately.

She began nibbling at the buttons on his shirt. His chest smelled warm and musky, PS took a deep breath to fully inhale him and could feel the little hairs on his shoulder stand at attention—Danny was perfectly still.

As she unbuttoned his shirt down to his torso, he gently grabbed her hands and held them to his chest. PS seized the opportunity to use his hands as a leash, and began pulling him toward her as she inched her way down the hall to the bedroom, kissing him along the way.

She sensed a hesitancy, like he wanted to follow, but was reluctant. She encouraged him with her lips and her tongue, pressing her body close enough to his to feel that he wanted her as badly as she wanted him.

She swayed back and forth, ever so gently so as to create enough friction to entice him to follow. He threw his head back and gasped, grabbing her by the shoulders to guide her as she stroked his body with hers.

She gently embraced his strong square buttocks and used them as rudders to keep him moving toward the bedroom. But when they got to the doorway he stopped. "I want to," he panted in her ear.

"Good." PS whispered, finding his right breast with her tongue and circling it gently.

He gasped again and threw his head back in pure pleasure.

"God, I want to," he said as he gently pulled away from her gratifying tongue.

"Then what's the problem? Are you teasing me?"

PS was confused and a little embarrassed. "What's the matter?" She asked with a sinking feeling.

"I'm afraid of becoming your slave?"

"What? My slave? You mean my looooove slave?" She taunted with a kiss and another nibble at his shirt button.

"No, that wouldn't be so bad, but I need to be able to control myself more. I need to have a handle on my feelings."

PS was becoming frustrated. She wanted this man with the full hot passion of a ninety degree summer day. "I've got some feelings you can handle," she said jokingly with as much coaxing ability she could muster in this waning battle.

411

Danny let go of her hands and embraced her. He kissed her hard on the mouth as if he were a starving man, and this was the first food he'd seized in months. It was a hungry, passionate, forceful kiss.

PS was mesmerized with the touch of his hands on her back, and the taste of his tongue as it slid expertly in and out of her mouth, around her lips and over her eyelashes.

She could still feel his mouth on hers as she heard the front door slam shut.

He was gone.

The next day at work PS dreaded seeing Danny.

She caught an early cab to work, just in case he decided to stop by to collect her at the apartment.

She was mad at herself for leaving her car at the station the night before. Just one more way she had blindly relinquished control to this man.

She moved quickly into the building and barely stopped to say hello to anyone in her path.

She saw Peter rounding the corner. He inhaled as though he were about to say something, but when she glared at him, he gurgled, and only managed a feeble wave. He wanted to ask if she was okay, but didn't dare.

PS sat at her desk and busied herself with phone mail. She kept her head down and closed herself off. She assumed he was avoiding her, too.

But still, she couldn't help but look up from time to time just to see if he was in the newsroom, just to check to see if he was somewhere looking at her—laughing perhaps. He wasn't.

She was both relieved and devastated at the same time.

Never again, she thought to herself. Never again will I be taken in like this.

Her heart ached.

She needed to pull herself together before receiving her daily assignment, so she walked out of the newsroom and into the back hall toward the vending machine. She wanted something chocolate with lots of calories and fat grams. She stood there considering her options when Danny sauntered around the corner.

Their eyes met and both stood there in uncomfortable silence for what seemed like an eternity.

"Good morning, beautiful," Danny mustered a halfhearted smile, and his eyes darted around to see if anyone else was around to hear.

There wasn't and he continued to talk to PS as he moved forward. He reached out to put his hand on her shoulder.

"Don't!" She spat.

"What?" Danny recoiled his hand as if he'd touched something hot.

"Danny, don't," PS continued. "I don't know what you're doing, or why you're playing with my feelings, but just don't anymore, please."

She turned back to the vending machine and forced herself to insert two quarters, realizing that she needed three. She scrounged around in her hand, but only had pennies. Danny reached out and handed her a quarter.

She snatched it from him without looking up, and shoved it into the machine.

Snickers. That'll take care of it.

"Please, you don't understand," he begged.

"Danny, what is it that I don't understand? What's the matter with you? How can you just turn it off like that? Do you have AIDS? Herpes? Some sort of sexually transmittable disease? You're damned right I don't understand. What's going on here?"

PS quickly hushed her voice, and looked around to make certain that they were still alone, though she felt red with anger, she didn't care. She almost wanted everyone to hear. As soon as she got to her desk, she was going to call Willina and tell her everything. Willina would understand what this all meant. She would know what to do. "I don't understand," PS whimpered.

"No, to all of that. I swear it. I told you. I explained it to you last night." Danny fell silent as an engineer walked by, shot the two a fleeting glance and then hurried along.

"What? That you didn't want to become my love slave? Well Danny, I think that explanation sucks. And since I don't feel like being a fool this year, let's just keep it professional, okay?"

PS reached down, snatched up her Snickers bar, walked back to her desk, and prayed the day would go by fast.

For the next five months, that's just what she and Danny did. They kept it professional.

But every time he walked by her desk, her heart skipped a beat. And his did too.

CHAPTER SIXTEEN

PS lay on her sofa. Her spirited kitten had found his way to the foot of the furniture and was scaling it like Spiderman, much to his owner's amusement who was watching the spectacle in the waning light of the moon, streaming through the window.

The diversion brought PS a little relief. Relief from her flashbacks of Lathan lying on that concrete slab with a bullet hole right through his forehead. For a moment, she couldn't imagine how his family would manage without him. She couldn't fathom the grief they must have been feeling that night. For a moment, she thought she would never have been able to withstand such insurmountable grief as a loved one's true absence. For a moment—but then her thoughts returned to Danny Rierson. And as Guernsey found his way to the crook beneath her neck, and nuzzled in for a good night's sleep, PS realized that she had once felt much like Lathan's family must feel. It was the night Danny left her for good.

She started to doze. Guernsey started purring lulling her into sleep where her dream had left off.

She tossed a little but then found comfort at her memories of Danny.

Terry, the photographer and PS had been sent Downriver to collect an interview.

415

A young man had been taken into custody for molesting and then strangling to death his cousin, a seven-year old girl. Larry Pink didn't even know about the story until he saw it on Channel Three.

Angry that they'd been scooped, the news managers got together to decide how they could best save face, play catch-up and even surpass the competition. They decided to send a reporter and a photographer to the house of the suspect's parents to see if they could get them to talk about what had happened.

The luck of the draw was Terry Franklin and PS Garrett.

PS was uneasy about the assignment, knowing that these were dangerous interviews to try and get. She didn't know who the boy's parents were, she hadn't seen them, hadn't had an opportunity to size them up, and this was an embarrassing, and dare say, mortifying position for them to be in. Not the kind of thing you want announced to the neighbors by the sudden appearance of a news crew.

With her left shoulder beginning to throb, PS suggested that the assignment desk call the family first, rather than to ambush them. Since the parents weren't the criminals, PS felt the station owed them the courtesy of warning them that they were coming. The assignment desk reluctantly agreed and told the TV crew to head to the neighborhood anyway so they could at least be in the area once contact with the family had been made by the station.

Terry drove around until they found the small rural neighborhood.

Most of the houses used what looked like saddle blankets for curtains. The yards were very large, there was spotty overgrown grass. The houses were rundown and old. PS thought she even saw an outhouse or two.

As the crew pulled up to the address that had been jotted on a sticky note, the reporter could see in the back yard an old white commode, some tires and some rusty automobile parts.

"These people are real class," she said as she turned to Terry, picking up the two-way radio, since the particular news vehicle she was in didn't have a working cellular phone. She dialed the station. "Okay, we're at the address, have you made contact with these people by phone?"

"Not yet," answered Janine, the assignment desk assistant. "So just go up and knock on the door and see what you get."

"I don't like this. I don't like it one bit," PS said to Terry as they got out of the car. The reporter took a second and looked around, and got an incredible sense of foreboding. Her mind wouldn't let her feet walk toward the front door. It was that sixth sense that every reporter either has or develops after years of being on the streets.

Those who don't develop it got injured, fired or made a career change to the nearest PR department.

She looked around the property. The nearest neighbor was a half-acre and a clump of trees away or across the road.

She continued to scan the area.

The home had the requisite saddle blanket in the front window. Behind the rusty junk in the back yard, she could see a doghouse, though, there was no dog in sight. She also saw what looked like the remnants of a target practice deer—one of those Styrofoam animals that you set up in the back yard for bow hunting practice.

Terry sized up the situation while stepping out of the vehicle, and reaching back to the rear door to retrieve the camera. "Do you think the logo on the side of the car is big enough?" The photographer asked.

PS looked down. "No, I think it should be a little larger. I don't think they'll be able to tell it's us from way over there," PS said sarcastically taking a few slow steps toward the front door.

"These people are hillbillies!" She said to Terry. A chill raced down her back and she shivered. "And it doesn't look to me as though anyone is at home. So let's just get back into the car."

Terry opened the car door and got back in just as Danny was trying to reach them on the two way radio. "Unit ten, I repeat, please come in."

PS picked up the microphone and answered. "Yeah Danny, what's up?"

"Are you at that address the desk gave you?"

"Um, yeah, but it doesn't appear that anyone is home. We just thought we'd wait here for a while to see if anybody drives up," PS said.

It was a lie, but she didn't think the station needed to know she had deliberately violated their order to go knock on the door because the very idea had given her the heeby jeebies.

"Oh yeah?" Danny sounded a little angry. "Don't wait. Get out of there now. Do you under-

418

stand. Do not approach the house, you've done enough. Now get out of there. Please return to base. I'll talk to you about it when you get here."

Oh great! PS thought to herself. Just what we need, to be yanked off one assignment and put on another. "Come on Terry, let's us news puppets get out of here."

"You're the boss." Terry said and put the car into drive.

"No, Ter. That would be the major malfunction here. I'm not the boss. I'm a soldier, not a general, and it's this very crap that makes me want to go AWOL. These people have no idea what it's like out here. That little chippie on the desk has never been on the street. Not once. All she knows is what was told to her by Bill Thorn and Larry Pink, who've also never been on the street."

"I know. You don't have to tell me, I'm in the trenches with you," Terry sighed.

"I'm sorry Ter, I don't mean to yell at you. I'm just venting. These guys send us out to redneckville to bang on some door of who-the-Hell-knows-who, and then they get pissed off when you decide maybe this time it's just a little too dangerous. You know the hair was standing up on the back of my neck? I don't know who those people are, and that dog house in the back was as good a no trespassing sign as I needed."

"Lower your voice a bit. Okay?" Terry said exasperated.

"I'm done. Good and done."

"You mean well done?"

"Well, I am done, so I guess you could say I'm well done."

The photographer and reporter laughed uncomfortably.

When they got back to the station from Downriver, Danny was waiting for them at the garage door. He was antsy and seemed angry.

PS didn't know how it happened, but obviously somehow, the station must have found out that they hadn't really gone up and knocked on the door of that house as they had been instructed to do.

"Will you and Terry come with me please?" Danny spoke steadily and professionally in a tone that made it perfectly clear he wasn't PS's friend, he wasn't the man she'd rolled around in the grass with one hundred-fifty days ago, he wasn't the would-be lover who ran out of her apartment when the moment of truth arrived.

He was her manager, and that's how he spoke to her.

PS's heart sank. *I guess it really is over between us*, she thought, her head and shoulders down as she followed Danny into the building.

She ached.

Terry and PS followed Danny as he walked into the conference room. Inside was the news director, Bob Tucker, managing editor, Bill Thorn, the assignment editor, Larry Pink, The executive producer, Mia Wiekstamer, and the assignment desk assistant, Janine.

PS was confused by the unusual assembly of people, but sat down in the chair, closest to the door.

Terry grabbed a chair next to her, and Danny walked over to the other side of the table with the rest of the managers and Janine.

Bob Tucker spoke first. "You were asked to go to a house Downriver to get an interview with Chester-the-molester's parents. What you didn't know was Janine here had already made contact with them. Apparently she got their number from the criss cross directory and gave them a call and was told by whom ever answered the phone, that if anybody from the media showed up and knocked on their door they would consider it trespassing and feel it was their right to shoot.

"Unfortunately, because of her inexperience, Janine didn't take the threat seriously and decided to withhold that information."

"I just thought it was an idle threat, I thought they were kidding." Janine piped in.

"Thought they were kidding?" PS jumped up and screamed, the gravity of why they were meeting setting in.

Her head was reeling. She looked the young woman squarely in the face. PS had had trouble from her before. She was absolutely, capital A incompetent—she got addresses wrong, and would send crews on wild goose chases on a fairly regular basis. She had no news sense whatsoever. In fact, she didn't exhibit that she had any sense whatsoever. She would take down phone numbers incorrectly, screw up messages, rudely answer the phone.

At that particular moment PS was having trouble recalling anything she had done right. The

421

entire news staff had complained to Bill Thorn about her, but he seemed to like her and always made some inane excuse for her.

In that job, apparently you didn't have to be good, you just had to be liked. So the newsroom had been stuck with her for the last eight months.

But this incident was going to far.

"Some redneck told you they'd shoot me, and you thought they were kidding? ARE YOU NUTS?" PS demanded.

"Well, I called them and they said they would shoot anyone who knocked on their door, but since you were already on your way I figured you could handle yourself."

"Apparently a neighbor across the street saw you as you got out of your car," Danny piped in. "The people in that neighborhood have had first hand experience with those people and know them to be extremely violent and dangerous. The neighbor contacted the sheriff's department, which contacted us. I happened to be the one who answered the phone when the police called. Thank goodness." Danny shot a chilly look in Janine's direction as he finished speaking.

PS's first instinct was to climb over the table that separated her and Janine and slap her squarely across the face. Obviously her intent was clearly expressed on her face, because Bill Thorn shifted to block the clear path between the reporter and the little harpy.

PS sat brooding for a moment. She collected herself as best she could, and then calmly spoke. "Fire the bitch," she said with a low growl.

Bill chimed in, "Come on, I don't think that language is necessary."

"Fire the bitch," PS said, in the same tone and tenor.

"She's young. She just needs a little more training," Bill pressed.

"Fire the bitch," PS said yet again.

Bill looked to the other managers to assess support.

But when the others returned blank stares, Bill slinked down in his seat a bit. "Well, I do think some sort of reprimand is in order, but I think firing her would be a little severe," Bill persuaded.

That's when Danny jumped in. "This young woman just needlessly put the lives of two crew members in jeopardy. I haven't been here that long, but I have been here long enough to know this is not the first time Janine has made these kinds of mistakes. But this is not just demonstrating bad judgment, this could have cost the lives of valuable members of our team. She's careless.

"I agree, she should be fired. I'm sorry Janine, but I think you could better serve our community if you did something else, perhaps selling shoes or something along that order."

"Now wait a minute, I don't think that's necessary," Bill protested.

But Danny could not be interrupted. "Imagine what would have happened if our reporter and photographer had been hurt. Think about the field day the newspapers would have had with us when they found out we had been warned and deliberately sent them into the line of fire. Imagine the lawsuits filed by the family members of this crew!"

"Oh C'mon. That's just ridiculous," Bill protested again.

But the look on Bob Tucker's face began to harden.

"Bill," PS said, struggling to contain her boiling anger. "What's going on here? Does this girl have pictures of you in compromising positions with animals or something? Why are you protecting her? This is a hanging offense. You know it! If this were anybody else, you would have bounced them. But why not her? Don't answer that. I don't really want to know, but I'll bet you Mrs. Thorn would be curious."

PS then turned to the news director. "Now, the way I see it Bob, you have three choices. I can beat her ass, and you fire the bitch, I can beat her ass and quit and you fire the bitch, or you can just fire the bitch. Which is it?"

The news managers looked at each other, as if they were considering her words. Danny struggled to stifle a smile. Then Bob Tucker spoke first. "This is a very competitive business. We live and die by the kinds of stories we bring in, and we go to great lengths, and sometimes risk personal safety to get those stories on the air. It's the nature of the business. Having said that, I also have to add, that at no time is any crew to be deliberately put in harms way to get a piece of tape. It's reckless, it's unconscionable and I can't allow it.

"Janine, I know you're young and inexperienced. I know you would not have knowingly risked the lives of two members of our crew. But at the same time, if you have so little judgment that you would not take that kind of threat seriously, I fear you may be a danger to all of our crews."

"I agree," Bill piped in conveniently after the boss had spoken. "Janine, I'm sorry but we're going to have to demote you. I think you'll have to learn the business as a production assistant and not as an assistant assignment editor."

"Actually Bill, I wasn't thinking of a demotion," Bob interrupted. "Janine, you're dismissed effective immediately. Actually, I think you owe these two people an apology and then you're dismissed."

Janine started to cry.

That did it! PS hated women who cried in the newsroom. There's no place in this business for sobbing females. That stuff should be done at home, in the privacy afforded by a closed door where no one can see you and hold it against the gender. By sobbing like a little sissy, she set all women in the newsroom back at least a decade.

She was evil and must be destroyed.

Janine apologized, "I'm so sorry. I didn't mean any harm. I swear, I thought they were kidding. Honest."

And then she ran out of the office weeping and sobbing.

PS turned to the news director and said, "Can I still beat her ass?"

"No, I would prefer that you not. But why don't

you take the next two days off."

"Sure, great timing Bob, it's Friday."

"That's right," he said with a smile and then pointed PS to the door.

Monday, when PS walked through the station's doors, Mia Wiekstamer, the executive producer called her in to her office.

"We have a really important assignment we want you to work on. Maria Swick is the next woman to be put to death in Ohio. She's in the women's facility in Dayton and has agreed to do an exclusive interview with us. We want you to do some background— track down family members and friends of her two victims, and then drive down to Dayton next week to interview her. I don't want you talk about this with anyone else, we'll just keep it hush-hush for now."

"Wow!" PS said excitedly. "This sounds big."

"It is big. We're starting to inch up to Channel Three in the ratings and we need a heavy hitting promotable story to run in our second block to hold the audience. We think if we can promo the Hell out of this we'll be able to grab our demographics and hold them through the quarter hour."

"I think this will hold them alright. I've got an idea," PS said. "Why don't I figure out a way to do a mini package, kind of like a super tease in the first block. I'll write it so you have just enough information, but not too much. Maybe you'll see her face but won't see or hear Maria talk until the second block. In the first block story, we'll give all the background and history,

426

maybe show me walking through the doors of the pen, sitting down and putting the mic on her but hold the good stuff for later. We'll give 'em a sip and then take the glass away until after the break. That oughta hold 'em."

"I love it. That's smart thinking. I'm so glad I came up with the idea," Mia said with a sly grin and a wink.

"Okay, sure," PS said. "I'll get right on it."

PS knew Mia could have held on to her smile and wink. She wasn't kidding. It was a good idea, and PS knew that it was Mia's habit to steal other people's ideas and present them as her own. It explained part of her meteoric rise and a little about her treachery. In the treachery department in the Channel Six newsroom, the only person who had Mia beat was Salina Kingsley

Maria Swick was a woman who'd killed two people in cold blood nearly eight years ago. She'd kidnapped an infant from Southfield, a suburb of Detroit. She led police on a lark for nearly three months.

Of course the FBI had released its character profile. Of course it had nearly no resemblance to the case, and didn't amount to a hill of beans when it came to solving the mystery of how this woman seemingly disappeared into thin air with a newborn. When police finally did catch up with her, it was a fluke. An off-duty Dayton cop recognized her at a grocery store where he was moonlighting as a security guard. He'd seen a description and composite of her at the cop shop just a few weeks before.

When the cops surrounded her hide-out, she slaughtered the infant and tried to hide its body in a freezer. And when police burst through her door she shot the first officer who came through.

Good! PS thought to herself. *Another project to keep me busy and my mind occupied.* That's exactly what she needed. An engrossing project to consume her every waking moment.

She began to walk out of Mia's office when the E. P. added, "Oh and by the way, because we want you to turn this in the next two weeks, I'm giving you a producer to help you out. Stop by Danny's desk, I've already briefed him. Have fun, and good luck."

The reporter's jaw dropped. She began to protest, but Mia had already picked up her phone, started to dial and given the reporter the shoo signal to leave her office.

Oh great. She thought. Just what I need. *To be, thrown in with this guy on a major story.*

She knew they made a good team, but all of a sudden, she wasn't looking forward to this assignment. It would be a lot of work. A lot of long hours.

PS sighed, stiffened her lip and put on her game face. The one she'd gotten so good at wearing.

She walked into the newsroom and stopped by Danny's desk and said good morning.

"I hear we're going to have a little project to keep us busy for the next couple of weeks," he said with a smile as he looked up.

PS leaned over close to his ear and whispered, "Remember, you said it first. Let's keep it professional."

"Actually, if I remember correctly you said that, not me," Danny was wearing a broad grin as he peered up at the reporter with those incredible twinkling eyes.

Her face felt red. She looked around to see if anyone else in the newsroom had noticed the little encounter.

Everyone had.

And Salina Kingsley's face was red too.

PS walked toward the vending machine. As usual when she had any encounter with Danny at all, she needed chocolate. Lots of it.

As she rounded the corner to the hallway, she said under her breath, "I hate my life today."

As usual, Danny was great to work with. He knew how to find contacts, he knew how to get people to talk. He even went out and conducted several of the interviews.

PS lost herself in the task as well, and regularly lost track of time. Often times she didn't know what was going on around her or what hour of the day or even what day of the week it was. She had gotten into a routine of working until she couldn't work any more—going home, grabbing a nap and returning to work.

Done correctly, this story might even win some awards.

She was sitting at her desk, pouring over some background information, and reading transposed logs of the interviews Danny had logged a few days before. He walked over . "Do you know it's nearly eight o'clock?"

"Oh yeah?" PS grunted not bothering to look up.

"Have you eaten today?"

"What are you, my producer or my baby-sitter?" PS sneered.

"Both," he answered.

PS tore herself from her computer screen and looked up. Danny flashed that sparkling smile. "Com'on stop playing hard to get. Let's go get a bite to eat and talk about this."

"There's really nothing to talk about," PS said, annoyed.

"Yes there is, we have to drive to Dayton on Friday, and I think we need to talk about what we have, where we are, and what still needs to be shot. We're keeping this professional remember?" He said with a slight smile and raised eyebrow.

His words stung. And PS could smell the scent of his skin, and feel the warmth of his breath. She felt the fever coming back.

"Yeah, whatever," she sighed, collecting her belongings and walking ahead of him out the front door of the station.

The two walked to a restaurant near the station, spread their papers out over the table, and ordered without even looking at the menu. They were both starving and exhausted. They were both also very excited about the project that had been tossed in their laps.

They chatted animatedly about the interviews they'd done, and what still needed to be shot. PS asked Danny about the arrangements for Friday's six hour drive to Dayton. He said the cameraman was going down the day before to shoot video of the corrections facility and to get some scenic shots to help weave the story. He explained there was some sort of convention in town, so hotel space was scarce. The station would be forced to put them up in an old Victorian Bed and Breakfast. He didn't know how crummy it might be, but at least everybody would have their own rooms and bathrooms. That much he was sure of.

They'd drawn an above average photog, Laurence. He had a nice eye for detail, and he loved to light things. It didn't matter how much energy it took, Laurence would pull out his light kit and make even the simplest of interviews look like a first class, two-camera shoot job.

By the time the food arrived, Danny and PS had slipped back into being friends. They talked about their work, what they'd been doing on their limited off time, which wasn't a whole lot.

PS was slurping her chilled cucumber soup when she realized Danny's foot had been gently tapping hers. She got a few butterflies and slurped her soup even louder. He started to laugh and so did she.

After dinner they walked back to the station. They were walking so close together, their hands brushed against each other as they swung. Danny grabbed at her fingers, but she gently pulled them away.

At the moment, she wanted another EMMY to sit on her mantel more than she wanted another failed shot at romance with this man.

When they got into the station's garage, PS walked toward her car. Danny touched her lightly on the shoulder. She turned to face him and caught him in a warm gaze. "Thanks for having dinner with me," he said.

"No prob, boss. I'll see you on the morrow," she said in a faux Shakespearean voice. She looked at him for a moment more and felt the heat returning to her face.

She jumped into her car without looking back. She just didn't dare.

"Call me," he yelled out behind her. "Let me know you got home safely."

"Don't worry, I'll get home safely. Go home, go to bed, get some rest."

PS revved up her engine, and busied herself with her seat belt, never looking up. She felt both relieved and pained as she heard his car finally drive out of the garage. She sat there for a moment, collecting herself with her head pressed to the steering wheel, and then drove out as well.

The next five days might be death of her.

They got an early start Friday morning. There was so much to prepare for, PS didn't have time to think about Danny Rierson, the man. The only thing on her mind was Maria Swick, the murderess.

For the entire six hour drive to Dayton, she and Danny talked. They planned the interview, plotted strategy, slipped in small talk from time to time. It was as though they had never misfired, never quarreled, never fallen out of love before admitting they'd fallen in. It was like a brand new beginning. And for the first time in months, when PS Garrett looked over at Danny Rierson, she saw the man, and not the producer and it didn't break her heart.

CHAPTER SEVENTEEN

By noon Sunday, the shoot was over.

The photographer, the reporter and the producer trudged into a fast food restaurant to eat and debrief. It wasn't the first time they'd sat down that day, but it felt like it.

They talked excitedly about the shoot, patted each other on the back and basked in a job well done.

As they started getting up to leave the restaurant, Laurence asked if they would be shooting anything else.

Danny and PS each pulled out their lists, made check marks, and looked up at each other with surprise.

"Are we done?" PS asked.

"I think so," Danny said, rechecking his shoot list. "Yeah, I can't believe it, we got this thing done in one and a half days. That's incredible."

PS and Danny raised their hands and gave each other a high five. Then Laurence said, "Well, today's my mother-in-law's birthday, and there's this really big family celebration. I had told my wife I wouldn't be able to make it because of this assignment, but if you think we're really done, I'd like to head back. If I leave now, and don't catch any traffic, I might be able to catch the tail end."

Danny and PS both furrowed their brows.

Danny looked over his shoot list one more time.

"Did you get the exteriors of the pen?" He asked.

"On tape one," Laurence said. "I shot those the day before you two got down here."

"Well, what about those photos I brought with me. We need to get those shot," PS added.

"Did it last night after you two sorry sucks went to bed," Laurence laughed.

"Sorry suck? Oh, Hell no, you can't go!" PS laughed.

"Well, wait a minute Laurence, let me think about this for a minute. If something does come up, we're going to be out of luck if you leave." Danny said. "Let's go over the list one more time."

"Hey, I'm going over my list," PS said. "And we have the exteriors of the facility. We have community shots for color. I have taped stand ups and even cut a few teases for the promotions department.

"The interview with Maria Swick is done, and that was the most important thing. We'd completed four interviews with the slain police officer's family members before we left Detroit. As near as I can tell, we couldn't find anything else to shoot if we were making it up as we went along. In fact, there is no need for any of us to stay. We could all head back this very minute."

"Laurence," Danny said. "Wish your mother-in-law a happy birthday for me, okay?"

"Thanks you guys, have a safe trip back," Laurence jogged to his car, and pulled off, waving as he disappeared onto the exit ramp.

"You wanna take off too?" PS asked Danny. "If you're too tired to drive, I'll take the first leg."

435

"You drive me?" Danny answered. "I don't think so. I see how you are when you're tired."

"I'm not that tired," PS said trying to stifle a yawn. "Let's go."

"Yeah. To take a shower and a nap. I'm exhausted. Then lets go to a couple of these little antique shops and have a nice dinner on Channel Six. What do you say?" Danny said.

"Antique shops?" PS squealed. "What, are you gay?"

"Hey, real men like antiques too, you know," he said. "Besides, I've been watching you. You can't wait to get into some of these shops."

"Well..." PS hesitated.

"I say it sounds like a plan," Danny said with a twinkle in his eye.

He left two twenties on the table to cover the twenty-five dollar bill, got up and walked out the door with PS reluctantly following behind him.

The first stop was a little shop that claimed to be an antique boutique, but it turned out to be a junk store.

PS loved it. She absolutely adored other people's junk.

She found a nice antique etched glass wine decanter, but Danny grabbed the matching wine glasses.

"Oh come on," she begged. "That's not fair."

They had a delicate filigree etched around tender rose buds. The stems were long and rounded. PS had never seen anything more breathtaking and she had to have them. They were in perfect condition, and the price was a steal.

436

"I saw them first," Danny teased.

"But they match my decanter," PS whined.

"Actually I like that decanter too. I'll flip you for them," Danny said.

"No way. Just give me the glasses." PS begged.

"Oh, I love it when you're begging me," Danny said with a twinkle in his eye.

PS's stare turned cold. She remembered the time she had tried to coax him into her bedroom, almost begging him and he'd left her standing there with her lips puckered as the door slammed. She felt foolish and flush. "Forget it." She said in a huff, and walked up to the cash register to pay for her decanter. "I have plenty of glasses at home."

"Come on, let's flip for them. They're a set and it would be a shame to break up the set. Heads you get the decanter and the glasses, tails, I do. Deal?"

Danny pulled a quarter out of his pocket and tossed it in the air. He caught it, and slapped it down on the top of his wrist. He un-cupped his hand and revealed tails.

PS handed him the decanter and walked out of the store.

"Oh, so now you're mad right?"

"Not mad, just disappointed. Buy your junk and let's go," PS said, wishing that she had hopped in the car with Laurence when he headed back to Detroit.

PS said she was too tired for dinner and skipped it all together. Instead she stayed in her well-appointed room and ordered some delivery food from down the street.

She was glad the hotels in the area had been filled. The large Victorian house was exquisite and had more than delivered during an otherwise grueling trip.

By ten o'clock she should have been exhausted, but couldn't make herself go to sleep. She called the hostess of the inn, hoping she hadn't retired yet. She hadn't so PS asked if she could come down and get some chamomile tea.

"Don't be silly," the inn-keep said. "I'll bring some up. You just relax."

PS sat by her screen door, and gazed out onto the veranda at the warm summer night waiting for her tea to arrive. She was excited, nervous, exhausted, lonely. Her emotions ran the gamut.

She had been so wound up in the Maria Swick interview, it hadn't hit her until that moment that Danny was staying in the room next to hers. She found herself wondering if he'd wandered up to bed yet.

She held her breath, to see if she could hear any movement beyond the wall, but only heard the sound of her own heart pounding in her head.

The night felt warm and romantic. A light breeze danced into the room, carrying with it the scent of wild flowers. PS started trembling.

She couldn't get that man out of her head. She felt the fever returning, and wiped her face with her hands.

As she gazed out the door, she felt a tear roll down her cheek. She hadn't noticed until then that she was crying.

She felt so alone.

She was in a house, filled with people and she felt absolutely alone.

She got up and walked into the bathroom. She looked in the mirror. Her eyes were puffy and red.

She hated being alone. She hated going to parties by herself or with girlfriends, or a date she cared nothing about.

She dampened a washcloth with cool water and wiped her face and checked mirror again.

No change.

She still felt hot, and more than a little uncomfortable. She turned on the shower, undressed and stepped in. The cool water felt good as it ran down, first her chest and then her back. The water became a little too cool, so she turned up the hot water and let the warmth run over her entire body.

She pretended to be in a tropical waterfall. She could see brightly colored birds dancing on the wind in her mind's eye. She could smell the wild gardenia, and imagined the lush green foliage lining the craggy shore.

When the water got too warm, she turned the cold back up and was immediately returned to a cool Massachusetts breeze.

She was actually enjoying herself and produced a loud chuckle a time or two. She continued to play with the faucet heads, changing the water from hot, to warm, to cool and back to hot again, until her skin became puckered and pruned.

Her toes looked almost ancient, and she wondered if that's what her feet would look like when she turned eighty.

She dried off gently, put on an oversized shirt she'd swiped from her father and walked back into the bedroom suite, a warm breeze still blowing through the open screen door.

It felt good.

She decided to sleep with the verandah door open.

She turned down the lights and went back to the balcony door to stare out at the night a little longer.

She felt renewed, a little drained, but still renewed.

She looked around to see if there was anything boring to read, *oh crap*, she thought to herself. *I forgot about my tea. I bet the hostess brought it by and I didn't hear her because I was in the shower. Oh well, what does it matter anyway?*

PS sat back down in front of the screen door and peered out into the darkness. Her head filled with pounding again.

She placed her head in her hands and waited for the fever to cool.

Go away. She thought to herself. *Go away.*

But the feeling grew stronger. She couldn't shake it.

She was startled when she heard a faint knock at her door. "Come in," she whispered hoarsely.

Thank goodness, the hostess hadn't forgotten her tea after all. She hoped she'd brought a second tea bag. PS was such a wreck she would have eaten the chamomile raw if it would help her get to sleep and forget the anxiety that was creeping through her again. "I'm sorry. I was in the shower. You can put the tea on the bureau. Thank you very much," PS said continuing to stare out across the meadow without looking up. She didn't dare. She knew there were still tears on her cheeks, and she didn't want to be noticed wiping them away.

The person at the door said nothing. But PS could hear breathing behind her so she knew someone was still standing there.

"I'm sorry, did you hear me?" She asked. "Thanks for bringing me tea. Just leave it on the dresser."

Still no answer.

She took a deep breath, wiped her nose with her sleeve, and finally turned around to accept the tea.

But when she turned around, it wasn't the hostess standing at her door. It was Danny.

Her eyes were red and damp, and tears had filled the crevices between her nose and her cheek. She strained, thinking she was imagining it, but she wasn't.

Danny was standing there with a bottle of wine, and two of the wine glasses he'd *stolen* from her earlier that afternoon at the antique shop. The etchings caught the dim light from the lamp and pranced off the wall and ceiling like sparkling laser beams.

Both stood perfectly still, trying to read the other—sizing each other up.

Finally PS blinked back the tears and spoke. "What are you doing here?"

"Can I stay?"

Before she could answer, Danny was across the room.

He picked her up by the shoulders and raised her to her feet kissing her hard on the lips and then neck.

She tried to pull away, but couldn't. She wanted him too badly.

She returned his passion with her own. Her tears mixed with their saliva. He kissed her as though he were a starving man. She could understand. She, too, was ravenous.

He held her face in his hands and stared into her eyes and up at her forehead. He kissed her so tenderly she felt as though she were a fragile china doll that might break.

She was.

Sometimes they didn't kiss at all, they just stood there with their faces so close they were inhaling each other's exhale. And then he would pull her to him and begin kissing her again.

PS Garrett's head exploded. She was sure she must be imagining this. She must.

But she wasn't. It was real. He was in her room, and in her arms and her whole person enveloped his. Her body temperature seemed to raise to four-hundred degrees. She was burning up. She couldn't get enough of him. She drank his kisses like water and with her own lips begged for more.

The more he kissed her, the more she needed. She was parched and he was an oasis. She could almost hear the waterfall in the distance.

When they had satiated themselves with kissing, and caressing and fondling, he led her to the bed, slowly and carefully. There he undressed her by pulling her oversized shirt over her head, not bothering to unbutton it.

He lay on top of her, beside her, behind her and beneath her. As they made love together, she looked at the differences in their skin tones. He was so pale. She was so dark.

She liked the contrast when their skin touched, almost becoming one.

Before then, she had never looked at Danny as being of a different race. But that night as they made love, it added to the excitement. It sweetened the flavor.

They laid there in each other's arms, entwining their fingers and kissing each other's palms.

Neither remembered when sleep finally came, but they woke with the sun, streaming in through the open verandah door. And Daniel D. Rierson was still cuddled behind PS Garrett.

After the Maria Swick story aired, PS and Danny were together every single night for the next five hundred and forty seven days. That's a year and a half.

They didn't keep their relationship a secret. It was too important to both of them.

They figured once they got past the usual station gossip—most of it fueled maliciously by Salina who was consumed with jealousy—people would get over it and move on to a new interesting topic.

The love affair didn't interfere with work. In fact, it made them a stronger team. They championed each other's causes and looked out for each other's best interests. They were a formidable force in the newsroom.

PS loved him as she had loved no other man before. She would have followed him to the end of the earth and back.

They would lay around on Saturdays in each other's arms and talk about everything under the sun, from nuclear proliferation to Family Circus and Snuffy Smith.

PS loved that they would fall asleep holding hands and wake up holding hands.

They made regular forays to Baskin Robbins, and every new flavor was an event, an adventure. She taught him just the right combination of Jamocha and Mint Chocolate Chip. She explained how you have to get the sugar cone on the side so it doesn't get soggy.

Once they brought home a half-gallon of Daiquiri Ice, mixed it with rum and slurped the whole thing. That night the two laughed about everyone at work including Janine and wondered where she might be selling shoes.

PS taught him the box step. Danny taught her the hustle. He sent flowers to her mother, thanking her for having a daughter he could love. They held hands in public and didn't care who stared. They sent birthday cards to friends and family and signed both names.

If PS was going to be home late he knew it and knew the reason why. He was almost never late. He flew home to her arms, and never seemed to tire of kissing her, and holding her, and talking to her and listening to her. They shared everything—their home, expenses, high points and low points.

Bringing Fido into the family completed the circle.

Before she met Danny, PS had been half a person, and didn't realize it until she'd met her other half—her better half.

One night they made love so enthusiastically that the bed collapsed, breaking into five pieces. *BOOM!* It sounded like an explosion. It was an antique they'd found after they'd moved in together. They both liked it because it had "character".

Their bodies were moving with such velocity and intensity, as Danny lifted up to enter her again, the bed just collapsed. They laughed so hard, it hurt.

That was the night Danny asked PS to marry him, and she said yes without even thinking about it. The question was just a formality anyway, they both knew that they belonged together. This was the kind of relationship you beg God to give you, and you generally only get it once in a lifetime—and only if your Karma is good.

PS wanted to bear his sandy headed children, five if he wanted. More if he asked.

This had not been a chance meeting, this was her soul mate. And PS Garrett thanked her Maker every day for sending him her way.

Her only regret was that they had wasted so much time in the beginning getting there.

They could have had five extra months together, had they not been so rational and professional—so stupid in the beginning. They would have had more time if they hadn't worn such impenetrable armor to protect their foolish pride.

PS wished they'd done a lot of things differently in the beginning, yet there were so many other things she'd do again in the same way a million times over.

When Danny left, PS was inconsolable.

Some friends who felt sorry for her told her Danny was in a better place now. Some said he sings with the angels.

PS didn't know what that meant exactly, but thought that's probably true since she knew in her heart he was a Godsend.

The day he left, she remembered wishing she had some deep rooted religious beliefs to comfort her at his departure.

She could remember many a time she had interviewed people who'd tragically lost a loved one, and they were rocks—solid in their belief system. Such people didn't have pseudo faith, they had the genuine article. They truly believed and it was a real comfort.

PS wasn't raised with religion, so when Danny left, she had nothing to hold onto—nothing to grasp. She simply slid down a slippery slope and only Willina understood enough to hand her a branch and pull her back.

Learning to breathe again was a process. PS Garrett ached. All she knew was he was suddenly and violently gone, and from then on she'd have to find her way alone.

And what broke her heart the most was, she never even had the chance to say "thank you", or "good bye".

In the news business he was just another statistic. Someone else gunned down on the streets of Detroit for fifteen dollars and the fake Rolex watch they'd picked up in New York, the weekend they flew up to see Sunset Boulevard and Forever Plaid.

The station ran his picture on the news for about a week. It offered a reward for the capture of the punk who killed him. But of course, "nobody saw nothing". To this day, three years later, Danny remains a blot of red ink on the wall of the homicide division. Another unsolved crime. Number two hundred, forty-three for that year.

Of course, PS Garrett saw him differently then just another murder victim. In her heart, he was the world.

The sun was coming up, and PS was sitting up on her sofa—the tears rolling down her cheeks and onto Guernsey's head. Each time a tear plopped onto his tiny noggin, he looked around in confusion to try to figure out its origin.

It made PS laugh a little. She missed Fido. She missed Danny. She missed being loved unconditionally by someone other than her parents or best friend.

That first year nearly destroyed her, personally and professionally. It was hard to concentrate, hard to do her job, particularly when innocent people were victimized by evil beings, reprobates, repeat offenders, demonic beasts. But eventually she grew stronger. Her focus returned.

Time became her band-aid—work her salvation.

Any reporter who'd been doing this as long as she had, learned years ago to hide the grief. Ignore it. Work past the pain.

Sanity depended on it.

Willina had learned all of the tricks of survival from her own rough childhood in the projects of Detroit. She'd lost several cousins to gun violence, one of her brothers was gunned down on the street looking for crack. Wil had learned to make it look like grief rolled off her back like duck water. And then she taught her friend how to internalize the pain, seek it out and destroy it.

"Take ten deep breaths of God," she would counsel PS.

Funny, PS had never figured Wil to be the religious sort. "Don't confuse loving God with fearing God," she'd say. "I have a relationship with God. And when I breathe deeply with God on my lips and in my heart, it clears the air passages. Allows you to think.

"Now, do it. Just close your eyes and take a deep breath."

PS tried, but the first one hurt too badly. She could barely draw enough breath to fill her chest. "I can't," she cried. "My heart is broken."

"I know, honey. I know. But try again. Keep trying until you can draw ten breaths that fill your chest cavity."

PS kept trying. But on every inhale, she could see Danny's face, or feel his touch, or sense his loss. Her lungs fluttered, flattened and ached. She didn't want to breath.

"Try again. Clear your mind. Take one long, slow breath and think the word "God", feel the word "God". You don't have to understand it. Just do it."

PS stifled her tears, set her shoulders and braced herself for the shooting pain of breathing. She stared at the ground, cleared her head and slowly began to draw in. It was difficult. But eventually, it worked.

She continued the exercise, day in and day out with Wil by her side—coaching her.

And after teaching her to breath again, Wil taught her to stand, and then walk. She taught PS how to be miserable without showing it on her face. She taught her to smile and talk, and even answer questions on autopilot without even hearing them. She helped her friend build a defense system, so impenetrable, that with almost no effort at all, PS could seek out and destroy any overt emotion she didn't care to display.

Wil taught her how to live again. Even if it was just an existence, it was still life.

With Willina's guidance, PS took her sadness underground, put a smile on her face, and feigned happiness. Whatever true sorrow she felt, she drove it so deep into her soul, her own personality could no longer detect it.

Willina taught her well.

When her mind wandered, PS chastised it and tightened and narrowed her thoughts so she wouldn't be forced to remember.

That's what saved her life. She became a better reporter because of it. But she hadn't become a better person. She had been permanently injured,and the fact that she had let Allen George worm his way into her life was proof of that.

Danny was never coming back. PS couldn't substitute him with this man who wasn't even a fraction of the man Danny was. Allen George had no character, no credibility. He was a liar, a thief and an impostor. Allen George had gotten into her home by default. He remained there because of the grief that had numbed her for so long.

PS could hear Allen moving around in her bedroom. He opened the door and walked out into the living room and toward the sofa where PS had spent the night. She immediately shut her eyes and pretended to be asleep.

He walked away and toward the front door, opened it and stepped out into the warm July air. As he moved out onto the stoop his foot grazed a small bouquet of weeds and wild flowers that had been placed on the ground near the door.

Allen angrily kicked them down the breezeway scattering leaves, stems and flowering buds across the concrete slab that opened onto the lawn of the back of the condominium complex. The note that offered a name and a place for a long awaited rendezvous that had accompanied the make-shift bouquet had blown away over night.

The stranger who'd been watching PS had grown impatient. His attempts to get her attention were failing and he was getting desperate to make personal contact. So he left her one more note on the bouquet of wild flowers he'd lovingly picked from the vacant lot across the street. If PS Garrett didn't respond this time, the man who'd been stalking her had decided he would have to be more forceful and direct in his approach.

As Allen stepped away from PS's door, he kicked at another remaining petal. He was annoyed. If he ever found out who was responsible for constantly leaving that crap in front of his door he would personally ring their neck.

He thought it might be the same pesky kids who killed PS's cat. He couldn't fault them for that. That little stunt had actually worked in his favor. But ever since that incident, the small childish offerings had been more of a nuisance than anything else, and his patience was running thin. And now there was another scroungy beast in his home. Every time he touched Guernsey, his skin crawled. He wouldn't have thought of bringing a cat into that house if he could have avoided it at all. He hated animals—cats in particular.

Allen walked down the breezeway and continued to scatter the stems and flowers with his foot as he had done almost every week since he had moved in. When he was satisfied that there was no longer a recognizable bouquet, he turned and headed for the street. He walked passed PS's car and kicked the front tire as he went.

"Selfish bitch!" He spat.

He walked across the parking lot toward the corner market to get a newspaper. He could tell his time was getting short and he needed to hatch a plan to tide him over until he found a new sponsor.

Several other people from the complex walked to their cars and greeted Allen cordially.

The man taking cover from a large tree at the far end of the parking lot took notice. From the distance, he couldn't see that once again Allen George had decimated his love offering. He'd been watching Allen George since he arrived at the apartment of his beloved PS Garrett. He wanted him out of the way, but didn't dare lay a hand on him. He was afraid of Allen George. But knew he would have to make him disappear if he ever wanted a chance to touch PS Garrett again, to feel her warm, soft brown skin against his own, to share a kiss and perhaps more. He knew PS would love him when she met him. He knew it for sure. She would appreciate everything he'd done to get her attention—all of the stories he'd nefariously *arranged* as *gifts* to his favorite police reporter.

The shooting at the Gas N Go in Pixley. That had been a crime of opportunity. He was as surprised as anybody that the beautiful and talented PS Garrett showed up. But he wanted more of her.

He realized that if he followed her closely enough he could create havoc that would bring his favorite reporter to the scene. But it had to be big. PS Garrett didn't cover small stuff. It had to be showy and violent to bring out Channel Six's ace.

The shooting on Tuxedo had been brilliant. He simply waited outside that Chop Suey place she often frequented. When he saw her leaving, he drove several blocks away and shot the first teenager he saw walking down the sidewalk. It was easy. The neighborhood was used to violence. To him, one more dead black teenager meant nothing to the world, but it meant everything to a police reporter hurrying to the scene to get the scoop. It was her gift, from him.

He'd actually gotten close enough to smell her perfume and touch her hair as she moved through the crowd.

The fire at the trailer park two weeks ago had been a stroke of genius. It was close enough to her home that he knew she'd be dispatched. Each dastardly deed was carefully crafted to bring her to the scene in an attempt to be closer to her. To make her a superstar.

He delighted in the suffering of others. When boredom set in while he waited for PS Garrett's appearances and disappearances at her stoop, he'd been amusing himself with the mutilation of small animals around the condo complex for months. He loved it when he could make *weaker* beings suffer. He'd taken delight in catching rabbits and squirrels. He liked the system he had devised to restrain them as he dismembered them, listening to their cries of pain. All his life, he had been in pain and he liked it when he could make others suffer too. He lifted his right hand to his nose to smell the imaginary blood on his fingers. That orange tabby cat had made the most noise as it was sliced from throat to anus. But humans had become his favorites.

The wheels began turning in his head. Perhaps his crimes had been too random. Maybe he needed to send a stronger message that he was doing this for her.

He needed a calling card. Every serial killer has a calling card.

The thought was exciting. "That's it. I will be a serial killer!" He quietly announced to himself as he watched Allen George round the corner at the bottom of the street. "What better way to show your love to a woman who reports on murders? I should have thought of it before."

He reached down to satisfy the need that had suddenly and desperately returned to the bulge in his trousers.

The mere thought of murder had become a powerful aphrodisiac. And as the man behind the tree watched Allen George disappear from view he said in a low, calm voice, "Watch, Watch, I'll start with him."

Inside her condo, PS opened her eyes and could see clearly for the first time in four months. For PS Garrett, it was like a lung had miraculously opened upand allowed fresh air in to clear her head. And at long last, a plan began to develop.

Allen George would be gone within the week.

To be continued...

About the Author

I wrote my first poem at the age of four. It went, "Sugar plum, sugar plum in the tree. Please get the sugar plum just for me." My mother tells me it went on for nine more verses.

I've settled in Detroit because I love the state and the people. In Detroit, we are hearty because of the winters and kind because the rest of the world beats us up, but Detroiters are a proud and spirited bunch and I'm happy they've adopted me, as I have them.

I split my residence between the suburbs of Detroit, Michigan and a rural farming community on a bluff overlooking Lake Huron in Ontario, Canada.

Many people consider me a closet geek. I collect rocks, minerals, fossils, rough gems (I do my own mining and faceting), and I'm a novice astronomer. For stress management I design pearl and gemstone jewelry. I enjoy horseback riding, am an avid cyclist and love motorcycles. Snow beckons me in my love of cross country skiing. I've raised hibisucs trees and calle lillies in my living room and orchids in my basement. As a farm girl, originally from the Chesapeake Bay Region, if Mother Nature made it, I love it.

I've done a lot of living, still get carded for alcohol, see as much of the country as I can, and would like to see more of the world. And the one thing that has been constant throughout my years is...I love to write.

Visit me at my website *deadlinethe book.com* for a sneak peak into the world of a working news reporter.

Also Available
from Dailey Swan Publishing

Confessions of a Virgin Scarifice $12.95
by Adrianne Ambrose

Beyond the Fears of Tomorrow $9.95
by Casey Robert Swanson

Revenge $12.95
by JH Hardy

The Lamp Post Motel $14.95
by Joe Gold

Bones of the Homeless $15.95
by Judy Jones

Endlight Event $14.95
by John P Cater

The Black Beast of Algernon Woods $15.95
by Nickolas Cook

Prisoners of War (Dupers Fork Vol.1) $14.95
by Andrew Winters

In Lieu of Light $12.95
by Wayne w. Jackson

www.daileyswanpublishing.com